Falling From Grace

Falling From Grace

PAMELA OLDFIELD

MICHAEL JOSEPH
LONDON

MICHAEL JOSEPH LTD

Published by the Penguin Group
27 Wrights Lane, London W8 5TZ
Viking Penguin Inc., 375 Hudson Street, New York, New York 10014, USA
Penguin Books Australia Ltd, Ringwood, Victoria, Australia
Penguin Books Canada Ltd, 10 Alcorn Avenue, Toronto, Ontario, Canada M4V 3B2
Penguin Books (NZ) Ltd, 182–190 Wairau Road, Auckland 10, New Zealand

Penguin Books Ltd, Registered Offices: Harmondsworth, Middlesex, England

First published in Great Britain 1995
Copyright © Pamela Oldfield, 1995

Typeset by Datix International Limited, Bungay, Suffolk
Printed in England by Clays Ltd, St Ives plc
Set in 11½/13½ Monophoto Garamond

ISBN 0 7181 3953 4

The moral right of the author has been asserted

FOR CAROLE AND DAVID
WITH LOVE

Acknowledgements

I would like to thank the Airship Heritage Trust
(RAF Cardington) and the Royal Aeronautical Society
(London) for their interest and guidance whilst I was
researching the book.
Any errors are my responsibility.

Chapter One

BEL LEANED BACK IN THE WHITE garden chair, drew on her cigarette and allowed three small but perfect smoke-rings to escape her lips. For a moment she regarded the tennis court, deciding it would soon need resurfacing. The winter frosts had been particularly severe and the asphalt, laid at great expense only three years ago, was already breaking up in places. She would have to mention it to Walter. Lazily she surveyed the rest of the garden. The rhododendrons were long past their best, but the new rose-beds were proving a success, providing a soft splash of colour here and there among the smooth sweeps of lawn. Her smoke-rings drifted upwards, wavering, towards a clear August sky, taking her thoughts with them. Walter, her husband, was up there somewhere, on his way to Canada in the airship R100. For a moment or two she imagined him among the distinguished passengers; he would be in his element, wining and dining in the luxurious surroundings offered by the pride of England's airship industry. Walter would be enjoying it all immensely. Airships were his life, she thought, with only the slightest trace of resentment. He was almost *married* to them! She, Bel, came a poor second. The other woman! A faint smile touched her lips, for it was a passion he had once shared with her father. As a child Bel had grown accustomed to her mother's resigned comments when the man she loved failed to return for his evening meal. Now, as Walter's wife, Bel too must accept the time her husband spent in the vast sheds at Cardington where the airships were housed, and she had grown accustomed to being alone on the nights when he 'stayed over'. In some ways his frequent absences from home were a relief from the interminable 'lectures' about aerodynamics and other technicalities to which she was subjected – and which she dutifully tried to understand.

On the other side of the small table Marie smiled. Her round face was flushed from her exertions on the tennis court and she held a glass of lemonade with both hands. 'A penny for them, Bel!' she said.

'I was thinking of Walter.'

'Too late now, my dear! You should have gone with him.' She glanced at her brother who sat between them, idly examining the strings of his racquet. 'Tell her, Larry. I'd have jumped at the chance.'

Larry shrugged. 'She's old enough to know her own mind.' He gave Bel a smile. 'Take no notice of her, Bel. She's always been bossy. Just because she was born a few years before me! I know how you feel. It's understandable. If Father had died in that crash . . .'

'Well, I'll admit I had tears in my eyes when we saw her go, and I wasn't the only one. All those people with their faces uplifted. It was almost religious.'

'Religious? Hardly that!'

'It *was*, Larry. People wept. Tears of pride. I know how Bel feels, but she should have gone anyway. No wonder Walter was proud of that airship. She was quite superb.'

'We were all proud of her,' said Larry.

'But did you feel it *here*?' Marie clapped a hand to her heart. 'That airship was so beautiful. Like a . . . a wonderful silver fish swimming in a blue sky! And she was *ours*! The largest and most modern airship in the world—'

'Except for the R101 which will eventually be even bigger!'

Marie ignored his interruption. 'Going to Canada and back! It will certainly knock the zeppelins into a cocked hat! The Germans have had it their own way for far too long . . .'

As brother and sister argued good-naturedly, Bel considered them without answering. Larry and Marie shared the same father as Walter but *their* mother, who had died some years ago, had been an Italian beauty. Unlike Walter, Marie and Larry were olive-skinned with gleaming, dark hair. Larry's curled naturally but Marie's had been coaxed into the deep waves which, in 1930, were the height of fashion. Marie had her mother's brown eyes but Larry's were an intense blue, inherited from his father. Bel was aware of the contrast she provided with her own blond waves and grey eyes. Briefly she regarded with approval her own slim hand and the cigarette in its ivory holder; she was attractive and knew it. Her tennis dress was expensive, her long legs clad in silk. She was pampered, but the thought caused her no pangs of conscience. Only her childlessness did that. A slight shadow crossed her face as the familiar guilt surfaced. She had failed to provide Walter with a son.

Marie said, 'Wake up, dear old thing!' She snapped impatient fingers in front of Bel's face. 'I said from all accounts it's been a perfect flight so far.'

Bel pushed the unwelcome thoughts from her. 'Hurrah for the R100!' she said lightly. She might admire it, but since her father's death on the fateful R38 she had developed a singular dread of the huge airships which she was still attempting to overcome. A few weeks earlier, to please Walter, she had agreed to enter the R100 as it neared its completion. Summoning all her courage she had accompanied him on a tour of inspection, but it had proved an unfortunate experience, best forgotten and unlikely ever to be repeated. Her fears had suddenly overwhelmed her and,

3

to her husband's disgust, she had left the airship in a state of near hysteria.

Marie shook her head despairingly. 'My dear, you're quite hopeless! Hundreds of people would give their eye-teeth to be on that flight. Canada, no less! It's so romantic. Imagine docking at wherever it is—'

'St Hubert's Airport,' said Larry, pouring himself another glass of lemonade. 'Honestly, Marie, you've got a memory like a sieve! St Hubert's, Montreal. And then there's the round trip over Ottawa, to see and be seen. Then Toronto and Niagara Falls before they fly back to England. I'd love to have gone but . . .'

Marie said, 'I don't see why one of us couldn't have gone with him instead of Bel. Walter is so proud of his beloved airships.'

'It's hardly *his*,' Larry protested.

Bel shrugged. The R100 belonged to the privately financed Airship Guarantee Company and had been built at Howden in Yorkshire. Walter, involved with the R101, had nevertheless invested heavily in her rival but had not been involved in her design. His talents had been invested in the R101, the airship financed by the British government. On this airship Walter had acted as design consultant and he was eagerly awaiting *her* first transatlantic flight, promised for late August or early September. There would be a prestigious and highly publicised flight to India, when it was hoped that the Secretary of State for Air would be on board. That, thought Bel, would be the icing on the cake.

She smiled suddenly at Larry. 'Why should Walter take you with him? You blotted your copybook,' she reminded him. 'You chose to study law instead of aircraft design. What can you expect?'

'Letting the side down!' Marie agreed. 'Who needs barristers? But you should be proud of Walter, Bel.'

'I *am* proud!' Bel protested. 'I don't go around trumpet-

4

ing my feelings for him, but I *am* proud of him. He's a very clever—'

'He should be proud of *you*,' said Larry.

Bel did not miss the subtle intensity behind the words and was careful not to look at him.

Marie said, 'Proud of Bel? Why, what has she done? Except be beautiful and rich and charming.'

Deliberately flippant, Bel asked, 'Isn't that enough?'

But Marie was not to be deflected. 'Beautiful, rich women are parasites!' she declared.

Larry gave her a little push. 'Hey! Bel could never be a parasite. She does a hell of a lot more than you do. Don't be so waspish; it doesn't suit you.'

'I was not being waspish. I was stating a fact. Ask Bel. See what she thinks.'

Not for the first time, Bel wondered why she was so fond of this difficult young woman. Marie, three years older than Larry, was twenty-four. She was utterly imposs-ible at times, and had once been suspended from boarding-school for her "unsuitable and unorthodox opinions". Eventually she had been expelled from a Swiss finishing school for bad language. Six months ago she had jilted her unfortunate fiancé, and was now being swept along by the current interest in spiritualism. Marie liked to shock and, secretly, Bel envied her her confidence. By comparison she considered herself conservative and unremarkable.

'So I'm a parasite,' Bel conceded with a nonchalant wave of her cigarette. 'I married your precious half-brother, and that makes me a parasite!' A lonely, childless parasite, she added silently, with an uncharacteristic flash of self-pity.

Marie said, 'You didn't have to marry him. Or you could have waited a few years. He's so much older than you. You could have had no end of fun with all those younger men. You didn't even have the teensiest fling. Or if you did, you kept it jolly quiet.'

'I fell in love with him. Is that so awful?'

'You could have fallen for someone younger.'

'You can't *choose* to fall in love,' Bel protested. 'Even you must admit that. Age doesn't alter things. It doesn't make people less lovable.' She was aware of Larry's gaze and wished Marie would drop the subject. 'Anyway, you are hardly the best person to give advice on matters of the heart. What about poor old Henry?'

'Henry? I did him a favour! He'll thank me for it one day.'

'But originally you *did* make a mistake.'

Marie narrowed her eyes slightly. 'Are you saying *you* did, too?'

'Of *course* not!'

'Methinks the lady doth protest too much!' said Marie triumphantly.

'Oh!, for heaven's sake!' Bel felt a growing desire to shake her. 'You're a troublemaker – always trying to set the cat among the pigeons.'

As though sensing her discomfort, Larry said sharply, 'Give it a rest, Marie. You can be such a bore sometimes.'

Marie glanced at him, a strange expression on her face. 'But surely *you* think she should have chosen a younger man!'

Bel said angrily, 'Oh, stop this nonsense! You don't really care who I marry; you just like to argue.'

There was a long, awkward moment and then Marie smiled at Bel, all contrition. 'Larry's right. I'm a bore and a troublemaker, and I talk nonsense. You're not a parasite. Think of all the hours you spend at that ghastly soup kitchen when you're in London. All those smelly down-and-outs with scruffy clothes and horrible bugs. Ugh! I couldn't do it.'

'That's because you've no heart,' Larry told her.

'And you've got too much!' Marie tossed her head. 'You're too soft-hearted, Larry. You'll never make a career as a barrister. You'll be so sorry for everyone, you'll believe all their hard-luck stories, and you'll end up doing the work for nothing.' She turned to Bel. 'But I am sorry, Bel. I don't know why I say these things. I don't mean them. Walter's not a bad old stick. Do you forgive me?'

'She shouldn't,' said Larry.

'But I do,' said Bel, eager to change the subject. She smiled at Larry, her self-professed champion. 'I think one day you'll make a very good barrister. A very compassionate one, and word will get round and people will flock to you.'

'I believe you,' he laughed. 'Thousands wouldn't!' He stood up and looked from one to the other. 'Anyone feel like another game?' His gaze lingered on Bel, but she shook her head.

Marie said, 'I'm melting already. Sorry, my dear.'

'What frail creatures you are!' he said with a smile. 'Then I'll be forced to write a letter. See you later – and don't talk about me when I've gone.'

'Don't flatter yourself!' said Marie. 'What could we possibly find to say?'

In silence they watched him walk across the lawn, swatting the odd daisy here and there with the head of his racquet.

Lowering her voice, Marie said suddenly, 'He's eating his heart out for you, Bel, and you don't give a damn!'

The accusation took Bel completely by surprise, and for a moment she was too stunned to answer. She had known for some time that Larry loved her, but had never by any word or sign encouraged him. Pretending ignorance had seemed the best course. She had not realised that Marie knew of her brother's devotion, and now that she did she wondered uncomfortably whether Walter also knew. For a moment she considered denying the accusation, but that seemed cowardly.

'I know,' she admitted quietly. 'I've always known. But

7

what can I do? I don't want to hurt him, and there can be no future in it. He knows that.'

'You could say something! You could give him the chance to tell you how he feels.'

'Encourage him?' Bel stared at her with genuine astonishment. 'But how would that help?'

'You could have an affair with him!'

Bel was dumbfounded. 'An affair? Are you quite mad?'

'What harm would it do? Walter need never know.' She fixed Bel with a cool stare. 'It might help Larry to get over it. You know how these affairs are – they burn themselves out.'

'No, I don't know – and neither do you. I can't believe you are suggesting such a thing. It's impossible.' She looked at Marie suspiciously. 'Did Larry *tell* you how he felt about me?'

'He had no need to. He's my baby brother, remember? I can read him like a book. When I challenged him he told me everything; just poured his heart out. He was desperate to confide in someone.'

Bel drew a deep breath, her thoughts whirling. 'When was this?'

'A couple of years ago. Don't you love him – just a little?'

'Of course I do, but not . . . I mean I don't—.' She was aware of Marie's eyes as she stammered and fell silent. She had never allowed herself to consider whether or not she found Larry attractive in that way. The idea had been forbidden. Dangerous, even. Now, trapped by Marie's accusing gaze, she was afraid to investigate her own feelings. She was married to Walter and, whether she loved him or not, he deserved her loyalty and respect.

She said defensively,' Larry is so young. He's six years younger than me.'

'He's twenty-one. Don't try to make him sound like a lovesick adolescent.' Marie's eyes flashed angrily. 'I think

you care for him. You're just too frightened to admit it –
even to yourself!' She stood up and began to slot her
racquet back into its case.

'Marie . . .' Bel searched for words to lighten the situation. 'Walter is also your brother. Do you really want me
to betray his trust?'

'He's my half-brother.'

'You're splitting hairs, Marie.' She looked at her, puzzled. 'Don't you have any affection for Walter? He's been
very good to you and Larry since your mother died. Don't
you feel you owe him anything?'

'Larry's closer – he's flesh and blood.' Marie's tone
was defiant.' And he's suffering. Walter isn't. Walter
hasn't a care in the world – except how his precious
"101" will behave on the trip to India. I don't think he'd
even notice anything was wrong. If he found the two of
you on the rug together, he'd probably just step over
you!'

Bel almost gasped aloud as the picture Marie painted
provoked a frisson of excitement within her. She opened
her mouth to deny the accusation but closed it again.
Marie was exaggerating, but there was a kernel of truth in
her statement. 'The two of you on the rug together'! The
explicit phrase rang in her ears and Bel struggled to stifle
her imagination. In desperation she searched for a way to
change the subject. 'Walter's precious 101, as you call it, is
at this very moment being cut in half,' she told Marie, her
tone deliberately light-hearted.' The poor thing! A major
operation from all accounts!'

Marie was not fooled. 'You're changing the subject.'

'Don't you think we should?'

'No – unless you promise to think about what I've said.'

'I've thought about it already, and it's quite impossible.
You know it is.'

They regarded each other silently for a long moment
while Bel held her breath. She was feeling shocked and

vulnerable, and desperately wanted to be alone with her thoughts.

At last Marie smiled. 'Cutting her in half? My dear, what fun! I think I did read something about it.'

Bel relaxed a little. 'They're extending her frame so that they can put in another gas bag to improve the lift.'

Marie rolled her eyes. '*Fascinating*!' she said. 'About Larry—'

'No! Don't say any more, Marie. Please!'

Marie regarded her with something akin to pity. 'I'm right. You know that, Bel. All it takes is a little courage.' She shrugged lightly. 'But then you never have been very brave.'

'It's not a question of bravery.'

'Isn't it?' She smiled. 'Poor Bel. You'll never know, will you?'

'I'm Walter's *wife*! Damn you, Marie!'

Bel snatched up her racquet and walked quickly across the grass, leaving Marie to lower the net and carry in the tray. Damn her! Marie's careless words still danced in her brain. 'Together on the rug . . .' Oh, God! It was impossible. Out of the question. Marie had no right to suggest such a thing. And she herself had no right to give the suggestion a second thought. So why was her heart thudding in this unaccustomed way with a desire which she was determined not to acknowledge?

'You *fool*!' she whispered. But she knew in her heart that it was too late for recriminations. The damage had already been done.

*

Larry and Marie returned to their home in Hampstead on the following Saturday and Bel was left alone with her thoughts. She tried resolutely to banish from her mind the outrageous suggestion which Marie had made but from time to time, unintentionally, she found herself considering

10

it. If she was honest with herself, the idea attracted her simply for its excitement value. Her life with Walter was relaxed and relatively uneventful; he spoiled her, in fact. He was a wealthy man and he indulged her taste in beautiful clothes; they entertained on a regular basis; they spent time in London to make the trips to the theatre which she so much enjoyed. Their main home was in Cardington, near Bedford, only a few minutes from the airfield, but they also had a London flat. In both they employed a resident housekeeper and a daily woman to do the rough work. Yes. Bel was pampered, as Marie was fond of telling her.

Her relationship with Walter was also relaxed and that suited her. She had known him all her life, for he had been her father's closest friend. Her mother had often teased Walter, insisting that his love affair with the airship left no room in his life for a woman. Walter and Geoffrey had been enthusiastic colleagues in the airship industry until disaster parted them for ever. Even now, nine years after the event, Bel remembered the newspaper pictures of what remained of the airship which had broken up in mid-air over the Humber in 1921. She recalled Walter's desperate expression as later he watched his friend's body being lowered into the earth. The horror of that time had left an indelible mark in her mind.

Walter was a man with relatively few physical needs, and their occasional lovemaking was pleasurable but hardly passionate. He lived for his work, and a wife and home were merely the necessary trappings of existence. Bel had long since realised, albeit with somewhat rueful acceptance, that her husband's idea of heaven was an earnest discussion with fellow enthusiasts about the merits and demerits of the latest innovation in airship design. Ideally, the conversation should be held inside the vast shed which housed the airship. A dozen or more men in overalls climbing around the airship's hull would also help.

To date, Bel had found her own languid existence quite satisfactory and had never been tempted to even the slightest 'fling' with any of the men who made up their small social circle, although several married men had hinted that they would be interested. Marie's oft-repeated challenge to 'Live dangerously!' had amused her. The occasional indiscretions of her friends had merely intrigued her. She was content with her life and saw no reason to disturb the status quo. To ease her conscience she helped out at a soup kitchen run by one of her friends in a particularly deprived area of Whitechapel, and this gave her a comfortable feeling of giving something back to society.

It disturbed her now to discover just how frequently her thoughts returned to Larry, and she laid the blame for that squarely at Marie's door. It also alarmed her to note how eagerly her imagination toyed with a variety of situations in which she and Larry were exchanging romantic comments. She would suddenly find herself wondering how his kiss would feel, what he might say by way of declaring his passion, how easily she might fall in love with him. The novel she was attempting to read frequently lay forgotten in her lap, the pages unturned, and on Friday Mrs Banks, the housekeeper, had to ask her three times whether or not blanquette of veal would be acceptable for dinner. Determined not to surrender to her wild imaginings, Bel did her best to fill the days that remained before Walter returned from Canada. It was finally a great relief for her, on waking one morning, to realise that it was Saturday the 16th August and that, if all went according to plan, her husband would be home before nightfall.

*

The R100 completed her record-breaking trip on the 16th August. She arrived back in England to an ecstatic populace who, waving and cheering, stood in her enormous shadow and watched her sail overhead on her way back to Cardington. There she docked just before half-past nine, to be greeted by a huge crowd of jubilant sightseers and reporters. Here at last was something Britain could boast about; here was good news to chase away the gloom of the troubles in Ireland, an earthquake in Italy and the spectre of spiralling unemployment at home. As part of the crowd waiting below the mooring mast at Cardington, even Bel could not resist a thrill of pride as the huge ship made a textbook approach and docked. She was also surprised by the strength of her delight as she watched her husband step on to the tarmac at the foot of the mast, to be immediately swept up in the rush of photographers. His handsome face was flushed with excitement and his eyes shone as he turned to wave to those still on the airship above him and then began to search the crowd for his wife. When at last Bel managed to reach him he cried, 'Oh, my dearest girl! You should have been with me!' and hugged her exuberantly.

Over an extravagant meal that evening Walter tried to inspire in her some of the excitement and wonder of his trip, and Bel made every effort to react in an enthusiastic manner. In spite of herself, she found his elation infectious and once or twice almost wished that she *had* been with him.

'Just imagine it, Bel,' he said, his eyes glowing at the memory. 'The first Atlantic crossing by a British airship since 1919. Eleven years! And there were those who said it would never happen again. And she was *beautiful*!' He put a spoonful of Mrs Banks' best lemon cream into his mouth and swallowed it heedlessly.

Bel smiled. 'She looked wonderful from the ground as she moved away. So graceful. Dignified, somehow, as though she knew how important she was. Like an animal that knows when you are talking about it. People were visibly moved, and the radio reports and the news bulletins

13

were so full of praise. I've kept all the cuttings for you. They're in a folder on your desk.'

'Thank you, my dear,' he said and his delight was obvious. 'It was good for morale, that flight. It's been a difficult year and the people needed something to lift their spirits.' He reached across the table and took her hands in his. 'You should have been with me, my dear. Do say you will come to India? Please think about it − for my sake, Bel. You can see just how safe it is. Things have moved on since your father died.'

For a moment Bel's mind went blank with shock. He was asking her to fly!

'Please, Bel!'

She saw the pleading in his eyes and wavered. 'I . . . I'll think about it.'

'You wouldn't regret it, Bel.'

'But I thought you had doubts—' she began uncertainly.

'Doubts?'

'About the 101. You've been so worried lately.'

He brushed her comment aside. 'Oh, that. There are always problems. We'll have those ironed out in no time.' He withdrew his hands slowly and looked, she thought, a little less sure. 'I daresay the extra bay will make all the difference. I shall know better when I've seen what progress they've made while I've been away.' He frowned, then forced a smile. 'We must all think positively about her.'

Bel raised a fist in a humorous gesture of support. 'The R101!' she said, forcing a smile. The idea of a trip to India terrified her, but she had no wish to spoil her husband's triumphant return. Uninvited, the memory of her talk with Marie surfaced and she felt a surge of shame. Walter was her husband and she had been unfaithful to him in her heart. Poor, dear Walter! Somehow she must make it up to him. She breathed deeply, fighting to suppress the usual symptoms of panic which were gripping her at the mere idea of the flight: a faint nausea and a speeding-up of her pulse. If it were humanly possible she would overcome her fear and go with him. 'I will come if I can,' she said as firmly as she could. 'It was a bit sudden, Walter. Give me time to get used to the idea.'

A broad smile lit his face. 'You're a good girl, Bel. I won't push you. You come to me in your own time. It will be such an adventure. The trip of a lifetime.' He gave a little shake of his head as though to bring himself down to earth again. 'Fifty-seven hours, thirty-six minutes – that's all she took to come home! Can you imagine that? And she still had fuel. 'He shook his head and took a mouthful of wine. 'Not that we didn't have some dicey moments. We did. On the way out we hit a bit of bad weather over the St Lawrence and she bucked about a bit. Like a frisky horse. Mind you, we were doing seventy knots at the time. Tore a few holes, mostly in the fins, but they were soon patched.' He laughed.

'Didn't do much for the diners, though. Sent the food flying!'

'Good heavens!'

'Oh, they took it all in good part. I wish you'd been with me,' he said, 'but that's not a reproof. Now where was I? Oh yes. Frisky's the word. A freak wind lifted her several thousand feet.'

'Several *thousand*?'

'Oh, yes!'

'Weren't people frightened?'

'If they were, they didn't show it. There was a wonderful spirit. A great patriotism, a feeling that we were all in it together, for England's glory.' He pushed away his plate. 'You may laugh but I was—'

'Why should I laugh, Walter? It must have been wonderful.' She leaned forward and laid her hand over his. 'I'm so pleased for you. I truly am. It was a terrific achievement and I can imagine how much this means to you and everyone else.'

15

As she looked earnestly into his blue eyes she was suddenly appalled to find herself thinking of Larry's darker ones. She said quickly, 'I'm so very proud of you – and the ship, of course.'

He nodded, obviously pleased by her remarks. 'I'm not ashamed to say there was a bit of a lump in my throat when we docked at St Hubert's. The crowds were huge and the welcome was tumultuous. Never seen anything like it.' A smile lit his face. 'But I hope to! Can you imagine the reception the 101 will get in Karachi?' He sighed deeply. 'If she does half as well . . . Mind you, there was one moment on the way back . . . For some reason I don't understand they'd given the elevator wheel to a youngster . . .' He shook his head, sobered by the recollection. 'This young rigger had brought her down too low. Must have been about five hundred feet from the ground!'

'Five hundred! Good lord!' Bel's stomach knotted instantly. She knew enough to appreciate the seriousness of the error. Five hundred feet was two hundred feet less than the airship's total length.

He nodded. 'It was a close shave, believe me!'

Recognising his very real concern, Bel's fear returned. She vividly remembered the newspaper pictures of the wreckage of the R38. She had been eighteen at the time and the accounts and photographs of the disaster had filled her with horror. So many good men had lost their lives, including her father. She thought again about Walter's casual description of the R100's lucky escape. Suppose the captain had *not* seen the danger in time or had been unable to help the airship regain the necessary height? The newspapers would have headlined another disaster and Walter might not be sitting here. He might, instead, be lying in his coffin or lost for ever in a watery grave.

'Oh, Walter!' she whispered, but he was already describing Niagara Falls in great detail and went on to enthuse over the city of Toronto which had impressed him tremendously.

Suppose he had not returned from this trip? She would have been a widow . . . Her thoughts reverted yet again to Larry, and she imagined him waiting for a discreet opportunity to offer himself in Walter's stead. Would she accept? Did she feel *anything* for him? Of course he was good-looking and good company, and she had always been fond of him but . . . Oh, God! She was doing it again!

She was so angry with herself that she threw down her napkin and jumped to her feet. 'Let's have our coffee in the drawing room,' she said. Anything to interrupt this insidious line of thinking. She was ashamed and angry with herself.

Walter looked at her in surprise. 'If you wish,' he agreed.

'And then – take me to bed!' she said, with a seductive toss of her head.

Walter raised his eyebrows, making no attempt to hide his surprise. 'Have you missed me that much?' he asked, smiling.

She could only nod. Her conscience was pricking her unbearably. How could she sit there imagining herself accepting another husband when Walter had so recently escaped death? What sort of woman was she, she asked herself in an agony of frustration. She would take her husband to bed and she would be to him all that a wife should be – and more! And tomorrow she would try especially hard to please him. In short, she would love her husband to distraction! That way, she would drive these foolish thought of Larry out of her head for ever.

Walter rose, smiling, and leaned across to kiss her. Bel, confused and guilty, longed to wring Marie's sweet little neck.

*

17

After a day's rest Walter was eager to be back at work and, knowing better than to try talking him out of it, Bel waved him off soon after breakfast. He was anxious to see what had been done to the R101 in his absence and Bel was aware of his growing unease. There was an unexpressed spirit of competition between the two companies and, although Walter was elated by the success of the Canadian trip, Bel knew he was desperate for the R101 to outshine it. At present this was looking less and less likely, as the government's airship was proving disappointing in several respects. Walter was sure she would never meet her required specifications and time was growing dangerously short. Soon after 8 o'clock he had left Bel with a hurried kiss, leaving her to return to the breakfast table for a last slice of toast.

By mid-morning she had bathed and was dressed and wondering how to spend her day. She had read the paper and had chosen the menu for dinner. She had written a letter to Walter's father who, cared for by a resident nurse, still shared his home in Belsize Park with Larry and Marie. Now seventy-two, he was crippled with arthritis and spent his days in a wheelchair, but his spirit remained indomitable and Bel had great respect for him. She knew how much the success of the R100 would have pleased him and, since Walter hated letter-writing, she had filled several sheets of notepaper with details of the flight.

A glance at the clock showed her that it was not yet noon. Lunch would be at one o'clock. Perhaps she would walk to the postbox? Perhaps not. She could go after lunch. Or she might do some gardening. The roses needed a little attention since Johns, the gardener, had been laid up for two days with what he called 'a nasty bout' and what Bel called a heavy drinking spree. She considered him without enthusiasm. She would like Walter to get rid of him but, as he held a driving licence, he was occasionally

18

useful when Walter was away and she wanted to go into Bedford.

There was a knock at the door and Mrs Banks bustled in. She was wiping her hands on her apron and her plump face was flushed with excitement.

'Ma'am, there's a young man wandering about in the garden. Do you know anything about him?' She crossed to the window and pointed. 'Look. Over there!'

Intrigued, Bel rose to her feet and joined the housekeeper. 'So there is. How odd! I don't know who he can be. Maybe Walter—'

'Had I best ask him, then, ma'am?' Mrs Banks suggested eagerly. 'You can't be too careful these days. Strangers and what-not. He might be . . . you know, a bit funny up here.' She tapped her forehead.

For a moment Bel made no answer. Puzzled, she watched the intruder as he made his way over the grass. He was stockily built, with broad shoulders and light brown hair. His hands were in his pockets and there was something in his manner of walking that disturbed Bel. Was it arrogance? She frowned. Whatever was he up to, she wondered. There was something about the tilt of his head . . . He suddenly began to whistle tunelessly as though defying anyone to challenge his right to be there.

Mrs Banks said, 'Cheeky young monkey! I'd give him whistle!'

Bel nodded. 'Yes, perhaps you'd better ask him what he wants.' But before the housekeeper could leave the room she changed her mind. 'No! Better still – *I'll* ask him.'

Ignoring Mrs Banks' obvious disappointment, she hurried along the passage to the front door and out into the garden. The young man was standing beside the rockery and turned to smile at her.

'Can I help you?' Bel asked with a polite smile.

'I shouldn't think so,' he said, 'but thanks, anyway. Nice

19

garden.' He pointed to the rose-bed. 'Those pale pink ones. Ophelia.'

'That's right but—'

'My father's favourite rose.' He looked straight into her eyes. 'My father likes roses.'

She stared at him, disconcerted. 'What are you doing here?'

He shrugged carelessly. 'Just wandering, you know. Nothing specific. Admiring the flowers. That sort of thing.'

Bel felt her face tighten and was aware that Mrs Banks was hovering on the front step, listening.

'You do realise you're trespassing, I suppose?'

His expression changed to one of exaggerated innocence. 'But I'm not doing any damage. I'm not trampling any corn and I haven't left any gates open. No cattle stampeding down the road.' He put up a hand to shadow his face and stared into the distance. 'At least, none that I can see.' Before Bel could counter this he turned back to stare at her with cold eyes. 'You must be the lady of the house. You're awfully pretty.'

Before she knew what she was doing, Bel had opened her mouth to thank him for the compliment. She quickly shut it again. She was certainly not going to be softened by sweet talking.

'And your name is—?' she asked coolly.

'Howard.'

Mrs Banks, unwilling to be left out of the little drama, waddled across the lawn towards them. 'Are you all right, ma'am?' she asked unnecessarily.

Bel said, 'Quite all right, thank you, Mrs Banks.' But, in fact, she was a little uncertain what to do next. The young man seemed harmless enough, but possibly looks were deceptive and she had no intention of putting herself or the housekeeper at risk. She said sharply, 'Well, perhaps you'd like to leave us now, since you say you have no business with us and this *is* private property.'

Mrs Banks folded her arms. 'Yes, you be off,' she said sternly.

He seemed quite undismayed by this show of resistance and, laughing lightly, ran a hand through his hair. To Bel he said, 'Do you really want to be rid of me? Mightn't you want to know me better? You might even "take" to me. You never know.'

Mrs Banks said, 'Don't you be so saucy!'

To the intruder, Bel said, 'Take to you? No, I don't think so. I don't care for your impertinence.' She felt that the conversation was getting out of hand and that she was losing the initiative – if she had ever had it. She was disturbed by his presence in a way that she could not explain. She did not expect him to produce a knife or pistol but she did feel threatened. The directness of his gaze unnerved her.

She said, 'Should I know you? I mean, is this some kind of joke you're playing?' There was something vaguely familiar about him, but she could not decide exactly what it was. His voice, perhaps? 'You're not a long-lost nephew just back from Australia, are you?' She made it sound like a joke, but Mrs Banks was not amused.

'He's an intruder!' she said scornfully. 'That's all he is. An intruder with a lot of cheek! If the master was here he'd soon—'

The young man reacted strongly to her words. 'Oh, the *master*!' His chin jutted just a little. 'Perhaps the *master* would treat me more kindly. He might even ask me in for a cup of tea and the odd "biccy".'

'I doubt it,' Bel told him. She was beginning to feel distinctly troubled. There was something in his manner that made her uneasy; it was as though he were totally in control of the situation and amused by her reaction. His confidence undermined her and this knowledge annoyed her. Suddenly she experienced a frisson of fear and wished that her husband was around. And had this young man

21

known that he was not present? How could he? Unless he knew Walter. 'Do you work for my husband?' she demanded. Perhaps he had been sacked and was now determined to make himself a nuisance. 'Or *did* you ever work for him?'

Mrs Banks asked 'Should I ring for the police, ma'am?'

Bel continued to stare at him. Was he perhaps a thief who for some reason had expected the house to be empty and was now bluffing his way out of trouble?

He stared back at her, his gaze intense and disconcerting. 'I don't think that's any of your business,' he told her.

Bel felt a rush of anger. 'Now that's enough,' she said. 'This is my property and I'm asking you formally, and for the last time, to leave.'

He looked at her thoughtfully for a long moment. 'Yes, you're awfully pretty,' he said. 'I thought you would be.'

While Bel was searching for a crushing remark he suddenly put up his hand in mock salute and walked briskly away. They watched in silence as he reached the drive and headed towards the gate. Bel was annoyed to notice the still defiant set of his broad shoulders and the arrogant tilt of his fair head. When at last he was out of sight she looked at Mrs Banks unhappily.

'Well!' said the housekeeper with a puzzled frown. 'What on earth was all that about?'

'I don't know.' Bel shook her head.

'And where did he spring from?'

'Maybe he is *from* somewhere. An asylum or a hospital, maybe. But . . .' Bel shook her head. 'He didn't look mad, did he? Not *mad* mad, if you see what I mean.'

At that moment they heard a motor-cycle start up, and Mrs Banks said, 'So that's how he got here!'

They listened intently as the engine roared and then faded into the distance.

'I think it's all very odd, ma'am, and you should notify the police.'

'Oh, dear! Do you really?' Bel hesitated. 'It's just that if he's really quite harmless I should hate to get him into trouble.'

'Harmless? What's harmless about making yourself at home in someone else's garden? There was a funny look in his eyes if you ask me. He might be dangerous!'

'He didn't hurt us. He could have done.' Bel stared round the garden helplessly. 'Oh dear! If only my husband had been here.'

At that moment they both saw the blue smoke of the motor-cycle's exhaust as it rose lazily above the rhododendron hedge. A final gesture, thought Bel. It was as though, even in his absence, he had wanted the last word.

Seeing the housekeeper's concern, she said, 'I'll talk to my husband when he comes home and he can ring the police if he thinks it necessary.' She frowned. 'How old was he, do you think? About twenty?'

'About that, I reckon.'

'Wearing? Oh, lord, I'm forgetting already. A darkish blazer . . .'

'And no hat!'

As they began to walk back to the house, Bel said, 'Do you think it *could* have been some kind of practical joke?'

Mrs Banks snorted. 'Joke? That was no joke, ma'am. I'll bet my last farthing on it. He was up to no good. A wrong'un. It was written all over him.'

'We may never know,' said Bel, but as they walked back into the house she had the strongest feeling that they had not heard the last of him.

*

That afternoon Walter stood alone in the vast shed which housed the two halves of the R101. The roof, almost two hundred feet above him, effectively shut out the sun's warmth and at this time of the year no one complained about the cool interior. It was a different matter in winter,

23

Walter reflected, when snow fell and there was no way to heat the shed. Then there were well-founded complaints from the men about the freezing conditions in which they had to work. Around him, the sound of metal on metal echoed and re-echoed in the space above his head and voices floated spectrally in the air. There were lights everywhere to combat the permanent gloom, some hung on wires, others fixed to metal frames. They came from every angle and all pointed to the stricken airship.

Walter stared at the creation on which he had lavished years of devotion. 'You've *got* to do it!' he muttered. 'You *must*!'

Nearby, to his left, a generator hummed, coughed and resumed its humming. To his right a small group of mechanics conferred, their heads together, engrossed in their discussion. Ahead of him a trestle table had been set up and on this large blueprints were spread out. A middle-aged man bent assiduously over his calculations while another watched him impatiently, hands on his hips, waiting for a verdict. To Walter the scene was as familiar as the back of his own hand.

He glanced upwards at the dozens of young men who clambered, like so many monkeys, amongst the vast curving framework of the forward half of the airship. The other half, temporarily abandoned, filled the dark space with its delicate metallic tracery. To an outsider the huge interior of the shed would appear as a starkly efficient work-place. To Walter it was a second home, a familiar and welcoming environment which demanded his unstinting allegiance. He was equally happy here in the middle of summer or the depths of winter, and he hardly registered the changing of the seasons. He was as comfortable in the middle of the day as he was in the early hours of the morning. The occasional emergency call which disturbed his sleep at home would be welcomed as a challenge rather than an intrusion. It was as though the outside world receded as soon as he set foot inside the huge doors and, Jonah-like, was swallowed up in the shed's cavernous maw.

Walter had returned from the flight on the R100 with mixed feelings. There was a deep satisfaction that it had been so successful and would undoubtedly reinforce the government's commitment to the industry as a whole. Their commitment was not in doubt. The Royal Airship Works at Cardington was proof of that, for although Britain now had a Labour government the R.A.W. was still funded entirely by them. But for how long? Walter suffered from a growing suspicion that his beloved R101 could not, and would not, prove equal in performance to the R100. All earlier hopes that it would actually exceed the 100's performance had long since evaporated, at least in Walter's mind. No one had yet admitted to such a treacherous opinion and Walter had no intention of being the first to utter such heresy. He had hoped that by the time he returned from Canada some of the faults would have been miraculously rectified, but now found to his dismay that this was not the case. There were too many things going wrong and too little time to put them right. It seemed that as soon as one problem was eradicated another surfaced, and his original frustration was rapidly developing into a deep unease.

The earlier trial flights had proved less than reassuring. Then her designers had been alarmed to learn that sharp-cornered metal struts were rubbing against the giant gas bags and in some cases fraying them badly. Small holes had appeared and these had been crudely patched. The rough edges had been padded, but to what effect? How safe was it now, he wondered anxiously. And how would the repairs stand up to an intercontinental flight lasting fifty hours in weather conditions that could not be guaranteed fine? So far the only trial flights had taken place in perfect weather because they dared not risk damage to the airship which would be costly and time-consuming to repair. Time was their enemy. Or one of them, he thought ruefully.

The various trials to date had merely confirmed the growing suspicion, secretly shared among the experts, that there were inherent weaknesses in her design. The airship did not behave well in rough weather, but pitched and rolled. When it rained her silver skin soaked up the water and added weight to a vessel that was already refusing to fly as fast as expected.

The gas valves were also giving concern. When the ship rolled heavily the valves opened, allowing the hydrogen gas to escape. In bad weather the flight could take longer than the fifty hours predicted, and if that happened the total loss of gas could be significant. Walter knew, too, that the original specifications for the airship had not been met. Her diesel engines were not as good as the Rolls Royce engines chosen by the designers of the R100, and on several occasions had actually broken down in flight. The airship itself was heavier than anticipated by several tons. It was for this reason that they were inserting an extra gas bag which meant that the entire framework had to be extended. Because of the airship's shape the new section had to go amidships and this work was now in progress. But would the extra bay give the additional lift that was needed? Walter was not at all sure.

As he stared unhappily around, he was joined by a foreman in white overalls whose expression was as sombre as his own.

'It's a bloody shambles, sir,' he said bluntly, 'and Thompson's digging his heels in, still hoping that we fly on time. Breathing down our bloody necks!' He shook his head morosely. 'We're breaking our backs as it is; working round the clock almost. We keep telling him it's touch and go, and to make it we'll need an awful lot of luck. But will he listen? Not bloody likely! Says he *must* be back in

England for the conference on the twentieth of October. Won't hear any arguments.'

Walter pursed his lips irritably. Lord Thompson, the Minister for Air, was putting additional pressure on to the ship's builders by insisting that he use the flight to India as a flag-waving occasion, timed to impress the various heads of state who would later be converging on London. Walter shook his head. 'And if she's *not* ready to fly, Allicks? If she's not fit?'

A shrug of the shoulders was the only answer he got and he went on, 'But if she doesn't get her Certificate of Airworthiness she won't be *allowed* to fly!'

Allicks laughed mirthlessly. 'It's a nice thought, sir. I wish I could believe it but I don't. Somehow they'll get her into the air. Someone will pull a few strings or turn a blind eye. It's bloody ironic. We only need a few more days – a week, maybe. I mean, look at her, sir. All that money, and they're willing to spoil the ship for a hap'orth of tar!' He sighed heavily, blowing out his cheeks. 'If you ask me, Thompson's got too much at stake. They say he's tipped to be the next Viceroy of India. You can see what a show he'd make – arriving in India in the R101. "Look! No hands!" Huh? A nice little feather in his cap!'

'If they arrive at all!'

As soon as he had spoken Walter wished the words unsaid. He heard Allicks' sharp intake of breath and cursed his own stupidity. He had gone too far. He had allowed his own disillusion to affect his judgement. Bad luck to even *speak* of such a thing, and awfully bad form to encourage despondency among the men. He should have known better, he reflected, annoyed with himself. He rested his hand on the man's shoulder and said quickly, 'Take no notice of me, Allicks. I'm feeling a bit gloomy today.'

'That's all right sir.'

'Are the men bearing up? Wouldn't want them to lose heart.'

'I reckon most of them think she'll make it, sir. They believe what they want to believe, some of them. Can't blame them, either. What can they do about it, poor sods? They do a week's work and take home a week's wages. It's a job to them.'

Walter raised his eyebrows. 'I hope she's a little more than that!'

'Well, maybe, sir, but you know what I mean. They don't carry the can.'

Walter nodded. 'We must keep up morale,' he said. 'Forget what I said just now. Put it down to indigestion or something!' He sighed heavily. 'I've got a lot on my mind at the moment.' To make this more convincing he added, 'Family troubles.'

Allicks gave him a quick look. 'Like that, is it, sir? I'm sorry.'

Walter shrugged lightly. It was not 'like that' but at least he had distracted the man's attention; had given him something else to think about. 'Nothing that can't be put right' he said cheerfully.

'Wish I could say the same about *her*.' Allicks jerked a thumb towards the airship. 'It's a bastard, sir, if you'll pardon my French.'

Walter nodded. He wanted to say something encouraging but could think of nothing that might convince Allicks; he was not a stupid man, and to pretend that all was well would insult his intelligence.

'Let's keep our fingers crossed,' he said. 'With a bit of luck it can all come together even at this late stage. If someone up there' . . . he pointed skywards, 'smiles on us!'

'He'll have to do a bloody sight more than *smile*!' Allicks grinned. 'He'll have to come down here, pick up a spanner and get his fingers dirty!'

Walter forced a smile and stuck up a thumb in the universal gesture of confidence. 'We'll do it!' he told him. 'We'll surprise them all! Hold on to that thought!'

If only he himself believed that, Walter thought, as the foreman, with a final shake of his head, moved away in the direction of the men at the table. Calmly, he tried to consider the worst possibility – a delayed or cancelled trip. Oh, God! If the trip had to be cancelled, the airship industry would lose face. Worse still, Britain would lose respect worldwide because the R100 had already raised such high expectations. Walter bit his lip. The thought of such a failure was abhorrent but he was a realist. In his own mind, the doubts were crystallising into an incontrovertible certainty, and his eyes dulled as he faced the brutal fact. His Majesty's Airship R101 could not possibly be ready on time.

Chapter Two

BY THE AFTERNOON POST, BEL received a letter in a familiar handwriting; a letter which immediately chased from her mind all thoughts of the mysterious trespasser. It was from Larry. Her first thought was, 'Thank heavens Walter is at work!' For a long moment she stared at the envelope without making any attempt to open it. Larry rarely wrote to her, and when he did it was usually a 'Thank you' letter, an invitation to a party or a suggestion that she and Walter join a group of friends for a trip to the theatre. Intuition warned her that this was different. Ignoring the rest of the letters, she went out into the garden and made for her favourite perch – the swing beneath the sycamore. It was here, beneath the sheltering branches, that she had somehow accepted the dreadful possibility that she was barren; here, two years ago, that she had wept at the death of her mother; here, also, that she had come to terms with the knowledge that she no longer loved Walter in the way he deserved to be loved. Now, sensing the importance of the moment, she sat down on the swing and reluctantly eased her finger under the flap of the envelope.

'Don't say it, Larry!' she whispered as she slowly unfolded the pages. 'Please don't *tell* me!'

While his love remained undeclared she could pretend it

did not exist, but once he had revealed the depth of his feelings nothing could ever be the same again. If Larry told her that he loved her she would have to respond in some way, and she did not know what to say. With the envelope open she resisted the urge to withdraw the folded sheets. Or was she afraid to do so? In her heart she felt that the letter heralded change and she was unprepared for that. As Walter's wife she was safe but as Larry's lover . . . She hesitated, turning the envelope slowly in her hands, wondering if she dare send it back unread.

'No!' she whispered. She owed him that much, surely. She was swept with a sudden compassion. Poor Larry! A young man who was wasting his youth in a hopeless passion. Was Marie right after all? She had made Bel feel mean-spirited, ungenerous. Guilty, even. Bel hadn't liked the picture of herself that Marie's words had conjured up. She had known Larry since he was a baby; he was born when she was six years old and playing with dolls. Then he had been 'Uncle Walter's baby brother.' She smiled at the memory. The two families had gone on holiday together when the children were little. She and Marie and Larry had built sand-castles together and fished for shrimps and searched for shells. A threesome, dubbed 'the terrible trio' by Walter who was bemused by his father's second family. Then Marie and Larry had departed for boarding school and they had seen less of each other. She next became aware of Larry when he was fourteen and she was twenty and engaged to marry Walter. She had been surprised by the eloquence of his eyes, a dark blue with great brilliance so that she fancied his very soul might be glimpsed in their depths. Over the years he had grown into an attractive man.

The first line of the letter destroyed any hope she might have entertained that it was not a love letter. In spite of herself her hands trembled as she read:

My very dearest Bel,

This letter is so hard to write, mainly because I had never expected to speak of my feelings for you. Now Marie has made it inevitable, and I cannot forgive her interference. She has told me of her conversation with you and I am shaken to the core. We have quarrelled . . .

'Oh, *no!*' cried Bel. A family rift would be unbearable.

. . . Of course I love you but I would never, never have done or said anything to come between you and Walter. You must believe me. But because of her meddling I felt I should put pen to paper, if only to assure you that I shall never refer to the matter again. I hope most sincerely that you will feel able to behave towards me as you always have done – to treat me as a brother – albeit a well-loved one!

Instinctively Bel closed her eyes, unwilling to read more. Already she could see problems arising. Either Walter or their father would learn of the quarrel between Marie and Larry, and would ask questions. He would suspect that either Marie or Larry would confide in Bel, and she could hardly explain the cause of the trouble.

'Damn you, Marie!' she muttered, as she read on:

Being near to you has always been a source of such joy to me that I could not bear it were we to lose that uncomplicated friendship. All I ask is that you allow me to love you. Don't reproach me, my dearest Bel, for I cannot help myself and a cold word from you would break my heart. I will never try to come between you and Walter – how could I even think of it? I am sure Walter loves you dearly. If he did not I

32

might dare to hope there was a chance for me, but you are such a wonderful person – how could he not love you? He has been so good to us since Mother died . . .

Bel sighed. Yes, it was true, she reflected. Teresa's premature death from tuberculosis had left Marie and Larry motherless while still very young and their father had withdrawn from them, shocked into a severe depression by his loss. Walter had done his best to fill the gap in their lives until George had recovered.

. . . and he deserves your love. If you can put this whole sorry incident from you, perhaps you and I can carry on as before. Although I would lay down my life for you, I ask nothing from you. I will settle most gratefully for a loving friendship.

Yours, Larry

Before she knew what she was doing Bel had pressed the letter to her lips and tears filled her eyes. She allowed herself a long moment's heartache and then, blinking furiously, she drew in a sharp breath.

'Don't be such a *fool*!' she told herself angrily. 'Larry is nothing to you. *Nothing*!' She stared at the letter. Walter must never see it. She would destroy it at once; with a quick gesture she tore it through and returned the fragments of paper to the envelope. Her heart raced, however, and confusing emotions swept through her. Slowly she began to push herself to and fro as though the gentle rhythm of the swing might somehow restore her peace of mind. Larry's letter had disturbed her fragile poise, had jolted her into an awareness of a passion that was new to her. Despite the problems which Marie's meddling had created Bel could not deny that something within her exulted at Larry's declaration of love. Inexplicably, his

33

words had comforted her: 'I would lay down my life for you . . .'

'Like the good shepherd,' she thought, and a faint smile touched her face and softened it. How wonderful to be one of his lambs, carried in those strong young arms; tended by those gentle hands . . .

'*No!*' she cried, thrusting the images from her. 'This is just crazy!'

With a fierce gesture of rejection she threw the envelope to the ground and forced herself higher. She must be sensible about this, she told herself earnestly. She must certainly not allow it to develop further. Larry was so young, she would need to be strong for both of them. 'Think!' she told herself as the swing took her higher. 'Stay calm and think it out carefully.' She was angry with Marie for precipitating this crisis between them and, for the moment at least, decided to do nothing to heal the rift between brother and sister. Marie must be made to see that she could not interfere in people's lives with impunity. But Larry was the innocent victim whose only crime was to fall in love with his half-brother's wife. The burning question was – should she answer the letter? To do so might be a mistake. Yet not to answer it might make him think that she blamed him in some way for what had happened. He had finally declared his feelings for her and she appreciated the compliment. She was not annoyed with him and she wanted him to understand that. On the other hand, by answering the letter she might encourage him, and that was exactly what Marie wanted her to do.

'Larry! *Larry!*' she whispered and his name produced an unfamiliar but highly pleasurable thrill within her. Frowning suddenly, she drew in her breath and let it out slowly. This was what she most feared – an awakening of interest on her part. This was what she must guard against.

Slowly the arc of the swing lessened until she was quite still and then she stared down at the offending envelope.

34

She had been too hasty, she could see that now. The letter was in pieces. Too late to return it unanswered. Impossible to pretend she hadn't read it.

'I'll have to answer it', she said aloud. A few well-chosen, kindly phrases would suffice. Then she would dispose of the letter and that would be the end of it. Full of good intentions, she slid from the swing and picked up the envelope, then crossed the lawn to the area beside the tennis court where the chairs and table stood empty. She sat down and, before she knew what she was about, had emptied out the torn paper and was reassembling the letter. When it was done she reread it; She read it several times until she knew it by heart. It was only when the tears fell on the paper that she realised she was crying.

*

Vera glanced across the small, neat kitchen. 'Serviceable', the estate agent had called it. Over the years she had tried to make it homely, with a plaited cloth rug and seat cushions and a few flowers in a vase on the windowsill. There were times when she looked at it with critical affection, but today she had eyes only for her son who, with his elbows on the table in front of him, was supporting his head between his two cupped hands. He had been very quiet all day and that, she knew, was a bad sign where Howard was concerned. She tipped the potatoes into the colander and watched the boiling water drain away. Two grilled chops waited in the pan and she had cooked plenty of onions – strong ones, the kind he liked. The meal was one of his favourites, but something told her that this evening he would scarcely taste the food. She guessed that he had something on his mind and was wondering how to break it to her . . . which meant that the news was not good. He had been this way exactly when he first told her about his girl-friend, May – a relationship which fortunately

35

had withered within a few months. He had been equally preoccupied when he failed his mid-term examination, and was frequently distracted and withdrawn whenever he thought about his father. Recently, however, he had seemed more withdrawn, more uncommunicative, and it was difficult not to feel anxious.

She tried to see his expression but his face was now hidden in his hands. Carefully she shared out the chops, added onions, potatoes and gravy and set the plates on the table.

'So what is it? What's up?' She sat down and reached for the salt and pepper.

'The matter? Nothing!'

'That's not true.'

He took the salt from her and applied it liberally to his dinner. 'How was the shop?' he asked.

For a moment, caught off guard, she was distracted. 'It was "middling", as Mr Carter would say. Mrs Barnes has been refused any more credit, but I could see it coming. Poor soul, she was so embarrassed. I couldn't bear to see it; I went out to the back.'

'What can she expect? She should pay her bills.'

'But can she? Mr Carter said her husband spends all the money on drink.'

He hacked at the chop, put a large forkful of food into his mouth and chewed absentmindedly.

Just as she had expected, thought Vera with resignation. It could be sawdust on the fork for all the notice he took. Sometimes she wondered why she bothered, but then he was her only child and he wouldn't always be with her. He was twenty, and would spread his wings sooner or later. He was ambitious, she knew; determined to 'make good', spurred on by his father's enviable position in life. Howard's one aim was to earn a great deal of money, and she could not find it in her heart to blame him for that. She worked three mornings a week in the grocer's shop on the corner. Their existence, though not meagre, lacked the sparkle which money could add.

After a long silence he said, 'I've got the job; the one I wanted. I can start next week.'

He was avoiding her eyes, she noted, and she was seized by a dreadful premonition. 'Which job?' she asked. 'You applied for more than one.'

'The best one, the one I wanted . . . in Bedfordshire. I told you about it. I said—'

'Bedfordshire?' Her voice rose. 'Bedfordshire?' Her own appetite disappeared and she laid down her knife and fork with a clatter. 'Oh, Howard! You haven't? Not Cardington? Not there? Oh, you didn't?' She stared at him, transfixed.

He gave a defiant toss of his fair head, a gesture that always infuriated her.

'But I have, Mum. At Cardington. They've taken me on as a trainee rigger. Not all that much to start with but—'

'The A.G.C.? Your *father's* company?'

He looked up, his face reddening. 'For heaven's sake! The A.G.C. is *not* Dad's company; he merely has money invested in it. I'm talking about the Royal Airship Works where Dad is a consultant. It's not my fault if he has a finger in both pies. I want to work with airships and Cardington's the place to be.' He forked more food into his mouth and ate furiously. 'There's no reason why I shouldn't get a job there . . .' he mumbled.

'Don't talk with your mouth full!' she said from habit.

'I will if I want! I'm not a child, Mum. I'll eat any way I like.'

'I taught you decent manners.'

'Who cares?'

'I do,' she insisted, but her heart was not in the argument. She looked at him helplessly. 'Oh, please, Howard! Not Cardington!'

'Cardington!' he insisted. 'Dad doesn't own the place

and he doesn't own me! I'm entitled to work anywhere I can—'

'But he'll be furious!' Her heart lurched with fear. Why did this son of hers have to persist with his vendetta? He won't want you there – you know he won't.'

'He won't *know*, will he? Unless you tell him. I'll be just a number to him.' You don't think he lowers himself to speak to the men, do you? He's too busy hobnobbing with the important people. You've heard him: Sir This and Lord That. Oh don't worry, Mum. I doubt he'll notice me.'

She picked up her knife and fork and toyed with some onions. 'But *why*, Howard? I don't understand. Why antagonise him?'

'Because I despise him! That's why.' The sullen expression she knew so well settled on his face. 'Because he doesn't want to know me. That's enough of a reason.'

'Doesn't want to know you?' Her own anger flared. 'How can you say such a thing? How can you even *think* such a thing? He has always known you; always cared for you. You've been to a good school and then college. He paid for all that – oh, Howard! How can you talk like this?'

He pushed back his chair and rose to his feet. 'I'm not saying any more, except that he's not the man you think he is. I know. He's a liar and a—' He bit back the rest of the sentence. 'I'm going up there on Sunday and you can't stop me. There's a room for me at Shortstown. It's all arranged.'

'Shortstown? Where is this Shortstown?'

'It's an estate just across the road from the flying field. They built it for the workmen. Some of the senior staff live there, too. A Mrs Croft is renting me a room and cooking me a dinner. She's a widow.' As he looked at her, his voice softened. 'Don't worry. I'll be OK, Mum.'

'But will you?' Vera was seized by a great sadness. Her

son was leaving her. She choked back tears. She wanted to shout at him but it would achieve nothing. He was like his father, stubborn and self-willed. On the few occasions when Walter did visit, it seemed she had spent her time refereeing their arguments and patching up their quarrels. And yet his father loved him. Did Howard know that? She had done her best to convince him.

Now, suddenly defeated, she knew that he would go and she would be on her own. She glanced down at the congealing food; gathering the plates, she said dully, 'The birds will be happy.'

Outside in the cramped garden she scraped the food on to the bird-table. Howard had made it as a present to her when he was thirteen years old, and it had always leaned sideways. Not that the birds minded. Before she had returned to the back door a starling had appeared and was rooting happily among the food scraps. It strutted about, stabbing at the food, gulping it down greedily She watched for a moment, struggling again to hold back tears. A rough, unmannered bird, rather like her son.

Howard still waited in the kitchen. As she closed the back door she sensed that his temper was cooling, but her own emotions were still agonisingly raw. All her life she had dreaded this moment, while working to avoid it.

He said, 'Look, Mum, I have to go.'

'Are you sure he doesn't know?'

'He doesn't.'

Vera hesitated. 'Maybe it would be better if we told him – before he finds out?' She looked at him anxiously.

'Why should we tell him? He doesn't keep us informed of *his* activities. We're left in the dark for months on end until he condescends to write to us or call in.'

She felt a great weakness in her legs and sat down shakily. 'But suppose he sees you – or hears your name mentioned?'

'Look, Mum, I'm not actually deceiving him. I'm simply

not telling him. If he asks I'll say I didn't think he'd be interested.'

She looked at the young, flushed face and knew that she was unable to help him. He was determined to test his strength against that of his father. Her days as peacemaker had come to an abrupt end and now he was alone.

'You'll regret this,' she said wearily. Another thought struck her, giving her further cause for alarm. 'Stay away from him, won't you, Howard? You must promise me that. Don't go looking for trouble. Oh, Howard! There's so much you don't know about your father and me.'

Howard's mouth tightened ominously. 'And there's a lot *you* don't know, Mum.'

'What's that supposed to mean?'

'I've found out things—'

'Found out? What do you mean?' Her heart began to race and she felt very cold.

He glanced away. 'Nothing!'

'You said you had—'

'I said *nothing*!' he shouted. 'For heaven's sake! I don't mean anything. It was just something to say. Forget it, can't you!'

For a long moment they stared at each other.

'Howard . . .'

'Stop it, Mum! Let it rest, can't you?' He took a deep lungful of air like a drowning man. 'Why you still love him is beyond me. He ignores you for ages, then comes here like a prodigal son and you – you practically *grovel*!'

'Howard!' She sprang to her feet, and before she knew what she was doing she had slapped him hard across the face. 'I won't have you say such things. You think what you will, but I know him. I understand him. I know what he has done for us and I know how hard it's been for him. He—' She broke off, biting her lip, not daring to look at her son. She had struck him across the face and he would never forget, probably never forgive her. Tears welled up

40

in her eyes. 'And I *don't* grovel. That was a wicked thing to say. Oh, Howard! Howard!'

Nothing she could say would express the depth of her anguish. Why did they all have to quarrel? All she wanted was to love them both, to be loved in return and to know that they loved each other. Was it too much to expect? Instead there was this gulf between her husband and her son, this terrible barrier. She didn't understand how it had come about. As a child Howard had adored his father and they had played together. She remembered him sitting on his father's lap, listening to a bedtime story . . . and the day he had taken them to Worthing. Watching them together, throwing pebbles into the sea, she had been so proud and happy. When had it all gone wrong?

Howard said, 'Look, I'm sorry.'

'No, you're not!' All her pent-up bitterness rang in those words. If her son and husband did not value her, what was she, she wondered desperately. She had never had any other role. Damn Howard – and damn his father! The suspicion surfaced that perhaps there had been a grain of truth in her son's comment. But *grovel*? No. She had never grovelled in her life. But perhaps she had been too pleased to see her errant husband, a little too grateful for his sporadic interest.

'Mum,' said Howard, 'about what I said just now. I didn't mean—'

She cut in quickly. 'Stop it! I don't want to hear any more.' Her voice shook and she realised she had a choice: she must end the conversation or burst into tears. Taking a deep breath, she gathered around her what little dignity she still retained. He was leaving her and she would have to stand alone. This was a good time to start, she told herself resolutely, ignoring the terrible ache in her heart. She saw the stricken look on his face but pressed on. 'You are so sure of yourself. You think you know best. So go. Take the job. I wish you well.'

And without giving him time to argue further, she turned on her heel and rushed out of the room. Stumbling blindly up the stairs to her bedroom, she closed the door behind her and leaned back against it, while tears coursed down her face. She heard him shout, 'Mum! Come back here!' and was tempted momentarily. But then, somehow, her resolve stiffened and she shook her head.

'No, Howard!' she whispered. 'Not any more!'

Let them both do without her! She groped her way to the bed and sat on it, sobs choking her. Then, still sobbing, she stood up, crossed to the door and turned the key in the lock.

*

Larry stuffed various files into his briefcase and buckled it securely. From behind his desk Stanley Meade, Clerk of Chambers, regarded him sourly over the rim of his spectacles.

'Off already?' he asked, with a disapproving glance at the clock on the wall behind him.

'That's right.' Larry ignored the unspoken suggestion that he was behaving improperly by leaving the Temple at half-past five. Normally he would have lingered awhile to talk to Edward Barnes when he returned from court, but this week Larry had found it impossible. He had left promptly, desperate to get home and see if a letter from Bel awaited him. So far he had been out of luck and the disappointment was agonising. He wanted a letter from her, no matter what it contained.

'I'm off then!' he announced cheerfully.

Meade regarded him balefully. 'I'll tell Mr Barnes that once again you were unable to wait for him. Something pressing, no doubt?'

'Very pressing!'

'Tomorrow, then. Nine sharp?'

'Of course.' Larry experienced a slight twinge of conscience. Meade was a decent enough fellow who was usually very helpful. It wouldn't be wise to spoil the relationship. He said, 'An affair of the heart, Mr Meade!' and rolled his eyes humorously, inviting sympathy.

'Ah!' The man smiled thinly. 'Mustn't keep a lady waiting. Women are such tartars about time. You don't have to tell me. My wife simply cannot bear—'

Larry glanced at the clock. 'Must go. She'll never forgive me if I'm late. Good night, then.'

A dismissive wave from Meade said it all and, thankfully, Larry ran down the steps and, ignoring the path, hurried across the grass where over the years countless similarly impatient feet had worn a track. On the far side of the green he rejoined the pavement and made his way around the corner to join the queue at the bus-stop. The congested traffic rumbled past, open-topped buses, trams, motor-cars and motor-bikes. A few carts rolled by, their horses blinkered, the drivers wary. Larry saw and heard nothing, so wrapped up was he with his problem. He longed for a few kind words from Bel; they would make him the happiest man alive. If only she would understand! Even better would be an admission that she felt the same affection for him, although he knew this would be dangerous. With the slightest encouragement Larry felt he would be lost. It would take so little on Bel's part to send him sliding down the primrose path to – to what? To everlasting regret? To eternal damnation? In his present mood even eternal damnation seemed a small price to pay for Bel's love. But she was Walter's wife and he was fond of Walter, too. How could he ever look Walter in the eye again if he had laid so much as a finger on his wife? The thought of touching her made him close his eyes in an agony of frustration.

'Oh, Bel!' he cried.

The woman in front of him turned enquiringly. 'What's that?'

43

He hoped he wasn't blushing. 'I'm sorry. I was talking to myself!'

The man behind him laughed. 'You want to watch that, mate! You know what they say!' And he tapped his forehead meaningfully.

Fortunately for Larry, the conversation was abruptly ended by the arrival of the bus and he climbed the stairs and made his way to the front. Clutching his briefcase to him like a shield, he settled into a seat and once more allowed his thoughts to dwell on the forbidden subject. He imagined himself alone with Bel, confiding his love to her. In this imaginary confession Bel told him that she no longer loved her husband and suggested that they run away together to find happiness . . .

'I said, "Where to?" You deaf or something?'

The bus conductor was eyeing him with a disgruntled expression.

'I'm sorry.' He handed over twopence and received his ticket without further comment.

The clumsy interruption had spoiled his dream and he turned his attention to another problem. What was he to do if Bel didn't answer his letter? As the bus wove its way between the other vehicles on the road, Larry considered the options without enthusiasm. He could stay away from Bel, although that would certainly provoke comment. He could go round to their flat and challenge her, but that way he ran the risk of a firm rejection. He could, if it were possible, ignore the whole thing and pretend that he had never written the letter. He stared unseeingly ahead, wishing away the next fifteen minutes of his life so that he could be at home, hopefully opening the letter for which he waited so desperately. A small round woman with a mass of parcels sat down next to him and began a conversation about the weather which effectively interrupted his line of thought. He was glad when he reached his stop and could hurry down the stairs of the bus and jump to the pavement. Would there be a letter or wouldn't there? He almost ran down the road.

'Bel! Darling!' he whispered. Surely she must know what agony this was to him, this not knowing.

Arriving home he was greeted at the door by Emily, the housekeeper who had been with the family for more than thirty years.

'Your father's not at all well,' she told him anxiously. 'He's had a bit of a fall and he's——'

'A bit of a fall?' Larry repeated. 'How bad was it? How did it happen?' All thought of the letter had vanished from his mind. His father's condition varied with the weather and sometimes, Larry suspected, with his state of mind. When he was feeling bad-tempered he would insist that he could do everything for himself; when feeling less irritable he would accept help with a reasonably good grace.

Before Emily could elaborate further, the nurse appeared at the top of the stairs and, seeing Larry, came hurrying down. Nurse Elton was large and competent, but today her face was creased by a frown.

'He would insist on getting the clock from the mantelpiece,' she explained breathlessly. 'I said I would get it as soon as my hands were free – I was carrying the washbowl at the time – but no! That wasn't good enough, he had to have the clock then and there. Said it needed winding, and before I knew what had happened he was standing up, clutching the back of the chair and' . . . She threw up her hands in exasperation. 'His legs gave way and down he went. It was his own fault, you see. He gets so impatient. Can't wait a minute once he's set his heart——'

'Any real damage?' Larry cut across the account, knowing from past experience how long-winded the nurse could be on occasions.

'Only to his pride!' she said, tossing her head. 'The doctor says there's nothing broken but – oh, that man!

45

Your father, I mean, not the doctor. One of these days he won't be so lucky. One of these—'

Larry smiled. 'Don't worry about it, Nurse. I'll go up to him at once and try and talk some sense into him.'

Emily said, 'And there's a letter for you, sir. On the sideboard in the morning room.'

The letter! Already half-way up the stairs, Larry paused in mid-step. He hesitated, but decided he must put his father first and went on up.

'Thank you, Emily,' he called over his shoulder.

But by the time he reached the landing and knocked on his father's bedroom door, his heart was racing. The letter *was* from Bel. He knew it.

'Ah, Father. I hear you took a bit of a tumble.'

His father sat in the chair beside the bed, propped up by pillows. His legs rested on a footstool and he was reading a book which Larry recognised as a new edition of *Middlemarch*. George had put on weight but his grey hair, parted in the middle, was still thick and his inactivity had given him a restlessness of spirit. Above all he abhorred self-pity and hated to be fussed over, and he and the nurse had skirmished many times because of this.

Larry said lightly, 'Glad to hear there are no bones broken.'

His father laid down his book as though a visitor was the last thing he wanted, but Larry knew better. His father enjoyed company and looked forward to a visit from either his son or daughter or one of his many friends.

Larry asked, 'Are your legs paining you? Worse than usual, I mean?'

'Well, of course they are! Damned legs. Weak as butter and aching like hell! But that's nothing unusual. What worries me is you and that sister of yours.'

Larry groaned inwardly. The old man missed nothing. He asked cautiously, 'What about us?'

'Why, this silly falling-out you've had. Oh, don't pretend

to me. I'm your father, for heaven's sake! I *know* you, dammit! Both of you. There's something wrong. And because of it your sister's taken it into her head to go away for a few days – to stay with that obnoxious Geraldine she's so fond of. Geraldine! Huh! The girl's a bad influence. She's got her teeth into this spiritualism nonsense and won't let go. According to Marie, she's trying to make contact with her father!'

'Plenty of people want to contact their dear departed. It's not a crime.'

'It's a nonsense, if you ask me. All I can say is don't bother to try and reach me once I've gone because I shan't be very pleased. The idea of Marie dragging me back from eternity to grumble about her lot is most depressing.'

Larry smiled. 'I'll tell her that, shall I?'

'Do! Geraldine! Huh! According to your sister, this Geraldine has some kind of ouija board. Nasty things.' He frowned up at Larry. 'If it *can* conjure up a ghost or a spirit or whatever, how on earth do you know you're getting the right one? Eh? Might be the ghost of a murderer.' He shook his head despondently. 'I sometimes wish I'd never sent Marie to that school. It was money down the drain. The friends she made there are quite intolerable. Geraldine Batt, would you believe. With a name like Batt, what can anyone expect? Batty would be more like it.'

Larry hid a smile. His father was an impossible snob, and the truth was that Marie appeared to have been drawn to any girl in the school of whom her father might disapprove. Geraldine was the daughter of an army sergeant and she now had a flat in Chiswick. So that, thought Larry, was where Marie had gone to sulk.

'She'll be back soon, Father,' he said mildly. 'You know how quickly Marie tires of people.'

'You haven't answered my question.' His father narrowed his eyes. 'You've quarrelled, haven't you?'

So Marie had said nothing. Better follow her example. 'Hardly a quarrel, Father. More a – a disagreement. It's nothing.'

'You should be more patient with her, Larry. She's only a child.'

'Nonsense! She's a grown woman. She's older than me.'

His father shook his head. 'Your sister will never be a grown woman!' he said with resignation. 'She takes after her mother. She'll be a wilful child all her life, like Teresa. Charming but wilful.'

Larry had heard this theory before, and was pleased that at that moment Nurse Elton entered the room with a tea-tray. Seizing the opportunity, he said quickly, 'Well, I must go, Father. I'll see you later.'

And ignoring the old man's protests, Larry slipped out of the room and hurried down to the morning room. One glance at the envelope confirmed his expectations. The familiar handwriting danced in front of his eyes and a great happiness filled his heart. Whatever the contents, the letter was from the woman he loved and he would treasure it as such. He sat down heavily on the sofa, took a deep breath, opened the envelope and began to read:

My dear Larry,

Please rest assured that Marie's foolishness can never spoil our friendship. Your letter made me both happy and sad. Happy that you love me, but sad that I can never be more to you than Walter's wife. I know you understand that and are wise enough to accept it. Walter is my very dear husband, and I love him, but there is room in my heart for you also.

I have known of your affection for me for some years, but hoped it need never be expressed. Now that it has, my greatest wish is that we should remain

48

the good friends we have always been, and that we do not speak of love again.

Dearest Larry, please understand that I cannot write more and that Walter should never find out that I have written to you.

Yours, Bel

'Oh, Bel! My very dearest Bel!'

At least she was not angry with him. He felt a wave of relief. And she had spoken so kindly, so *lovingly*. With eager eyes he scanned the letter again. What exactly had she said? 'There is room in my heart for you also . . .' What did that mean precisely? Was she trying to tell him something that she could not put in writing? 'Room in my heart . . .' Was she telling him that she returned his love? He hardly dared to hope, but surely it was a possibility. He read the letter again, searching for clues that might reveal her true feelings — if indeed she had any deeper feelings that she dare not express. Oh, God! He was tormenting himself with the slim chance that she loved him in return. For a moment his hopes soared, but almost immediately plummeted. She had said something about Walter. . . . 'He is my dear husband and I love him . . .' No, no. '. . . my *very* dear husband . . .'

'Oh, Bel!'

His sigh was heartfelt. This was a straightforward rejection, couched in kindly words and phrases, designed to soften the blow to his pride. Unless . . . could it be a plea for him to take the initiative? She had known of his love for *years*! It was incredible. She had never given the slightest hint . . .

'Do you *truly* love him?' he asked in an agony of indecision. The letter had come at last but he was no nearer knowing the truth. Did Bel love him? She had said she loved Walter, so perhaps that was true. And maybe a woman could love two men. He read the letter again in a fever of impatience. Somewhere within its bland phrases there must be a glimpse of the truth. If he thought for a moment that she returned his love . . .

Larry drew a deep breath, closed his eyes and dared to hope.

Chapter Three

THE TWO YOUNG WOMEN sat in Geraldine's small living room which had been furnished quite simply but with good taste. Three prints hung on the walls and a small display cabinet contained several pieces of Meissen china. In deference to the August weather the lower half of the sash window had been pushed up and a slight but welcome breeze ruffled the lace curtain. Geraldine was petite, with fluffy auburn hair which defied the hairdresser's attempts to subdue it into a fashionable style. She sat on the sofa with her feet tucked beneath her, her grey suede shoes discarded on the floor. A tea-tray set for two rested on the oak coffee table. Opposite her Marie sat in the armchair, one leg crossed elegantly over the other, pressing dainty fingers on to the remaining crumbs of the chocolate cake she had been eating. On a second, larger table, the ouija board waited for their attention. This particular model was a flat, pear-shaped, wooden board with a small wheel at either side of the wide end. At the narrow end a pencil rested, point down, in a small hole.

Marie wiped her fingers on her napkin and glanced eagerly towards the board. 'So!' she said with a smile. 'The hour has come! Shall we try for your father again?'

Geraldine shook her head. 'No, not today,' she said. 'I tried it yesterday with Mrs T. – the woman who lives in

Flat 3. She has only just discovered that I have a "planchette" – as she calls it. She was frightfully keen, a real believer, but we didn't have any luck. The first words were meaningless, but then we got S, T and A and she thought it might be her uncle who died some years ago – his name was Stanley – but it didn't finish the word so we couldn't be sure. She didn't like him much when he was alive, so she didn't particularly want to make contact with him.'

'Maybe he changed his mind half-way through!' Marie suggested. 'Perhaps he didn't like her much, either.'

'Very likely.' Geraldine shrugged. 'Then there was something that looked foreign – I forget exactly what it was, but it looked as though it might have been German. Lots of capital letters in funny places, and part of a word that might have been "strasse", which Mrs T. says is German for "street".'

'Do either of you know any dead Germans?'

'Not one.'

'So much for that, then. We might have better luck. Did you ask it any questions?'

'No, just waited to see what it would write. Left it to its own devices, really. Poor Mrs T. was frightfully disappointed; she was hoping to receive a message from her husband, but he either wasn't able or wasn't willing! So then we tried for my father.'

'And?'

'Nothing.'

She picked up the tray and carried it out into her kitchen, and while she was doing that Marie moved the coffee table and replaced it with the larger one.

Geraldine returned with a large sheet of white paper which she spread over the table beneath the board. When the curtains had been drawn the light in the room was reduced, and the ambience thus created met with her approval. Cheerfully they settled themselves on either side of the board and regarded each other expectantly.

Marie said, 'You first.'

Geraldine smoothed back her hair, placed one forefinger against her lips and looked pensive. After a few moments' thought, she said, 'I'll be a bit more subtle today. It thinks I'm going for my father, but I'll ask it about my grandfather instead. On my mother's side. Grandfather Brooks, I used to call him. Ready, then?'

Both women placed the fingers of their right hands lightly on the board and closed their eyes. The room was quiet except for the ticking of the clock on the mantelpiece. In spite of her reservations, Marie felt a prickle of excitement as she waited for the familiar tremor in the board which would herald the start of the proceedings. They concentrated in silence for a while until they were distracted by a noise in the street outside. Raucous voices were suddenly raised in dispute and their carefully contrived atmosphere was immediately shattered.

'Oh, blast!' cried Geraldine. She jumped to her feet, crossed to the window and closed it with a little more force than was necessary. 'We'll have to swelter for a little while,' she said.

They resumed their positions and both women closed their eyes. Then Marie opened hers slightly and was amused to see the expression on her friend's face. With her lips compressed and her eyes screwed tightly shut, Geraldine looked slightly ridiculous but Marie, feeling somewhat disloyal, hastily closed her own eyes again.

Geraldine said softly, 'Grandfather Brooks. Grandfather Brooks? Are you there? Can you hear me?'

The board trembled on its little wheels but did not move. The pencil remained idle.

'Grandfather Brooks! This is Geraldine.' She had raised her voice a little. 'Are you with us? Do you have a message?'

Without warning the board suddenly swivelled slightly beneath their fingers and Marie drew in her breath. The board continued to move, and as it did so, the point of the pencil left a trace across the paper. The board made a few sharp movements across the paper, stopped for a moment and then resumed its activities, circling around and making unexpected changes of direction. It paused, moved, paused again and finally ended in a flurry of activity. Only when it was obviously finished did they dare to withdraw their fingers from its polished surface.

'Golly!' cried Marie.

Carefully, Geraldine slid the paper from beneath the board and together they considered the 'writing' the pencil had produced. At first sight it appeared to be a random jumble of curving lines, criss-crossing the page, but after a moment Marie stabbed a finger triumphantly.

'That could be a "B", she said. "B" for Brooks. And if you turn it round a bit, there's something that could be a small "h" and then a small "o" and then a capital "A"—' She frowned with concentration. 'And could that be a capital "P"?'

Geraldine regarded it hopefully. '*It could* be,' she agreed. 'H.O.A.P. But what does it mean?'

'Hope?'

'Marie! I like to think my grandfather *could* spell "hope"!'

Marie shrugged. She hated the occasional disappointments when they could make no sense of the pencil's scrawl. 'Maybe it's an anagram?' she suggested eagerly. Geraldine said, 'Hapo . . . Poha . . . Poah or Phoa.' Her face fell. 'Not very likely, is it?' She rotated the paper, searching for fresh ideas. 'There's something there,' she pointed, 'that might or might not be a capital "G". "G" for grandfather, perhaps? Or there! That could be a small "h" followed by an "o" and an "n" . . .'

'Hon . . . Honour. Was his honour ever questioned?'

'Not that I know of.'

'Honorary. Was he ever the honorary anything?'

''Fraid not.'

54

Marie tried again. 'Honey. Honesty—'

Geraldine looked up. 'Honey!' she exclaimed. 'Grandfather kept bees! Perhaps that's it. That's how he's letting me know it's *him*. Oh, Marie! Do you think so?'

'It's possible.' Marie thought it a long shot, but didn't want to put a damper on the proceedings. 'Do you want to ask him something more specific? Like his favourite flower or something. That would prove it was him.'

Geraldine's eyes were round 'His favourite flower. Yes, that's marvellous!'

She seized upon the idea with enthusiasm, and once more they concentrated their efforts. Geraldine turned the sheet of paper over and after a reluctant start, the ouija board responded with its erratic gyrations. It began to move faster and with apparent purpose.

'You're pushing it!' cried Geraldine.

'I'm not! I swear it!'

The board finally slowed down and then stopped and the two women regarded each other with growing excitement. Then they bent their heads over the paper, scrutinising the results.

They found the capital letters 'O' and 'E' in separate areas of the page, and a small 'sr' together in the middle.

'Rose!' cried Marie. 'His favourite flowers were roses!'

But Geraldine shook her head. 'They were dahlias,' she confessed. 'He grew masses of them. He was a bit of an expert in his way, always messing about in the potting-shed and tramping soil into the kitchen. The housekeeper used to get very cross.'

'Never mind,' said Marie. 'At least it proves we aren't cheating; we aren't influencing it in any way. It must be someone else who likes roses. Not much point in going on with this one.'

Somewhat grudgingly, Geraldine agreed.

Marie said, 'It's my turn now and I'm going to ask it about Larry.'

'Larry?' Geraldine looked at her in astonishment. 'Your brother? But Larry isn't dead. How can you try to contact him if he—'

'Not him. I want to ask someone *about* him. Anyone who knows anything.'

'But why Larry?'

'Never you mind!' Marie tapped the side of her nose. 'Let's just try it.'

Geraldine lifted the board and Marie replaced the paper. Suddenly Geraldine hugged the board to her chest. 'We won't try anything unless you tell me what you want to find out. It's my board and—'

'Oh, really, Geraldine! You're such a baby sometimes. Look, it really is the most desperate secret, but if I learn anything of interest I'll tell you. If not, wild horses won't drag it out of me!' She stared fiercely at her friend. 'I mean it. I daren't tell you. Not yet. Now put the board in place.'

After a moment's hesitation Geraldine laid it down on the table with a bad grace and they placed their fingers on the board and, with closed eyes, bent their heads earnestly.

Marie said softly, 'Is there anyone there? Can anyone help me?'

Nothing happened.

'Please!' Marie insisted. 'I want to ask about Larr—, about Lawrence Roberts. Is there anyone there?'

Nothing happened and Geraldine said smugly, 'I told you it wouldn't because he's not dead. How—'

She stopped abruptly as, almost lazily, the board moved and the pencil slid across the page in loops and angles. Marie held her breath. Someone was *answering* her! The board gathered speed and she resisted the temptation to open her eyes and watch it. It stopped, moved once and stopped again.

'Heavens!' said Marie, opening her eyes at last.

Geraldine was eyeing her excitedly. Together they searched the pencilled squiggles. They found a capital 'N' and four letters which might, with a stretch of the imagination, be 'trou'.

Geraldine said, 'Trout? Does your brother go trout fishing?'

Marie ignored her. 'TROU . . .?'

'Or troupe?' Geraldine stared at the ceiling in search of inspiration. 'If we include the "N", it could be trounce? Or trousseau . . . or trousers . . .'

Marie said, 'You're being silly, dear old thing!' but her mind was racing, full of possibilities. Ignoring her friend's pretended sulk she said, 'I'm going to ask it a direct question.'

They both concentrated once again on the board.

Marie whispered, 'Will Lawrence be satisfied?'

'I can't hear you!' Geraldine protested.

'Shh!' She repeated the question.

There was a moment's silence and then, without warning, the board spun so suddenly that they instinctively withdrew their fingers in alarm and watched in amazement as it careered off the table and crashed on to the floor.

Horribly startled, they stared at it nervously.

Geraldine said, 'Now you've done it!' As a light-hearted remark it failed utterly. She swallowed. 'Well, that's your answer – whatever it means!'

Marie saw her own agitation reflected in her friend's expression. 'I don't know what it means.'

'What did *you* mean? Will Laurence be satisfied? Satisfied with *what*?'

'It doesn't matter.' She retrieved the fallen board and replaced it on the table. With an attempt at humour she added, 'I think that's enough for today.' Hopefully Geraldine would not realise how shaken she was. The suspicion deepened in her mind that she was going to regret her rash remarks to Bel about Larry. Already she and her brother were at odds over the matter, and for once she acknowledged that she had been at fault.

'Satisfied with *what*?' Geraldine insisted.

'I told you it doesn't matter. I don't want to talk about it. Please, Geraldine.'

'You're *scared* of something! You *are*!' Her friend regarded her soberly. 'The ouija board's frightened you.'

'Don't be ridiculous. It's only a piece of wood on castors.' But in spite of her brave words she was uncomfortably aware of her father's warning. The occult and the supernatural were not to be trifled with, he had insisted. She pushed the board away from her.

Geraldine picked it up. 'Then it's something to do with Larry. What's happening, Marie? You said you'd tell me.'

'There's nothing to tell,' said Bel and then, seeing the disbelief in her friend's eyes, she sighed heavily. 'Well, there is something but I can't tell you just now. But I will – later on. You'll have to trust me.'

'You've gone all pale and interesting.'

'Thanks!' She was aware of Geraldine's searching gaze. 'You couldn't bring yourself to offer me a sherry, could you?' she asked shakily.

As Marie sipped her drink the four letters danced before her eyes. TROU . . . Was it possible they did mean something? And if so *what*?

It was only later, as she lay in bed that night, that the word 'trouble' entered her head and that thought kept sleep at bay until the early hours of the morning.

*

Two days later Bel made her way down the steps into the gloom of the crypt of St Saviour's Church where a small group of women were already busy, preparing a meal for the down-and-outs of Whitechapel. For some inexplicable reason the sight of her friends' worthy activity failed to stir her the way it normally did, and she had to force a smile.

'Good morning!' she cried with false cheerfulness and was answered by several of the women.

Sensible aprons covered the expensive clothes and a variety of cloche hats protected immaculate hair styles. If there was anything incongruous about the sight it was lost on Bel, who today found it dispiritingly familiar. The cavernous room, with its cold stone walls, remained crypt-like, for no attempt had been made to soften its harsh atmosphere. Margaret Hart, the driving force behind the scheme, had decreed that none of the money they raised was to be wasted on decoration. The donations, she insisted, were intended for the sustenance of the poor and needy, and she was adamant that the money should go nowhere else. Food, heating, light and rent and a few necessary sundries were all she allowed. The only splashes of colour in the gloom were the bright check tablecloths, but these had been given to them. Margaret was a wealthy widow whose children had long since married and scattered to the far corners of the Empire. The soup kitchen, Bel knew, was more than just a hobby to her. It was her life, Margaret's reason for living. She badgered her friends for donations and organised fund-raising events. The monthly luncheons at her home in Belgravia were enjoyed by twelve people at a time, and the profit this engendered swelled the fund.

'Good morning, Bel! It's good to see you again.'

Margaret's face, flushed from her exertions, broke into a welcoming smile and some of Bel's enthusiasm returned.

On a large gas-stove a huge cooking pot belched savoury steam, while behind it two women bent industriously over a growing pile of carrots and potatoes. These had been precooked elsewhere to save time and were being cut into smaller pieces to be added to the soup. Both Mabel Westhorne and her daughter Frances glanced up at Bel and added their greetings. Margaret began to unpack the tin soup-bowls from a large cardboard box.

Without looking, Bel knew that the cooking pot contained simmering beef bones donated by a sympathetic local butcher. Half a pound of lentils and some pearl barley would have been added as well to thicken it. On a nearby trestle table Agatha Corby was cutting bread into the thick slices known to their regulars as 'doorstoppers'. There would be no butter.

As Bel hung up her jacket, Margaret hurried forward with a voluminous apron and kissed her cheek briefly.

'Bless you!' she said. 'I thought perhaps you weren't coming,' Her tone suggested the mildest reproach.

Bel tied the apron round her waist, smiling. 'I'm sorry. I was held up for nearly ten minutes when an elderly man stumbled in front of our tram. Drunk, they thought. His leg was broken, but he was lucky he wasn't killed.'

Margaret tut-tutted, but Bel could see that her interest was not with the dead but with those still living who waited eagerly in the street above: thirty or more hungry bellies waiting to be filled with their first hot meal in days.

Margaret said briskly, 'Work with Agatha, will you, Bel? You'll find a rice pudding in the oven and some cold semolina under that blue cloth. Everything well with you, my dear?'

'Yes, thank you.' Bel hesitated. 'What makes you ask?'

'Intuition. I thought you seemed a mite distracted.'

'No, not at all,' Bel lied. 'A little tired, actually.' That was another lie.

Margaret went to the corner of the crypt where a pile of chairs had been roughly stacked. She began to arrange a motley collection of these around two trestle tables. Once these chairs had been filled, the floor would suffice for the unlucky ones at the end of the queue.

As she joined Agatha at the table Bel made an effort to appear brisk and businesslike. Arranging the thick slices in rows on a tray, she asked, 'How's your mother, Agatha?'

Agatha's pale blue eyes filled with tears. 'No better,' she said in a low voice.

'I'm so sorry.' Bel knew that for Agatha, a spinster in

her fifties, the death of her mother would be a great blow. To distract the older woman's thoughts she said brightly, 'My husband is newly returned from the wilds of Canada. He made the trip on the R100. Did I mention it last week?'

Agatha wiped her eyes and swallowed hard. 'I think you did, but it had slipped my mind. How very wonderful for him. Did he enjoy it?'

Mabel glanced up from her vegetables. 'Lucky man! It was an outstanding success from all accounts. It just goes to show that England can do it. Germany shan't have it all her own way!'

Frances laughed. 'Who is this man Zeppelin? Barnes Wallis will get my vote of confidence any day! *There* is a man who can design airships. Or should I say *the* man?'

There was an appreciative murmur of agreement.

Bel said, 'I'm sure it was teamwork but yes – he is extremely talented. My husband was tremendously impressed with the design. The trip was a huge boost for the industry as a whole.'

Agatha said, 'My brother's always wanted to fly in an airship. It's been an ambition of his for as long as I can remember.'

Bel smiled at her.' Well, you can tell him that it was all very luxurious. Just like an ocean liner, according to Walter. And so smooth and comfortable. Flying over the sea, they could always see the long, slim shadow of the airship – and from that height they could watch whales and dolphins splashing about in the water. And they could see people on the decks of ships waving up at them.'

Half-heartedly, Margaret said, 'How fantastic! Oh! The rice pudding!' She knelt to check on it and, seeing that it was done, turned off the gas.

Frances said, 'I think I shall have to try it one day. I rather fancy floating through the air, looking down on everyone else. Quite literally!' She laughed. 'It must make one feel frightfully superior!'

Margaret wiped her hands on her apron and gave her staff a last-minute inspection. 'Are we all ready, ladies? Oh, good. Then let them in, Frances, will you? I see poor old Neville is first, as usual. I sometimes wonder if he camps out there overnight!'

Frances hurried eagerly to the steps and went up to open the door while those left below braced themselves for the onslaught. Almost at once there was the sound of scuffling feet and an old man made his way unsteadily down the steps, clinging like a drowning man to the wooden handrail. Like most of those who would follow him, he was dressed in an assortment of ragged, ill-fitting clothes. He was unshaven and his hair was matted. As he reached the bottom of the steps and began to shuffle slowly forward he was overtaken by another, slightly younger, man. At once Neville let out a hoarse roar of protest.

'Oy! Charlie! I was first, you old bastard! Don't serve him, ladies! I was first!'

'There's plenty for everyone!' Margaret reminded him sternly as Charlie's grimy hand reached for the first bowl of soup. 'Good morning, Charlie,' she said, but received only a scowl by way of answer. Margaret offered him bread and reminded him to take only one slice.

He moved away to the nearest chair and began at once to drink from the bowl.

Bel, waiting her turn to be useful, looked around her at the familiar scene. The hungry poor, so alike to look at, were nevertheless distinct personalities and her eyes flicked from one to the other. There were a few new faces but she recognised most of them. Old Mary caught her eye and Bel smiled. Mary was subject to periods of religious mania and now she crossed herself before each mouthful. Barney, a young but very tall man of limited abilities, ate slowly and deliberately. His round eyes surveyed the world around him with brilliant vacuity, and no one had ever heard him speak. Her gaze rested on Gappy, so called because of his lack of teeth. He said, 'Bless you, ma'am,' again and again to no one in particular. Janey, beside him at the table, continued to surprise them all by somehow surviving a diet which consisted mainly of methylated spirits. William, known as 'Fatty' to his friends, dipped the bread into his soup and sucked on it noisily. It amazed Bel that someone who teetered on the edge of starvation could possess such a huge body. 'Fatty' had to be watched as he was liable to snatch the food from the less wary of his fellow diners.

When everyone had been served, Margaret banged for silence with a large spoon. 'We will now give thanks to the Lord,' she announced. Everyone except Mary ignored her completely, but the latter laid down her spoon and put her hands together.

'For what we are about to receive, may the Lord make us truly thankful. Amen.'

Only Mary offered an 'Amen' and she quickly resumed her meal. Margaret, accustomed to their lack of social graces, had long since given up the task of insisting on respect for the Lord.

Now, as always, the noise level rose – a disturbing medley of uncouth laughter, curses and whimpers which Bel had once found somewhat alarming. Now, she still could not quite come to terms with the raw misery and the half-veiled aggression that she sensed beneath the surface.

Margaret turned to her suddenly. 'Bel! I nearly forgot. There was someone here earlier on, asking for you. He said he knew you but when I pressed him, he refused to give his name. Rather mysterious, really.'

'For me? Are you sure?'

'Quite sure, my dear.' Margaret's mouth tightened slightly at Bel's unintentional slur on her reliability. 'He particularly asked for Mrs Roberts. Mrs Isobel Roberts.'

'Well, I can't imagine who that was.' Bel thought about it with nothing more than passing curiosity until a sudden idea made her cheeks burn. Not Larry, surely! She was annoyed to discover that the prospect of meeting him in their changed relationship excited her immeasurably. Trying to hide her sudden elation, she asked, 'Was he dark? With deep blue eyes?' What on earth had possessed him to come in search of her here, of all places, she wondered.

Margaret raised her eyebrows, faintly mocking. '*Deep blue eyes?*'

Bel felt her colour deepen. How stupid of her! That one careless word hinted at more than a passing interest in the man.

But Margaret promptly crushed her newly aroused hopes. 'Not *deep blue*, no. Sorry to disappoint you, Bel. His eyes were grey, actually. Rather nice. With light brown hair. Quite young. Twenty, maybe.'

Agatha said, 'You're a sly one, Bel! Fancy keeping such a jolly young man a secret!'

Margaret went on, 'I said you'd be along if he cared to wait, but he laughed and said . . .' She paused, for effect. 'He said, "Just tell her an admirer called." Yes, that's it. His exact words. An admirer!'

Bel's disappointment gave way abruptly to an uncomfortable suspicion. Margaret's description fitted that of the young man who had trespassed so recently in the garden at Cardington. But that made no sense. Cardington was miles away, and he could not possibly have traced her to London – unless he had a very good reason for doing so.

'Was he . . . pleasant-looking?' she asked cautiously. 'Or . . . cheeky?'

Margaret's smile faded. 'You look worried, Bel. I hope I did nothing wrong in talking to him. He seemed – well, shall we say cheerful. Jaunty, almost. Hands in his pockets. Whistling. That sort of thing.'

'Good heavens!' Bel said weakly. It *was* him; it must be. For a moment she was tempted to explain about the unwanted visitor in Cardington, but then she thought better of it. Best to say as little as possible about the wretched man until she knew what was going on.

Mabel said, 'Aren't you going to tell us, Bel?'

'I can't. I don't know — for certain, I mean.' She searched her mind for a reasonable explanation that might satisfy their curiosity.' It sounds a bit like my cousin. Or rather, second cousin. He turns up from time to time.' She fancied this sounded unconvincing so she added, 'Usually to borrow money.'

Fortunately, an argument at one of the tables distracted their attention and by the time it had been dealt with, the matter of her visitor had been forgotten. Except by Bel. She knew that she had no skeletons in her cupboard, so her conscience was clear in that respect, but the thought of an unknown man following her around, *knowing* her movements, was not a comfortable one. She wished now that she had remembered to tell Walter about him, and made up her mind to do so when next she saw him.

When the time came for her to dole out generous portions of rice pudding, she tried to give it her full attention. Margaret had found her 'a mite distracted' earlier and Bel had no desire to arouse interest in herself. She wanted time to think about Larry. Now that she was back in London they were not far apart and it was usual for Bel to visit her father-in-law at least once a week. George Roberts looked forward to seeing her and she did not want to depart from this routine. Having known Walter's father for many years before she and Walter had married, their relationship had always been very relaxed. Bel could recall George teasing her when she was still a child. He had told her outrageous stories, guaranteed to give any child nightmares, and had brought her weird and wonderful presents from his various trips abroad. She still treasured a Spanish fan and a particularly ugly buddha carved out of dark wood.

The problem now was that if she called at the house

65

when Larry was in chambers, he would think she was deliberately avoiding him. If she called when he was at home, they would come face to face for the first time since their exchange of letters. This meeting was one which Bel both longed for and dreaded. As she ladled a helping of the sticky white pudding into yet another bowl, she came to a decision which seemed a reasonable compromise. She would call the next day, late in the afternoon so that the visit would be almost over by the time Larry returned. Having George, and maybe the nurse, present might lessen the tension. For a few heady moments she imagined Larry following her to the front door to insist that they meet somewhere, away from prying eyes. To accept would be a very rash step, she knew. But if he *did* make such a suggestion, Bel knew that she would find it almost impossible to refuse. There was also the possibility that Marie would be at home, and that too could prove awkward. She did not know whether Marie knew of her correspondence with Larry. Bel sighed. Not so long ago her life had seemed uneventful, even tranquil – to the point of dullness, she had sometimes thought. Now she felt that her problems were multiplying and life was too exciting. She was unsure which state she preferred.

'Bel!'

She glanced round guiltily. 'Sorry!'

Margaret was looking harassed. 'I said could you take a look at William?'

Bel turned her head and saw that the large man had slipped sideways in his chair and was slumped forward with his head resting on the table. Asleep, she thought with a resigned shake of the head. A combination of food and warmth frequently affected them this way. She set down the ladle and crossed the room. Laying a hand gently on his shoulder she said, 'William! Wake up.'

To her surprise he failed to react but instead slipped further sideways. She grabbed his arm, but he was too heavy for her and slipped awkwardly to the floor. He ended up on his back, his arms outstretched as if pleading for help; his mouth was open, his eyes stared unseeingly and his limbs twitched feebly.

'Oh, my God!' she cried, shaking him desperately. 'William! *William!*'

Was he *dead*? Bel was aware of a growing horror. She had never seen anyone die; had never seen a dead body. Her father's coffin, like those of the other victims of the disaster, had been nailed down, denying her a chance to say a last goodbye. Everyone had assured her it had been 'for the best'.

'William!' She took his head in her hands, willing him to open his eyes. He moaned quietly, and then she felt him go limp. She sat back, appalled by the suddenness of the tragedy. 'Oh, God! Please!' she whispered but by this time Margaret, Mabel and Frances, alerted by the tone of her voice, had hurried to her side. Incredibly, after a first cautious glance, the other diners continued their meal, apparently undeterred.

It did not take long to ascertain that William had enjoyed his last meal.

Mabel said, 'Poor soul. Oh, that's terrible!' Her voice trembled.

Margaret gave her a sharp look. 'Pull yourself together, Mabel. At least he went with a full stomach. I suppose he was as happy as he could expect to be. He didn't die alone in the gutter.'

They knew for certain that William was dead long before the hastily summoned doctor arrived at the scene. When he confirmed their diagnosis they covered William's body with a spare tablecloth to protect him from prying eyes.

The doctor stood up, brushing his trousers fastidiously to remove the dust. 'Well, he's well out of it. Not much to live for, his sort.' As he wiped his hands on a clean white

67

handkerchief, he glanced around the crypt with an expression that made his audience aware of his disapproval. 'I don't know that you do them any favours,' he remarked, returning the handkerchief to his pocket. 'Simply prolongs the agony, don't you think?'

Margaret reddened angrily. 'No, I don't think! That's a rather callous attitude, if I may say so. Particularly coming from a doctor.'

He shrugged. 'Without the food their merciful release by death would come that much sooner. I think it's a valid viewpoint.' He began to rummage in his bag.

Bel felt a wave of anger at his indifference. 'Put yourself in their shoes, doctor. Would you prefer to wait for your "merciful release" hungry and cold? Or would you allow an occasional nourishing meal to brighten your day?'

His smile was as bleak as his charity. 'I hardly think it worth an argument, madam. I'm sure you ladies mean well.' He took a small pad from his bag. 'Now, if you'll excuse me.' He scribbled something indecipherable and handed the sheet to Margaret with the words, 'Death certificate'.

Bel said caustically, 'No point in asking you for a donation, then.'

He gave her a withering look. 'Hardly,' he said. 'To whom shall I send the bill?'

Margaret gave him her address and they watched in silence as he made his way up the steps.

As the door clanged to behind him, Frances said, 'What an unpleasant man!'

Bel shook her head. 'That is the understatement of the year!' she said. 'He was an arrogant, selfish, cold-hearted—' She searched for a word that was strong enough.

Mabel said, 'Pig?'

'I was thinking more of *bastard*!' said Bel defiantly.

There was a shocked silence as the ladies stared at her.

Margaret said, 'Bel! My dear girl! That's not like you.'

68

She laid a hand gently on Bel's arm. 'Are you all right? It has been rather a shock.'

Generously, Mabel, Frances and Agatha agreed that no doubt the trauma of the death had unsettled Bel and no further reference was made to her lapse. As soon as the meal was over and the room emptied of diners, they began to wash up and clear away, discussing meanwhile the matter of William's interment. Agatha expressed the thought that a pauper's burial for William would be a sad thing, but Margaret was adamant that not a penny of her 'kitchen fund' would be deflected from its purpose.

Bel recalled suddenly the doctor's disdainful expression as he looked into William's lifeless eyes. Had he seen too many 'Williams', perhaps? Had he ever felt the smallest stirrings of compassion for his patients, or or had his own comfortable lifestyle immured him to the small griefs of others? Would *she*, cocooned in her life of ease, ever think that way? It was not a pleasant thought. She shivered, drawing in her breath sharply. 'I'll pay for the funeral. A basic coffin. Nothing fancy.'

'Oh, Bel!' Margaret grasped her hands warmly. 'That's so generous.'

At once the others congratulated her on her kind gesture, but Bel brushed their comments aside. Suddenly she wanted only to be free of all of them. She felt tremendously tired and aware of a great confusion. Pleading another engagement, she made her escape and hailed the first taxi that appeared. More shaken than she had at first suspected, she sat back against the leather upholstery and tried to relax. She had given Larry's address but it was George she wanted to talk to. It was at times like these that she most missed her father.

*

'Oh, it's you, madam.' Emily's face brightened. 'Just the thing he needs. He's a bit bad-tempered today. Didn't sleep well, so Nurse says, and with Master Larry at work and Miss Marie away he's got no one to talk to.'

So Larry was out. Bel didn't know whether to be glad or sorry. Perhaps it was as well, for now she and her father-in-law could talk freely. She allowed Emily to help her off with her jacket. Both Emily and Nurse Elton adored the old man, Bel knew, and with good reason. As an employer he was very fair and paid good wages. The staff tolerated his occasional irritability because, although he could be exasperating, he had a kind heart which he was not always able to conceal.

As Bel tapped on the bedroom door she could hear the nurse chiding him in the special voice of authority she kept for certain occasions.

'I know it's hot. It's August. What do you expect? But you must fasten your pyjama jacket properly. She'll be here at any moment . . . There! That's better. You look a little more presentable.'

Bel knocked a little louder.

'Come in, ma'am.'

The large, familiar bedroom was pleasantly decorated and airy, with none of the cloying smells which were the hallmark of so many sick-rooms. Nurse Elton was a firm believer in the benefits of fresh air and Bel saw with relief that the window was wide open. A hint of Pears soap lingered in the room from the early morning ablutions, competing with the scent from a bowl of yellow roses which stood on the table beneath the window. Her father-in-law was propped up in bed wearing striped pyjamas. His reading glasses hung on a cord around his neck and a book lay beside him on the coverlet.

The nurse stopped fussing with the bedclothes to turn and beam at the visitor. 'I saw you from the window, Mrs Roberts, and I was just saying to—'

'Good morning, Nurse. I—'

'I was just saying that although it's hot—'

70

George gave her an impatient little push and said, 'Stop talking, woman, for God's sake! You'll wear me out with your incessant chatter. Leave us. I'm in good hands now.' He held out his arms and Bel crossed the room to kiss him.

The nurse retreated to the door saying, 'Don't stand any nonsense, Mrs Roberts. He's in one of his moods!'

'I won't! Thank you, Nurse.' To the old man she said, 'One of your moods, eh? That sounds ominous.'

He laughed. 'That's the way she likes me. A bit of a challenge – it gives her a chance to throw her weight about. I keep telling her, she's wasted here. Should have been a general in the army!' As the door closed George looked at her carefully. 'Is something wrong, Bel? You look so pale.'

'I've just had a shock,' Bel admitted. 'A rather nasty one.' She sat down on the chair beside his bed. 'But what about you? Not out of bed today?'

He shrugged dismissively. 'A bad day. Back aches. That's all. Sometimes I feel lazy and then I think, why bother? And then Nurse Elton decides I *must* get up and I defy her. Today *I* won. I'll stay here.' He grinned almost boyishly. 'But this nasty shock. Tell me about it.'

As Bel began her account of William's death, some of the horror faded. George said very little, but he listened attentively and Bel was aware that his eyes did not leave her face.

'It was all so . . . sordid and dreadful,' she finished lamely, 'and I felt . . .' she swallowed. 'I don't know what I felt but I was surprised by –' she searched for words '–surprised by how bad I felt. Not for him alone but for *me*. Does that sound ridiculous?'

'No.'

'Selfish, though.'

'Why should it be ridiculous? Death is a reminder to us all that we're only mortal. That one day it will be our turn. Poor Bel.'

71

He reached out and took her hand in his. It was warm and surprisingly strong – and immensely comforting. Her eyes filled with unexpected tears and before she knew what was happening she was crying. 'Oh, this is dreadful,' she told him between sobs. 'I'm supposed to be cheering you up!'

George pulled her towards him and stroked her hair. 'My mother used to say, "Tears are better out than in!"' he said gently. 'When you've finished, you'll find a *sensible* handkerchief in the drawer beside you. Those frilly confections you women carry are useless for mopping up tears. Useless for blowing the nose, too. I don't know what they *are* for, to tell you the truth.'

Like an obedient child Bel opened the drawer and found the handkerchief. Fine linen with a monogrammed 'G' in the corner. 'We're so lucky!' she said, wiping her eyes.

'The luck of the draw!' he answered, understanding her train of thought.

'But is it fair?'

'Of course not.'

'But shouldn't it matter?'

'The poor are always with us. You do what you can. There are those who don't care at all. If you must feel guilty, find something more reasonable to be guilty about.' He smiled.

She stared into the faded, kindly eyes. *If you must feel guilty* . . . She was overcome by a need to confide in him. 'I want—' Immediately she bit her lip, panic-stricken. He was Walter's *father*. How could she tell him how confused she felt about his other son? Shaking her head, she realised that she had been dangerously close to blurting out her feelings for Larry and that would have been disastrous. 'It doesn't matter.'

He raised his eyebrows. 'When someone says that, I know it *does* matter. When someone says, "The fact is . . ." they are usually about to lie. But take your time, Bel. I won't press you.' His smile was rueful. 'I know more than you might imagine, Bel, dear. And I can be a source of comfort in times of trouble. And I have had two wives. You can't marry twice without understanding something about how the world wags. I haven't always been a helpless old man.'

'You *aren't* helpless!'

'Not entirely, no.' He stared into space for a moment or two, looking into the past. 'Walter came to me once many years ago. In quite a state, I may say. He needed to confide in me and I wanted to listen, but sadly his courage failed him. I wouldn't press him and maybe that was a mistake. I never did find out what it was that was so terrible. Money, I suspect; he liked to gamble in those days. Well, to be truthful we all enjoyed a flutter on the horses, but I suspect Walter had got into debt.' He shrugged. 'He made a couple of unexplained trips to France and obviously managed to sort things out without my help. At least I suppose he did. Maybe he was the better for it. We all have to learn to manage. We have to stand on our own two feet. Poor Walter.'

'I do love him, you know.' The words tumbled out.

'I hope so, Bel.'

She dared not meet his gaze. She *had* loved Walter, but had she ever been *in love* with him? She was beginning to realise that there was a difference.

'I sometimes worried about you, Bel.' Once again George's hand sought hers. 'When your father died, it was natural enough for you and Walter to share the grief. Walter and Geoffrey were such good friends; they meant so much to each other. Then when he told us that you and he . . . that you wanted to marry, I thought, "Please God, let it be for the right reasons". Do you see what I'm getting at, Bel?'

She could only nod.

He continued, 'I wanted you both to be happy and you

73

seemed to need each other so. You were so young when Geoffrey died, but somehow you grew up overnight. The shock and the sense of loss, I daresay. I was relieved when you agreed to wait a year or so, but then it all went ahead. I did so pray it was for the right reasons.' He looked at her anxiously.

Bel drew a shuddering breath. If only she could tell him. She almost had, but now he was making it harder for her. 'George, I—'

He waited. Looking into his eyes, she saw his need for reassurance. How could she confirm his worst fears, she asked herself silently.

'I hope I've been a good wife.' She was startled by her own words. Was that what she had meant to say?

He smiled. 'I'm sure you have – and are. And probably always will be.'

She looked at him sharply. *Probably?* What was he trying to say? It was true that until now she had never thought of anyone but Walter. After her father's death she had missed the comfort of an older, wiser man, and in a way Walter had stepped into her father's shoes. Had she, then, married him for the wrong reasons?

To change the subject she said, 'I know Walter longs for a son. I'm not too old. There's still time, although the doctor doesn't . . .' She busied her fingers with the handkerchief. 'They don't hold out much hope. Poor Walter.' She thought about the burden of guilt she carried because of her childlessness. Walter had assumed the fault to be hers. To Bel that had seemed most unjust, but he had been so certain that he could father a child. A man's pride, she thought resentfully.

He drew in a long, slow breath, watching her intently. 'Let me just say this, Bel, dear. Your parents are dead, and I know you have no close woman friend. Marie is not the most mature person – although I love her dearly – and she certainly lacks discretion. If you ever need someone to confide in – for whatever reason – remember that I'm here.'

'Thank you. You're such a comfort!'

'I mean it. Life can be hard and . . . and somewhat unpredictable. We can't always be perfect, you know. Everyone makes mistakes and things happen that we don't expect. If only we could see—' He stopped in mid-sentence and threw up his hands in dismay. 'But that's enough of that. I'm in danger of making a speech!' He laughed, to break the tension. 'Let's talk about something else. That foolish daughter of mine, for example. She is home again, you know. Got fed up with Geraldine, I expect. Or vice versa. Anyway, she and Larry appear to be reconciled. Thank goodness. I can't abide an atmosphere. Still, they never did stay enemies for long, even as children. Oh, speak of the devil!'

As though summoned by the power of her name, Marie appeared in the doorway. Without bothering to knock, she whirled into the room, kissed her father and then Bel, and threw herself on to a chair.

'You'll never guess!' she exclaimed. 'Geraldine and I are going to a seance! A proper one at the Wigmore Hall. Next Saturday. There'll be hundreds of people. Thousands, probably. The medium is a woman – Alice Threadmore.'

George groaned. 'Oh, no, Marie! You're not falling for all that fiddle-faddle, surely? First the ouija board and now seances. I thought you had more sense.'

'It's not fiddle-faddle. Just because you don't believe in it you assume it must be nonsense. Geraldine says that—'

Angrily he said 'Geraldine! Geraldine! I'm sick of the sound of her. I should think you've seen through Geraldine by now. A silly, empty-headed little thing—'

'You've never even met her!' To Bel, Marie said eagerly, 'Tell him, Bel. About Alice Threadmore. Talk some sense into him if you can.'

'I only know what I read,' Bel protested.

75

'Then you'll have read about Hinchcliffe, the flyer who disappeared with Elsie Mackay.' To her father she continued excitedly, 'They say he came back – *after* he was dead. His spirit just materialised in the room of a friend and he said they were lost. He didn't even need a medium. Absolutely everyone believes in it now. It's called spiritualism and—'

George snapped, 'I *know* what it's called, Marie. I just think it's a lot of hocus-pocus.' He looked to Bel for affirmation.

She hesitated. 'I don't know much about it but—'

Marie swooped. 'There you are, then. You can't pontificate, can you? I *do* know something about it because Geraldine has some books on the subject and I've read them, and because *I* keep an open mind. And for your information, Father, Arthur Conan Doyle believes in it, so there!'

For a second or two George hesitated, but then he snorted angrily. 'Conan Doyle? But he's a writer, dammit! They're given to flights of fancy. It's what they're paid to do. Conan Doyle, indeed!'

'An intelligent man, though.'

'Being intelligent doesn't necessarily make you an expert on life after death.'

Marie grinned. 'But you're shaken, aren't you, Father? A great many people respect his opinions.'

'Well, I don't. And you should be very careful, meddling in the unknown.'

Bel agreed. 'I believe there are a great many charlatans, Marie. This woman – whatever her name is . . .'

'Alice Threadmore.'

'Are you sure she's genuine? People who have been bereaved are very vulnerable and easily convinced. They tend to believe whatever they want to believe.'

'But I haven't been bereaved, dear old thing, and neither has Geraldine, so we won't be vulnerable.'

She shot Bel a defiant look and suddenly Bel had had enough of her company. She stood up. 'On that challenging note I shall have to love and leave you both.' Ignoring Marie's pout of disappointment, she kissed George and gave him a wink. 'I leave you in good hands!' she said.

George rolled his eyes dramatically. 'Good hands? Oh, God! Couldn't you take me with you!'

To Bel's surprise, Marie did not rise to his bait but said instead, 'I'll see Bel to the door. See she doesn't steal the silver, that sort of thing.'

Half-way down the stairs Marie stopped and whispered, 'I'm sorry about Larry. He was terribly angry and I suppose you are, too. I can be such a fool, sometimes. Do say you forgive me.'

Taken aback by the unexpected apology, Bel could only murmur a half-hearted, 'Of course I do.' She wondered whether or not Marie knew about the exchange of letters, but could not bring herself to ask. If Marie did *not* know, she would rather not enlighten her.

Chapter Four

A FEW DAYS LATER HOWARD slowed his bicycle to a halt as he approached the impressive gates which led to the Cardington flying field. The main building was to his left, imposing in red brick with large windows. At the gates, a man asked his name, handed him a pass.

'To your right,' he said tersely.

Howard wheeled his bicycle while his eyes devoured the territory he had imagined for so long. So this was the Bedford Airship Station – or R.A.W. Cardington as it was sometimes known. Cardington! This was where his father's heart lay and where his passion burned. At any moment he might *see* him! He took a deep breath and moved on, his eyes missing nothing. Behind the main building large sheds housed the Shorts factory where some of the components for the airship were made. Howard had been well briefed by his landlady who, it seemed, was also a mine of information on the R101 – as was everybody, she had assured him. Within a five-mile radius of the R.A.W. no conversation was complete without at least one reference to the airship's progress. A faint smile twitched at the corners of Howard's mouth. Soon he would be part of that, one of the believers and, unbeknown to the rest of them, he would have a greater claim than anyone. His own father was a consultant designer on the airship. How sad it was that he could never boast such an enviable link; could never bask in the reflected glory that was rightfully his.

Unaware that he sighed deeply, he paused to take his bearings. To his right he saw various small sheds, no doubt housing plant of some kind, and beyond them what looked like gas storage tanks. From these various installations a narrow railway track snaked out across the grass, disappearing in the direction of the vast sheds which Howard had seen from a distance on his visit the day before. Above him the vast sky was blue and cloudless and there was not a breath of wind. A lark struggled upwards, spilling his song, and in the distance he could hear an engine throbbing. Mounting again, he cycled slowly on, savouring his first impressions.

'Oh, boy!' he whispered suddenly and stopped again.

The two Cardington sheds reared up majestically from the flat landscape like twin cathedrals. They towered upwards, diminishing everything around them. Constructed from girders with metal cladding, they stood outlined darkly against the sky. But they were not identical. The first one, Howard's landlady had told him, was known familiarly as 'No.1' and had been enlarged from an earlier shed to house the R101. Immediately beside it was 'No.2'. This hangar had been erected at Pulham but later dismantled and brought to Cardington for the R100. It had undergone some extension and its green cladding was less faded than that of No.1.

As Howard proceeded he saw, to his far left, a kite balloon floating some way above the ground. Below a small huddle of men watched it, their heads tilted back as though weighing up its performance. If they turned their heads, thought Howard, they would see a lone figure pushing a bicycle. It would surprise them to know that it was the son of Walter Roberts. His face darkened moodily. They never would know. His mind wrestled with the

problem that he faced; the dilemma he lived with. Sometimes he longed to be recognised and respected as his
father's son, but at other times he tried to hate that very
same father. The tug of these opposing emotions kept him
continually off-balance, although Howard was unaware of
the fact. He sensed only that his inner turmoil was like a
chronic disease that frequently exhausted him.

As he approached the sheds he waited breathlessly for a
first clear view from the front, and when it came he was
not disappointed. Vast doors stood wide open, supported
by a complicated 'buttress' of girders. He shook his head
in wonderment at the sheer *weight* of the doors and looked
for the machinery for opening and closing them. Having
found this and inspected it to his satisfaction, he turned his
attention to the vast darkness of the interior which no
number of light bulbs could lighten sufficiently. No.1 shed
was a hive of activity. Everywhere within its cavernous
recesses there were men at work, some on the ground,
others apparently suspended in mid-air or clinging, spider-
like, to the silvery framework of the airship. Howard
feasted his eyes upon the enormous curved hull for which
nothing had prepared him. One glance and he was capti-
vated by the huge, vulnerable creature and could see at
once how a man might fall under its spell. He felt a thrill
of pride that he, too, was to be allowed to contribute to
her success.

'Oh, boy!' he muttered again and was at once struck by
the inadequacy of the comment. 'Jesus Christ!' he
amended.

At the far end gas was being pumped into one of the gas
bags which was slowly inflating. From the vast roof space
far above him layers of silvery cloth hung down and this,
he guessed, would be the outer covering, or envelope,
which would shroud the curved shell of the ship.

'Oh, God!' he whispered and a beaming smile lit up his
face. For so many years it had been no more than a

blueprint, an idea bandied about by a succession of governments and constantly in danger of cancellation. Now, after years of back-breaking effort, it was a reality.

'You're going to be beautiful!'

From No.2 shed the nose of the triumphant R100 jutted from the dark interior into the sunshine, and Howard wished suddenly that he had travelled to Cardington to see her return from Canada. He was aware of a great lightening of his heart. His decision had been the right one. Before too long he would see the new airship finished – would be part of that dedicated team that put her into the air. He turned his head to the right and there was the mooring mast, exactly as his father had described it: the mast to which the nose of the airship would soon be connected. Around the mast was a circle of anchor points. To these the trailing ropes from the airship would be fastened to steady her during the docking procedures. His father had—

'Oy! You with the bike!'

He turned guiltily to see a man in white overalls surveying him from the apron of No.1. 'Coming!' he shouted and made haste to present himself to his new foreman. His first working day had begun and within minutes he was totally absorbed. He did not realise until later that evening that, for the first time in months, he had – for a few hours – forgotten his father's existence.

*

That evening Mrs Croft greeted him at the front door with a cheerful smile. The little hallway smelt of Ronuk polish, which reminded Howard of home. Delicious cooking smells wafted from the direction of the kitchen and he realised he was starving.

The landlady tucked up a few wisps of grey hair and wiped her hands on her apron. She said, 'Your supper's all ready and waiting, Mr Roberts. I thought we'd eat together,

81

if that suits you. My other young men had no objection and it's no fun eating alone. A nice bit of steak pie and a cabbage fresh from the garden – not mine, I should say, but a friend who has a vegetable plot down the road.' She hovered at the bottom of the stairs as Howard went up to his room. 'I'll be serving it up then, shall I?' she called after him.

Taking the hint, Howard hurried down again as quickly as he could and five minutes later was seated opposite his landlady, telling her, between mouthfuls, about his day.

Mrs Croft leaned forward and waved a fork at him. 'Mind you, there's not much you can tell me but what I haven't already heard. Oh, yes! Those young sparks! I've heard how they race each other, up and over the roof.'

'Over the *roof*?' Howard stared at her, a forkful of pie poised half-way to his mouth.

Her homely face crinkled in delight at his obvious surprise. 'Well, not *over* it but *under* it. They climb up the stairs on one side, run full pelt across the thing in the roof—'

For a moment Howard frowned, then he grinned. 'The catwalk?'

'That's the thing, and down the other side.'

'But that's hundreds of feet up!'

'You tell *them* that!' She laughed. 'Course, it's not allowed. Strictly forbidden, really. I mean, you could break your neck if you fell and—'

'Has anyone ever fallen?'

'Not to my knowledge. And don't you go getting any ideas, neither. I don't want my new lodger brought home in pieces, thank you very much!'

Howard grinned. 'You never know!' he said. 'No! I'm only kidding. But she's so enormous. It's breathtaking. It's funny – when you're up there you don't notice the height so much, but from the ground! Gosh! You stand underneath her and she's like . . . like . . .' He laughed. 'Well, words fail me. And that's before she's finished. I can't wait to see her completed.'

Mrs Croft patted his hand. 'She's going to be even bigger with that new gas bag they're putting in. She'll be the biggest airship *ever!*' Seeing his surprise she added, 'Oh, we all know what's going on inside those sheds. In Shortstown everyone knows everyone and word gets round. You've heard of the bush telegraph? Well! That's nothing to this place, believe you me. And she was over seven hundred feet long *before the new bag went in!* Seven-seventy I think it will be. Imagine that taking to the air. You just wait until they walk her out,' she told him. 'That's a rare sight, that is. They . . .' She paused in mid-flow. 'I forgot the mustard. My last young man—'

'I don't like it,' said Howard.

'Don't like it? Well, I never!' She frowned. 'Now where was I? Oh, yes! Walking her out of the shed. They get hundreds of people from somewhere – don't ask me where! – and they all hang on to these ropes and it's inch by inch, step by step! *So* careful! You've never seen anything like it. I watched the 101 walked out on her trial flight last year, and a few weeks back I watched the 100 walked out. My hubby used to be a walker. He'd volunteer. Loved the excitement of it, you see. It's a blooming miracle every time. There's so little room, and the winds do billow round that shed. If a gust caught her nose and whipped her to one side she'd do herself a mischief. She'd be damaged against the side of the shed – could get a nasty tear if that happened. Not that a *little* tear would matter that much because the riggers would be up there like a shot to patch it. Still, it would be a shame and in the air, of course, a small tear can soon become a big tear and so it goes. If the tear went through her skin to the gas bag – well! You can imagine!' She paused for breath, filled her mouth with pie and ate it as quickly as she could. 'I don't mind telling you when the 100 was walked out I held my breath, and so did everyone else. But she made it, bless her. Oh, Mr Roberts, she was a sight for sore eyes, as they say. She brought tears to my eyes and that's the truth.'

Howard nodded. It was clear that comment was unnecessary and he was content to eat his food before it grew cold. After supper he would write a short note to his mother to cheer her up and after that . . . An idea came to him suddenly, unbidden, like a flash of lightning; an idea from the darker corners of his mind. He savoured it, tightening his lips briefly. For a moment he wavered, then decided he liked the idea. Yes, he would write a second note – to *her*. To the woman who had ensnared his father. Nothing too definite, just hints. She was intelligent. Let her work it out for herself; let her worry the way his mother had worried over the years. Not that she had ever uttered a word of reproach. His mouth twisted briefly at the memory of his mother's face as the postman came and went and the familiar envelope did not arrive. Not that it was often more than a few days late, but every time was like a small death to his mother. He guessed, rather than knew, that she must always be wondering if one day, one dreadful week, there would be no money folded into the terse note. Her eyes would darken and her voice would be tight. Yes, his mother had worried and now he would see to it that *she* had something to worry about. His mother would never know that her son had avenged her. He smiled suddenly, liking the idea; seeing himself as a modest, unsung hero.

Mrs Croft asked, 'What's so funny?'

He said quickly, 'I can see you're a bit of an expert on airships, Mrs C.'

The compliment pleased her. 'I ought to be,' she told him. 'We lived for years at Howden, in Yorkshire, before we came here. My hubby worked on the R38 alongside my father. He really loved that ship, my hubby did. I used to tease him. "Who'd you rather lose, me or her?" I said. And d'you know what he said? "I can always remarry, but we couldn't build another 38!"' She laughed at the memory. 'Course, he didn't mean it. But that's how you get about them.'

Howard said cautiously, 'But didn't she crash, the 38?'

Her expression changed and she sighed. 'Sort of,' she admitted reluctantly. 'She broke up over the Humber. Just broke in half in mid-air. People on the ground *saw* the envelope rip open and *heard* the girders tearing apart. "Screeching metal" is how one man described it. Then down came the front half into the water, all in flames. The rear half came down a bit slower and fell into shallower water. They say the tail fins slowed it down, but fifteen hundred feet is a long way to fall. We lost forty-four men that day. Only five survived.' She sighed again. 'I said to my hubby, "Thank God you don't fly." He was ground crew, you see. My father worked on the R34, too. He cried when she broke up. I've never forgotten it. To see a grown man cry! It was terrible. He was an engineer – knew all there was to know about engines, he did.'

She broke off to offer Howard a second helping of pie and the remains of the cabbage, which he accepted gratefully. His exertions in his new job had made him ravenous.

'I do like to see a man eat,' she told him. 'I can see we're going to get along like a house on fire. One of my young men was a vegetarian. No meat, just vegetables. I told him straight, either you eat what you're given or you go elsewhere. He soon knuckled under. *And* it did him the world of good. Got rid of all his pimples. But where was I?'

'The R34.'

'Oh, dear me, yes! My father was on the rear engine. Proud as punch he was. A real disaster that, although no one was killed. Poor old 34. She'd gone up and got herself lost in the dark over the North Sea and drifted about for hours. Somehow they came down too low and scraped the high ground at Guisborough, but then she bounced back up again. What a carry-on! And the weather got worse and worse. She made it back to Howden, though God alone knows how. The poor old ship was so battered it seemed impossible she could ever get home safely. But she did. They left her at her mooring then, but the storm was so bad it smashed her against the ground, time and again, until in the morning she was a wreck. I can see my father – white as a sheet, his face.'

'Terrible!' said Howard dutifully. He thought again about what he would say in the note to the woman at Cardington. 'Haven't you ever wondered . . .', perhaps, or 'Ask your husband how he enjoyed his stay in Paris . . .' Just hints. Nothing definite. He wondered how much she knew. Had his father told her everything? It was most unlikely. He narrowed his eyes. Maybe just worrying her was not enough. Maybe he should *scare* her a little. Yes, a nice little threat . . . He could imagine her reading the note. Her expression would change and her legs would buckle under her; she'd clutch at the nearest chair and sit down. there'd be a sheen of sweat on her forehead . . . And serve her damn well right! She deserved it. But should he sign his name? Or would 'A well-wisher' be more dramatic? Not that he did wish her well – quite the opposite, but there was plenty of time. He might send her a second note, worse than the first. She'd show it to his father and – and what? What exactly would his father do?

'I said, what does your father do?' Mrs Croft leaned forward, waving a hand in front of his eyes to attract his attention.

For a moment he was caught off-guard, confused, staring at her anxiously. His father? What does he do? Quick. Think. 'He's dead,' Howard improvised. 'Died a year or so ago – in a road accident. Yes, a road accident. Fell off his bike, his *motor*-bike, and went straight under a bus. In London, it was. Just before my birthday.'

'Oh, dear. You poor thing!' She tutted sympathetically.

'Still, you know what they say. The world's a vale of sorrow!' She stood up carefully and reached for his empty plate. 'A bit of currant duff with custard?'

'Please!' He rather wished his father *had* fallen under a bus. It would be easier to mourn a dead father than hate a live one. He rather liked his little deception. When Mrs Croft returned to the dining room she carried a huge steamed pudding. Howard said, 'He didn't die instantly, my father. He lingered for weeks in terrible agony — hovering between life and death.'

'Oh, my!' She set the pudding on the table, picked out a currant and popped it into her mouth. 'Still, these things are sent to test us. That's what I always say.' She heaped a plate with the spongy mass and indicated the custard jug. Howard helped himself. For some reason the harrowing mental picture of his father in hospital didn't please him as much as he felt it should.

'Still, she was a lovely ship, the 34,' Mrs Croft told him, effectively dismissing his family tragedy. 'The whole world said so. I mean, to get to America and back! That was a tremendous achievement. The King sent them a telegram, you know. Still, you wouldn't be old enough to remember it. A wonderful trip with the eyes of the world on her. That's what the papers said. "The eyes of the world!"'

Howard nodded vaguely, his thoughts drifting.

'The first crossing of the Atlantic from east to west and the first *double* crossing! That's hard to beat. Nineteen-nineteen, it was. You'd have been a baby then. I remember my father saying it would have been much earlier if it hadn't been for the war, but then we—' She stopped abruptly as Howard, his plate not cleared, pushed his chair back.

'If you'll excuse me? I have some letters to write.'

Her face fell as she noted the unfinished currant duff. 'But you haven't—'

He stood up, ignoring her protests. Suddenly he could

wait no longer. His letter to his mother would only take a few moments, and then he could get down to it. His revenge! He had a clear image of himself, head bent, poring over *her* letter. He liked what he saw. With a muttered 'Excuse me,' he left the room and took the stairs to his room two at a time.

*

That same afternoon Bel found herself standing outside a jeweller's shop in Bond Street. Her eyes ranged unseeingly across the various items – the rings, necklaces and bracelets glittered and winked to no avail. One of the watches told her that it was ten to two, although she knew it was almost 4 o'clock. She was thinking of Larry and wondering how *not* to think of him. He was in her thoughts from the moment she woke up until the moment she fell asleep at night. She worried in case she spoke his name in her sleep and Walter heard her. She craved the luxury of talking about him, but there was no one in whom she could confide. Since their exchange of letters she had not seen him, and she began to suspect that he was keeping away from her. The idea was unbearably painful, although she realised that she also was being careful to prevent a meeting. Her confusion alarmed her. Earlier in the day she had gone to the Inn of Chambers where Larry worked and had walked about aimlessly for an hour and a half hoping to catch a glimpse of him. Not that she had intended him to see her. That was not the point of the exercise, but she . . .

A shadow was cast suddenly across the display of jewellery. A man was standing beside her, standing very close. She closed her hand over her clutch bag in case he was a pickpocket and then stepped to one side, pretending to study the price tag on one of the watches. To her astonishment he took another step towards her, until his shoulder touched her own. Indignantly she turned to face him, summoning a few sharp words. As she opened her mouth

88

the words died in her throat. Instead she said faintly, 'Larry!' and then, in a hoarse whisper, 'Oh, Larry!'

Her knees went weak with shock and she knew that her excitement was written all over her face. The suddenness of their meeting had given her no time to prepare herself. She was both pleased and dismayed to see his own feelings reflecting hers so closely.

She said, 'How did you find me? That is, how did you— Why did you . . .' Her voice faltered and her throat was dry as he put an arm through hers.

'I saw you from the window,' he told her. 'I was due in court, so I couldn't come down but I guessed – at least I hoped – that you'd wanted to see me. Or maybe I was wrong.'

'No,' she stammered. 'At least, I didn't intend to *speak* to you. I only wanted to . . .' She bit her lip, repressing the final confession.

'To *see* me? Oh, Bel!' He began to lead her along the pavement, his arm wonderfully warm and firm through the cloth of her jacket. 'You did want to see me, didn't you?'

'Oh, Larry, I did, but it was foolish of me. I—'

'I thought, "Where will she go next?" and thought of here because I know you love window-shopping. You said once that window-shopping was "soporific". I was about fourteen at the time and frightfully impressed. I thought you were wildly sophisticated.' He laughed, looking down into her face, unaware of the other shoppers who jostled past them. 'So I dropped everything and came after you. And don't pretend you're angry with me because I can see in your face that you're not at all put out.'

Bel's heart thudded uncomfortably. He was right, she thought, conscience-stricken. She had undoubtedly engineered this meeting, by her own stupidity. Hadn't she said something in her letter to him about 'remaining good friends'? Then why had she mooned around an area where he might possibly catch sight of her? It was her own fault entirely.

'I'm not put out,' she told him. 'Of course it's good to see you. It's always—'

He laughed again. 'Bel! You're a terrible liar. I never realised that before. You're just as pleased to see me as I am to see you! Admit it. I dare you to!'

Bel was looking anxiously from side to side, terrified that someone they knew would recognise them. Arm in arm and *looking so terribly happy*! They might as well shout it from the rooftops, she thought, and for a moment panic flared. A man or a woman in love cannot hide the fact from a discerning woman, though she could not vouch for men's perspicacity.

'Go on, Bel! Say it. What does it matter? There's no one else to hear it.'

Looking into his familiar, handsome face it was hard to resist his pleading. It was also impossible to pretend any longer. The sight of him confirmed her worst suspicions – that she had loved him for a long time without ever acknowledging the fact.

'Larry, I – I don't want to hold out any hope. That's all. If I admit it you'll—'

'So you do! I knew it!'

To her consternation he pulled her close and put his arms around her.

'Oh, Larry, don't!' she cried fearfully.

But it was too late. He was kissing her and after an initial urge to resist, she quite forgot the shoppers around them and kissed him back. Not the kind of kiss you give to a younger brother-in-law at Christmas, but the sort of kiss a woman gives to the man she loves. Held tightly against him with her mouth on his, Bel felt a wild surge of joy. So this was being in love, she thought faintly. This was what had been missing from her relationship with Walter. At the thought of her husband she struggled suddenly, pushing them apart. It was no use expecting Larry to be circumspect; she was older and wiser and must be sensible for both of them.

'Larry, we mustn't do this,' she gasped. 'We mustn't let this happen.' But looking into those ardent eyes she knew with a tremor of fear that she had set in motion something she could not control. 'Oh, God, Larry! What have I done? I'm so sorry!' Unexpectedly tears pricked at her eyelids as her mood changed from one of exhilaration to one of apprehension. But her words had no effect on Larry. The bright excitement still lit up his face and she saw that his eyes – his *deep* blue eyes! – were soft with adoration. That look! She drew a deep breath and stared into his eyes, and knew intuitively that her own expression matched his. Many times she had seen and envied that expression on the faces of others, recognising instantly the emotion behind it, but had never expected to experience it herself. She wanted to weep for joy, but still her natural caution restrained her. For Larry's sake she must try to make amends for her initial mistake.

'Larry, we must be careful,' she began nervously but he was still talking, his face animated, his eyes so luminous with love that she longed to throw her arms round his neck and kiss him again. An unfamiliar longing struck her now somewhere far below her heart, and with an urgency that brought a flicker of shame with it. It was lust, not love. It was sexual attraction. With a growing helplessness, she acknowledged it as such. But lust was such an ugly word. 'Need' was kinder. Perhaps love plus need became desire. Was that the right equation? With an effort she tried to regain her crumbling composure, but it was difficult for now Larry was hurrying her through the dawdling crowd at breakneck speed.

'Where are we going?' she asked breathlessly. For a moment her imagination soared. Thank goodness he lived at home with his father and didn't own a bachelor flat!

91

'To my *lair*!' he answered with a brief grin.

'Larry!' This was getting out of hand. 'Seriously, Larry, we must be sensible!'

'You be sensible if you like but me, I'm going to be just a little bit crazy!'

'But where are we—'

He stopped so abruptly that an elderly woman cannoned into them and Larry spent the next minute apologising profusely and gathering up the shopping she had dropped.

'To Selfridges to the tea-room,' he told her. 'Is that innocent enough for you?'

'Yes, but—'

'It's OK, Bel. We just *happened* to meet in Bond Street and I am taking you for a cup of tea and a cream cake. What could be more innocent than that?'

She felt her face break into a reluctant smile. Selfridges! It would give her a chance to collect her thoughts and talk to him. Perhaps she could convince him of the madness of their behaviour and the need to put an end to it before too much damage was done. 'Tea and a cream cake. Wonderful!'

'So you'll stop fussing and come with me?'

'You are my half-brother-in-law, so why not?'

He leaned closer and whispered in her ear 'I love you!' and then before she could protest he was once more propelling her along the street. Soon they had reached Selfridges and were going up the stairs to the tea-room.

They ordered tea and eclairs but when it arrived Bel ate her pastry without tasting it. This new Larry amazed and secretly delighted her. Gone was the shy young man, silently worshipping her from afar. Her letter appeared to have unleashed a new man, one who was assured and happy, with a sense of fun she had never suspected. His enthusiasm was infectious and Bel was rapidly surrendering all her good intentions. She told herself that this was to avoid spoiling Larry's pleasure, but in reality she knew that she no longer had the will power, or the wish, to cast even the smallest shadow over their new-found joy. One stolen meeting would hurt no one, she assured herself, and she would see to it that the affair . . . The word brought her up sharply. Was this an *affair*? Surely not. An affair had all sorts of unpleasant connotations and frequently resulted in a scandal. A year or two back, Margaret's brother had been involved with a young dancer from the ballet and it had ended in a messy divorce which rocked society and kept the gossips happy for months. She, Bel, would see that this was their first and last such meeting. . . .

'Bel! You're not listening, are you?'

The blue eyes held hers once more and immediately she felt her resolve slipping away. Maybe one more meeting. Or once a month. Or fortnightly, perhaps. . . .

Larry went on, 'I said we won't do anything to hurt Walter. I mean it, Bel. Only promise to *be* with me from time to time – just the two of us, to talk and share things and – I love you and you love me and all I ask—'

'I haven't said so! Oh, Larry, did I say that I loved you?' She was at once a mass of uncertainties.

'You don't need to say it, Bel. Your letter hinted at it and your kiss convinced me, so there's really no point in denying it. I simply had to know, and now I do know I'm the happiest man in the world. Corny but true.' He put his hand over hers. 'Can't you be glad that you have worked this miracle in me? Please don't worry about it. I want us to be happy. Can't you allow yourself a little happiness?'

'I wasn't *unhappy*,' she protested.

'But were you *happy*? Like this? Did you feel about Walter the way you feel about me?'

She was silent, afraid to meet his eyes. How could she tell him she had never in her life felt so complete, so much a *woman*. If he ever guessed at the depths of her longing she would be lost.

'If we just meet occasionally . . .' she said.

'It's a start'. His smile broadened. 'How about *regularly*? Does that sound too dreadful?'

'No, but—'

'Regularly once a day!'

His handsome face mocked but there was a tenderness that took the sting out of it and, seeing her consternation, he shook his head in amusement. 'I was joking. As often or as little as you decree. It's up to you.'

Bel could no longer deny the appeal of secret meetings. Yet even as she considered the possibilities her anxiety grew. 'But how can we arrange it? I can't keep telephoning you at home. George would quickly suspect something. If Walter ever finds out he will be heartbroken – and angry. Understandably angry. He might forgive me, but would he ever forgive you?'

'I'll take my chances. I don't want to hurt him any more than you do but Bel, *dearest* Bel, I've waited years for this and I won't give you up without a struggle . . . You could ring me at chambers. If I'm not there, leave a message.'

'Oh, no! That's too dangerous. They'd know the name.'

'You could be Mrs Smith.'

'Larry! It's no joking matter.'

'It is to me, my sweet Bel.'

Her panic grew. 'And don't get into the habit of calling me "sweet" or "dearest". It might slip out in an unguarded moment.' She hid her face in her hands for a moment, then looked up at him soberly. 'Larry! I'm not going to be very good at this. If only there were just the two of us, but I can't and won't hurt Walter. He has done nothing to deserve it. Oh, why is life so difficult?'

'And why is it so *short*?' He looked at her closely, watching her face as as his meaning dawned.

God! Yes, it *was* short, she reflected. And this might be her one and only chance of real happiness. But was that excuse enough for betraying Walter's trust? Suddenly she was exhausted by the dilemma. If she refused this new relationship with Larry he might – he just might – find another woman. And if he did not find someone else she would be forced to stand by and watch him waste his life, lonely and unloved. Maybe Marie had been right after all. Maybe this would be a brief affair which would harm no one and then blow itself out. She wanted to scream out in an agony of frustration and indecision. If only her father had lived; then she would never have been drawn towards Walter and maybe she and Larry would have fallen in love with no hindrance and with everyone's blessing. She uttered a deep, heartfelt sigh. There was nothing to be gained by 'If onlys'. Her father *had* died, and she had turned to Walter who had given her what she needed. She swallowed hard. She had been a good wife and she would continue to please him in any way she could; but she would allow herself the luxury of loving Larry. They would meet once a week, here, and then they would carry on their respective lives. It could be done, she was sure of it.

She looked at Larry, who was waiting silently for her to resolve her inner crisis. 'Suppose we meet once a week,' she suggested. 'And each time we part we fix the next meeting. Then there will be no need for letters or telephone calls. Nothing to betray us.'

The word 'betray' troubled her. She thought suddenly of Anne Boleyn and Henry's other wives. They must have been very much in love to risk being beheaded. The women, for so long dry as dust, suddenly sprang to life and she felt a moment's rapport with them. Was this what the history books meant by 'risking all'?

When at last they parted it was arranged that they would meet at the same place at intervals of *eight* days' time, as a weekly meeting might mean that they would be seen together too often by regular shoppers. On the way home Bel leaned back in the taxi and tried to make sense of what was happening. Her whole life had been turned upside down in the space of a few hours, but she could not wish it otherwise. As she paid the driver and went up the steps to the front door she was still smiling broadly, and she could not imagine that anything could dim her newly discovered happiness.

Chapter Five

THE FOLLOWING DAY WALTER returned from Cardington to find Bel in a state of some alarm.
He had hardly set foot in the door when she
produced an envelope from her pocket and asked him to
read it.

'Who's it from?' he asked.

'That's just it. I don't know. I thought you might. It's
quite frightening in a way. That this total stranger is—'

'Total stranger? For heaven's sake, Bel. Let me at least
take off my coat and settle myself with a drink. Why
should total strangers write to you?'

'I don't know. It came this morning and I've been
racking my brains ever since. I tried to reach you at
Cardington—'

'We had a meeting which lasted most of the day. I'll tell
you about it over dinner. What's on the menu tonight? We
didn't even stop for lunch and for once I'm starving.'

He followed her into the lounge and waited impatiently
while Mrs Parks served drinks, producing a dish of salted
nuts to accompany them. Walter took a large mouthful of
whisky and water and swallowed it gratefully. The troubles
at R.A.W. were multiplying like rabbits and his unease was
growing deeper as each day passed. He needed time to
think, and was annoyed by Bel's immediate demand on his

time and energy. She was a grown woman now and really should be able to cope with these matters herself, he reflected irritably. He sighed, his eyes closed, aware that as soon as he opened them Bel would pounce. He sometimes wondered if it was his fault that she relied so heavily upon him. With another mouthful of his drink he pushed the thought aside. The subject of his relationship with Bel was one he chose not to pursue, for it invariably led to memories of Geoffrey Hammond which still had the power to hurt him. Geoffrey's death had left a terrible void and his daughter had stepped in to replace him. Poor Bel! He had done her a great disservice and had lived to regret his selfishness.

And yet at one time her dependence on him had been more than pleasing. As well as lover he had been both father and tutor to her, and that had satisfied him tremendously for reasons he could not explain. He had taught her all he knew about literature and music but now, because of his commitments elsewhere, he had lost touch and she had overtaken him. They no longer shared the same interests. He no longer had time to keep up with the newer writers — Henry Williamson and Evelyn Waugh were no more than names to him whereas Bel spoke knowledgeably about them over the dinner table. She played records of songs he had never heard and danced in a way that he found entirely frivolous. Her fascination with the movie industry had developed and she now expressed a liking for Ben Lyon, Jean Harlow and Edward G. Robinson, whoever they might be. And the 'talkies'! What a ridiculous word that was. Gradually he had begun to feel that life with a capital 'L' was passing him by, and now when he looked at Bel he felt for the first time that the difference in their ages was widening the gulf between them.

But if he was becoming insecure he tried not to dwell on it. He was not a man to investigate his feelings, and to do so was unfashionable. He considered such introspection unmanly and thoroughly undesirable. Constantly reminding himself that he had a job of work to do, he concentrated his efforts in that direction. He was what he was and when uncomfortable doubts surfaced he repressed them. Cardington and the R101 had first call on his time and that was the way he liked it. Dealing with stresses and lifts and thrusts was his escape from the niggling doubts which he occasionally experienced about his marriage. Bel was Geoffrey's only child, and he owed it to him to care for her as lovingly as possible. He could not tolerate the thought that Bel might not be happy. There was no reason for such an assumption, he argued. She had everything money could buy – two homes, beautiful clothes, servants, time to spend as she chose. She had no worries as far as he knew, and not many women were so fortunate.

Suddenly he became aware that she was waiting for his attention.

'Do please read it,' she said and reluctantly he put down his drink and took the proffered letter.

Dear Mrs Roberts,
    I am so sorry I missed you at St Saviour's. The soup smelled quite tasty. You really are doing a splendid job. Three cheers for the 'do-gooders' of this world.

Walter frowned. 'Who is this idiot?'

'That's what I'm telling you, Walter. I don't know him from Adam. He turned up one day in the—'

' "Wait! Wait!" ' He held up the letter with an imperious gesture. 'One thing at a time, dear, please. Let me finish the letter.'

You seem quite a good-hearted person. A pity you are married to a less-than-worthy man . . .

Walter felt a stab of anger. 'What the hell does he mean by that, dammit? Less than worthy? I'll give him "less than worthy" if I get my hands on him!' He glared at Bel. 'So what is all this?'

'I keep telling you, Walter. I don't know who he is or anything about him.' She hesitated. 'You might as well read to the end.'

> . . . Ask him if he has any skeletons in his cupboard. His answer may surprise you. Ask him if the letter 'H' means anything to him? Or the letter 'V'. I will be in touch again soon.
>
> A well-wisher.

Walter's anger gave way abruptly to fear. He felt a wave of faintness and then his body grew hot and a sweat broke out on his skin. The letters 'H' and 'V'. That could only mean one thing. Howard! His hands shook so much that he dropped the letter and sank to his knees to retrieve it. But he must say something; he could sense that Bel was looking at him, waiting for an answer. Desperately he groped around for an explanation that would convince her, but nothing suitable sprang to his shocked mind. After all these years his son was going to turn on him. The boy's love was turning to hate and he had only himself to blame. Vera had tried to warn him; had tried to alert him to the boy's growing hostility. He was neglecting the boy, she had told him in her timid way, but he had never wanted to listen. Being Vera, she had never had the courage to persist. And now *this*. His nightmare was becoming a reality. Gratefully he realised that Bel was talking.

'I'm sorry,' he stammered. 'What was that about the garden?'

'I said he just strolled around the garden as though he had every right to be there. There was something about him that was vaguely familiar although I couldn't for the life of me say what it was. And he whistled. He wasn't exactly rude and he didn't threaten me or anything but it was – well, I suppose it was a bit unnerving. Mrs Banks wanted to call the police but—'

'The police?' Oh, God! This was worse than he could have imagined. 'I hope you didn't trouble the police.'

'No, we didn't. But if he had refused to go or had come back again I think I would have done so.' She was frowning with the effort of recollection and he had a sudden picture of Bel and Howard talking together on his lawn. It was preposterous – and yet it had happened.

She went on, 'I meant to tell you about it but then forgot. I didn't give it another thought until suddenly he popped up again. At least I assume it was him from the description. He had called at the soup kitchen, asking for me.'

The soup kitchen? How on earth could he have known where to find her? He felt dizzy with fright. Was the young fool following Bel around? Did he intend her some mischief? *Was he going to pass the information on to his mother?* Oh, God! Poor Vera! And how, in God's name, had he tracked them down? Even Vera did not have his Cardington address, although he had given her his telephone number at R.A.W. for use in an emergency. There had never been one, fortunately, and he had considered himself safe. What on earth had inspired Howard to show his hand at this late stage? He reached for his drink and finished it in one gulp.

Bel said, 'Are you all right, dear? You look terribly pale?'

'I do feel a bit queasy,' he lied. 'I – I might go and lie down.'

She looked surprised. 'I thought you said you were starving.'

He ignored the comment and rushed on. 'Probably something I ate at lunch. The canteen's gone downhill a bit lately. Used to be very hot on hygiene. I . . .' What on earth was he saying? The canteen was superb. He was rambling. Pull yourself together, man! She doesn't suspect, and you can make sure it stays that way if you keep your nerve.

'Do you know about "H"?' she asked. 'Only when I asked him his name in the garden he said it was Howard, so I think the letter might be from him.'

He said, 'I don't know any Howards.' His voice sounded hoarse and he coughed hastily.

'Or "V"?'

He shrugged without comment.

'The bit about the skeletons is a bit melodramatic, isn't it?' She laughed nervously and he could see that she was rattled. Any woman would be. The idea of a stranger prying into your life – and a rather odd one at that – would unsettle most people.

He said, 'The man's obviously deranged, but I doubt if he's dangerous.'

Bel hesitated. 'But suppose he is? What worries me most is that he seemed to know about us. In the garden he said I was beautiful and then added, 'but then I knew you would be'. Or words to that effect. But how could he know such a thing? And he went on about the roses, saying that they were his father's favourite flowers. Do you think "V" could be his father? Victor, perhaps. Do you know any Victors? Or maybe his mother? Veronica? Valerie?'

Walter could only shake his head, not trusting himself to speak. He was seized with an overpowering weakness and his stomach churned ominously. He would have to think carefully about this, he would have to contact Vera urgently – oh, no! He couldn't do that without telling her about Bel, and so far he had managed to spare her that knowledge. But his first priority was to recover his confidence; overcome this terrible fear. Then he would think it out carefully so that he did not cause an even bigger disaster. Damnation!

He would have to do *something*. The boy deserved a good hiding, he told himself, but even as his mind formed the phrase his heart ached in the old familiar way. They had been such marvellous friends in the early years; Howard had loved him unequivocally. Walter sighed deeply for those long-gone, golden days. In his mind's eye he could see the boy asleep in bed, hair tousled against the pillow, his left arm thrown out from the blanket; the right clutching the battered old bear. Now what did he call that teddy bear? Rufus! That was it. He smiled faintly.

'What?' Bel asked. 'What are you smiling at?'

'Nothing. It doesn't matter.'

She gave him a strange look. 'You must have been smiling at something.'

'The fact is I didn't realise I *was* smiling. I was remembering something that happened at work.'

Her voice rose a little. 'I don't believe you. Your father says that anyone who starts a sentence with the words, "The fact is" . . .'

'I know . . . "is lying."' He tutted. His courage was slowly returning now that the subject had shifted slightly and he was recovering from the initial shock. 'My father is hardly the oracle on these matters, so don't bother to quote him to me, dear. Which reminds me – I must pop in there tomorrow, now that I'm back. He does love a bit of company and I feel rather remiss.'

Bel shook her head as she took the letter from him and reread it. 'I wondered if perhaps you had had to sack one of the men. He might be a young rigger who has a grudge against you. Have you sacked an "H" or a "V" lately?' She was trying to speak lightly and he felt a flash of admiration for her. It must be rather worrying for her, especially with Mrs Banks fussing and adding to the tension.

'Not possible, dear. I don't do what the Americans like to call the hiring and firing. I doubt it we could afford to sack anyone at the moment. In fact, I think we've taken a few more men on. We're working flat out to get her ready for her flight trials.' For a moment his concerns about the airship resurfaced, blotting out his other problem. 'She ought to have a proper test flight of forty-eight hours to include a speed test, manoeuvring and so on. I've been talking to Will Charlton, the chief supply officer. He's worried. So are we all, to be truthful. The damned engines are so heavy, and we can't seem to replace the lift we've lost. Let's hope the new gas bag does the trick. Not that I hold out much hope. The designers wanted ninety tons useful lift, and we'll be lucky if we get thirty-five. Forty at the outside! And we still think she's underpowered.'

'Is it too late to change them? The engines, I mean.'

'It's not too late, but the top brass have vetoed the idea. We had asked for the lighter gasolene engines, but it's no go. The trouble is, as always, that the cost is escalating all the time and the Treasury are getting jumpy. If only we weren't getting so much publicity ... but we are. The irony is that in the normal way of things we'd be welcoming interest from the press, but because we are beset with gremlins, press coverage is becoming a huge bugbear. Everything we do, every minor error, is immediately under the spotlight, and it looks bad to be constantly retracting. R100 was fortunate in that respect.' He sighed, rubbing his face tiredly.

'Poor Walter.'

He smiled at her. She seemed genuinely to care about him.' I wish to God your father was still alive,' he said wistfully.

Bel gave him a strange look. 'So do I,' she said.

'I could always talk to Geoffrey. He'd have understood perfectly. Poor old Geoff. I wonder what he'd make of all this?' He waved a hand vaguely to indicate the mess he had made of his life, and unexpected tears sprang suddenly at the back of his eyes and he brushed them quickly away.

Bel laid a hand on his arm but he brushed her aside,

104

afraid that her sympathy would undermine him totally. He saw the hurt expression on her face but could do nothing to explain.

She folded the letter and slipped it into her pocket. 'Forget the R101,' she told him. 'Forget this stupid young man. If you're really not hungry you should get some rest. Sleep, the great healer!'

Her smile was lopsided and he longed to take her in his arms. But that was out of the question. Given the slightest encouragement, he would break down and tell her everything. At least he must spare her that.

She said, 'Get some sleep, Walter, and you'll feel better in the morning. And try not to worry. I'm sure the new gas bag will work the magic.'

'My dearest Bel!' He managed a fairly convincing laugh. 'You always were the optimist.' Briefly and with reluctance, he considered the new gas bag. 'Mind you, it's not just the new one. The final report on the overall design of the bags was never totally positive. It's all very well to introduce a new design, but they're untried. We know the old-style bags worked perfectly. Or as near as dammit. It was always the frames that—' He shook his head. 'Now all it needs is one bad tear.'

Bel said, 'Don't even *think* about it!'

Walter pursed his lips. Ten thousand cubic feet of hydrogen could be lost through a one-foot hole. Bel was right; it didn't bear thinking about. He said, 'Today's meeting was not a happy one, I can say *that* hand on heart. We shall know more after the trials, of course – but then there's the . . .' He put a hand to his head. His earlier lie was proving prophetic – he *was* feeling unwell. 'I think I shall go straight to bed. It may be a chill; it was surprisingly cold in the shed this morning – not what you expect at this time of the year. Ask Mrs Parks to bring me up some hot milk, will you, dear?' Her look of concern touched him and he cursed Howard inwardly. 'And forget about the letter. I'll

105

make a few enquiries. Might be something in what you said about sacked employees. I'll sort it out, dear.'

As he made his way towards the bedroom his heart hardened. If Howard wanted to play silly beggars, he would find he had picked on the wrong man. Two could play at that game and Howard must be made to see the error of his ways.

*

The Wigmore Hall opened its doors at precisely 7.30 p.m., and the long queue of eager people was allowed inside. Among those entering the vast auditorium were Marie and Geraldine who had booked seats in row ten. Marie was having second thoughts about the evening ahead. A session with an ouija board in the privacy of Geraldine's flat had been fun, but this was different. She sat down in a slightly subdued frame of mind and surveyed the audience nervously. People were passing the time in a variety of ways, some with their heads bent in silent meditation, others talking eagerly, rustling the inevitable sweet papers or wriggling themselves out of coats and jackets. Newcomers like Marie and Geraldine studied their surroundings with cautious interest. Geraldine, however, appeared to be treating the event as a joke, laughing too loudly and too often so that even Marie was embarrassed.

Finally Marie hissed 'Do keep your voice down, dear old thing. This is a church, remember.'

'A church? Of course it's not. They give concerts and—'

'I mean this evening's event is . . . well, it has religious undertones, surely.'

Geraldine gave her a withering look. 'Religious undertones? Honestly, Marie, you can be so pretentious at times.'

Marie bit back an angry retort. There were times when her father's opinion of Geraldine as an 'empty-headed female' appeared apt but then, she reflected, who was she

106

to stand in judgement? She herself was rash and thoughtless, and she deeply regretted her interference between Bel and Larry, although she would never admit it. She sighed.

Geraldine snapped well-manicured fingers in front of her face. 'You're miles away! Not scared, are you?'

'Of course not.' With an effort she pushed the unwelcome train of thought to the back of her mind and turned her attention to the present. The audience was settling and Marie was aware of an air of repressed excitement. The stage was in darkness, the auditorium gently lit. Suddenly the house lights dimmed and a spotlight lit up a single chair which stood on a small rostrum centre stage. Behind this was a backcloth of filmy grey material, artistically draped. As music swelled suddenly from an unseen organ, a tall woman walked on to the stage. At first the audience fell silent, then they greeted her with subdued applause.

Alice Threadmore was disappointing, thought Marie. A very ordinary woman in a long grey dress. Now she clasped her hands and bent her head; she did not look like someone who could contact the dead, and Marie did not know whether to be pleased or sorry. Stealing a quick glance at those around her, she saw a rapt expression on every face. When at last the famous medium spoke, Marie thought she detected a trace of cockney in her accent and was again disappointed.

'Ladies and gentlemen – or may I call you friends? Let us for a moment remember those loved ones who have passed over to the other side.'

There was a long silence and then Alice Threadmore made her way to the chair and sat down. She appeared to be breathing deeply and then, somewhat dramatically, she held out her arms in an expansive welcome – presumably to a host of invisible spirits. Marie felt the hairs on the back of her neck stiffen.

'There are so many of you,' Alice said. 'All so eager.

Wait, please. I will do what I can for you . . . one at a time.'

Marie realised that the medium was no longer addressing the audience but speaking in this natural way to . . . to what exactly? Were there really spirits around her?

Alice continued. 'Yes, I hear you, madam. Your name is? Dorothy.' To the audience she said, 'She is very faint. Rather nervous. She has only recently passed over.' She touched the side of her face. 'I see a scar, here. Now, Dorothy, who do you want to speak to? Your sister. Wait just a moment, my dear . . .' She addressed herself once again to her eager audience. 'I have Dorothy, who has a scar on her face and has recently passed over. Does anybody here have a sister, Dorothy?'

Marie swallowed hard. If it was a trick, it was very well done.

There was no response from the audience.

'What's that? . . . Oh, I'm sorry. It's not Dorothy, it's *Dorothea* . . .'

At once a woman in a blue cloche hat stood up. 'It's my sister-*in-law*,' she said. 'She had a scar there. She fell as a child.'

Alice smiled. 'Your sister-in-law says you called her Dottie and she hated it.'

'That's right. We did. I mean, she did.'

'Dorothea says she went peacefully. You weren't there.'

'We didn't get to the hospital in time.'

'You're not to fret about it . . . Ah! I'm getting a gentleman . . .'

The woman in the blue hat sat down, whispering urgently to her companion.

The medium continued. '. . . Albert what? I can't hear you very well . . . Oh dear, I've lost him . . . Here's a young woman. Don't be afraid, dear; tell me your name. Ida Bridges. No? Oh, Bridger. Ida Bridger is here with me. She passed away three years ago. She wants to talk to her mother . . .' She searched the audience for a response. 'Is that you? Lady in the balcony? It is. Good. Ida wants you to know she's happy about the baby. Does that make sense to you, dear?'

Marie craned her neck but could not see into the balcony. She heard a woman's voice, though, and waited impatiently, hoping for an interpretation of what was happening.

Alice Threadmore was smiling. 'She died giving birth and you are raising the child? How splendid! Ida is thanking you. She's smiling at you.'

From the corner of her eye Marie saw Geraldine dabbing at her eyes with a handkerchief. So, she thought in surprise, she *did* have a compassionate side to her nature.

Still Marie could not entirely surrender her doubts. 'It could be an elaborate piece of theatre,' she whispered. 'They could have planted people in the audience and coached them in their replies.'

'Do you think that's what they've done?'

Marie was silent, unable to pronounce judgement, but as time passed her suspicions faded. By the time the interval came round she was nearly convinced and almost prepared to admit it.

After the half-hour interlude Alice Threadmore returned to the stage and the messages continued, although it soon became obvious that she was growing tired.

'Just one more,' she told the audience, 'and then I must stop. Yes, sir – I can see you very clearly . . . Your name is Gerry? Oh, dear. You mustn't be so impatient. I can see you're upset but . . . You are talking about trouble. In the past? Oh, in the future. I see . . . You want to speak to a young woman named Mary or Marie. He wants to warn her about something . . .' She frowned. 'He's giving me another name. I think it's Walter. Now he's pointing up into the sky. I don't know what it means, but I feel this terrible urgency.'

Geraldine shook Marie's arm. 'It could be Geoffrey instead of Gerry. And you know a Walter. It's you, Marie. He wants to talk to you. Stand up!'

'We don't know anyone called Geoffrey.'

'You do! There's that man who died in the crash. Stand up, you idiot!'

Marie felt a flash of panic. 'I can't! It's not for me!'

'Marie, *think*! Your sister-in-law's father was Geoffrey, and your brother is Walter. Stand up before she loses him!'

Desperately Marie glanced round the audience in the hope that someone else had risen to claim the elusive Gerry or Gerald. No one moved and, nudged again by Geraldine, she reluctantly rose to her feet. Immediately she was aware that thousands of pairs of curious eyes were suddenly focused upon her. 'I'm ... that is ...' she stammered.

Alice turned to look at her. 'Speak up, dear,' she said.

'My – my friend's father was a *Geoffrey*. My name is *Marie*. I don't know if ...' She faltered to a stop, embarrassed and uncertain. It was hard to believe that Bel's dead father had anything to tell her.

Alice closed her eyes. 'Is it Gerry or Geoffrey? ... Oh, it *is*! Ah! Good. Then ... What are you saying? Left? ... What is left? I don't understand you. Forgive me. I am very tired. What's that you say ... not enough *what* left? I can't make any sense of this ...' She turned to Marie. 'He seems to be saying there's not enough left? Does that mean anything?'

'I'm afraid not.'

'He's pointing upwards ... yes, yes, sir. I'm *telling* her ...' To Marie she said, 'He's very impatient with me. Very disturbed about something ... Oh dear, I wish I could understand ... Ah! What's this now? He says something that sounds like time ... yes, that's it. Oh! Not enough time ... not enough left and not enough time for what? ...' Abruptly she put both hands over her face and shud-

110

dered. The audience murmured anxiously as she fell back in her chair, apparently exhausted. From the side of the stage an elderly man hurried towards her and touched her arm gently.

Geraldine said, 'Oh, no!'

Marie didn't know whether she was pleased or not that her embarrassing ordeal was at an end. To her relief, Alice finally opened her eyes and nodded in answer to the man's whispered question. He turned to the audience and said, 'My wife is desperately tired. I simply cannot let her continue.' He looked harassed, as though the situation was a familiar one, and the audience made sympathetic noises.

Marie sat down, her legs suddenly weak. She felt a strong desire to throttle Geraldine. None of the message made any sense, and she was convinced that 'Geoffrey', if his spirit existed, must have been seeking someone else. Her stomach churned with nerves and she suddenly wanted the entire evening to have been an elaborate hoax.

Geraldine patted her arm. 'Bad luck,' she whispered. 'If only he had come through earlier on, before Alice became tired.'

'Oh, stop this nonsense!' Marie snapped.

On stage Alice Threadmore rose slowly to her feet while her husband hovered beside her. 'My husband looks after me very well,' she said with a tired smile. 'I must confess I am extremely weary.' She glanced towards Marie. 'I'm so sorry I couldn't be more helpful. When they are upset they speak so quickly. It is all so urgent, you see, but I couldn't quite grasp his meaning.' To the audience in general she went on, 'I know many of you will have been disappointed, but it is possible to see me privately. The address is in the programme if you care to write to me. Now I must bid you all good night and God bless!'

Some people in the audience returned the blessing and loud applause echoed from every corner of the hall. Marie, ignoring Geraldine's protests, was already on her feet. She was thoroughly confused and more deeply affected than she would care to admit. Her one thought was to escape and call a taxi. She wanted to reach the welcome familiarity of her own home as quickly as possible and put the whole worrying episode behind her.

Chapter Six

VERA WAS NO LETTER-WRITER, but her son's letter had galvanised her into action. She had found a small pad of Basildon Bond notepaper, and a pencil which she was busy sharpening with the vegetable knife. Her sense of loss at his departure had brought her low, and for days she had stayed indoors grieving and sick at heart. But now, with his cheerful, chirpy letter, her sorrow had turned to anger. Her whole life had revolved around him, and what thanks did she get? He had simply thrown the years of devotion back in her face. He had waltzed off without a by-your-leave and had the cheek to write that he was well and happy and that 'Mrs C'. was a good cook. As though her own efforts had already been forgotten . . . So he was well and happy. Three cheers! She sat down and stared grimly at the notepad, then arranged the lined sheet so that she would keep the writing straight. She *hated* letter-writing. There was always the matter of the punctuation which she had never really understood. She frowned and thought of her son. She missed him terribly, but that made her angrier than ever. Was he missing her? It was so unfair. Of course she was glad that he had settled down, but where did that leave her? Was she supposed to sit around, twiddling her thumbs, waiting for his occasional visits? Well, she had had enough of that with his father.

Years of waiting and hoping and taking an interest in his blasted balloons. She was through with all that. They could build an airship and fly to the moon for all she cared!

She wrote 'Dear Howard'. Not that they were *balloons*. Walter would object strongly to that word. Balloons were saggy things, full of air or gas. Splendid when filled but limp and insignificant when deflated. He had used that word 'insignificant' to Howard when he was barely three years old. No wonder the boy had grown up difficult. Hot-air balloons were balloons, he had told the boy, as they knelt together on the floor with sheets of paper Walter had stolen from his office. He took a balloon from his pocket and blew it up and tossed it into the air. It had made that funny, rude noise as it came down and the cat was terrified. Walter had been determined the boy would understand. Balloons were light, he said, and they floated but they went where the wind blew them. Airships were different; they were 'steerable'. Vera permitted herself a smile. Poor Howard. He had tried so hard to understand his father's big words. She could still see Walter's face as he talked to the boy, his expression so earnest as he searched for the simple words which his son would understand. 'An airship is a dirigible, you see, Howard? Say it. Di-ri-gi-ble . . . No, no! Not *didgible*. Di-ri-gi-ble . . .' But it was always 'didgible' with Howard even when he knew the correct word because it became a family joke. That, of course, was when they *had* jokes, before it all went wrong. She sighed. Poor Walter. He had never understood why the boy became a stranger to him; never could see that his occasional, hurried visits and the dreadful arguments about the school reports were all that Howard could remember. As Howard grew older he became tongue-tied in front of his father, and that irritated Walter.

Her throat ached as she thought about it. Poor Howard! Walter made him feel such a failure, although he didn't

114

mean to at all. He wanted the boy to be someone he could be proud of. She took out her handkerchief and wiped away a tear that had somehow escaped.

'This is no good!' she scolded herself. 'Think about the good times.'

Walter had ruffled the boy's hair that day – one of the rare signs of affection he ever showed. He wasn't very good at showing people that he loved them, but it wasn't his fault and she understood. 'An airship is very heavy, Howard, and it can't fly unless lots of gas is pumped into it to make it lighter than air. So we have lots and lots of big bags fixed side by side inside the hull . . .' Walter had turned to Vera, smiling. Did she think he understood? Not really, she had told him.

He had got the boy all excited about airships, and then the R38 crashed and Geoffrey was killed and everything was suddenly different. After the funeral he had suggested that Howard join the Marines. He had a cousin, he said, who was a bandsman who might be able to get him in, as long as he could play an instrument. He had spent pounds on a trumpet and insisted on lessons, but the boy hated it. Oh! The battles they had had!

But it was all in the past now. Over and done with. Drawing a deep breath, she reminded herself about her new resolution. She must write this very important letter. She had been gripping the pen so tightly that her hand was beginning to ache. How best to break the news that his mother was no longer a doormat? As if she hadn't slaved away all her life cooking his favourites – toad-in-the-hole, sausage and mash, fish and chips and God knows what. She let out a short, sharp sigh of regret. Mrs Croft's meat pie and Mrs Croft's apple tart, indeed! Carefully she squeezed in the date above the 'Dear Howard' – 17/8/30. 1930! Amazing where all the years had gone. She was thirty-nine going on forty, although she still felt like a little girl inside.

'Thank you for your letter,' she wrote carefully. 'I hope this finds you as it finds me.'

She was rather pleased with that line. Staring at the small wireless cabinet, she awaited further inspiration. Walter had given them the wireless one Christmas and they had both been so thrilled and grateful. Huh! The extent of their gratitude now embarrassed her. Grovel? Was that the word Howard had used? Had she really grovelled? How dreadful if she had. She had only meant to let Walter know how much she appreciated everything he did for them. Wasn't that his due? Well, perhaps Howard was right. But if so those days were over.

'Over!' she said loudly. She was sick to death of the pair of them. They had used her and abandoned her. She caught the eye of her tabby cat and her expression softened slightly.

'We don't need them, do we?' she demanded rhetorically.' Blow them! Blasted men!' She continued: 'I am glad you like it there,' and added defiantly, 'Time will tell . . .'

The cat purred loudly and Vera smiled. 'They think the sun shines out of their ears; well, it doesn't!'

She thought about her supper. Perhaps she would have a boiled egg. Howard had never liked them boiled so it had been fried or scrambled, fried or scrambled, until there were times she could have screamed. And always mashed potatoes. Of all the ways you could cook a potato! Not on Sundays, though. She *had* put her foot down there. At least she had been firm about that: roast potatoes with roast meat. Today it would be *boiled egg* with a runny yolk and fingers of toast, the way she used to have them when she was a child.

'Don't write to me here any more', she wrote. 'I shall be visiting.'

Yes, that was a lovely touch. Visiting! It sounded really romantic. But it was true. Men weren't the only ones who could wander around, fancy-free. Women could do it too,

116

and she would go to see her sister. They hadn't seen each other for years, but Evie always sent a card at Christmas and said, 'When are you coming over to see us?'

'Well, it's *now*!' she told the cat.

It would be a lovely surprise. She had already written to tell them and she had booked her crossing on the ferry. Only the second time in her life that she had crossed the Channel, but she didn't care if she was seasick like last time. She would be travelling, she would be seeing the world. Doing exciting things with her life instead of sitting at home, moping.

'I am going to stay with Evie . . .'

Evie and her husband Pierre had a smallholding near Beauvais in France. They had met when the two sisters had visited Paris more than twenty years ago, and Pierre had been a steward on the ferry. He had been on the return ferry, too, and had been so smitten. He had pursued Evie with such gusto, writing long letters in terrible English and sending her perfume. Vera smiled at the memory. Evie couldn't bring herself to refuse him. And why should she? He was an honest man, hard-working, saving for a little farm. He couldn't help being French, and Vera had never held it against him. She had always envied Evie. Now she drew in a long breath and let it out slowly. That had been an eventful trip. Walter had been in Paris with his friend Geoffrey and Geoffrey's wife, Elaine, and their daughter, sitting on the next table. Because they were English it was natural they would get into conversation. They were a nice family, and Walter had been so shocked when the wife died. It seemed to bring the two men closer together. Then when Geoffrey was killed – well! That was such a blow. The daughter was a funny little thing, shy but quite pretty for her age. Girls of that age are always either podgy or gawky. She was gawky . . . but lovely eyes. She didn't have much luck, poor child. But that had all been in the future and at that time in Paris they were all so happy together.

Vera smiled. They had teased Walter, saying that he was scared of women. A confirmed bachelor. Well, he hadn't been scared of *her*! They had talked and talked. And the conversation between her and Walter had led to other things. Vera's smile wavered. Her cheeks still burned at the memory. *She* had been chasing *him*! Not that he had minded – far from it. She sighed. Poor Walter. It had all been so exciting at the time, but later there had been a price to pay.

Afterwards Walter had said that Paris had cast its spell on him. Not that Howard wasn't worth it. He was a lovely baby. A beautiful baby. Everyone said so. For a moment her determination wavered. Perhaps he would want to come home for the weekend? Or not, as the case may be. No! She *would* go to Evie's. Let them all wonder about her. They might even worry about her. Or *miss* her. Now that would be nice.

'I will let you know when I get back,' she went on.

Yes, that was nice and vague. She let her imagination run ahead and saw herself helping to feed the pigs and scattering corn to the chickens. She might even milk a cow . . . On second thoughts, maybe not. It sounded rather *personal*.

'If you do see your father, give him my good wishes . . .'

Vera sat back and smiled at the cat. 'Give him my good wishes,' she muttered, 'and a kick up the bum!'

For all the long lonely nights and worrisome days. For the best years of her life. For her mother and father being so upset and it all being so awful. Not that he hadn't done his best, but it was so cat and mouse and no white wedding. That had really hurt. Not that they had any money for that sort of thing, but every girl dreams of floating down the aisle looking radiant.

She sighed. 'I could have had him adopted, but I couldn't bear the idea. I thought they might be unkind to him or not love him the way he deserved to be loved. And at least

I knew Walter would support us. I'll say that much for him. Moneywise anyway.'

The cat blinked affectionately and Vera stared at the letter. Enough said. That was it. All finished. Damn and blast them all!

'Your loving Mum,' she finished, adding a few kisses, then a few more. She addressed an envelope, folded the letter and tucked it inside, fixed the stamp on with a few thumps from the heel of her hand and almost ran to the end of the road to post it. Tomorrow she would take some money from her savings account and go shopping for a new coat and hat. She fancied something in navy. Or maybe she would go to the Co-op and have it on the never-never. That way she would make her money last.

Vera was buttering the toast when her new-found confidence began to slip away and two large tears fell. Then, as she forced down the egg and toast her stomach suddenly churned with fright. She remembered that she had not told Howard to take care.

*

Walter sipped his tea thoughtfully. His father looked very frail these days. That fall had not helped, although he made light of it. Nurse Elton had called in the doctor, apparently, but there was little that could be done.

'I was chatting with Major Scott earlier today,' said Walter. 'A very decent man. Very clever. So wonderfully enthusiastic. He quite cheered me up.'

'Scott? Now isn't he the chappie who invented the coupling for the mooring mast?'

'He designed the entire head. Brilliant engineer, and modest with it.'

'I heard him talk somewhere. Some do or other. I can't remember.'

'He'll be officer in command of the flight. He'll have a lot of good men with him, but the responsibility will rest

119

on his shoulders. The speed at which they travel, the exact course, the height and so on. I shouldn't like to be in his shoes.'

'But you will be on board?'

'Oh, yes. God willing!' He smiled. 'I'd like to see them try and keep me away. India! Can you imagine? I'll bring you back some tea, Father! Richmond's another man I admire. His mind is crystal clear; he has a great knack of making the most complicated system appear simple. He'd have made a wonderful teacher. You have to take your hat off to men like him. Mind you, they ribbed him a bit about his original estimate for a hundred passengers. We know now that's out of the question, but his priority is the safety of the airship and if we have to modify our passenger list so be it.'

'You've got a first-class crew for a first-class ship.'

Walter held up both hands, each with fingers crossed, and said again, 'God willing! I was asking about her wireless. Scott says the range is extraordinary: nine hundred miles during the day and nearly twice that at night. When we lose Cardington met. office we'll be able to contact the one at Malta.' He looked at his father. 'Are you tired? Is this stuff too much for you?'

'No, no. It gives me something to think about. Does me good. I'm a bit tired, that's all. I didn't sleep well. I had your sister in here yesterday just as I was settling myself down. In a very funny mood. Mind you, it was her own fault. Been to see Alice somebody-or-other. A medium! At the Wigmore Hall. Says someone tried to make contact with her. Or Geraldine thinks he did.'

Walter groaned. 'Time that girl grew up,' he said. 'So who was trying to contact her? Her grandparents. Her mother?'

George hesitated. 'Geoffrey. So she says.'

'*Geoffrey?*'

The old man spread his hands in a helpless gesture.

120

'That's her story. Something about something he'd left, apparently. Not enough left or lift. Don't ask me to make sense of it all; I was half asleep at the time. But it had shaken her, I could see that, and it takes a lot to shake Marie.'

'Geoffrey?' Walter snorted angrily. 'I can't see poor old Geoff wanting to say anything to Marie. Bel, maybe, or me even, but not Marie.' He swallowed the last of his tea.

George asked 'How is Bel?'

'Very well.'

George gave him a quick look. 'You don't sound very sure.'

'She's all right, I tell you.' Walter groaned inwardly. His father didn't miss much. 'She's a bit upset about an old down-and-out at her precious soup kitchen. He practically died in her arms apparently.'

'So I heard. Poor Bel. Enough to upset anybody.'

Walter did not meet his father's eyes. Bel was not all right, she had been on edge ever since that damned letter from Howard. Not that she'd made a fuss, but she must have felt a bit suspicious. Took it rather well, on the whole, but certainly it had not done her any good. She was not cast down exactly, but not her usual self. Strangely volatile, somehow. He had wondered whether she might be pregnant at last. Pregnancy can alter a woman's moods, but she had snapped his head off when he asked. Damn Howard and his letter! He was beginning to think this was Howard's way of putting pressure on him, but if so he would be disappointed. There was no way Howard was coming to work at Cardington The boy had a decent qualification and could get a job anywhere Walter was more than willing to pull a few strings for him if necessary, but Cardington was out of the question. So were Howden and Pulham. As far as Howard was concerned, the entire airship industry was out of bounds.

'Something on your mind, Walter?'

'No.' He forced a smile. His father was no fool. Quickly he cast around for a new subject with which to distract him. 'We were looking at the artist's impression of the passenger quarters on the upper deck. Twenty-something cabins, and not as cramped as you might expect. They're in the process of ripping out the original bunks which were wood. They've been redesigned in lightweight metal and canvas to save weight; it's going to be all-important, this weight ratio.' He fell silent for a moment, thinking. 'Crew's quarters are down below, of course, also the smoking room.'

His father raised his eyebrows. 'A smoking room in an airship filled with hydrogen gas!'

'Sounds dangerous, doesn't it? But the ceiling and floor are aluminium and the walls are asbestos. Absolutely no risk there – that's why it's on the lower deck, well away from the gas bags.' He frowned. 'The useful lift is all important. The heavier the passenger and crew quarters, the less lift the ship has, and with so much fuel to carry it's a matter for serious concern. In fact it's given us one of the greatest headaches. The fuel alone is going to weigh about thirty-five tons . . .'

'But that weight will decrease as the fuel's used up.'

Walter nodded. 'Of course. She should have a bit more lift on the way back. The R100 brought back some of her fuel but you can't be sure, that's the problem. Bad weather, say head winds, and you use more. Rain means more weight because the envelope absorbs it. More weight means less lift, so we use more fuel to get her up to a safe height. They're planning to fly her at twelve hundred feet.'

'Twelve hundred above sea level, you mean?'

'Yes. It's going to be a close thing, but I must admit they've been very clever at keeping the weight down. For example, the lounge floor is covered with aluminium, and the elegant columns which look so solid are actually duralumin covered with balsa wood. Strong but very light. The walls are painted canvas. And all very handsome, especially the dining room. All the furniture's wicker, of course. Nothing solid. Rectangular tables to seat six, eight or ten. And the lounge is so spacious. Sixty by thirty feet, near as dammit, with one wall all windows. There'll be room to dance.'

'Dance? Good God! Who's going to want to dance? Can't they look at the view?'

Walter smiled. 'There's a limit to how long you can look at the Atlantic, Father.'

'Read a book, then.'

Walter laughed. 'You know what the newspapers are saying – you can tango your way to India!'

'Oh, that! A lot of damned nonsense!'

'Of course, the press are buzzing round like flies. Only a few weeks to "the off" and they can't get enough information. They want photographs, they want quotes, they want press handouts. We had the editor of *Aeroplane* with us a few days ago. Asking a lot of damned awkward questions. He knows a sight too much, that man, and he has a reputation for speaking his mind. His article will appear on the seventeenth of next month and I'm not looking forward to reading it.'

'But it will be supportive, surely? I mean, waving the flag and all that!'

'Not everyone thinks like that, Father; you know they don't. Some people feel there's too much money going into this project, with too little prospect of a commercial return. The economy is shuddering and there are those who believe the money could, and should, be spent on other things. Maybe this particular editor is one of them. But there you are . . . We've a free press and he can print what he likes. Not that I think he'll act from malice; he's got no axe to grind. He'll just write it as he sees it.'

'And you don't think he was impressed?'

'I know damned well he wasn't.'

'Never mind. For all the doubting Thomases, there'll be plenty who *do* want to see her fly.'

'Oh, don't get me wrong, Father. He wants a success story, he just doesn't think he'll get one. But you're right. We're getting plenty of the other kind of attention. Too much, really. We don't need it right now, but it's too late. They've waited years for this flight and they mean to do us proud. Touching in a way, all that trust.' He sighed. 'Let's hope it's justified.'

'Of course it will be justified,' George told him. He frowned. 'What day is it, Walter? I get so confused.'

'It's the seventeenth of August. Sunday.' He pointed to the *Sunday Times* which lay on a nearby chair. 'See?'

'Of course. How silly.' He was annoyed with himself. 'And when is it Lord Thompson wants to fly to India?'

'He insists the airship must be ready by the end of September. As soon after the twenty-fifth as we can manage.'

'And will she?'

Walter shook his head. 'I can't see it, myself, but we have to try.'

The old man reached out suddenly and touched Walter's hand. 'Do you *have* to go to India?'

Walter stared at him in astonishment. 'Do I *have* to? I damn well *want* to! I've invested half my life in that airship. Don't worry, Father; she'll do it. There are always these last-minute panics and doubts. But she'll get us there and back. Just think about the R100. There were worries about her, but she did us all proud.'

'If you say so.'

'I do, Father. Now I really must go.'

'I'll take a nap. I do, these days. I cat-nap. It passes the time. Give Bel my love. And be nice to her, Walter. I sometimes wonder –' He waved a hand irritably. 'No, you just go. But – Walter—'

Walter waited in the doorway, hiding his impatience.

124

'Tell her you love her.'

'Good heavens! She knows that by now, surely.'

The old man gave him an odd look. 'It bears repeating, Walter. It bears repeating.'

Before Walter could reply he turned away and slid down under the bedclothes, effectively ending the conversation.

'Trust you to have the last word,' muttered Walter and he closed the door softly and went downstairs.

*

Tuesday dawned bright and clear and Bel stared up at the sunlit ceiling with her heart racing. A week had passed since her meeting with Larry, and now they were to meet again. She had been giving the matter of their relationship some serious thought and knew she should end it now, before they became too closely involved. Now it was *just* possible to kiss and walk away, but later it would be out of the question. She had rehearsed speech after speech and had composed several letters. The trouble was that she wanted with all her heart to continue. Knowing how wrong it was and aware of the risks they were taking, she still longed to be near Larry; to know that he was in her life. Never before had she felt so happy with herself and the rest of the world. It was all she could do to hide her elation. For the first time she knew what it was to yearn physically for someone and although that made her vulnerable, she could not wish it otherwise. She appreciated, however, that that was the aspect of the relationship which she must keep under control. She would allow herself to love Larry, and she would give herself permission to be extraordinarily happy, but she would never give in to the demands of her body – or Larry's. She was older than him, and would be strong for both of them.

If only she could believe that Marie was wrong when she said Bel was the only woman he had ever looked at. She did not want him to be a virgin; she hated the idea that she was responsible for the terrible frustrations a man must experience without sexual release. The times were changing and morality was being undermined by modern thinking on the subject. Bel was well aware that for someone like Marie or Geraldine, perhaps, the conflict between desire and satisfaction would be less intense. They were younger than she was, and had grown up through the more permissive years that followed the end of the war. They were modern women with a different set of values.

Perhaps Marie was wrong about Larry's virginity? She might even have invented the story to put pressure on Bel. Marie was not always reliable and that she told white lies without flinching whenever the need arose. Her remark about Larry might easily be one of them.

A glance at the bedside clock showed seven-thirty, but Bel could not bear to be still a moment longer. She threw off the covers and reached for her slippers. In the bathroom, as she watched the hot water cascade into the bath, she felt again the fierce urge that until a week ago had been so new to her.

'Oh, Larry! My love!' she whispered.

Only a few more hours and she would be with him. As long as they did not hurt Walter, no harm would be done. She desperately wanted to believe that. Dear Walter! If only loving Walter had been like this, but it had been quite different. Their lovemaking had been gentle, unremarkable and, for her, often dutiful. The emphasis had always been on the production of the son Walter wanted so desperately. She dared not imagine how it would be to lie in Larry's arms.

'I mustn't *think* like this!' she cried. 'It must *never* happen!'

As long as she clung to that thought they would survive. The affair could not last for ever; Bel knew she would suffer when that time came, but she was prepared for it. She lay in the water, luxuriating in the fragrant foam that reached to her chin. She imagined waking in the morning with Larry beside her, and saw the curve of his chin and the long lashes and darkly curved brows. It seemed incredible that she had only just fallen in love with him after all these years. And it was Marie's doing. Now, of course, she felt no antagonism towards her sister-in-law. Without her, Bel would not be in this hazy, heady state of exhilaration. She could no longer bring herself to blame Marie. Despite all the problems which threatened, Bel was more inclined to thank her!

*

Larry was waiting for her in the tea-rooms, sitting at a small table tucked away in a discreet corner. As Bel entered she quickly surveyed the other diners and was relieved to see no one that she recognised. Relax! she told herself. There's no need to look guilty. He's your brother-in-law and that makes it acceptable to other people. Except for the love that blazed in Larry's eyes! And no doubt in her own.

'Larry, how nice to see you.'

As he stood up she offered her cheek for a polite peck, but he put his arms round her and held her close.

'I love you a hundred times over!' he whispered, then said aloud 'Thank you so much for coming. I've ordered,' he told her as they seated themselves. He began to hum the popular song, 'Tea for two . . . And me for you . . .'

'Please!!' she begged. 'Someone will hear you. And don't look at me like that!'

'Like what? Do I look as though I want to carry you off to my bed? Because I do!'

'Larry!' She wanted to beg him to be circumspect, but the mention of his bed had startled her and she had to take several deep breaths. 'If you go on like this I'll have to leave you here!' she warned, but the smile on his face showed how little conviction her words held. And of

127

course she would not leave him. She would stay with him for as long as she dared – for ever, if only it were possible.

'Tea and tea-cakes,' he said, for the benefit of those around. Then lowering his voice he went on, 'Oh, Bel, I adore you. It's killing me! Do I look pale and wan?'

She said softly, '"Why so pale and wan, fond lover? Prithee why so pale?"'

'"Will, if looking well won't win her, looking *ill* prevail?"' Larry smiled. 'Now I know what the poor devil meant. I'm pining away.'

'You're not doing anything of the sort. You look wonderful on it. It's me that should look haggard.'

'You look wonderful. Oh, Bel! You look positively blooming.'

'You've done that to me.'

'I haven't *touched* you!' He adopted an expression of great innocence. 'But not for want of thinking about it. Have you—' He stopped as the waitress arrived with the tea-tray. Impatiently they waited until she had finished setting out the table.

Larry said, 'You be mother!'

She dared not look at him so busied herself instead with milk, sugar and tea.

'Larry, we must try not to get carried away. We must—'

'Stop it!' he told her. 'I'm not going to listen to you any longer. I've never been in love before – at least it's never been reciprocated – and I'm damned well going to enjoy it. There's only one thing we have to do and that's be happy in each other's company. As far as I'm concerned the sky's the limit. I know I may be jumping the gun, but I've been thinking.'

Bel looked at him, startled by his vehemence. This Larry was not the young man she had expected to lead gently by the hand. He was not prepared to be reasonable. With a moment's panic she knew that all her pleas for caution would be swept aside. Larry was racing ahead. And every fibre of her being cried out to follow him.

'Now don't take this the wrong way, Bel. I would never say anything to hurt you. You know that—'

Oh, God! What was coming next?

'But you and Walter have been married for a long time now and—'

Panic seized her. 'I won't leave him, Larry. Please don't ask me to do that because—'

'I wasn't going to. Hear me out, sweetheart.'

'Larry!' She looked round anxiously. 'Do *please* be careful what you say.'

'Sorry, darling.'

'*Larry!*'

'Sorry – Bel. Does that suit you?' His smile lit up his face and somehow Bel resisted the urge to hug him.

'And in all these years, Bel, you have never had a child . . .'

Bel felt the beginnings of apprehension.

He went on gently, 'So, putting two and two together to make five—'

'That I can't have children. I still won't leave him, Larry. I—'

He leaned forward and put a finger over her lips. Without knowing why, she touched his finger with the tip of her tongue and he jumped back as though scalded. 'Bel! You don't know what you're doing to me!' he exclaimed. 'I'm likely to throw you down right here among the diners and make love to you.'

'I'm sorry.'

'Don't be! It was unnerving but wonderful.'

For a few moments they regarded each other warily – like two naughty children, thought Bel.

'Which brings me,' Larry continued, 'to the point of my story. If you are not going to have a child, why shouldn't we—'

'Oh, don't tempt me!' cried Bel seeing what was coming. 'Do you think I haven't wanted to – to . . .'

He leaned forward. '"To fly with me and be my love—"'

She nodded. 'But you're *free*, Larry. I'm a married woman. Who would *you* be betraying?'

'My half-brother.'

'Well, yes. I suppose so. But a husband is another matter entirely. Not that I don't want to. You must believe me. It's what I want more than anything in the world, but—'

She stopped, appalled. She was encouraging him by that admission and he didn't need any encouragement. But a small voice within her argued that what Larry said was true; there would never be a child to prove their misconduct to the world. She swallowed. Misconduct was such a hateful word. It smacked of deceit and worse. Were they really sitting here, buttering tea-cakes, and discussing *misconduct*? The thought sobered her.

'What is it, Bel?'

How quick he was to read her mind, she thought, awestruck. Did lovers ever have any secrets from each other? She could not imagine how.

'It's all happening too fast,' she said earnestly. 'I'm afraid that it will run away with us and the sky will fall on us. It will all turn sour—'

'Of course it won't.' His smile was so gentle, so reassuring. 'I'm sorry if I frightened you. I'm a hasty devil.'

'You never were before.'

Again that wonderful grin. 'I was never allowed to be in love with you before. It's like walking into bright sunshine after years of shadow.'

'Larry! Oh, God, Larry. I love you so much.' She took a deep breath. 'You're right, of course. What you said about – about me and Walter. But suppose with me and you – suppose things happened differently? It would be too terrible.'

He shook his head. 'It would be marvellous' he insisted. 'Walter would have to know, and he would divorce you and we could go anywhere in the world and be together with our child.'

She stared at him, rocked to the depths of her soul. A child? Divorce? Was he that far committed? It was incredible in so short a time. But then it had been years for him, she reflected. For her it was just a week.

He was laughing softly. 'You look just the way you did when we found that snake in the garden at St Tropez. Do you remember? I was about fifteen. You stared at it and didn't move and I thought you were scared but when I teased you, you said you had never seen anything so perfect. It was quite a big one, but you didn't run away. It could have bitten you.'

'Walter said it was harmless.'

'Yes, but you didn't know that at the time. I thought all girls were scared of snakes.'

'Wasn't I just wonderfully brave!' she mocked.

'You were just wonderful full stop. And still are. Look, Bel I have to tell you this, so I might as well get it off my chest right away.'

He looked so serious suddenly that Bel's heart seemed to stop beating.

'I've always loved you, and I've always known that if I can't have you then I shall never marry. It doesn't matter; I shall always be here for you if you need me. Walter is older than me and might well die before me. I can wait. I just want you to know so that you don't ever start trying to interest me in another woman. I'll never stop loving you, but I shan't be lonely because I will always see you and I can learn to be satisfied with that. But it's not what I want, Bel What I want is you.'

'Larry, I—'

'You in my arms. You in my heart. You body and soul if that were ever possible. Probably it won't be. I just want you to know exactly where I stand.' Seeing that she could not answer he said, 'You don't have to tell me where you stand. I realise this is all very sudden for you and I'm not expecting miracles . . . just yet.'

'I wish I could kiss you,' she whispered and her voice was hoarse with longing.

Before he could answer someone loomed up beside them and, tearing her gaze from Larry, Bel looked round in alarm. A large woman stood beside them, dressed expensively, with a small pekinese tucked under her arm. She looked vaguely familiar but Bel, startled and confused, could not think clearly. Had she overheard? Was it all over before it had begun? As she stared up into the delicately rouged face, apprehension gripped her.

Smiling, the woman said, 'It's Isobel Roberts, surely? I was sure it was you. You don't remember me?'

Bel tried to assume a look of polite interest but her heart was hammering. She dared not look at Larry. Had this wretched woman heard her totally explicit comment to him? 'I wish I could kiss you!' It did not leave any margin for doubt. If she *had* heard, then there was no way she could have misunderstood Bel's meaning. 'I'm afraid I don't,' she stammered. Don't blush, Bel, she told herself frantically. For God's sake don't blush!

The woman flashed a smile at Larry who had risen politely to his feet. 'I'm a friend of Margaret's', she told Bel. 'You were at a fund-raising meeting once, for the Whitechapel soup kitchen. You were with your husband, I recall?'

Her smile was sweet, but was there an edge to her voice? Or was she imagining it? Bel felt the fear tighten within her.

'Oh . . . Mrs . . .'

'Lampitt, dear.' She smiled at Larry and Bel fancied she read a hint of enquiry in her expression. She tried to think, but her mind was filled with a succession of possible disasters which must inevitably follow this ridiculous meeting. Walter would be devastated, her marriage would be over; the family would be torn apart. And the press! They would have a field day. Bel cursed her stupidity. Why on earth had she and Larry not planned for such an eventuality? They were rank amateurs and deserved to be discovered. For a moment she toyed with the idea of giving Larry a false name, but her courage failed her and she said weakly, 'This is my husband's brother, Lawrence.'

Larry now shook hands with Mrs Lampitt, murmuring something complimentary about the dog.

'Oh, Bootsie. She is a darling, isn't she?' Mrs Lampitt beamed at him.' She gets compliments wherever we go. And she's so intelligent. She knows every word I say to her, bless her. Such good company, dogs, don't you think?'

Bel and Larry agreed wholeheartedly, effusive in their praise for dogs. Anything, thought Bel, to keep the attention on the dog. Rashly she put out a hand to pat Bootsie, but the dog promptly made a half-hearted snap at her fingers.

'Oh, Bootsie, *darling*!' cried Mrs Lampitt. 'Who's a naughty girl then?'

Bel, conscience-stricken, almost said, 'I am!' but managed to suppress the words in time.

Mrs Lampitt was apologising for Bootsie. 'She doesn't usually do that, but she is *so* perceptive.'

Perceptive! Bel stared at her in horror. *Perceptive*! Mrs Lampitt *knew*! She felt sick. A word from Mrs Lampitt in Walter's ear . . .

Larry said, 'Perceptive to what, exactly?'

Bel sneaked a look at him and though his smile was sweet his eyes were steely. Oh, God! He was going to bluff it out.

Mrs Lampitt hesitated fractionally. 'Why, to atmosphere,' she said.

Larry's gaze did not falter and Bel felt a flicker of hope. 'Atmosphere?' he challenged.

Mrs Lampitt looked a little less sure of herself. 'And to *people*.' She switched her attention to Bel. 'Sometimes people pretend to like dogs; they're just being polite, you know, but Bootsie can tell.' She smiled. 'Perhaps you're a little nervous of dogs. She would sense that immediately. They can smell fear.'

'They can smell fear . . .' Bel felt the nudge of hysteria. If that were so, Bootsie should have been overcome by the fumes! But Bel had been thrown a lifeline and she seized it eagerly. 'I suppose I may be a little nervous. Deep down, that is. I – I was bitten once by a poodle. When I was a child. My aunt's poodle, Trixie.'

'Ah, then! That explains it.' Mrs Lampitt gave the dog a small slap on the nose and it immediately growled a warning. 'She's rather grumpy at the moment because I didn't give her a cake. Sometimes I do, but the vet says she's getting a little too fat and I mustn't spoil her. Poor Bootsie. She doesn't love Mummy today.'

That makes two of us, thought Bel!

Mrs Lampitt smiled. 'Well, I can't stand here chatting, much as I'd like to. I'm on my way to the hairdresser's. I've got this little man in Regent Street who understands my hair – the only one, I might add. I'm not going to interrupt your tête-à-tête any longer. I just wanted to say "Hello".' She smiled at Bel. 'I did contribute to your little venture in Whitechapel, and I shall do so again. Such a deserving cause, and one does feel for those poor wretches. But for the grace of God and all that. Oh, and do give my regards to your husband.' She gave Larry an arch smile. 'Goodbye, Mr Roberts.'

With a farewell flutter of her plump fingers she was gone and Bel sank back in her chair, suddenly aware that her whole body had been tensed. She stared helplessly at Larry, whose face was lit by a broad smile.

134

It's not funny!' she protested. 'I'm a nervous wreck and you sit there like a Cheshire cat. Oh, Larry, that was *awful.*'

He laughed aloud.

'Larry! Don't! I was so frightened. You were marvellous.' She mimicked his voice: 'Perceptive to *what*, exactly? How did you dare? I thought we were finished.'

He put his hand over hers but she snatched it away. 'For heaven's sake! God knows who else is lurking in the shadows.' She looked round fearfully.

'Darling, don't let her—'

'Larry!'

His amusement irked her. She felt exhausted, emotionally drained, and he appeared to have found it *humorous.*

'Bel, I'm sorry you were scared, but you mustn't let the Mrs Lampitts of this world upset you. So she was suspicious. So what? We weren't *doing* anything for which we could be arrested.'

'But I had just said to you—'

'Go on!' He grinned.

'Well, you know what I had just said and if she heard that . . .'

'If she did, she did. We can't undo anything, so let's just try to see the funny side of it. Drink your tea before it gets cold.'

'I could do with a large whisky topped up with a double brandy!' she confessed, but she reached out with a shaking hand and obediently picked up her cup. She tried to finish her half-eaten tea-cake, but her throat was still so dry she couldn't swallow. Suddenly she smiled faintly. 'I almost gave you a false name. How would you like to be Milton Trout?'

'I'd need an American accent.'

Bel's panic was slowly retreating. 'But would you believe we could be so unlucky? What have we done to deserve it? Oh, don't answer that!'

He fluttered his fingers in a fair imitation of Mrs Lampitt and Bel relaxed a little, smiling.

'And dear Bootsie!' she said.

'We can only hope that Mrs Lampitt is discreet', said Larry, 'although I didn't like the way she said "tête-à-tête", did you?'

Bel shook her head, her sense of humour finally coming to her rescue. 'And Bootsie had that look in her eye. I bet she'll tell all the other dogs.'

She poured second cups of tea and gradually she felt better. Larry was with her and he had proved his mettle in the face of the enemy!

They finished their tea and, somewhat recovered, left the tea-rooms to wander round the shops. Larry wanted to buy her things but she wouldn't let him. Too hard to explain away, she told him. Mrs Lampitt's unexpected appearance had made one things uncomfortably clear – that wherever they went together in public they were taking a most tremendous risk. When Larry finally suggested that next time they met he should borrow a car for the day and escape to the country, she was more than happy to agree.

'Who knows?' he suggested. 'If we're lucky the car might run out of petrol. We might have to spend the night in a little wayside inn, where time stands still.'

'And another Mrs Lampitt will be staying there, booked into the next room to ours!'

'You're such a pessimist, Bel. But I still love you.'

'And you're quite incorrigible, Larry. But ditto, ditto, ditto!'

Chapter Seven

ON THURSDAY 21ST AUGUST, Walter travelled down to Deal to visit Vera, determined to have a serious talk with her about their son. He did some thinking on the train and was reluctantly prepared to accept some of the blame for his son's behaviour. Howard, however, was a grown man now and it was probably too late to do more than appeal to his better nature. He would be glad, he told himself, to talk the matter over with Vera and hear her comments. Since he did not know whether or not Howard had spoken to his mother about Bel, Walter decided not to mention her unless Vera herself raised the subject. He would tell Vera how sad he was that he and his son had grown so far apart, and would say that although he genuinely loved the boy, Howard seemed intent on spoiling the relationship; he had made it his business to pry into Walter's private life and that was not to be tolerated. Howard no doubt hated the idea that he and his mother lived where they did, while Walter and Bel owned a large house in the country as well as a comfortable flat in London. Walter could sympathise with this reaction, but there was nothing he could do about it.

But had Howard informed his mother of his discoveries? If so, she had never mentioned it; had never reproached him. Of course, she might be waiting to ask him face to face, and if she did Walter decided to hide nothing. On balance, though, he suspected that Vera had been kept in ignorance. Howard would not want her to know that he had appeared on the lawn at Cardington or had made his presence felt at St Saviour's. She would most certainly have disapproved. Now Walter would have to tell her, and was going to insist that the harassment must be stopped. If necessary he would use the ultimate deterrent: he would threaten to stop Vera's weekly payments. He had never before been tempted to do so, and had no wish to do so now, but if Vera took the boy's side against him, as she often did, he might be forced into it. He would do whatever it took to protect Bel. She must never know the true situation. She might hazard a guess, but she must never gain incontrovertible proof. That would be disastrous. Somehow he had kept the two women apart all these years, and God knows, it had not been easy. He had no intention of allowing a vindictive boy to ruin things now.

He took a taxi from the station and told the driver to drop him off in the street next to the one in which Vera lived.

'Come back for me in a couple of hours,' he instructed the driver. 'Wait for me here. D'you understand?'

'Right, guv!'

Walter straightened his shoulders and walked to Vera's little terraced house. He had sent her a telegram, as usual, to say that he was coming. He knocked on the door, waited and knocked again, but there was no reply. He put his face to the front-room window and peered in. There was no sign of life and he frowned. Vera was always ready and waiting for him, wearing her best dress, a cake baked especially for him. He waited, then knocked again. Strange. She was never out in the afternoons. She had no job; she had no need to work because he provided well enough for them.

After another knock the door of the adjacent house opened and a woman appeared on the step. She was somewhat unkempt in appearance and she folded her arms over a large bosom.

'Who are you?' she demanded.

Walter gave her a cool look. 'That's really no business of yours,' he said.

She seemed unmoved by the snub. 'I'm Mrs Sidney. Want Mrs Roberts, do you?'

'Yes, I do, as it happens.'

'Well, she's gone away, so you'll be unlucky.'

Walter scowled. Stupid woman! Vera did not 'go away' and if she did, she would have told him she was going. Anyway, where could she go? She only had her sister and she was in France.

'What do you mean "gone away"?' he asked, a trifle testily. 'Do you mean she's gone out shopping? Gone to the doctor? What, exactly?'

'I mean "gone away".' Her expression was triumphant. '*Right* away. I'm looking after her cat until she gets back.'

He almost said, 'I don't believe you' but hesitated. If she was looking after the cat . . .

She said, 'You her old man?'

Walter bit back an angry retort. It seemed unlikely that Vera had talked about their relationship against his strict orders. More likely that this objectionable woman had made an assumption about him.

Before he could answer the woman laughed. 'Not that it's any business of mine, but I'm not blind. She never said, like, but I guessed. It happens; it's the way of the world, as they say. The papers are full of it. Things have changed and not for the better, if you ask me.'

Walter thought rapidly. He had no intention of becoming involved in a conversation with this awful woman. Presumably Howard would be able to tell him Vera's whereabouts. He asked, 'Do you know when the son will be back?'

'Howard, you mean? Oh, he won't be back either. Don't tell you much, do they? He's been gone a week, or maybe

139

more. Got himself a job at long last. About time, I told her. My two boys were out earning before they was sixteen. Both of 'em – and earning decent money. I don't hold with them colleges. Makes 'em lazy. They think the world owes them a living.'

Walter stared at her, completely at a loss. Howard had got a job without telling him, and Vera had gone away! It was incredible. He felt a flash of anger. How dare they behave like this? After all he'd done for them, they should have had the decency to share their plans with him. He felt a complete fool.

'Do you happen to know where Mrs Roberts has gone?' he asked as politely as his growing temper would allow.

'*Mrs Roberts* has gone to France. To stay with her sister, Evelyn. I think that's her name. Don't ask me when she'll be back because I don't know. She didn't know either. "I'll be back some time." Those were her very words. I asked her, like when? "I don't know and I don't care," she said. Those were—'

'Her very words. I understand,' he snapped. But he did not understand. If anyone had seemed a fixed star in his small firmament, he would have expected it to be Vera. How on earth had she found her way to France, alone, when she rarely set foot out of the door except to go to the shops? She had always struck him as unadventurous. Set in her ways – and he had never criticised her for that. In fact he liked the fact that her life had revolved around him and Howard. Now he was astonished and dismayed. And where the hell was Howard? An uneasy suspicion entered his head. No! The boy would never dare. Not Cardington! He felt a sudden weakness and leaned against the door jamb for support.

'You all right, Mr Roberts? You look a bit peaky.' Relenting a little, she smiled. 'Want a cup of tea?'

'I'm perfectly all right, thank you.'

'You don't look it. You look as if you've lost a shilling and found a ha'penny!'

'I tell you I'm OK!' Unintentionally he had raised his voice.

'Please yourself!' She tossed her head, said, 'Pompous ass!' and flounced inside. As the door shut with a bang, Walter cursed his stupidity. He had offended the only person who knew anything about Vera and Howard. He felt angry and very shaken, and more upset than he cared to admit. Her last words hurt him. Pompous? Was he pompous? He hated women like Mrs Sidney, and he wondered how Vera had put up with her for all these years. Suddenly he needed a cup of tea, but his pride kept him standing there until the weakness passed. He would find a café and have something to eat, and come back in time for the taxi. As he walked away, he glanced back at the little house where his son had grown up and there was a lump in his throat. Everything was changing. The status quo had been disrupted and there was a hollow feeling inside him which would never be satisfied.

'Oh, Vera!' he whispered. 'I'm sorry!'

With a heavy heart he faced up to the knowledge that nothing would ever be the same again.

*

Howard was eating a tasty supper of soused herrings and mashed potatoes when the back door suddenly opened and a young woman came in. She was a thin, small creature – twig-like, he thought – but pretty enough with bobbed brown hair and large brown eyes. Her mouth was a little too wide for her face, but Howard found her more than passable. He stopped in mid-chew and they regarded each other warily.

'My aunt not in, then?' she asked.

Howard swallowed hard. 'Er, no. She's gone to a meeting at the Baptist Hall. Whist, I think. You her niece?'

'Must be if she's my auntie.' She perched herself on the edge of the only armchair. 'She goes every Friday.'

'How come you didn't know, then? Why ask me?'

She raised finely plucked eyebrows. 'Oh, we are sharp! You'll cut yourself if you're not careful. My name's Margaret Clark, but they call me Peggy.'

'I'm Howard. I'm—'

'I know who you are. You're the new lodger. Auntie's new "gentleman".'

She smiled and Howard saw an immediate improvement. Not bad-looking, he thought with interest. He had only ever been with one girl, and she had been less than forthcoming. Pansy. That was her name. Pansy Gardner. Kept her legs crossed. His mother had liked her, but then she would. He had once called Pansy 'Little Miss Prim' and had had his face slapped for his trouble This one might be different.

'She's a good cook, your aunt. First class!'

'First class!' she mocked. 'I can cook as good as her. Pastry and stuff. There's nothing to it. We did it at school. And laundry, but that was boring. All about starch for collars and blue for whites.'

He grinned. 'You'll make someone a good wife, then, since you know so much.'

'Happen I will.' She winked and Howard nearly choked on his fish. Maybe his luck was changing. He had got his father on the hop, had found himself a job and this girl was making eyes at him. He wondered how old she was.

'What do you do?' he asked. 'Not still at school, surely?'

'No. I work for the R.A.W., like you. Like all of us here at Shortstown. Mum worked in the canteen before she got TB, then she had to give up. They found her a job in the main building, in the mail room; they're good like that. My cousin Hilda's on the gas bags. Or was. She was always moaning about the smell! Not of the gas but the glue stuff they use. Now they've done the last one she's laid off temporary. But they'll find her something.'

'So if the airship industry ever came to an end . . .'

She pulled her face into an expression of exaggerated horror. 'Don't even *think* such a thing! If the jolly old 101 doesn't make it to India we're sunk! Mum always says it's our bread and butter and Dad says, "*And* our cake!" Every time, he says it! We pull his leg about it. I work on the envelope. Machinist. It's not bad. You meet lots of people.'

'Men, you mean.'

'Them, too.'

'Chat you up, do they?'

'I can handle them.'

'Ooh! That sounds a bit naughty.'

She blushed. 'Don't be so rude. You know what I meant.'

Howard considered this. A blush meant that she was not the easy virtue sort, but it might also mean another Pansy. It would be fun finding out. He smiled. 'Sorry. Only kidding. Got a young man then, have you?'

She hesitated. 'I'm not short of admirers, if that's what you're getting at, but I'm really, really choosy. I don't go with just anybody.' She crossed her legs, revealing a glimpse of stocking top. 'You got a – a lady friend?'

'Did have,' he lied, 'but I gave her the push. Too pushy and always making eyes at other blokes.' He thought this was rather clever – let her know exactly what he expected.

'Where's your folks?' she asked.

That took him aback. What had he told her aunt? 'My father's dead. Motor accident. Knocked down by a Rolls Royce.'

'Oh, the poor thing.'

He thought frantically. 'No, I'm kidding!' he amended hastily. 'It was a bus. He fell off his motor-bike.'

'Make up your mind!'

143

'He fell off *under* the bus.'

'When was that then?'

Another difficult one. He would have to remember all these lies. 'Some time ago – but I still remember it. The funeral and everything.' Might as well go for a bit of sympathy, he thought, seeing her expression change. 'I still miss him. He was a wonderful man. Him and me, we were more like brothers really. It knocked me for six when he was killed.' For a moment Howard saw clearly how it could have been. A boy and his father. Good friends. Thinking the world of each other. Going fishing together. 'We used to fish,' he told her. 'At Broxbourne. Just the two of us.' Suddenly there was a lump in his throat. Why hadn't his father been that sort? Why hadn't he been a wonderful man?

'Catch much, did you?'

Why hadn't they gone fishing together? Or done something together? Anything. They could have played tennis. He knew his father played because he had given him an old tennis racquet. And he had a tennis court at the house in Cardington. He imagined his father teaching him to play, and Howard succeeding beyond his wildest dreams. 'That boy of mine!' he could have said. 'He's *dynamite* on the court. Plays like a champion.' He could have boasted to his posh friends – except that none of them even knew Howard existed, so how could he? The rosy vision faded abruptly.

'Howard!'

'What?'

'I said "What did you catch?"'

'Fish. What d'you think we caught? Rabbits?' He sighed. If only his father had been someone else, it could all have been so different.

'I mean *what* fish, silly.'

Damn! Reluctantly he gave her his full attention. What had they caught? He had aroused her interest, but what fish were there to catch? He said cautiously, 'It was a long time ago.'

'But you *must* know what you caught.'

'Course I do.' He thought of the fish he had eaten over the years. 'Mackerel mostly, and . . .' He looked at his plate. 'And herrings. Cod, sometimes.' He shrugged. 'I haven't had the heart since he died.'

She looked properly respectful of his tragedy. Then she said, 'It sounds fun, fishing. You could take me. I'd like to go fishing; you could teach me.'

Crikey! Women! He didn't know one end of a fishing-rod from the other! He took a deep breath. 'Look, women don't take to it. I mean, they're not natural fishers. Fishermen are like it says – *men*.'

She looked hurt and he wished he had never mentioned fishing.

'My grandfather died,' she said at last.

'Well, they do, don't they? I mean, they're old. You expect that.'

'I didn't say I didn't expect it. I just said he died.'

'Oh!' He finished the soused herrings and reached for the banana custard. 'You want to make a pot of tea?'

'Not particularly.' She gave him a challenging look and he revised his opinion accordingly. Not exactly willing; might even be lazy. Or one of these new sort of women who thought they were as good as men. That would be just his luck.

'Go on!' he said. 'Just for me!' He threw in a wink for good measure.

'Just for you, then.'

As she stood up he said, 'They go all the way up, do they?' and stared at her legs.

'Course they do! Cheeky devil! Yours stop half-way, I suppose!'

She leaned back slightly to adjust a suspender and her small breasts were outlined briefly against her blouse. Two of everything, he thought, and all in the right place!

By the time she came back with the tea-tray Howard had finished his pudding and turned his chair round to face her. They sat in silence while she poured milk into the cups.

'How d'you like it?' she asked.

Howard grinned wickedly. 'As often as possible!' He hoped he looked like Douglas Fairbanks in a particularly swashbuckling mood.

'Howard!' she protested. 'Not so much cheek, please! You're not a bit like Auntie said you were.'

He took that as a point against him. Mrs C. must have given him a good build-up to bring the niece scampering round to have a look. Perhaps he would go a bit careful on the wisecracks for a while. He searched his mind for a safe subject. 'My mother's going to miss me,' he said. 'She's got no one but me now. She's gone abroad to stay with relations – got a sister in France who married a rich farmer. She couldn't bear the empty house, she said, so she's gone away. You'd like my mother. Quiet. Sort of elegant.'

'Must be awful being a widow.'

'A widow?' For a moment he had forgotten that he had killed off his father. 'Oh, a *widow*! Yes. Pretty awful, but at least he left her a lot of money. Me, too. He left us both money.'

'Was he rich then?'

'Pretty rich.' He thought she looked impressed.

'I've got some savings,' she told him. 'In the Post Office. Thirteen pounds ten shillings. I keep all the money I get for birthdays and that. I never spend it. Mum says I'm a miser! But money's not everything, is it? Your mother must be lonely.'

'I suppose so – but she's been awfully brave and she's got me. It must be awful if you've got no children and you're a widow. That's real loneliness.'

'I suppose she'll be looking forward to you giving her some grandchildren?'

Howard gave her a suspicious look. 'Not just yet, I shouldn't think.' But her expression was entirely innocent. 'But I suppose you're right. I shall have to think of settling down some time.'

She gave him a bright smile. 'I'd like to meet your mother one day,' she said. 'She sounds really, really nice.'

Howard swallowed the last of his tea and held it out for a refill. This time she did not protest but filled it dutifully and his spirits rose. Perhaps this was the beginning of something good? Perhaps his luck really had changed for the better. He accepted the cup, winked at her again and watched the faint colour come into her face. She was quite a pretty little thing. As he sipped his tea, he was filled with hope. A new job *and* a girlfriend. The future had never looked so promising.

*

The following day was Saturday and Bel was still in her dressing-gown when Marie arrived, bubbling with excitement and full of apologies for the early visit. Bel stood in the morning room and surveyed her with dismay.

'I know it's early, but I've been awake half the night,' Marie exclaimed, throwing herself into an easy chair. 'I worried and worried, and I know you'll be cross, but it's terribly important. You'll think I'm mad but I must talk to you. I rushed out of the house without any breakfast and I've—'

Noticing the gleam in her sister-in-law's eyes, Bel's stomach churned fearfully. Terribly important? This *had* to be about Larry. But so *soon*! Was it possible Marie had met Mrs Lampitt? Or had the gossip started already? She felt hot at the very idea. 'Look,' she interrupted, stalling for time. She must have a moment to compose herself and prepare for the worst. 'I've only just got out of the bath. I'll get dressed—'

147

'I don't mind you *déshabillé*,' Marie told her. 'It's just that—'

'No, I'd rather,' Bel insisted. 'You find Mrs Parks and tell her we'll both have breakfast at . . .' She glanced at the clock. 'At nine. That'll give me fifteen minutes to dress and comb my hair. I'll see you in the dining room.'

Without giving Marie time to argue, she hurried back into the bedroom and shut the door. She leaned back against it, breathing deeply in an effort to remain calm. It was so unfair, she thought bitterly. She and Larry had hardly had time to fall in love but here was the rest of the world pressing in, pointing accusing fingers. If Marie had already heard rumours, then the affair was over before it had begun. There was no way she and Larry could brazen it out and no way Walter could remain in ignorance of their relationship. Oh, Larry! *Larry!* She took a deep breath and then another. And what was she to say to Marie if challenged directly? And knowing Marie's tendency to call a spade a spade, she *would* challenge. Dare she admit the truth and ask for her sister-in-law's discretion? Was it fair to do that? Suppose Walter approached Marie . . . but, no. He would never humiliate himself that way. Could she confide in Marie? For a moment she was tempted by the idea, for she longed to talk to someone about Larry. Perhaps she should simply admit everything and throw herself on Marie's mercy. After all, Marie had brought all this about and must accept at least some responsibility for the impending disaster. But Marie might tell Geraldine and then it would be everywhere. Still in a turmoil, she pulled on underwear and a simple dress and ran a quick comb through her hair. She dispensed with the usual touch of lipstick and did not bother with stockings.

When she went into the dining room the breakfast had appeared and Marie was already attacking her grapefruit.

'Sorry, dear old thing, but I was starving and I couldn't

148

wait,' she told Bel apologetically. 'I knew you wouldn't mind.'

This was going to be difficult, thought Bel as she sat down at the table. She stared at her grapefruit without enthusiasm. 'Marie, I don't know what you've heard—' she began, but Marie interrupted her.

'I want you to come with me to a clairvoyant,' she told Bel. 'And before you start to argue, this is no ordinary—'

'You want *what*?' Bel stared at her in confusion. What had a clairvoyant to do with Larry? 'A clairvoyant?' She felt a glimmer of hope. Perhaps this wasn't connected with Larry. *Please let it not be to do with him!*

Marie pointed her spoon accusingly. 'I *knew* you'd make a fuss! But just listen to me, Bel, before you say anything. This clairvoyant is not a quack.'

'A clairvoyant!' Hope soared. So it was nothing to do with her and Larry! Presumably, then, Marie had heard nothing. She felt weak with relief. *Thank you!* She suddenly recovered her appetite and took a spoonful of grapefruit. 'Go on.'

'I told you that we went to Alice Threadmore's séance thing and that Geoffrey – your father – had spoken to me. Well, I've been thinking it over and—'

'Hang on!' It was Bel's turn to wave a spoon. 'You only said it was *possible* and that *you thought* it might have been my father. As I recall—'

'Bel!' Marie scowled. 'Will you please shut up and listen?'

Bel stared at her. 'Marie! What on earth—'

'*Shut up!* And listen. This could be very important. Don't you understand? And take that look off your face! I've got to tell you this and you've *got* to listen.'

Bel finally realised that there was more than excitement in Marie's eyes. 'I'm sorry. I'm listening.'

Marie said slowly, 'I think your father was trying to tell me something important. He was not talking about anything that was *left*. Alice misunderstood because she couldn't know about airships. He was talking about *lift*. Don't you see, Bel? *Airship lift!* He was trying to tell us something about the R101 because Walter will be on it. Walter was his dearest friend, and your father knows there is something about the lift of the airship that isn't right.' She stared earnestly into Bel's eyes. 'I'm worried, Bel. I believe Geoffrey was trying to warn Walter.'

Bel felt her heart sink, but for a different reason. Poor Marie! This was all that stupid Geraldine's doing.

'Bel! Answer me.'

'What was the question?'

'The question is – Do you believe me? Don't you think I'm right? Your father was saying "Not enough lift". In other words—'

'No. The answer is I don't think you're right.' Ignoring Marie's expression, Bel spelled out her disbelief. 'If my father had a message about the R101 – and it's a big if – he'd give it to Walter, not to you.'

'But Walter wasn't there!' Marie's tone was triumphant. 'Don't you see? Only I was there, so he spoke through Alice to me. Bel, you must believe me. Hand on heart.' She suited action to words. 'I've got this terrible feeling that something awful is going to happen to the airship.'

Although thoroughly sceptical, Bel was reluctantly impressed by her sister-in-law's obvious conviction. Her round face was flushed and her usual veneer of sophisticated indifference was totally absent. She truly believed what she was saying.

'I was so sure, Bel, that I thought of asking Walter to visit Alice privately, but then I knew he would never agree. So I went round to the address on the programme and tried to make an appointment for a private séance – for you, me and Alice. But they were booked up for months ahead. She's so good, you see. So famous. I didn't actually speak to her but to her secretary, who was an awfully decent sort of man, and he said that if there was a cancellation he would let me know. He put me on the top of the list, but I couldn't just sit around while your father is trying to reach us, so . . .' Her voice rose nervously.

'Marie! Please. Do calm down!' Bel put a hand on hers, but Marie shook it off irritably.

'Don't patronise me, Bel. Oh, you needn't shake your head like that. I know you, Bel, and I can see what you're thinking: that I'm a scatterbrain and it's a crackpot idea. But it's your husband I'm worried about, and it's your father's spirit who's trying to contact us. So I've arranged a sitting with a clairvoyant – no, let me finish, damn you!'

Her face was white with suppressed emotion and Bel bit back a slightly caustic comment.

'The secretary told me that this woman is very good, one of the best in London. Because I told him all about the message and he understood about airships, he *personally* arranged this for us.' She waited to see if Bel appreciated this and Bel nodded hastily.

'This woman's name is Karma – yes, Karma – and before you say anything sarcastic—'

'I wasn't going to say a word!' Bel protested. She could see the anxiety in Marie's face and, against her will, was disturbed by the strength of Marie's beliefs. For the first time she wondered if there could be anything in what her sister-in-law was saying.' So—?'

'So, Bel, the meeting is on the 25th, that's Monday, at three and—' She set her lips determinedly. 'And if you don't agree to come with me I – I shall tell Walter all about you and Larry!'

'*Marie!*' Now Bel was really shocked. The flippant young thing had vanished, this *concerned* individual was a comparative stranger. Marie had always been impetuous, fond of saying that she 'didn't give a tuppenny damn!' This new Marie was vulnerable and, Bel realised suddenly, close to tears.

'I'm sorry, Marie,' she said gently. 'I'm sorry—'

Marie grabbed her by the arm. 'You *are* coming!' she insisted, tight-lipped. 'Don't tell me you're sorry but you can't. Your father—'

'I meant I'm sorry I didn't take it seriously,' Bel told her, disentangling her arm from Marie's grip. 'Give me a moment to think it over. Tell me more about—'

'But you *will* come? You promise?'

'I haven't said that exactly.'

'Promise me!'

'I promise.'

Marie fell back in the chair, exhausted. 'Thank you. A thousand times.'

They looked at each other warily. Marie's lips trembled and she was making an obvious effort to control herself.

Bel said, 'But not because of your threat about Larry.'

Marie swallowed uncomfortably. 'I shouldn't have said that, I didn't mean it. I never would have told him.'

'I should hope not . . . Have some toast and marmalade.'

Marie's smile was a trifle forced. 'Thanks . . . Karma isn't her real name, of course. It means fate. The secretary said it's theatrical, to provide atmosphere, that's all. So don't mock her on that score.' She buttered her toast, spread it thickly with marmalade and then pushed the plate away impatiently. 'I'm not hungry.'

'It doesn't matter. Go on.'

'She doesn't have a crystal ball or anything; just a pack of cards. You cut the cards and give them back to her and she lays them out. He told me all this – the secretary, that is. She doesn't get in touch with spirits, though – that's the only snag – but he thinks she would be able to hint at anything important. And if anything was going to happen – well, she might see it and warn you. Your father's spirit might be there with her, telling her things or putting the thoughts into her mind. It's not quite as good as a medium, but he says she's a remarkable woman. So what do you think?'

152

Bel said slowly, 'I suppose it wouldn't do any harm.' She was glad to hear that she would not be making contact with her father – not that she didn't love and miss him, but the idea made her distinctly nervous.

'Well?' urged Marie. 'You promised.'

'I'll come,' Bel told her. She wondered if Karma might see a little too much – she might see something about Larry and that would be disconcerting. But she would have to risk it. She smiled at Marie and held up a hand, the palm flat. 'I promise to come. Three o'clock Monday.' She pushed the plate back towards Marie. 'Now that's settled you can eat your toast. Waste not, want not!'

Marie again protested that she could not eat a thing, but by the time Mrs Parks came in to clear the table she had eaten four slices of toast and drunk three cups of tea. The more Bel reflected on the forthcoming appointment with Karma, the more intrigued she became, and by the time Marie left she was looking forward to the sitting with curiosity and a growing sense of excitement.

*

Vera sat in a sheltered corner of the little courtyard, enjoying the last of the day's sunshine. Not that there was much warmth in it, but according to Howard the sun had vitamins in it so perhaps she would feel better. Since arriving here she had felt rather listless and tired, but Evie said it was all the excitement of travelling and she hadn't liked to tell them about all the upset at home. That sort of thing was best kept to herself. Evie was not very taken with Walter, although she had liked him at the beginning. She said she couldn't understand why he would never live with Vera and Howard as a family. Vera had tried to explain that Walter was a confirmed bachelor and had never wanted a wife and family. It wasn't that he had anything against her personally or against the child; he simply did not relish domesticity. Those had been his exact

153

words, and Vera had been impressed at the time in spite of her situation. Some men were like that. But he had done the decent thing by her, and the house in Deal was in her name; when she died it would be Howard's. Walter had been very generous, but Evie couldn't see it that way. She thought Walter didn't think Vera was good enough for him, and she called him a snob, and he certainly could be sniffy about things but Vera put that down to his upbringing. Once Evie had suggested that living alone as he did was unnatural, and he probably had another woman. They had had a dreadful row about that, and Vera hadn't been in touch with Evie for three years . . . not even a Christmas card. Not that Vera hadn't wondered about it, but she had never wanted it put into words.

Still, it had blown over, and now they were both being so kind and she liked her little room in the farmhouse (except for the spiders), but she didn't think she would stay too long. France wasn't England, and that was all there was to it. But if she stayed until the end of September she would see Walter's airship go over. Pierre had read it out to her from the newspaper: the exact route – depending on the weather, of course. She liked Pierre, but he had changed so much. He now had a large greying moustache and not much hair. Not as good-looking as Walter, but Evie seemed fond enough and that's what mattered. Vera had tried to see the young French steward in the lined face but without any luck. Still, they had a good enough life and Evie had said she could live with them if she wanted to. For ever! She said Pierre had suggested it . . . they were both so kind.

But England was home and she didn't think she could ever settle in a strange country. And there was Walter. She couldn't really leave him. A few weeks was one thing, but he expected her to be there. And Howard. She might be feeling cross with him, and he could be very exasperating, but she couldn't *leave* him. She thought about them all the time and wondered if they had met. There would be fireworks then! Well, at least she was well out of it – until the end of September, anyway. It would be rather wonderful to watch the ship fly past ... she would be able to wave to Walter, and later she could tell him how it had looked to the people on the ground. Evie said the whole village would be out watching for a glimpse of it, as long as there wasn't too much cloud. And if it left on time. The route Pierre called the 'favoured' route would come down to London across Potters Bar and the Isle of Dogs and over Greenwich. Then down past Sevenoaks and Hastings and across the Channel. Then it was Abbeville, Beauvais, Paris and so on. Pierre had shown her on the map. Evie said he was map-mad; he had even made a little map of the farm, with the house and trees and fences marked in different coloured inks. Not that it was a farm exactly. Very small, but they grew all their own vegetables and plenty to spare to take into the market at Allonne.

Vera smiled suddenly, thinking of Edouard who was Evie's nearest neighbour. He was nearly sixty, but had taken rather a fancy to her. Or so Evie said. He was a widower whose wife had died three years earlier. He was a lively sort of person and he made her laugh. He could speak quite a bit of English, but his accent was terrible. It made Vera feel rather clever to be able to speak good English among all these French people. Even Evie spoke French most of the time except to her, of course. Edouard had taught Vera a few phrases.

'Bonjour! Bonsoir!' she said aloud. 'D'accord!' She had teased him, 'Don't teach me anything saucy!' and he had laughed his booming laugh, throwing back his head and thumping the table. They were funny like that, the French. They waved their arms around quite a lot. But she would tell Walter her little bit of French when she got back. And Howard, of course. When she next saw them. Maybe she would invite them both to tea one Saturday, and see if she

155

couldn't get them to be nicer to each other? She could make a lemon sponge which Walter liked, and some raspberry buns which Howard liked . . . She checked herself abruptly. No! She sat up briskly. She mustn't start that again.

'I am not a doormat!' she declared.

No lemon sponge. No raspberry buns. She would make a coffee cake which *she* liked, and they could like it or lump it. And she would do cucumber sandwiches with the crusts cut off, and maybe a bit of sliced ham. Suddenly she could not wait to see them again. But there was all the time in the world. She was in France for only the second time in her life, and she must make the most of it. And Evie agreed it would do Walter and Howard good to know that Vera was no longer at their beck and call. And she was getting used to France, and soon she would begin to feel at home. And Edouard was teaching her to play chess. Now that *would* impress Walter. She leaned back in the old rocker Pierre had carried out for her. They were making such a fuss of her. Closing her eyes, with the sun warm on her face, she could almost feel the vitamins doing her good.

Chapter Eight

SUNDAY 24TH AUGUST
My lovely Bel,
   I know we agreed not to write to each other,
but I cannot bear these long absences from you and
putting my thoughts into words is the only way.
When I saw you yesterday with my father it was such
a joy, although there was no chance to be alone with
you. What can I say? I know you must visit him – he
does so enjoy your visits – but to have to pretend you
are no more to me than 'family' is so difficult for me.
All I wanted to do was take you in my arms, and that
would have been a shock to him. Or would it? He has
given me some rather odd looks lately, not hostile
exactly – more in sorrow than anger, unless I am
imagining things. He also asked me if there was
anything he had missed! When I asked him what he
meant, he said I looked as though I had won a
lottery! I found myself stuttering and stammering and
I am sure I looked as guilty as hell!

   You see what you are doing to me, dearest Bel? I
shall never be the same again, but I would not have it
any other way. When I go to sleep at night I see your
sweet face, and it is still there when I wake. In my
imagination, I mean, of course. If only it could be

reality. I love you so much it hurts. Why did we arrange to meet every eight days? The days go so slowly they are an agony to me. I cannot wait for Wednesday to arrive, to see you again. I have arranged to borrow a car from a friend – a lovely Jowitt with cream leather upholstery. We shall cut a terrific dash in it, and I shall be the happiest man alive. It *must* be a fine day, I shall arrange it with God. Surely he can sympathise with us in our plight? He cannot have meant the world to be one long vale of tears. There have to be some wonderful moments, and Wednesday will be one of them.

Forgive me for rambling on like this, but I feel nearer to you this way and cannot bear to stop. Walter told Father that he would be in Cardington most of the week, so I am entrusting this to the post. I did think of sending it by hand, but that might arouse the suspicion of your nice Mrs Parks and that would never do, would it? I try to imagine you reading this letter and pray you will not be angry with me for sending it. I would love a letter from you that I could read and re-read in the lonely days between our meetings. Would you write to me and give it to me on Wednesday? It would be such a comfort to see in black and white that you love me. When I am without you it seems impossible that after all these years we can mean something so wonderful to each other.

I must stop. No, I will just say this. I am desperate to spend a night with you. There! Very shocking! Unforgivable! Say it, Bel. I am a total cad! But it's true and I want you to know it. Maybe you will never be mine, but it is what I want more than anything in the world. I want to love you and care for you, and comfort you in sickness and in health as long as we both shall live. But that doesn't tell you the half of it. Why are words so inadequate on the subject of love?

My dearest Bel, goodbye for now and God be with you. How I envy Him!

Your loving Larry

*

Bel locked the bathroom door and sat on the edge of the bath. One part of her mind told her how ridiculous this was, the other half applauded her caution. She now felt safe to read Larry's letter and she did so again and again, luxuriating in its contents and wondering desperately if she dare answer it. From years of reading fiction she knew that love letters have a knack of getting themselves lost and being found by the wrong person. This one from Larry burned like a hot coal in her hand, and she could not decide where to hide it for safe keeping. Her first instinct had been to learn it by heart and then burn it, but she could not bear to part with it. The thought of Larry, pen in hand, bent earnestly over the paper made her senses swim, and the sight of his hasty scrawl moved her almost to tears. The contents of the letter also excited her. The idea that they might one day be lovers haunted her, too, but seeing Larry's desire couched in such loving terms increased her longings.

For the first time she allowed herself to wonder how, if ever, it might be possible. Just one night together, she argued. Larry had said that there would never be another woman in his life. If that were true, then it was surely selfish to withhold from him the body he so craved. Was her body so sacred that she could not be a little generous? If she truly loved Larry, perhaps she should be prepared to flout convention and give him what he wanted . . . and what she herself wanted. This battle with her conscience gave her little peace of mind until only one fact deterred her from taking that last step. She knew in her heart that once would never be enough. Once they had made love, it would be impossible to hold back. It would happen again and again, and they would be lost.

'No, Bel!' she told herself sternly. 'Walter is your husband and you owe him everything you have and everything you are.'

If only she could have loved Walter this way. How different her marriage would have been. Presumably Larry would still have loved her, but there would have been no room for him in her heart.

'Stop this, Bel!'

Reluctantly she refolded the letter and put it back into the envelope. She would put it under the mattress. No, she would put it in with letters she had kept from her father – funny, tender epistles he had sent to her while she languished in the hated boarding-school . . . No, that would not do either. She did not think her father would appreciate that. He would only see the situation from Walter's side. She felt an immediate stab of conscience. Whatever would he think if he knew? This question brought to mind the visit to Karma.

To banish that unwelcome thought, she turned her attention from both Larry and Karma and considered instead the letter from 'H' and Walter's reaction to it. He had been extraordinarily unwilling to pursue the matter, she reflected. He had pretended to dismiss the sender as a 'crank' and insisted that there was no need to involve the police. And, more disturbing, he had appeared unable or unwilling to meet her eyes while the matter was being discussed. She had a strong suspicion that he knew Howard's true identity and the reason for the harassment. She could no longer dismiss the possibility that her husband was being blackmailed. But what had he done? He always professed the highest moral virtues, and decried those weaker mortals who fell from grace. Had he made a mistake in his work on the airship?

160

A mistake that someone else had discovered? It seemed highly unlikely.

Perhaps Walter had been involved in a financial deal that had been less than legal? A loophole in the law, maybe, that was questionable. If none of these hypotheses answered the question, that left only one and that, to Bel's mind, appeared the most likely: Howard was Walter's illegitimate son. She was sure there had been a fleeting likeness, although at the time when he appeared in the garden it had somehow eluded her. If Walter had fathered a child out of wedlock, it would account for the fact that he insisted that the fault for their lack of children could not lie with him. Strangely, the thought of Walter with another woman did not hurt her as much as it might have done before she had fallen in love with Larry. Now she understood how powerful desire could be, and how rapidly it could blur the edges between right and wrong. Had Walter had an affair all those years ago? If so, it had happened before their marriage and her husband had been guilty of no infidelity. Guilty of deceit, yes, and over many years, but he had not been unfaithful. She felt curious about the other woman. She was shaken rather than devastated; intrigued rather than shocked.

'And it evens the score!' she whispered with a feeling approaching relief. If, as Howard suggested, this was the skeleton in Walter's cupboard, the fact that Walter was as fallible as the rest of mankind lightened the burden of guilt and remorse that Bel laboured under. If Walter had been less than honest with her, he could hardly condemn her for a similar failing.

With arguments like this she sought to ease her conscience. She longed to confide her suspicions to someone, and Larry was the only one she could turn to, but she would not be seeing him until Wednesday and that seemed a lifetime away. Suddenly she made up her mind. She would answer his letter and send it to him at his chambers.

That way it could not fall into the hands of Marie or George. She unlocked the bathroom door and went in search of her writing materials.

*

If first impressions were anything to go by, Karma was a fraud, thought Bel uncharitably. The room into which the clairvoyant led them was small and cramped and full of old-fashioned furniture, including an enormous aspidistra that was thick with dust and a firescreen in which woodworm had been particularly active. The faded velvet curtains were closed and a stick of incense burned in a jar on one corner of the mantelpiece. On one wall a large astrological chart had been pinned; on another a large bunch of dried herbs hung from the gas bracket; this was unlit, but three candles burned in a pewter candle-holder on a small card-table next to the one at which Karma now seated herself.

Bel avoided Marie's eyes, but she knew intuitively that her sister-in-law would be disappointed by what she saw. Alice Threadmore's secretary had not prepared them for this decidedly tawdry background.

Marie said, 'This is my sister-in-law, Isobel, who is going to consult you.'

Karma pointed to a stool in the corner of the room and Marie retired to it – with relief, Bel fancied.

'Do sit down.'

The clairvoyant's voice was husky and low, and there was the slightest hint of an accent which Bel could not recognise. Phony Russian, perhaps. She sat down and studied the woman opposite her, this woman by whom Marie set such store. Karma was small and round and her face was incredibly lined. It was impossible to guess her age, which might be anything from fifty to ninety. The cliché 'like a wrinkled apple' fitted her perfectly. Her eyes were small and dark as sloes, and she wore a red-fringed scarf over her head. The rest of her was swathed in a shapeless garment somewhat Arabic in shape which reached to her feet. Her hands were small and clawlike and in them she held a pack of playing cards which she shuffled from time to time. Bel was unimpressed, but tried hard not to show it. She kept her eyes on the woman in front of her, aware of Marie somewhere behind her. Marie was paying a quite exorbitant fee for this mumbo-jumbo, and Bel was afraid she had been hoodwinked. It was entirely possible that Karma and the secretary were in cahoots and shared the profits.

With a sudden snap the cards appeared to have reached a point at which the clairvoyant found them satisfactory. She set them on the table, face down, and said, 'Please cut them and hand me the ones you pick up.'

Bel did so and without preamble Karma began to lay the cards down, face up, in rows of three. Bel watched. A three of Spades, a seven and a nine of Clubs . . .

There were nine cards in all, all black save one. Bel hoped that was not a bad omen. Karma put the rest beside the candles, then she leaned forward, studying the cards intently. Bel found herself holding her breath and let it out in a soft hiss of irritation. Karma appeared not to hear; she was closing and opening her eyes in a series of fluttering movements. Then she drew a deep breath and raised her head from the cards. She stared straight into Bel's face with unfocused eyes and slowly rocked forward and back. Bel felt vaguely disorientated, as though the gloom and the candles and the incense were weaving some kind of spell upon her. She was glad that Marie was in the room with her, although she did not know why. Suddenly the clairvoyant stopped and leaned back in her chair. Her eyes were closed and she was breathing deeply.

'I'm feeling a huge sense of confusion . . .' she said slowly. 'Such terrible confusion . . . and this confusion is in your mind . . . and it has a dark side to it . . . Very dark . . .

But there is light and joy, somewhere in the future . . . Maybe months, maybe years. . . .'

Bel wondered whether or not she was expected to corroborate this state of confusion, but the clairvoyant had not opened her eyes. She glanced over her shoulder at Marie, who shook her head, so Bel remained silent.

'. . . I can see two letters intertwined . . . Two capital letters, one of which is a "W"—'

Bel started forward in her chair. Walter!

'. . . the other . . . Let me see . . . The other is an "H" . . . Why do I see these two letters so closely entwined? Perhaps it is a monogram . . . No, I think not . . . A coming together after many years . . . Ah! Here they are . . . coming together in eternal peace . . .'

Bel felt a sudden chill. Eternal peace? Surely that meant death. No, she would not even consider it. She shivered, unprepared for a catalogue of woes.

Apparently unaware of Bel's reaction, Karma steepled her fingers, the two forefingers pressing into her chin. She continued in her husky voice, '. . . . I see loss and I see sorrow. . . .' For a moment or two Karma was silent. She looked as though she had fallen asleep; her head was back and her mouth was partly open as she breathed noisily.

Bel turned to snatch another glance at Marie who was hunched forward on the stool, her arms clutched protectively across her chest. She put a finger to her lips and Bel faced the clairvoyant again, trying unsuccessfully to make sense of what she had been told. If the "W" was Walter, it could mean that he was going to die. She swallowed fearfully. Did that mean the airship? Oh, God! She shivered again and there was ice in the pit of her stomach. Had her father *really* made contact with Marie, trying to warn of a possible disaster, trying from the grave to save his friend Walter's life? It was all too incredible. An "H" might mean Howard, and if she was right about him being Walter's son then they were entwined in a way. But Howard was

164

young. How could *he* find eternal peace? There was no reason why he should die. That would make no sense. Bel took a deep breath to try and calm her frayed nerves. She had suddenly ceased to be sceptical. Karma was in touch with *something*, although precisely what this was remained unclear. She might be tuning in to Bel's thought processes or be particularly receptive to the waves of guilt flowing from her conscience. Whatever it was, Bel respected it and feared to hear the rest. It was very quiet. A clock ticked the minutes away. A moth flew from the curtains and fluttered past Karma who, without opening her eyes, reached out and clapped her hands over it. When she opened her hands the dead moth fell into her lap. To Bel it seemed an unhappy omen, pointing to the frailty of life.

Karma opened her eyes suddenly and reached for the cards she had discarded earlier. She laid out the next three and studied them carefully. A Queen of Clubs, the King of Hearts and the Ace of Spades.

'Black, black and more black!' she muttered with a shake of her head. Once more she placed the remaining cards on the side table and closed her eyes. 'I see letters . . .'

Bel froze.

'Not letters, headlines. Yes, large headlines,' she said. 'Headlines, headlines . . . So many headlines, but I cannot read them . . . I feel this great loss . . .' She crossed her hands over her stomach and doubled up, as though in pain or shock. When she straightened up she said, 'Oh! It's terrible . . .'

Bel felt a tremor of real fear. She wanted to tear herself away, to get up and leave the table but, almost hypnotised by the low, husky voice, she felt unable to summon the required energy.

'Someone is falling from a great height . . . Oh! . . . There is so much confusion here. So many dark threads tangled together, one with another, that I—' She put a hand over her mouth and stopped speaking. There was a long silence during which nobody moved. It seemed to Bel that nobody *breathed*.

Karma opened her eyes abruptly and said, 'You were married but not married. How can that be?'

Startled, Bel stared at her. 'I – that is we – were married at sea. We were on a cruise.'

She was severely shaken by the question. There was no way Karma could have access to that information. 'The captain of the ship . . .' she began but fell silent as the clairvoyant once more closed her eyes. How could she have known of the unusual wedding ceremony – unless Marie had told her. But why should Marie even *mention* her wedding? It was hardly relevant although Marie had pretended to be a little upset at the time, claiming that she had hoped to be a bridesmaid at some stage.

'I see something here . . . it's very colourful . . . blues and reds . . . Blues and reds and whites. . . .'

Bel thought suddenly – red, white and blue! The Union Jack! The Union Jack would fly from the stern of the R101. She had seen the airship's pennant, a large rectangle with both the Union Jack and the R.A.F. roundel together on a blue ground. She found herself nodding although it seemed unlikely Karma could see her.

'Red and white, blue . . . So many of them . . . and green and yellow. . . . Flowers everywhere and music . . .'

Of course! The reception in Karachi. There would be flowers and a military band to welcome the airship. Bel clutched at the idea thankfully, grateful for a ray of hope. There would be no disaster. They might even be the flowers and band at Cardington to welcome her home. She was aware of a great lightening of her heart. There would be no disaster. Some of the tension left her and she drew a deep sigh. She had lost all sense of time, but now made an effort to relax. Presumably the session was nearing its end, yet Karma had not once mentioned love – which seemed odd since she was obviously no charlatan and Bel imagined the cards must have something to say on the suject.

As though reading her mind Karma said, 'Ah! Here is a heart. I am feeling a happiness at last ... I see the letter "R" – Richard or Robert, maybe ... his heart is very full ...?'

Bel smiled for the first time since she had entered the little room. She wanted to say, 'It's Larry *Roberts*! And yes! His heart is full of love.' She could imagine what Marie was making of it.

Abruptly Karma opened her eyes and the unfocused look had gone. She stared at Bel for a moment and then smiled. 'I hope you are satisfied,' she said. 'I hope you found what you sought and heard what you wanted to hear.'

Bel said, 'Yes, indeed.' Had she, she wondered?

Karma stood up and unashamedly held out her hand for the promised fee.

Marie came forward, fumbling in her clutch bag, smiling uncertainly. She produced a five-pound note; the claw-like hand closed over it and offered no change. Five pounds! Bel hoped that Marie had been prepared for that.

Marie said, 'Well, thank you.'

'Yes,' said Bel, 'Thank you very much. You've been – it was . . .' The sentence died.

In silence they followed the woman out on to the landing and down the poorly-lit stairs. Their final goodbyes over, Bel and Marie found themselves on the pavement with the door closing firmly behind them.

They exchanged a long look and Marie said, 'Well, I'm glad that's over, dear old thing!'

Bel noticed that her voice shook slightly. She put a reassuring hand on Marie's arm. 'Let's go home,' she said. 'I need a strong drink!'

*

Walter received Howard's letter when he returned home to the house in Cardington on the Tuesday evening. Mrs Banks handed it over, her large frame shaking with indignation.

'Came right up to the back door, bold as brass!' she told him indignantly. 'Handed the letter over and said, "That's for his nibs!" His nibs! I said, "None of your cheek, young man." It was the same chap that came before and traipsed all over the lawn without so much as a by-your-leave. I can tell you, sir, it gave me a bit of a funny feeling, with the mistress in London. I mean, just me and him. He has that way of looking.' She helped Walter off with his coat, shook it and hung it on the hallstand. 'There's something shifty about his eyes, if you know what I mean – as though his thoughts aren't very nice. As though he's up to something. I said, "If by his nibs you mean Mr Roberts—" and he said, "His nibs will do" and I said, "That's enough of that sort of talk. I'd have the law on you if I had my way!" I told him straight, but all he did was laugh. I wouldn't trust him farther than I could throw him, sir, if you know what I mean.'

Walter, sick at heart, cut short the tirade. 'I understand. Thank you, Mrs Banks.' He took the letter reluctantly.

'I do think we ought to tell the police,' she said, her face creased with worry. 'I mean, he might mean us some harm. You or the mistress or anybody. When I got your message yesterday that you were going to sleep at the office again, "Well," I thought. "I'm all alone in this big house with that mad man roaming around." I didn't sleep a wink, sir, and that's the truth! Every little noise sounded like footsteps up the stairs and it was such a windy night. In the end I locked my bedroom door, if you must know. I was that scared, I was just longing for daylight. He shouldn't get away with frightening folks like this. We should tell the police.'

'I'll think about it,' Walter said lamely. 'I'm sorry you were so worried. I'm sure there is no need to be. I was working, and it got so late I thought I'd use the camp-bed in the office.'

'But did you eat?'

He shook his head. 'I was too tired to do anything but sleep. And I wanted to get an early start this morning before the others came in.'

'Something wrong, is there, sir?'

'No, no! At least, nothing that can't be put right. But time is against us. Only a few weeks left, and she must be ready for her forty-eight-hour test flight. Still, that's my worry.' He smiled. 'I was at work by six and sorted out my little problem. Then I snatched a bit of breakfast in the canteen. They actually do quite a good kipper.'

'Talking of food, sir, I'm afraid dinner will be a bit late. Ten minutes or so – and I'm very sorry but after such a terrible night I overslept this morning and I was late—'

Walter had a sudden thought. 'When did he come?'

'Yesterday. Early. You'd just gone off in the car. I'm surprised you didn't pass each other.'

'I see. Well, I'd better read what he has to say.'

Hiding his apprehension as well as he could, Walter took the letter into the study and closed the door. He poured himself a brandy and sat down. For a while he stared at the envelope, at his son's untidy writing. Howard had been left-handed as a child, but the school had said there was no need to worry; he would grow out of it and they would insist that he used his right hand. He had a momentary vision of his son on the one occasion when he watched him struggling with his homework, his pen held awkwardly, ink spattering across the sheet. His handwriting had never recovered.

Inside there was an address in Shortstown. God! He felt a rush of anger. So he had defied him and had come to Cardington. The message was clear enough:

169

Dear Dad,

I need ten pounds for something which I cannot explain just yet, but I will tell you later. Never fear. I will pay you back. It is MOST important, so please do send it round this evening or first thing tomorrow. Mum has gone to France and when she comes back I will send her some money every week. She will not need anything else from you. You can spend all your money on HER. So it looks as though you are rid of both of us at last. That will please you. I shall keep out of your way, so do not come looking for me. I have nothing to say to you. Your housekeeper was very rude to me. She should mind her manners or she might regret it. You all should. Even a worm will turn.

Howard

The letter bore the previous day's date, so there was no way Walter could have given his son the money, had he wished to do so. He had only just returned to read it, and today was Wednesday the 26th. And ten pounds was a lot of money.

'Oh, Howard! What have you done?' he muttered. How could he owe money already? Or . . . He shook his head. He had hardly had time to get a Cardington girl into trouble – unless it had happened in London. That might account for his hasty removal from that area. He groaned. Poor, foolish lad. Was the money for some seedy back-street abortionist?

He felt sick with anxiety. The letter both irritated and upset him. The pathetic attempt to be aggressive made Walter want to cry. His son seemed determined to alienate all those who loved him; he appeared hell-bent on self-destruction. Walter rubbed his eyes and stared unhappily at the fire. He poked it, reached for the tongs and added a few lumps of coal, then sat back, staring into the blaze. What on earth should he do, he wondered. If he sent the money now, it might be the first of many such demands. If he didn't, the little wretch might offer Bel a few home truths about her husband. Was it blackmail? He wished that he could talk to Vera about it all. He should have done so a year ago, before it all got out of hand, but the airship made so many demands on his time and – he smiled wryly, catching himself out in the lie. He could have made time to see Vera, but the truth was he did not enjoy discussing the boy with his mother. She always took it as a criticism; was always so defensive, blaming herself, convinced that somehow she had failed. Poor timid Vera. Like a little rabbit. Soft and warm and trusting. The brandy glass blurred and he brushed tears from his eyes.

He refilled his glass and took a large mouthful. The brandy warmed his stomach but it could not reach his chilled heart. Of course there must be no further mention of the police. Somehow he must convince the housekeeper that Howard's bark was worse than his bite. Apart from the ensuing scandal, he did not want his son hauled ignominiously to the local police station. He did not want to make a martyr of him. And whatever would Vera think if he had the boy arrested? She had been a good mother, at least she had done her best. He himself must accept the blame for the boy's rebellious nature. In Howard's eyes his father had deserted him, and nothing would ever change that. But he *loved* the boy! In spite of this stupid letter. Perhaps he would send the money, and with it he would send a friendly letter. No recriminations. He would ask to meet with him – at a pub, perhaps. Not in Cardington, naturally, but within cycling distance. They needed to talk before matters went too far. Or had they already reached a point of no return? He did not like the tone of Howard's remark about Mrs Banks. 'She might regret it.' A blatant threat, but he could be bluffing. Was the boy *violent*? The idea shocked him. The thought of his son as beyond control was the stuff of nightmares. He wanted him to have a good life, free of the tensions which filled Walter's own life.

He emptied the glass. 'By tomorrow morning at the latest', Howard had said. So now Howard would be thinking that the money was not forthcoming. The question was, what would he do? Walter frowned. He could take it round now . . . but it might be too late, and he quailed at the thought of the row that could follow. And bad news travels fast. It would be all round the RAW within twenty-four hours. He felt a sweat break out on his forehead as a new possibility presented itself to him: the press might get hold of the story.

'Hell and damnation!' For once in his life he had no idea how to proceed. Give him a mathematical problem and he would solve it. Ask about thrust and lift in an airship and he could work it out to the nth degree. Ask what was to be done about a recalcitrant son and he was stumped. Relationships were not his forte. 'Damn the boy!' Why did it have to be like this? He poured a third brandy and picked up *The Times*. He would sleep on it; he would think more clearly when he was rested.

He went down to dinner when summoned and was halfway through a succulent pork chop when he was startled by a loud crash. He jumped to his feet and hurried into the hall. From the sitting room the housekeeper called to him shakily.

'Sir! It's in here!'

He found her in a state of shock, her apron held to her face as she stared at the floor in horror.

'What the hell was that?' he demanded.

Mrs Banks pointed a trembling finger. A rock the size of a coconut lay in the middle of the carpet.

'From our own rockery!' Mrs Banks stammered. 'It was *him*, it must be!'

There was broken glass all over the floor. On its way in the rock had smashed the lower half of the window-pane, and had then knocked over a large fern which now lay on the carpet, its earth loosened, its fronds broken. The net curtain billowed inwards and upwards, revealing a jagged hole. Mrs Banks looked as though she might faint at any moment.

She said, 'There might be a note with it.'

Walter gave her a withering look. 'Of course there's not a note. Who do you think it is – Robin Hood?'

As he hurried past her towards the window, Mrs Banks made a futile grab at his arm. 'Oh, don't look out, sir! He might be out there, waiting. He might throw another one!'

Ignoring her, he pushed up the sash window and peered out. He dare not call Howard by name but he suspected the boy was out there, watching, waiting to see what would happen. There was no sign of any movement.

'I'm going out there,' he told the housekeeper. 'You wait here.'

'On my own? Oh, no, sir!' Her face creased with dismay. 'Suppose he comes into the house and you're out there—'

'He won't. He'll be legging it as fast as he can.'

'Should I call the police?'

'No!' He was almost shouting and that would never do. He must try to play down the whole incident. 'If I think it's necessary I shall do it myself.'

He hesitated, torn between finding the perpetrator and calming the housekeeper. Seeing how frightened she was, he took her firmly by the shoulders and guided her to a chair. Handing her a brandy, he said a few words of reassurance and went outside by way of the front door.

'Where are you?' he shouted. 'What do you want? Come here where I can see you. Where we can talk.'

There was no sound. Perhaps Howard had taken off, suddenly fearful of the consequences of his action. But Walter did not think so; he sensed that the boy was nearby. If only he would come forward, they could stop this foolishness from going any further. If only he had had the courage to tell Bel the truth – but that risk was one he dared not take. She might never forgive him. Might even leave him. Bel was his Achilles heel, for he had never expected to fall in love, had never expected to *want* to spend his life with a woman.

He went further into the garden, across the lawn, away from the steps. He raised his voice. 'I know you can hear me. Please! Let's talk.'

Silence greeted his words and he stared round, baffled by the darkening sky and a garden full of convenient shadows. After one more futile attempt, he admitted defeat and went back into the house.

Mrs Banks jumped to her feet when she saw him. 'It was him!' she insisted. 'The one who brought the letter. It must have been. Oh, Lordy! I told you he was up to no good and now look what he's done!' She looked nervously round the room, peering into the corners as though he might somehow be lurking there undiscovered. 'Who'd have thought it? And oh!' She clapped a hand to her mouth. 'Thank goodness the mistress is in London. She'd be scared out of her wits, poor thing. Oh, dear! What next, I wonder? Whatever is the world coming to!' She stared into her empty glass. Walter refilled it and poured one for himself. He was annoyed to see that his hands were shaking.

'Maybe he's trying to kill us,' the housekeeper suggested.

'Don't talk nonsense! He threw a rock into an empty room. How could that kill anyone?'

Walter swallowed his drink in one gulp, picked up the rock and threw it out of the window. Mrs Banks watched, horrified.

'That was *evidence*!' she told him. 'That might have had his fingerprints on it. We should leave everything exactly where it is until the police come.'

When he told her that they were not to be called, she

was rendered momentarily speechless. When she rallied she asked, 'But why not? He could do anything. He might come back later. We could both be murdered in our beds.'

'They are not to be called,' he repeated. 'I – I have an idea who it might be. A local lad. I'll see to it myself; it won't happen again.' Seeing her look of outrage he hurried on, 'I don't want to frighten my wife. If she knows what has happened she will never have a moment's peace. We wouldn't want that, would we, Mrs Banks?'

She hesitated and for a moment he thought she would agree, but then she shook her head. 'I don't like it, sir. He's a dangerous man. He might be a lunatic escaped from somewhere. I shan't sleep easy. As like as not he's out there, waiting his chance to get in. Please, Mr Roberts. Let's tell them.'

'They are not to be told,' he insisted.

'But the broken window?'

'I'll fasten a piece of board over it for tonight, and I'll have it fixed properly first thing tomorrow morning.'

She stared at him unhappily and he could see her mind working. 'But we should tell the mistress. She should be on her guard. If she doesn't know and—'

'I will see to everything, Mrs Banks. I will decide what to do. All you need do, when you are recovered, is sweep up this mess – and don't cut yourself on the glass.'

Before she could protest further he went in search of something with which to secure the window. When he came back she was nowhere to be seen and the earth and glass had not been cleared up. Ominous, he thought wearily. He went to the foot of the stairs and could hear her moving about in her room. Sulking, no doubt.

In the morning when he came down to breakfast the room had not been touched and there was no breakfast prepared. She appeared almost at once, however, dressed in her coat and hat and carrying a small bag. Angrily she informed him she was not going to stay another night with that madman on the loose. If he was not going to notify the police, she was giving notice. Hesitating on the doorstep she waited for him to protest, but when he remained silent she walked out and slammed the door behind her.

'Go to hell!' he told her retreating footsteps. He rubbed his face tiredly and wondered how on earth he was going to explain her disappearance to Isobel?

*

While Walter was eating a belated breakfast in the R.A.W. canteen, his son was two hundred feet up among the girders of the R101. Below him on the ground of the shed men moved about like miniatures, dwarfed by the distance between them. Above him other riggers moved lithely, three and four hundred feet up, inspecting the connections between each girder and the next, tightening screws, testing the joints, searching for flaws of any kind which could develop into a hazard once the airship was in flight. Once checked and found satisfactory, the joints would be padded to prevent them from chafing the gas bags. Holes previously rubbed in the bags were already being patched. It was all looking what his mother would have called 'make-do-and-mend', Howard thought with a smile. If he looked down he would see the roof of the passenger deck, the tanks which would hold water and others that would be filled with fuel for the five engines. If he looked to his right he would see the greyish-white of the vast gas bags, to his left a row of windows in the shed wall and an array of electric lights which supplemented the daylight. To a newcomer the sights would be marvellous, but Howard was already familiar with them and this familiarity bred a certain contempt.

He had also become used to the heights at which he was required to work, and these held no fears for him. He climbed amongst the metalwork like a monkey and, once straddling a girder, felt as safe as though he were only ten feet from the ground. His tools were suspended from a leather belt and on his feet he wore the obligatory rope-soled shoes.

'You got it?'

Howard turned to see Alf Comber settling himself on the girder beside him. Alf was a loser, in Howard's opinion, but Howard was not averse to making use of his present distress. Alf had taken a few too many liberties with a certain young barmaid and now she was 'missing her whatsits'. Alf had not cared to explain this phrase and Howard had not cared to admit his ignorance. He assumed it meant 'in the family way' because Alf was going to have to marry her before her folks found out. But she wanted a white wedding and that cost money. A dress, flowers, church bells – none of it came cheap, he had told Howard bitterly. He already had a little money saved up but he needed more. Before Howard could say that he never lent money Alf had made him a tempting offer. It seemed that Alf, on account of his long service with the R.A.W., had been one of the few lucky riggers selected to go to India. He had offered Howard the chance to take his place (albeit secretly) if he could come up with ten pounds. This would pay for the wedding and leave a very small amount to put towards the honeymoon – a weekend in Blackpool.

'Have you got the money?' he repeated.

'Not yet – but I will. I told you, I'll get it.' A great surge of anger rose within Howard as he thought of his father's meanness. Stingy baskit! What was ten pounds to him? What did he care? *He* would be travelling in luxury, stuffing himself with gourmet food and smoking expensive cigars. Well, bugger him! For a measly tenner his son could travel as crew, but no! The great Walter Roberts was too tight-fisted. Howard felt a brief glow of pleasure as he remembered the way the rock went through the window. Beautiful. He wished he had thrown a dozen rocks instead of just one. He wished he'd broken every window in the

177

place! Serve the mean old sod right. He hoped he'd scared the living daylights out of him – and that *she* would kick up merry hell when she found out. Not that he had finished with them. He would think of something else, something *she* would hate: a dead rat in a box. He could send it through the post wrapped in pretty paper with a bit of ribbon!

Alf pretended to adjust something with his spanner for the benefit of anyone who might be watching. 'You said your rich uncle would fork out.'

'He can't.' Howard searched for a reason. 'He's in hospital. How was I to know?'

'So?'

'So I know someone else. I'l let you have it by the weekend.'

'You said by today.'

'OK! So now I can't. What's a few days?' He looked into the weaselly face, hating it. The man was a loser. It was written all over him. He would have to get some money out of someone. 'Saturday morning. That's definite. Take it or leave it.'

Alf tutted but agreed half-heartedly. Howard thought frantically and an idea came to him suddenly. He would ask Peggy for a loan. She had said she had some savings: thirteen pounds ten shillings. Well, he could have ten of that and pay her back later.

'Saturday for sure,' he said.

*

'What! Ten pounds?' Peggy stared at him, shocked.

He had waited for her by the main building and now walked beside her, wheeling his bicycle. On either side of them the rest of the workers streamed in to the Royal Airship Works – the men, like Howard, in cloth caps; the foremen in bowlers; the women, like Peggy, in headscarves tied turban fashion. On bikes, on foot, a few in cars, tooting their way through the crowd. Some would find their way into the Shorts factory; some to the offices in the main building, the rest to the sheds themselves.

Alarmed by her reaction, Howard experienced a moment's uneasiness. She *had* to say 'Yes.' He had to be on that flight. His father would be so furious to think that his son had shared the triumph. Howard planned to get one of the lads to give Walter a note – or he might even sneak down to the passenger quarters and allow his father to catch a glimpse of him. Then he would disappear again. Keep him guessing. Keep him on edge . . . Peggy *had* to lend him the money! It would ruin the flight for Walter, knowing that Howard was around and wondering what he would do.

'It's only a loan,' he insisted. 'Go on, Peggy. Just for a few days?'

'But what's it for?'

He tapped the side of his nose and grinned. 'Can't tell you that!'

She was obviously thinking about it; he could see the slight frown on her face. She was a nice little thing really.

'Mum would kill me,' she said.

'How would she know?'

'You going to buy something with it?'

'Sort of.'

'You don't owe it to someone, do you?' She looked at him anxiously.

He smiled. 'Course I don't. Do I look daft to you?'

'But you've got all the money your father left you!' She had stopped walking and now regarded him suspiciously.

He thought rapidly, wishing he hadn't told so many lies. 'Can't get at it. It's tied up, as they say. Bonds and stuff.' He searched his mind for the right terms. 'Stocks and shares. You have to give them notice and it takes ages, but I'll be cashing some in so then I'll let you have it back.' He looked at her from the corner of his eye. She still didn't seem very happy. Women!

'I'm sorry, Howard. I don't think I'd better. It's a lot of money.'

But she *had* to! He grabbed her arm. 'It's only ten pounds!' Unintentionally he had raised his voice.

'*Only?*' She pulled her arm away, glaring at him. '*Only* ten!'

She was going to refuse him, he thought frantically. 'I thought you trusted me. I thought you loved me.'

She was startled. 'Loved you? I never said—' She stared at him. 'Why, Howard! D'you love me?'

He swallowed hard. This was getting out of hand.

'You really love me?' Her eyes were shining.

Better say 'Yes', he thought, but he crossed the fingers of his right hand. 'Course I do! You don't think I'd ask to borrow money if . . . What sort of man d'you think I am?' He shrugged. 'Well, there it is.'

'Howard!' Her expression changed slowly from one of suspicion to one of delight. Her eyes were soft and she looked positively pretty. 'You – but you hardly know me! I mean – well, I mean we've only known each other—'

'How long does it take to fall in love?' he asked and gave her what he hoped was a quizzical look.

She said, 'I don't believe it!' in a squeaky voice and both hands went up to her mouth. Suddenly she said, 'Oh!' and her eyes widened further. 'Oh, *no*! The money's for a—!' She stopped in mid-sentence but her glance fell on her ringless left hand.

A ring, thought Howard! Crikey! She thought he was going to buy her an engagement ring. Perhaps he should let her think so. Perhaps he could wriggle out of it later, after he got back from India. If he didn't want to marry her, he could always drop off in India and make a new life for himself. That way he'd never have to pay back the ten pounds. And it would upset his father no end. It would be in all the papers: 'SON OF FAMOUS DESIGNER MISSING IN INDIA'. Except that his father wasn't exactly famous; he just thought he was. But if it was in all the papers he would have to tell *her* all about Vera and about his son. Unless she had wormed it out of him already. He'd given her enough clues!

Peggy squeezed his arm and said, 'Oh, Howard! I don't know what to say!'

Grinning, he put an arm round her shoulder. 'So will you?' he asked.

'Will I marry you?'

'Will you lend me the money?'

Her face fell and he said hastily, 'I wouldn't propose to a girl on the way to work, now, would I!'

'Oh! I see.' She was suddenly all smiles again. 'Well then, I suppose I will. Lend you the money, I mean.'

He felt weak with relief. At last things were going right for him. His father could keep his rotten money. He gave her a beaming smile and she said archly, 'Aren't you going to ask me if I love you?'

'What?' His mind was already on the flight to India. 'Oh! Yes! I mean, do you?'

'Yes, I do.' She looked at him from beneath lowered lids. 'And Howard, if we're in love and everything and going to be married – I mean I know you haven't really proposed but you are going to – well, if you want . . . well, something in advance, you know what I mean . . .' She lowered her voice. 'Well, as long as Mum doesn't find out you can have it.'

Something in advance? He said, 'Thanks, Peg. How long does it take, then, to get money out of a savings account?' He'd thought she would just ask for the money and they would give it to her. In which case he could ask her to come in late tomorrow and go to the Post Office first. But maybe she had to fill in a form or something. He began to sweat.

'Thursday,' she whispered, 'when Auntie's gone to whist.'

He looked at her blankly. Surely the Post Office would be shut by then?

'We could do it up in your bedroom.'

Do it? *That*? His mouth fell open with shock. Did she mean——?

'I'll get the money for you and we'll . . .' She rolled her eyes expressively.

The money and that, too? His breath seemed to catch in his throat as a thousand possibilities danced tantalisingly before him. As easy as falling off a log! What a girl! He smiled as they walked on, with Peggy hanging on to his arm. His luck really had changed for the better. He swallowed.

'Thanks!' he said huskily.

Chapter Nine

THE CAR WAS A BEAUTY. Bel sat back against the leather seat, enjoying the feel of the wind in her hair and oblivious to the overcast sky which hinted at rain later. She had no idea where they were going and did not care. She was with Larry and that was all that mattered. She would cheerfully freeze with him in Antarctica or melt with him in Africa, and had told him so. Just to be with him satisfied all her needs, and she was astonished how little the rest of her life mattered now. If they were both destined to die tomorrow, she could bear it if she was in his arms at the time. Discovering her love for him had turned her world upside down and her values had somersaulted. She woke each day counting off the days, hours and minutes until they could be together again. It both frightened and delighted her, and she had given up trying to rationalise her feelings. The raging of her heart was a mysterious, alien force within her which seemed to provide a new view of the world and everyone in it.

He turned his head towards her briefly and at the sight of his eyes she felt ridiculously weak. 'Nothing on the grapevine à la Lampitt?' he asked.

She smiled. 'We'd be the last to know, I expect. But I've heard nothing.'

'Fingers crossed, then. We may have ridden out that particular storm. I suspect—'

Suddenly he braked hard and stopped, cursing mildly under his breath, as a large lorry loaded with sacks swung across their path, narrowly missing them.

'Idiot!' Larry put his finger on the horn and kept it there. 'I don't think Freddie would be very keen if I returned his motor with a large dent in it!' he remarked with a shake of his head.

With a shudder Bel thought, 'It could happen. Just like that! A moment's carelessness and we could have been killed.'

'Fool!' she shouted as the lorry pulled away.

Larry laid his hand briefly on her knee. 'Quite the little hoyden!' he said and she saw the corners of his mouth twitch.

As he continued to manoeuvre the Jowitt through the traffic, he began to talk enthusiastically about buying himself another car. Bel listened with rapt attention. He could have been talking about a voyage to the moon or the intricacies of Renaissance architecture for all she cared. She loved the sound of his voice, and that alone would have held her spellbound.

'That old banger I had at university gave up the ghost and I keep meaning to replace it.'

Bel allowed him to talk without interrupting. She was enjoying the changing view from the window as houses, people and other vehicles flashed past.

He glanced at her suddenly. 'Don't you want to know where we're going?'

'You said it was a secret.'

'We're going to Hampton Court. We're going to spend the day on a house-boat. I've brought a picnic: delicious, mouthwatering chicken, succulent honey-cured ham, the very best champagne—'

Her heart began to thud as she looked at him. 'Wait! You mean, *alone?*'

'A wonderful mayonnaise, a fantastic Waldorf salad with walnuts, apple and celery—'

'Larry!'

'We'll sit in the shade of a weeping willow—'

'Alone?'

He pulled up at traffic lights but stared straight ahead. 'Absolutely alone. Separated from the rest of . . .'

She resisted the urge to laugh. 'Ah! *That* alone!'

'Smoked salmon, a coffee gâteau from Harrods. The sort you like, with—'

'Larry!'

He laughed.

'A houseboat! How did you manage it?'

'Freddie's mother lives on the boat, but she's away at the moment in Germany so – you don't mind, do you?'

Her imagination was way ahead of the conversation. 'Mind what? Being on a houseboat? I shan't be seasick or anything, will I?' She was being cowardly, playing for time.

'You won't be seasick. There are no waves on the Thames – a little wash from passing boats, that's all. But you'll be alone with me and—' He shrugged and gave her a sideways glance as the lights changed and they moved ahead.

She tried to think about it sensibly, but her body was already crying out for him. Alone in a houseboat there was no way either of them would be able resist this fierce longing. She doubted if either of them would even try. No wonder Larry had insisted on keeping their destination a secret. He was making it easy for her. If he waited for her to suggest it, she would never say the words; they would never be lovers. He was making her mind up for her.

'Oh, Larry!' she said breathlessly. 'I want to, but should we? So soon, I mean. Oh, God! I—'

He said, 'You can say "No", Bel. If that's what you want. We could find a third-rate hotel without a willow

and have shepherd's pie with gristle and watery cabbage
followed by semolina, surrounded by dozens of unpleasant
people. Then we could drive straight home to London.
And no harm done.'

'Sounds wonderful when you put it like that!'

He kept his eyes on the road ahead so that she could
not see his expression. Bel thought frantically, fighting
her instincts. This was her last chance. She could still
refuse, could still choose to be faithful to Walter. And
that is what she ought to do. Duty and morality tugged in
one direction; that way she would sleep at nights with a
clear conscience. Her love for Larry and her own desire
tugged the other way; that way she would enjoy
the delights of an illicit passion and would be no better
than a—

He said softly, 'Poor Bel! I do understand, you know.
I'm asking an awful lot, but I'm a thoroughly selfish
wretch and I've waited all my life for you.'

'Larry—'

'I won't beg. It's not my way.'

'*Larry*! I want it just as much as you but—'

'And I shall still love you just as deeply if you say "No"
because I can't help myself.'

She looked sideways at him and was immediately moved
by the angle of his jaw and the shape of his nose and the
way his hair curled against the nape of his neck. He was a
beautiful man and he deserved the excitement of a woman's
body. The words 'waited all my life' echoed in her brain
accusingly. He deserved a woman who would give him all
he wanted in the world, and she was the one; she could
give him everything or nothing . . . She thought suddenly
of the lorry which had so narrowly missed them. Supposing
it had struck the car and one or both of them had been
killed? Their love would never have been consummated.
They would never have tasted the wildest joy the world
had to offer. The prospect filled her with a bleakness that

momentarily swamped her doubts and before she could change her mind she said, 'I've never been keen on shepherd's pie.'

He turned to her and the brilliance of his eyes was all that she needed by way of reassurance. Life was short and it could be cold and full of disappointments. But occasionally the chance came for something wonderful. She would take it.

'I love you, Bel!'

'I'm rather fond of you!' she said shakily. And now that the decision had been made she felt a great rush of exhilaration. Come what may, she was in love with Larry and she would give herself wholeheartedly.

'With cream,' he was saying, 'and those little toasted almonds . . .'

For a moment she stared at him.

'The coffee gâteau,' he said. 'Very seductive, pâtisserie!'

She began to laugh and then, suddenly, to her great consternation, she felt two large tears roll down her face. Within moments she was sobbing. 'I'm sorry! I don't know why—'

'It's allowed,' Larry said gently. 'An optional extra.'

He said nothing else and she cried softly until the anxiety and tension of the last few weeks had left her. By the time the tears had passed she was filled with a deep calm which left no room for guilt or regret.

*

Once they were out of London and on their way to Hampton Court they were able to talk more easily. Bel told Larry what had happened at the meeting with the clairvoyant, and as she had expected he was inclined to be sceptical.

'This "H" and "W",' he said. 'You seriously think that the young man who trespassed at Cardington is Walter's illegitimate son? It's a bit far-fetched, isn't it? I mean, you don't have a shred of evidence. Even *I* could claim to be someone's illegitimate son if I wanted to cause trouble.'

'But why should he want to cause trouble?' Bel asked. 'Whoever he is, he must have some kind of grudge against Walter, and Walter says he has never sacked anyone so it can't be that. And what did he mean about skeletons in Walter's cupboard? I know this is going to sound stupid but there was someone once, years ago. A woman we met in France – an Englishwoman on holiday. I was quite young at the time, but I do remember that Walter went out with her a couple of times without the rest of us and my mother and father teased him about her.' She thought for a moment. 'I was about fifteen or maybe fourteen, and my nose was rather put out of joint! Walter had always been so kind to me. He never treated me like a child – even when I *was* a child. He used talk to me about grown-up things and, of course, I was terribly flattered. You know, about the government and what was happening in Ireland. And about the airship industry, of course. On and on about it. I found it rather boring, actually, but I pretended I was interested just to keep his attention. When he went out with this woman I suppose I was rather jealous. Her name was Veronica, or something like that. If she had had a child by Walter, he would have been about the right age.'

'Sounds a bit thin to me.' Larry slowed right down to allow a flock of sheep to jostle their way across the road in front of them. The shepherd waved a 'thank you' and Larry drove on.

Bel sat beside him thoughtfully. 'And there was this other amazing thing Karma said – that I was married but not married. And Marie swears she hadn't told her, not a word. When I said we were married at sea—'

'*You* said that?'

'Yes.'

'So she didn't know that until you told her.'

Bel drew her brows together in concentration. 'I suppose

188

not. But she knew . . .' Or did she? Larry was right; Karma had not known they were married at sea.

Larry glanced at her, smiling apologetically. 'Am I spoiling it for you? I'm sorry. But you did ask for my opinion.'

'But she knew about you. She said a heart with an "R" and that's you!'

'But she also said she saw people falling from a great height.'

'No, she said some*one* falling.'

'But if you say she saw flags and heard music in Karachi, then obviously the R101 is going to get there.'

'She might not get back again.'

He was silent and Bel thought hard about what she remembered from the sitting. She was reluctant to give up her theories and yet Larry was making sense. Perhaps she had read too much into it – although Marie had not thought so and Marie had actually been there. 'She said right at the beginning that there was dreadful confusion that had a dark side to it – oh!'

He had pulled, bumping and jolting, off the road to park beside a bridge. 'We're there,' he announced, pulling on the brake.

'Oh!' she said again.

He grinned. 'The moment of truth!'

She followed him out of the car and watched as he took a hamper from the boot of the motor. She could see the river, broad and smooth, and the small, brightly painted houseboat moored about twenty yards along the towpath. It looked very innocent, but Bel thought, 'So this is where we will make love for the first time.' There was no sun to sparkle on the water, but at least the rain was holding off. She thought, 'This is where I shall commit adultery!' And she didn't care.

Larry helped her on to the deck and together they explored the little boat. It did not take long and then, somehow, they knew the moment had come. They could

189

no longer hide their need for one another and suddenly the last of Bel's reservations fled.

She looked into Larry's eager eyes. 'Shall we?' she asked. 'Please.'

Slowly Bel began to unbutton her blouse. A few moments passed as they took off their clothes.

'I didn't say it would be comfortable!' Larry teased as they lay close together on the narrow bunk. 'I can only guarantee the picnic. The rest is anybody's guess!'

She kissed him. 'I'm not complaining.'

Oblivious to everything except the fact that they were alone together, they faced each other, their arms entwined. For the first time since she had married, Bel felt conscious of her nakedness.

'You're so beautiful. So perfect,' Larry whispered. 'You smell and feel exactly as I knew you would.' He drew in a long shuddering breath and his arms tightened round her. 'I'll be as slow as I can, my sweet Bel, but—'

She laughed softly, aware of his hardening body. 'I don't think you'll manage it!' she whispered. 'It doesn't matter at all. Don't worry about me. I want you to enjoy it. I'll be happy if you—'

'Oh, Bel! Oh, God!' He buried his face in her shoulder. 'I don't think I can wait – Bel!'

Clumsily he moved on the narrow bunk until he was above her, his weight pressing down on her, one hand cupped beneath her head, covering her face with kisses.

With practised hands she guided him and then he was inside her. Her own body leaped in sympathy as he gasped her name, gulping for air, moaning with the pleasure for which he had waited so long. 'Bel! *Bel!*' he cried, in an agony of suspense.

'My dearest Larry! My *love!*' she cried as he released himself into her, and at that moment there was nobody else in the whole world. Just the two of them, who were now one.

190

He lay breathless, crushing her, as she stroked his head, feeling the curls springy beneath her fingers. She ran her fingers over his neck and across his shoulders. She could not think of a single moment of her life when she had felt so utterly and completely happy.

'Sweetheart!' she whispered.

With an effort he raised himself on his elbows and looked into her face. 'You're incredible!' he said. 'God Almighty!' he shook his head. 'When I think what I've been missing all these years! That was worth waiting for.' He let out his breath slowly and she moved sideways to give him room to lie beside her. Gradually his rapid breathing slowed. He grinned. 'Is it always like that?'

'Nearly always!' she assured him.

'I knew Walter was lucky, but I never realised just how lucky!'

Bel felt a moment's panic and said quickly, 'Don't talk about him, Larry.'

'I can't imagine you and him.'

'Don't try.'

He ran his finger around her nipple. 'He can't possibly love you the way I do.'

'*Please*, Larry!' She kissed his shoulder. 'I just want to think about the two of us.'

'Oh, God, Bel! I'm sorry, I'm a thoughtless brute.' His eyes were full of remorse.

'No, you're not.'

'I am, Bel. It was tactless.'

'So you were tactless? Nobody's perfect and I still adore you.'

'I'm so desperately jealous,' he whispered. 'Say you forgive me.' He kissed her mouth and throat and breasts. 'Say it!'

When at last she was able to speak she said, 'I forgive you' and then, 'This is so wonderful. I want it to last for ever.'

For a long time they clung together until at last Larry sat up and swung his legs to the floor.

'Champagne!' he said. 'And then we'll do it over all again – with you in mind.'

Lazily she watched him release the cork. It popped and fizzed out of the top.

Larry laughed. 'I know how it feels!' he said.

They sat together on the bunk, sipping the champagne and smiling at each other in secret delight.

'It's like a midnight feast in the dorm at boarding school' Larry told her. 'Forbidden joys!'

'Not *quite* the same, I hope!'

He stroked the side of her face. 'Not quite!' He grinned suddenly. 'I bet this boat was rocking! Anyone passing would have a good idea what was happening down below. Give them something to think about!'

'Probably reporting us to the police this very minute!'

'Let them find their own women! I'm not sharing you!'

Immediately the realisation flashed between them that that was exactly what Larry was doing. He *was* sharing her with Walter. For a moment she saw his eyes darken and then he had swallowed down the last of his champagne. 'Drink up!' he told her. 'There's plenty more where that came from!' He refilled their glasses. 'I love you, Bel. Why are words so damned inadequate? Here's to you and me and us! Now and for ever.'

'Amen.'

'You've given me a taste of heaven and I shall never let you go!'

'I shall never want you to.'

When they had finished their drinks Larry was as good as his word. Their lovemaking was for Bel and, despite his inexperience, he proved himself a gentle lover. When she had come, sighing and crying his name aloud, he came for a second time and then they both slept the sweet sleep of exhaustion.

Nearly an hour later they woke and dressed. They discovered that they were hungry and, sitting one each side of the tiny table, set out Larry's picnic.

Larry grinned. 'You've been a very good girl,' he told her. 'You've eaten all your dinner, so you shall have some dessert!'

With an exaggerated flourish he lifted the coffee gâteau from the hamper and placed it in the centre of the table.

'With nuts on!' said Bel.

He kissed her. 'With nuts on!'

*

On the way home they discussed whether or not Walter should be told. Bel was against the idea, terrified of him knowing, fearful that in some way he might prevent her from seeing Larry again. Afraid, too, of what it would do to George and how it would affect their family. She was also reluctant to hurt Walter and, on balance, favoured caution and felt that it was better to say nothing just yet. If the affair came to light, then they would be forced to take action. In the meantime, she pleaded, let their relationship remain a secret. What she did not actually express was the desire for their friendship to remain untarnished by public disapproval.

Larry disagreed. He wanted to tell Walter outright that they loved each other and wanted a divorce. This was the more honest way, he insisted, and she could not deny that. He preferred to speak out, to avoid what he called 'skulking in corners'. Loving her was something to be proud of, not something shameful. The only shameful part was the deceit.

'Think, too,' he urged Bel, 'how much worse Walter will feel in a year's time if he suddenly finds out. Or we tell him. Wouldn't it be more honest to tell him now?'

Bel regarded him soberly. 'Are you really thinking of Walter, Larry? Or are you afraid that in a year's time we

193

might feel differently about each other? That, like so many affairs, ours will lose its intensity?'

He was silent.

Bel went on, 'Suppose we tell Walter now and he thinks it a "flash in the pan." He might say he'll consider a divorce in a year's time. Would that be too long to wait?'

'Much too long! A month is too long for me.'

'I know. For me, too, but Larry – it's all happened so quickly and I feel rushed. You're scaring me when I want just to be happy.'

'I could make you happy. You don't love Walter.'

'I do – in a way. Oh, Larry, please let's delay all talk of divorce. You know I love you. Isn't that enough for now?'

'I would tell him. I wouldn't put you through that.'

'No, Larry. Not yet.'

'But you do love me. You do want us to be together, don't you?'

'When the time's right.'

He glanced at her as he turned into the road next to hers and parked the car. Bel was filled with compassion as he reached for her hand. 'Bel, I want you so much. More than ever after . . . after what's happened today. And I can't bear to think of you and Walter—' He swallowed. 'You know what I mean, Bel. I don't want anyone else to touch you.'

She hesitated. 'He rarely does, Larry. That's all I can say.'

'I'm so *jealous*!' he groaned. 'I'm not pleased with myself but . . .' He spread his hands in a gesture of helplessness. 'I never expected to feel this way, and that's the truth.'

'I understand, but I can't help you. I think we should carry on as we are for a while. Let a little time pass, Larry. Please, darling, for my sake. And today has been so wonderful. We mustn't spoil it.'

'And you do love me – even though I am a—'

Bel put a finger to his lips. 'Whatever you are is fine by

194

me,' she told him. 'I love you, remember? Now I really must go.'

After a final kiss she left him, with nothing settled between them except that they would meet again on the following Monday. Larry had agreed that she could write to him again at his chambers as long as she marked the letter 'Personal'. At the corner she turned for a last glimpse of him. As she approached her own steps she felt tremendously lonely and, with a flash of insight, realised for the first time that love brings pain as well as joy.

She was still considering this unpalatable truth when Mrs Parks appeared from the direction of the kitchen, and one glance at her face told Bel that something was wrong. Everything else was driven from her thoughts, to be replaced by a sense of apprehension.

'What is it?' Wild thoughts rushed through her mind. Walter had found out and was waiting to confront her! She lowered her voice. 'Is it my husband? Is he here?'

'No, ma'am, but—'

'There's been an accident! Is it Mr Roberts?' She was swamped with guilt.

'No, ma'am. It's Mrs Banks. She's in the kitchen and she's—'

'Mrs Banks? From Cardington?' Bel stared at her, astonished. 'Whatever is she doing here?'

'She's been here since eleven o'clock, so I gave her a bite to eat. Just a bit of ham and—'

'Oh, yes. Good.' She handed her coat to the housekeeper. 'Did she say what was wrong?'

'She wouldn't say anything except that no one had died. Shall I send her to you in the sitting room?'

'Yes. Send her through, please.'

She hurried upstairs to the bathroom and closed the door. Mrs Banks should be busy about the house at Cardington, and the fact that she was here was ominous.

Bel went downstairs and paused outside the sitting room,

breathing deeply to calm her nerves. She wanted to look as composed as possible in the circumstances. It had been the most exceptional day of her life, and she wanted only to sink into a chair and think about Larry and the time they had spent together. That pleasure was obviously going to be denied her. The world, it seemed, was determined to intrude on their happiness.

'Mrs Banks—' she began as she entered the room, but the housekeeper gave her no time to complete her sentence. Struggling to her feet, she clutched her handbag to her defensively. Her face was pale, her expression one of outrage. Bel could not imagine what had happened.

'I can't stay – that is, I've given my notice, ma'am,' she stammered, 'and nothing you can say will change my mind. I *won't* stay in that house with that madman around. I don't feel safe and that's the truth.'

'Madman? My husband?' Bel stared at her in astonishment. 'What on earth has he done to—'

'Not Mr Roberts, ma'am, although he's to blame as well. At least – that is – what I mean . . .' Her face crumpled suddenly and she fumbled in her bag and produced a handkerchief. She blew her nose while she struggled with her faltering composure. Bel watched with concern. The housekeeper was *frightened*, she thought with dismay, and Walter was somehow to blame.

'Sit down, Mrs Banks,' she said firmly, setting an example by seating herself. 'Then take a deep breath and start at the beginning. At the moment I don't understand what you're talking about.'

Slowly Mrs Banks lowered herself into the chair, but her fingers around the handbag were white at the knuckles. 'It's him again – that young man. The one called Howard. The one that trespassed.' Her voice was high with suppressed anger.

Bel said quietly, 'That young man. I see.' She gave the housekeeper an encouraging smile. 'There's no hurry, Mrs

Banks. Please take your time.' But the knot in her stomach had tightened.

'He's a madman, that one. Dangerous. He threw a rock through the window and Mr Roberts—'

Bel's assumed calm was shattered momentarily. 'Threw a rock – good heavens!'

'You may well say that, ma'am! Right through the sitting-room window. He broke the pot of ferns, and you should have seen the mess. The windows all smashed and glass everywhere and – and that lovely carpet. Ruined, I wouldn't wonder.'

'Never mind the carpet. Tell me what happened next. Were you in the house on your own?'

'No, ma'am, but in some ways I wish I had been!' Mrs Banks told her, 'because *I'd* have called the police and no mistake! That's what the police are *for*. Wouldn't *you* have called them?'

'I think so. Yes, I would.'

'A man like that – he could do anything. But no!' She trembled with rage. 'Mr Roberts goes outside looking for him. "Where are you?" he's calling. "We must talk."' She snorted. 'Talk? I'd give him more than talk, if I had my way. And going out there alone! I was terrified, ma'am, and I'm not ashamed to say so. If that madman had wanted to kill Mr Roberts, it would have been dead easy and then it would have been my turn. Because I'd have been a witness, ma'am.'

'You *saw* him?'

'Not exactly, but I was there. I don't mind admitting I stood there and I shook in my shoes. I mean, while the master was out in the garden the wretch could have come after *me*! I was all defenceless, I was.'

Bel could imagine it all happening. 'Poor Mrs Banks. How dreadful for you.' But why had Walter refused to call the police – unless her suspicion was correct and they were father and son? For a moment, in her mind's eye, she saw

Walter wandering the garden, calling for Howard, and felt a stab of sympathy for both men. With an effort she returned her attention to the housekeeper.

'Dreadful's the word, ma'am. You were well out of it. I said to myself at the time, "Thank goodness poor Mrs Roberts isn't here." At least *you* were safe.'

Bel thought this noble sentiment a little unlikely, but she let it pass.

Gaining confidence now, Mrs Banks went on, 'But would Mr Roberts phone the police? No, he would *not* – although I begged and pleaded with him. He said he "sort of knew him and didn't want the police involved." And I was not to tell you. He was most insistent, I was not to worry you. Well, ma'am, I didn't like the sound of it and I . . . well, I didn't stop to think. I got up this morning, packed a bag and—' Her face crumpled again. 'I – I gave in my notice.'

'Never mind, Mrs Banks. We can always sort that out. I'm sure you didn't mean it.'

'Well, yes and no, ma'am. I don't mean it now, but I did at the time. I thought if he wants to lie in his bed waiting to be murdered, that's his lookout, but he ought to think of me. I tossed and turned all night, frightened to close my eyes in case he came in at the window. That rock could have killed one of us. And it was *from our own rockery*! What cheek! I could have wrung the young devil's neck. And to think he was out there all that time, watching and spying on us. I mean, suppose one of us had gone outside to fetch something and he'd jumped on us? It gives me the collywobbles—'

'Poor Mrs Banks.' Bel crossed to her and patted her shoulder. 'I'm really sorry you've had to go through all this. I must admit I don't understand it, but of course I'll talk to my husband.' She thought quickly. Perhaps she should go up to Cardington and find out from Walter just what was going on. She hated the thought of leaving

198

London because she would be so far away from Larry, but she knew she ought to go. Walter might need her and, apart from her desire to establish Howard's identity, she didn't want to lose the housekeeper. In his present mood, Walter might need to be persuaded to take her back.

'I think the best thing is for us both to have a good night's rest here and then we'll travel to Cardington together tomorrow.' She smiled. 'I'll brave the lion in his den and solve the mystery. I expect there's a perfectly good explanation for everything. How does that sound?'

Mrs Banks brightened a little. 'Well, if you think so, ma'am. I'd be ever so grateful. I really do like Mr Roberts, and I hate to think of him eating at the canteen all the time. But I can't do with being in that house on my own if that young thug is—'

Bel held up a placatory hand. 'Not another word. I'm truly sorry that you have had such a dreadful experience and I understand how you feel. I will deal with everything, Mrs Banks. You will be in no danger, I promise you.' She forced a cheerful smile 'Now, is it agreed?'

It was.

*

Next morning, after a delayed start, they caught the 10 o'clock train to Cardington. Bel had telephoned the house to find out whether or not Walter was there but, having received no answer, she decided against ringing his office. She hoped to have a chance to see for herself what had happened and to have some time to think it over. The first thing she saw when she opened the front door of the house was a hand-written envelope with no stamp.

'I'll take that!' she exclaimed and scooped it from the mat. It bore the words 'MR ROBERTS' and she quickly thrust it into her pocket.

Mrs Banks looked at her sharply. 'Is it from *him*?'

'I don't know. It doesn't matter for the moment.' She

prayed that the housekeeper had not had time to read the envelope.

A quick tour of the house convinced her that her husband was not at home. The window in the sitting room had obviously been re-glazed and the carpet, thankfully, had suffered very little. Bel listened impatiently as the housekeeper delivered another lengthy account of the incident.

Finally she said 'Well, back to work, Mrs Banks.'

Mrs Banks looked nervous. 'But when Mr Roberts comes home and finds me here?'

'I'll say you came to me because you were worried about his safety, and I persuaded you to return. How does that sound?'

Mrs Banks' face brightened and she nodded eagerly. 'That sounds about right,' she said. 'I mean, I *was* worried about him.'

'That's settled, then. Now, it must be nearly lunch time and we had no breakfast. See if you can find something for our lunch, will you?'

'And leave me to read this letter in peace!' she thought as the housekeeper hurried away. It was, as she suspected, from Howard and it started with the word 'Dad'! For a moment the word danced before her eyes. *Dad*! She forced herself to read on

> How did you like a rock through your window? You should have given me the tenner, you miserable skin-flint. And *her*. She's as bad. It won't be the last you hear from me. And you are in for a nasty shock. But not just yet. Being your son is about the worst thing I can imagine. I hope that being my father is not so good either.
>
> Howard

The letter was hastily scribbled in pencil, but the spelling was correct. What struck Bel like a physical blow was the venomous tone of the message. How could a boy hate his own father as much as this one did? And Walter *was* his father; that much was clear. Horribly clear. And the word 'her' had been underlined. She supposed uneasily that it was natural the boy would hate her, too. In Howard's eyes, she and Walter were presumably tarred with the same brush. And it had been delivered by hand, which meant that he must be living in the neighbourhood – unless he spent his time rushing between London and Cardington.

She said, 'Howard! *Howard*!' as if by saying his name she could conjure him from wherever he was hiding. She thought suddenly of Karma's comment about the 'W' and the 'H' intertwined. Father and son – You couldn't get much closer than that. She recalled that first encounter with Howard in the garden. She had found him difficult though hardly a menace, but maybe Mrs Banks had been right about him. He had looked pleasant enough, but it was now apparent that his feelings towards Walter were spiteful in the extreme. So was he unbalanced?

'. . . It won't be the last you hear from me . . . you are in for a nasty shock . . .'

She stared unseeing out of the window. What was he going to do next? Set fire to the house? Or was it a bluff? And if so, did Walter know the boy well enough to call his bluff? Howard had thrown a rock through the window, risking police involvement. Unless Howard had *known* that his father would not pursue the matter? If so, then *how* did he know? Unless he had trapped Walter between a rock and a hard place! She saw the unintended pun and did not find it amusing.

Walter would not want to risk any kind of scandal just before the R101 was due to fly to India . . . She frowned, turning the offending letter over and over in her fingers. Poor Walter. Suddenly her heart ached for him; he wouldn't know how to deal with this. She would have to show him the letter, but was there anything she could do to help?

Perhaps the best course of action would be to ask the police to find Howard and caution him. They need not make any formal charges. A caution might be a sufficient deterrent.

'Damn him!' she cried.

If only she and Walter had been closer he might have confided in her earlier and this could have been avoided.

Mrs Banks came to the door of the sitting room and said' There's a bit of ham and I could fry up some cold potatoes. Would that do?'

'Yes, fine.'

Bel tried to think of Larry, but the few stolen hours on the river now seemed a million light years away. A fantasy. Worse, she felt a terrible burden of guilt. While she and Larry were betraying Walter, he had been struggling alone with the problem of his son. The timing was cruel. She almost wished she could turn back the clock and undo their lovemaking, but that would be to deny Larry and she loved him. Damn them all! she thought miserably. She had fallen deeply in love for the first time in her life. All she really wanted was to enjoy the thought of him, remember their time together and make plans for their next meeting. But that was selfish and fate was conspiring against her; putting every conceivable object in the way.

'Damn and blast them!'

Suddenly she screwed up the letter and threw it across the room. Then she followed it with a cushion. Then, in a moment of rising frustration, she snatched up a glass ash-tray and hurled it against the opposite wall. It narrowly missed one of Walter's favourite pictures and fell to the floor, where the carpet saved it. At that moment she knew exactly how Walter's son had felt when he threw the rock.

Badly shaken, she sat down, dismayed by her uncharacteristic behaviour. She might have broken both the ash-tray and the picture. She could never recall having behaved so badly. Marie, perhaps; she could imagine Marie's fiery temper erupting. Her sister-in-law could no doubt hurl things – and with unerring aim! But not me, Bel thought, appalled. She sighed heavily. When Walter talked to her about his son she would try to understand, she would try not to condemn the boy out of hand. No doubt Walter would be upset and ashamed of Howard's behaviour, but he must surely feel some love for him? She was aware of a great sadness. Had things been different, Howard could have been so proud of his talented father and could have shared with him the excitement of the airship's development. Instead he had been forced by circumstances to stay out of sight if not out of mind. Oh, God! What a mess. And the woman, Howard's mother. She too was hidden away somewhere, perhaps bribed to remain silent with a weekly cheque. Poor woman ... And all the time Bel herself had enjoyed a pampered existence, taking her good fortune for granted, unaware of the unhappy undercurrents in Walter's life. She bit her lip, ashamed of her lack of perception. Perhaps she had never cared enough to wonder at his moods?

She murmured, 'Walter! My poor darling!' She had been shallow and unthinking, wrapped up in her own selfish pursuit of pleasure. And now she had compounded all her earlier mistakes by being unfaithful. The thought was like a knife thrust, but there was no way she could deny her love for Larry. That would never change. She might live the rest of her life as Walter's wife, trying to make up for all those miserable years, but the thought of Larry would be there, burning brightly into her soul. They might have to part, but he would know that she loved only him. She drew a long breath and felt years older. On leaden legs she crossed the room, retrieved the cushion and replaced it on the sofa. Then she picked up the ash-tray and returned it to the coffee table. Reluctantly she took up Howard's letter and sat down again. She felt so tired, as though her life-force was draining away.

'Think, you fool!' she told herself angrily. She needed a plan of action. She smoothed out the letter and stared at the crumpled sheet. At once her thoughts reverted to the boy's mother. Was it that woman they had met on holiday, all those years ago? Veronica. Or was it Vera? One or the other. If so, where had Walter been hiding her all this time? And did she know that he had married? And had *she* ever married? A new thought struck her. Was Howard the *only* child Veronica had borne him? If it was Veronica. If not, then who had given Walter the son he had always wanted? She put both hands over her face, exhausted by the unending possibilities and unwelcome revelations. Her throat was tight with misery and she longed for the relief of tears, but her eyes remained dry.

'I must talk to you, Walter' she whispered. Perhaps she would tell him everything about Larry, and he could confide in her, and then there would be an end to all the secrets. Whatever followed would spring from knowledge and understanding instead of deceits. Wearily she got to her feet and picked up the letter. She and Walter must talk, and the sooner the better.

Chapter Ten

THAT SAME EVENING Walter stood in the Personnel Office, smiling at a middle-aged woman who was searching through the drawer marked 'P–T'.

She said, 'Roberts . . . Roberts, D . . . F . . . Ah! Here it is. Roberts, H.' She pulled the sheet clear and said, 'Roberts, Howard W. Is that the one?'

He nodded. 'I thought I might as well drop the letter in at his door. It's no trouble.'

'Are you sure?' She looked vaguely surprised – no doubt aware that the high-ups did not normally trouble themselves to redirect mail. She handed him the sheet and, with a start, Walter saw his son's particulars – height, weight, physical description, age, education . . . He memorised the address in Shortstown and handed it back with a 'thank you.'

The woman moved to the window. 'I might be able to point him out to you,' she suggested, eager to help. 'I'd recognise him; he's one of the new ones.' Peering down through the window she narrowed her eyes, and Walter obligingly moved to stand beside her. The shift had just ended and dozens of men and women were making their way home. For a moment she said nothing, studying the faces, then suddenly she pointed. 'Look! There he is, just rounding the corner with the bike and his arm round the girl.' She stared hard. 'It's Peggy Clark. They've soon chummed up.' She smiled. 'He must be a fast worker; she was arm-in-arm with the Scotts' eldest boy a few weeks back.'

Surprised, he said, 'Do you know them all?'

She laughed, flattered by his interest. 'Most of them. I've been here for years and I've got a good memory for faces. It helps in this job. People come storming in with a grumble and I say,' 'Oh, Mr Green – or Brown or whoever! How nice to see you again. How can I help you!' She laughed. 'It takes the wind right out of their sails.'

After exchanging a few more pleasantries, Walter thanked her for her help and hurried downstairs. He had come to a decision. He would stay on and work late, and then when it was dark he would drive round and park the car and wait for Howard. They would almost certainly go out for a beer, and then they could sit in the car and talk it out. He would give him the money on condition that Howard stopped his campaign of harassment. If he was desperate for money – if he had got a girl into trouble, perhaps – he would make it more. At least he would understand *that* predicament, he thought wryly. A case of history repeating itself with a vengeance. But he would be firm with the boy. Grow up, he would tell him. Live in the real world; you're an adult now. If he loved the girl he should marry her and *live* with her. Howard must not make his father's mistake. And whatever happened he must not lose his temper with him, nor would he threaten or cajole. He would talk to him as honestly as he could.

He felt a slight lightening of his heart. It was going to be difficult, but he thought he could handle it, that he could resolve the problem and then go down to London and tell Bel the whole truth, knowing that they had nothing more to fear. He could avert the threatened catastrophe, he promised himself with a glimmer of hope – as though wanting could make it so.

Back in his office, he realised that he could do with a bath and some clean pyjamas. There was nobody at home, so he would go back and get what he needed. He was sorry about Mrs Banks, but she had behaved very badly. It was her decision to leave, but there would be plenty of willing souls ready to take her place. That Bel would grumble was the least of his worries. He hummed to himself as he climbed into the car. The new fern should have been delivered by now – he had told the fellow at the nursery to leave it in the greenhouse. By the time Bel next came up to Cardington there would be no trace of the disturbance.

He had parked the car and was hanging up his coat in the hall when he realised with a sinking heart that he was not alone in the house. Someone was moving about upstairs in the main bedroom.

'Howard!' he whispered and his heart began to race, thudding painfully against his ribs as all his good intentions fled. He was filled with a bitter anguish as he saw the end of all his hopes. '*Howard!*' he repeated and the word seemed to mock him. He would thrash the young fool. Anger flared murderously as he took the stairs two at a time, and his hands were clenched into fists as he burst into the bedroom.

A few steps inside the room he stopped in shocked surprise and the furious phrases withered on his lips. Bel was sitting by the dressing table, brushing her hair. Her reflection smiled nervously at him and then she turned towards him.

'Walter!'

For a moment he could only stare at her wordlessly. She had been crying, he noticed, and all his carefully made plans fell apart. She would be wondering where Mrs Banks was.

'Isobel!' he said weakly.

To his surprise she stood up and moved to him at once

207

and put her arms round him. 'Walter. I've been such a selfish pig. Do say you forgive me.' Her beautiful face was very pale.

He tried to say something, but suddenly his throat was dry; he was confused and resentful at the ruin of his carefully laid plan. Reluctantly he felt the initiative slipping away from him and experienced a prickle of fear. He needed to be in control but instead he felt terribly vulnerable.

He stammered, 'Of course you're not selfish. Whatever do you mean?'

She stood back and looked at him and he felt uneasily that she was searching for something in his expression.

He asked, 'Why are you here? Has something happened?'

'Dear Walter, I would have understood. At least I think so.'

He thought he saw compassion in her eyes and that frightened him. 'You're talking in riddles,' he snapped. 'Tell me—' He heard another sound from downstairs.

She anticipated his question. 'It's Mrs Banks. I talked her into coming back.'

Again he felt the pain in his heart. He was not ready for this. He pulled away from her and sat on the bed. 'Just tell me!' he said hoarsely.

By way of an answer she handed him a crumpled sheet of paper and sat down again at the dressing table. She tried to brush her hair but he saw that her hand trembled.

He read: 'Dad . . .'

'Oh, Bel!' he whispered, stricken.

'Read it all, Walter, and then we'll talk.'

He read on while his heart continued its uneasy rhythm and there was a roaring in his ears. He felt very cold and heavy and the words danced before his eyes.

'Bel, dear,' he stammered. 'I – I want you to know—'

She said gently, 'You don't have to tell me, Walter. He's

your son, your illegitimate son. I put two and two together and it wasn't too difficult. I want to say that there's no need for us to quarrel over this. I want to help you to sort it out . . .'

He closed his eyes, barely able to hear her for the noise in his head. Was it his blood rushing round? He felt faint.

Her voice came as though from a great distance. 'I've thought about it, Walter, and I think it's too much for you to deal with alone. You must let me help. I could meet your . . . I could meet Howard and talk to him. Try to befriend him, maybe.'

Walter shook his head as his earlier euphoria vanished. She had no idea. The boy hated them both and nothing she could say would save the situation.

She was frowning. 'Walter? Do you hear me? Are you ill? *Walter!*'

'What . . . ?'

'You look terrible!'

He said, 'I'll be all right. Don't fuss.'

But would he, he wondered, his panic growing. The thudding in his heart had become a fierce ache. It was the shock, he told himself. Nothing more than that. She *knew!*

She pulled the stool towards him and sat close, holding his hands, and he realised how much he loved and needed her.

'Walter, I want you to know how sorry I am about – about all this.' She waved a hand vaguely. 'We can talk it over. You're not *alone* any more – that's what I want to tell you. And I'm not angry. Shocked, of course, but I'm trying to understand. Walter? Are you listening?'

He nodded. The pain in his chest was definitely getting worse. Suppose this was a heart attack and he died? Suppose he had only hours, only *minutes*, to live. He felt a desperate urgency to unburden himself completely. 'Howard . . .' he began.

'Yes?'

'You're wrong, my dear. How on earth can I tell you this?'

'He *isn't*?' Her beautiful eyes were full of confusion and he felt a rush of panic. He would lose her. He closed his eyes to avoid seeing the pain he must inflict. 'He isn't my illegitimate son ... The boy is *legitimate*.' As the silence lengthened he was forced to open his eyes and saw the disbelief on her face.

'*Legitimate?* But that would mean – If he is ...' She swallowed. 'You were *married* to his mother? To Veronica?'

He took a deep breath and bent over, doubled up with pain. This is what he had never wanted her to know; it would crucify her. And yet he needed to confess, to be honest, whatever the consequences. 'Vera *still is my wife*,' he said hoarsely.

She snatched back her hand and he heard the quick intake of breath as the realisation finally dawned.

'*Walter*! My God, Walter! You're not saying ...' Her voice became a whisper. '*We're not married?* I don't believe it!'

She slipped from the chair to her knees so that she could look up into his eyes. She said, 'Say it isn't true! Oh, God, Walter! All these years we've lived together and—'

He saw her fall back, her hands over her face. He wanted to comfort her, but his thoughts were whirling darkly and the room seemed to tilt. He felt very strange and then his vision deserted him and he knew no more.

*

The doctor smiled. 'Well, Mrs Roberts ...' She seemed to flinch, he thought, surprised. But shock does strange things to people. He glanced down at the sleeping patient. 'Your husband has had a lucky escape. It was a heart attack, but a mild one.'

Bel nodded dully. She was very pale and had been

crying. Probably quite a stunner when she was at her best, he thought. Pretty figure and that lovely hair. His senior partner had teased him. 'You take the call', he had said. 'Give your eyes a treat. Mrs Roberts is a knock-out!' Not that she was looking too good today, but he would give her a sedative. Thank goodness the housekeeper seemed a sensible soul. He snapped his bag shut. 'Plenty of rest and loving care,' he said. She did not smile. Had she heard what he said?

The houseeper said, 'He'll get that, doctor. Don't you worry.'

They both looked very distressed, but it was natural enough. He said, 'Mrs Roberts—' She gave him a strange look. 'I'll call in first thing in the morning to see how he is. We won't take any chances. But no excitement. None at all. You must keep him calm.'

The housekeeper glanced quickly at her mistress and the doctor had a feeling that he was missing something. Having a wife like Mrs Roberts must be something of an excitement for a man twenty years her senior, he reflected. Could that have brought on the attack? He had heard his partner tell of a patient who died 'on the job'. Mind you, *he* was about eighty, so he'd had a good innings.

He went on, 'What the Victorians called "bed rest" and a light diet.' He was puzzled. Still no real response from Mrs Roberts. The housekeeper took a few steps forward and asked, 'Fish, a jelly, a custard?'

'Exactly. Bit of poached chicken. I'm sure he's in good hands.' 'Don't worry, Mrs Roberts. Your husband is in no danger. Given a little time, he'll be his old self again.'

She looked at him. 'Will he?'

'Oh, yes!' He smiled at her; he wouldn't be averse to a little loving care from this one. Her expression had not altered and he frowned slightly. Suddenly it dawned on him. Of course, this was *the* Walter Roberts, one of the boffins involved with the Cardington airship. They were probably concerned that he would miss the prestigious flight. He said, 'He'll be fine in a week or two. She's not due to leave until the end of September, according to the papers, and it's only the twenty-eighth of August. He won't miss the flight. You can reassure him on that score when he wakes up.'

He expected sighs of relief all round, but was disappointed. The housekeeper still looked uncomfortable. Perhaps there had been a row of some kind. Perhaps the housekeeper had been at fault and an argument had developed. When an attack followed a row the survivors often felt guilty, blaming themselves for what had happened. And they rarely disclosed details to the doctor. The more he thought about it, the more likely this appeared.

He said, 'He'll still see India, Mrs Roberts. You, too, perhaps. You know what they say. You can tango all the way to Karachi! I read yesterday that they are taking a supply of Ambrose's records to dance to.' He gave her a long look and went on 'I wish I were going with you!' Then he laughed boyishly but still elicited no response. Trying for the last time for some reaction, he smiled. His smile had been known to melt the coldest women. 'I'll send a lad up with the two prescriptions. Your husband will sleep now, probably right through the night. If he wakes and is in any discomfort, give him one of the tablets in the small bottle. *Your* pills will be in a little box. Take two on retiring, but only until you're over the shock. Don't make a habit of it.' He held out his hand.

Bel shook it and smiled faintly. He held her hand a shade longer than was necessary, then nodded to the housekeeper who led the way downstairs.

At the door he paused. 'Mrs Roberts seems to be taking this very hard. Keep an eye on her, won't you? We don't want two patients for you to look after instead of one!'

'I will, doctor.'

The door closed before he was half-way down the steps.

212

He swung the starting handle and climbed into the car. Very odd, he reflected, slamming the door. He usually won the wives over. Perhaps he was losing his touch! He grinned and released the brake. Perhaps he would have better luck in the morning.

*

Two days later Larry re-read Bel's letter with a sense of deepening confusion. What she had told him was almost unbelievable.

> My dearest Larry,
>   I love you. Hold on to that thought as you read this hurried letter. I know it will cause you much grief and anxiety, but I beg you not to do anything hasty. I must have time to think.
>   To start at the beginning, there has been trouble here with the boy, Howard. I once told you I suspected he was Howard's son. He is, but he is his legal heir. Walter married the boy's mother years before we fell in love and he has never divorced her. Karma was right. We were *not* married! You will see where this leaves me! Unfortunately the boy has threatened us and has even thrown a rock through the window and Walter, for obvious reasons, refuses to notify the police. The strain of all this for Walter has brought on a mild heart attack, so I know no more details. The doctor has sedated him and we are all very upset. I have been able to send this letter to your home instead of your chambers, as you can say I was writing with news of the above. I hardly know what to think or where to turn, but you must, please, stay away until you hear from me. Naturally I was tempted to tell Walter about you and me, but now the moment has passed. Mrs Banks is afraid of what the boy might do and gave in her notice, but fortunately I persuaded

213

her to change her mind. So I am not alone in the house with an invalid, and you are not to worry.

If Walter is well enough I shall come to London as usual, as it my turn at the soup kitchen again. I will stay overnight, so we could meet. I am so desperate to see you again and to feel your arms around me. My instinct, when I first knew the whole truth, was to leave Walter and come straight to you, but he collapsed almost as the thought entered my head and now I cannot abandon him. But when he recovers we shall have to do some serious thinking. And, my dearest Larry, it is rather pleasant to think that when we made love we were *not* betraying my husband. I don't *have* a husband! It is such a strange feeling. I look at him, and he is still the same man but neither kith nor kin. I can't get used to it. I am a single, unmarried, spinster lady! Walter, however, is still a husband – but the husband of someone else. It goes round and round in my head and drives me crazy!

Write to me, here, my love, and tell me that you still love me. I am desperately in need of comfort. Without you there would be no light at the end of this dark and dreary tunnel!

There is no chance that Walter will see the letter as he is confined to bed. God bless you, my sweet Larry.

From your loving Bel

Larry whispered, 'Oh, *Bel!*' She was not Walter's wife; she was *nobody's* wife! She was a free woman! 'I can marry her!' he said, astounded. But a moment later his face fell. In the eyes of the world Bel and Walter *were* married, and in order to marry Larry she would have to tell the truth – that Walter was a bigamist – or *pretend* to get a divorce. And Walter must presumably have committed a crime. Bigamy was against the law and possibly he could be sent to prison. That would be disastrous. The resulting press coverage would destroy all those concerned in the deception, however innocent they might have been. Including Bel . . . And Walter was ill.

'God knows where it will all end!' he said despairingly. After a while he stood up. He must break the news to his father about Walter's heart attack – but it would be only the tip of the iceberg. The rest of the tragedy was still to come.

*

On the evening of the 1st of September, Walter was sitting up and looking a much better colour. The doctor had pronounced him 'the perfect patient' and Mrs Banks was given plenty of credit for the light but nourishing meals she had provided. Bel had tried to behave as though nothing untoward had happened, but she knew that each day brought them nearer to the inevitable discussion which she dreaded. As soon as Mrs Banks whisked away his supper tray, Walter said, 'Please, Bel. We must talk.'

She hesitated beside the bed. 'Are you sure it's wise?' she asked. 'Can we talk calmly? You mustn't get upset again'

'This silence – this pretending – is worse than talking. I must try to make you understand how it all just . . . happened. Dear Isobel! Please hear me out.'

She sat down reluctantly. 'Keep calm,' she told herself. 'Don't lose your temper and don't say anything you will regret. And *don't* tell him about Larry!'

He took several deep breaths and she said quickly, 'You must stop if you feel the slightest pain. Promise me!'

He said sadly, 'Do you really care? Does it really matter to you if I live or die? After what I have done to you . . .'

She glanced down at her clasped hands without comment.

'You must hate me. I deserve that.'

She said, 'I don't hate you. Just tell me, Walter.'

215

For a long time he struggled to begin and then the words came slowly and painfully. She listened silently, intrigued and dismayed in equal proportions.

'You remember the holiday we took in Paris with your parents? You recall the girl I met? A very shy girl, but she rather fell for me and, to tell you the truth, I was flattered. I took her out a few times and Geoff and your mother ribbed me about her. I had never had a girl-friend. I really wasn't interested in women.'

'But you've always said you wanted a son.'

'That came later, when I saw how it could be. I wanted a son I could *claim*, a son I need not keep hidden away like a guilty secret. At the time when I met Vera I wanted to keep my life uncomplicated. I was interested only in my career, in making a name for myself . . . Does that sound pretentious?'

'Not really.'

'I wasn't particularly interested in the opposite sex.' He paused. 'I was not in love with Vera and I never have been.'

Bel simply nodded her head. She could not watch the agony in his eyes as he spoke of the youthful folly that had somehow led them all to this impossible situation.

'Poor Vera. She was such a funny little thing and so vulnerable. One night we went out on our own and . . . and drank too much.' He lowered his voice. 'You can guess what happened. I admit it; I took advantage of her. Afterwards I was ashamed, but I went back to England, expecting that to be the end of it. A foolish holiday romance. She wrote to me saying that she loved me but I didn't answer. I thought she would get over it. I told Geoff and we had a bit of a laugh; it didn't seem terribly important. To tell you the truth, I forgot all about her. Then a few months later she wrote to me in such a state. She was – she was pregnant, and terrified to tell her parents. I sent her some money to get rid of the child.'

216

'Oh, Walter!' The reproach was uttered before she could restrain the words. 'I'm sorry,' she said quickly. 'I don't mean to reproach you.'

He swallowed and she could see the misery in his eyes.

'You may look at me like that,' he said, 'but these things happen all the time and I was equally terrified – of the responsibility. The thought of having a wife and child was anathema to me. It was the most frightful time for both of us.'

Bel said, 'But Howard survived to throw a rock through our window!' She regretted the bitter words as soon as they were out, but Walter merely nodded.

'I almost told my father, but then my courage failed. I was afraid he would despise me for my stupidity, and that all my friends would see what a fool I was to be trapped that way. Geoff was a tower of strength. He assured me it would all blow over; he said all the things I needed to hear.'

Bel sighed. 'It was all very human,' she said. Poor Walter. She was beginning to imagine his dilemma.

'Vera sent the money back,' Walter told her. 'She said she loved me and she wanted the baby. She asked me to marry her: *she* asked *me*. It was such a sad, humble little letter and it touched my heart. Not for herself, she said, but for the child. And for her parents who were so upset about everything. I felt terribly sorry for her and for them, and for the baby and –' He swallowed again. 'This is so difficult. Thinking about it in retrospect, I should have done the decent thing. I should have married her and lived with them, but I was selfish; I talked to Geoff, but your mother never did know. We worked out a compromise and I married her. We went to France for a "holiday", just the two of us. We stayed with Evie's Pierre and his family and were married in a little church on the outskirts of Paris. No music, no confetti, just a few smiles and plenty of heartache. I hadn't had the courage to tell her that I was

217

never going to be with her.' He shook his head, anguished. 'Oh, I was going to look after them financially, but apart from that I didn't want to be involved. We spent a few days together and then I told her. Vera was heartbroken when she realised. I borrowed some money and put a down payment on a house in Deal, and I moved her in.' His mouth trembled. 'I've never forgotten the expression on her face as I left her there.'

Bel heard the tremor in his voice and her own throat was tight as she said, 'How dreadful for you both.'

Walter flashed her a brief glance, acknowledging her sympathy and then, with a visible effort, went on with the sad tale.

'She had the child, a boy—'

'Howard?'

'Yes. She and her parents made the best of it. They told their friends that I worked abroad a lot, and they probably tried to believe it. But financially Vera was secure and the house was in her name. I visited from time to time and suddenly – much to my surprise – I began to enjoy the boy.' He glanced at Bel, almost apologetically. 'He was a loving little soul. Hard for you to imagine, but he was. I blame myself for the change in him. He needed me and I wasn't there. He loved me, they both did, and I neglected them. Oh, God!' He wiped tears from his eyes.

Bel said, 'You're getting upset, Walter. Perhaps you should finish it some other time . . .' She put some conviction into her voice, but she hoped he would continue.

'No. I must finish now. I've wanted to tell you for such a long time. It's been a burden for so long.'

He struggled with his emotions, and Bel knew that a gesture of sympathy was needed but found it impossible to reach out to him. His evident affection for his abandoned family hurt her more than she had expected, and made her realise that she had lived with a stranger all these years. *Her* Walter Roberts was a respectable citizen; a pillar of the church. The real Walter Roberts had been leading a double life. She, Bel, had never been his wife; she had never known him at all. Trying to imagine the countless lies he must have told her over the years made her feel a fool, and that angered her.

He went on, 'Nobody in my family knew, and I wanted to keep it that way. I began to think that I had got away with it. I saw no reason why I shouldn't maintain the deception indefinitely.'

His expression was one of self-loathing and Bel felt an unexpected pang of compassion. How, she wondered, could she have loved the man and not seen his pain? How could she have failed to see the agony he was going through? She must have been blind – or heartless. Swallowing hard, she felt a wave of guilt. She had not cared enough, not loved him enough. She said, 'Walter, I've been so—'

But he held up a hand imperatively. 'Don't stop me, Bel. I must tell it all while I still can. Please!'

She nodded. Then impulsively she leaned over, took one of his hands and kissed it.

He said harshly, '*Don't*! I don't deserve it . . .' After a moment he went on, his voice raw with regret. 'The R38 crashed and Geoff was killed. You began to figure in my life – just a sad, lonely young woman who had lost her father. I was so desperately sorry for you, losing him, and we both missed him so much it drew us together and suddenly . . .' He looked at her. 'Suddenly the unthinkable happened. I was in love – for the very first time. I was in love with you. Head over heels! I didn't know what had happened to me. It was so wonderful. All I wanted was you, maybe partly because you were part of Geoff. You can see how appalling that was for me, can't you?' She smiled faintly and he went on, 'In the circumstances, I mean. Falling in love when I was already secretly married.'

'Yes, I can.'

219

'You seemed to love me in return, and everyone was so pleased and happy and no one but Geoff had known about Vera. What could I do? I was desperately afraid of losing you, but I couldn't find it in my heart to abandon Vera. She'd been so brave, struggling alone to bring up my child, and never once reproaching me. I was almost out of my head with worry.' He sighed. 'I couldn't believe that I had messed up all our lives so thoroughly. Finally I thought that I would take a chance and pretend to marry you. I knew it was a risk, but I was desperate. I arranged for us to go on that cruise and persuaded the captain to marry us.'

Bel sat silent, remembering the spur-of-the-moment excitement. One of the passengers had lent her a white evening dress, and Walter had produced a wedding ring left to him by his grandfather. They had stood together on a moonlit deck with the ship's band playing appropriate music. Bel had thought it the most wonderful, most romantic day of her life. Now she saw it as a fraud, a criminal offence.

She put a hand to her head. 'So we are *not* married and never have been.'

'Oh, Bel! What can I say?'

A thought struck her. 'But Walter! Suppose I – suppose we had had a child!'

'I thought of that. Then I *would* have told Vera everything and arranged a divorce. Then you would have had to know and, hopefully, because of the child—'

'I would have forgiven you and agreed to marry you legally?'

He nodded. 'I was trying to ensure that if you had a child, neither your child nor Vera's would be illegitimate. I wouldn't have had *that* on my conscience.' He glanced up. '*Would* you have married me? If I'd been forced to tell you the truth?'

For the very first time she was grateful that they had

never had a child. 'I don't know.' She thought about it, frowning intently, trying to see herself pregnant and faced with such devastating news. 'I suppose so, for the child's sake.'

'God! What a bloody awful mess! You must despise me. When Vera knows, it will break her heart.' His eyes filled with tears and for a moment he sobbed uncontrollably. Bel put her arms around him but they both knew that nothing and nobody could ever bring him solace or the peace of mind he craved. The mistakes had been made and there was no way to undo the harm he had inflicted; no way to unravel the tangle. The most terrible remorse would follow him to his grave.

When at last he had recovered a little, she managed a smile. 'Somehow we'll sort this out. There must be a way—' But she could not see one and the expression on Walter's face showed her that he, too, knew the hopelessness of the situation.

After a while she asked, 'And does Vera know about me – about us?'

'I've never told her. But Howard, of course, has made it his business to find out. He believes that I was never married to his mother. He hates me and you can hardly blame him. I understand that he is goaded beyond endurance, seeing what luxury you and I enjoy. I suppose he sees himself as the avenging angel—'

'He's doing it rather well!' said Bel and, unintentionally, her tone was a little sharp. 'I can see why he feels that way, but what worries me is the hostility . . . the violence. Do you think he intends us any *real* harm? Physical violence, I mean? You must tell me honestly, Walter, because if so I would like to call in the police, just to caution him. Not to bring any charges against him—'

'Vera would be horrified!'

She hardened her heart. 'Vera isn't being threatened,

221

Walter. I am and you are – and indirectly Mrs Banks. Suppose he carries out his threats?'

'He won't. I shall talk to him. I intended to, but then this happened.' He indicated his bedridden state. 'But as soon as I'm about again . . .'

Bel hesitated. 'Could we ask him here? To meet and talk with us? To try and explain about this whole mess.'

Walter shook his head. 'I know you mean well, Bel, but I don't think he'd come. And if he did it would be rather like rubbing salt in a wound. Look at our elegant home – and so on. It might make things worse. I just don't know. You may be right but . . . I don't seem to know anything any more . . .'

He fell silent, breathing heavily.

Bel said, 'That's enough for one day, Walter. You're tired, I can tell. Try to doze again if you can. Try to think about something else. Think about your work, the airship, the flight to India – anything to keep your mind off the immediate problems.'

He said, 'The airship? Oh, God, Bel! If you only knew—'

Startled, she asked 'Knew what?'

He shook his head. 'I hardly know myself. It's just a growing feeling that—I can't explain it. All that I touch is . . .' He shook his head, searching for the right words. 'Is *flawed*! Each part of my life – for the first time in my life I'm *afraid*!'

'Oh, Walter! Don't!' she cried, fearful in her turn.

But he continued as though he had not heard. 'Everything looks so dark. Dark, and darker still. As though storm-clouds are gathering. As though I'm waiting helplessly for the lightning to strike. It's like a bad dream from which you can never wake.' He closed his eyes, exhausted.

Bel felt a shiver of apprehension at his words. He had always been such a confident man, so sure of himself and the rightness of his opinions. A powerful, effective man.

222

Well-respected, and in control of his life. But all that had
been a sham and Howard had exposed the lie. Somewhere,
somehow, the son had overtaken the father, to strike him a
blow from which he could never recover. When – *if* – the
bigamous marriage became known, Walter's career would
be over. The airship industry would shudder amidst a
storm of scandalous publicity. Her heart lurched with
dread. Was that Howard's intention? To threaten his father
with exposure? And would they have to buy his silence?
Financially he could cripple his father . . . Walter's fear was
infectious and for the first time she saw what the boy could
do to them. None of them would survive unscathed. Her
own life would be blown apart, her future with Larry
threatened. What had Karma said? 'I see loss and I see
sorrow . . . A great confusion with a dark side to it . . . A
very dark side . . .' Well, her words had proved most prophetic. Terrifyingly so. 'Black, black and more black . . .'
Bel shivered.

Abruptly she faced up to an idea which had been at the
back of her mind for some days. Should she, without
telling Walter, find Howard and confront him? Should she
– *could* she – persuade him to give up this terrible vendetta?
Was there anything she could say that would turn him
away from his determination to inflict suffering? Walter
had said that he was a sweet child. Was that sweetness
there still, buried under many layers of resentment and
rejection? If so, then it was remotely possible that she
could bring about a miracle. The idea of seeking him out
scared her, but was it worth a try? Or would Howard seize
the opportunity to hurt her in order to hurt his father?
Perhaps she would talk to Larry about it – on second
thoughts, maybe not! Larry would almost certainly forbid
her to go anywhere near the boy, and probably he would
be wise to do so. And he might decide to approach
Howard himself and that, too, might prove a fatal mistake.
She shrank from the idea that Larry could be hurt. Damn

Howard! She sighed. But the thought of Larry cheered her momentarily. Her love for him and his for her were the only redeeming features in a complex and baffling situation. Somehow, some day this must all be over, resolved one way or the other, and then she and Larry could be together. She would cling to that.

Bel stood up. Walter had fallen into an exhausted sleep; he looked frail, broken both in heart and spirit, and she was jolted by a sense of irretrievable loss. The husband she had – no! She bit her lip fiercely – the *man* she had lived with all these years was almost a stranger.

Chapter Eleven

WHEN BEL ARRIVED At St Saviour's the following day and made her way down to the crypt, it was like returning to another life. Astonishing, she thought, that despite all her troubles at Cardington, life for the rest of the world still continued normally. Agatha was not there and Bel, tying on her apron, learned that Agatha's mother had finally died and she was arranging the funeral. A merciful release, they all agreed and Bel nodded, smiled and chatted to Mabel and Frances as though nothing untoward was happening; as though her whole life was not about to be turned upside down. The topics then ranged from their children to their pets and other interests, while Bel said as little as possible about hers.

On this Tuesday Margaret had cajoled the local fishmonger into giving them some cod, and this she had converted into a gigantic fish pie with the aid of a white sauce and a thick layer of mashed potato. The pudding was a bread pudding made with stale bread and some currants donated by Mabel's niece whose husband ran a restaurant. If anyone noticed Bel's distracted air no one commented on it, and she thought she was coping rather well until Margaret shocked her with a chance remark.

'I saw a friend of yours yesterday,' she said. 'Somebody Lampitt. We met at the theatre.'

Bel felt her face freeze. 'Oh – yes?'

'She sent her best regards. Said she had seen you and your brother-in-law enjoying a tête-à-tête in Selfridges. Or was it Dickens and Jones? Somewhere. It doesn't matter.'

'She's not exactly a friend,' Bel protested. 'It was – I mean she seemed to think we . . .' She broke off. How could she proclaim their innocence? Eventually she and Larry would be married and then Margaret would know. If Howard had his way, the whole world would know *everything*.

Margaret said, 'Oh, sorry! I didn't mean to say anything out of turn.'

She sounded surprised and Bel realised she had protested too vigorously. 'Mrs Lampitt – she's a . . .' Bel wanted to say 'terrible gossip', or suggest that Mrs Lampitt exaggerated, but her conscience intervened. Mrs Lampitt had seen them and had jumped to the correct conclusion. Hardly fair to blame her. Her words faltered in mid-sentence but she was saved by the clock. Upstairs the door was opened and their customers poured down the steps, so that the next ten minutes passed in a confusion of greetings and Bel was kept busy serving fish pie. Most of the regulars were there, with the addition of four new faces.

'Bless you ma'am!' said Gappy and she smiled at him.

Neville was once again the victim of an injustice. Charlie, he insisted, had a larger helping and it wasn't fair. Resisting the urge to shake him, Bel slapped another spoonful of potato on to his tin plate.

Mary crossed herself as she received her pie and whispered, 'Hail Mary!'

Barney, of the limited intelligence, was missing and they all worried about him.

Bel tried to concentrate on the work in hand but her thoughts strayed rebelliously. At least, she thought somewhat guiltily, she need have no fear that Walter would hear about herself and Larry. He was confined to bed and even

Mrs Lampitt could not reach him there. But that lady had obviously guessed the truth and she was busy sowing the seeds. The sooner they were able to tell Walter the truth, the better it would be for all of them. At the thought of Larry her spirits rose a little. Only a few hours and they would be together. Alone and together – for the entire night if they wished, for she had given Mrs Parks the night off. She would be able to wake in the morning and see him there beside her. And, as a single woman, she need not fear the fierce prickings of conscience she had suffered on the houseboat. She felt that after everything she had endured lately she was entitled to a few hours of happiness.

*

That evening she and Larry sat beside the fire and ate the cold meat and salad that they had bought from the local delicatessen. They had made love earlier and no doubt would do so again later – if, as Larry teased, his strength held out. For a few hours they had been content to enjoy each others' bodies and revel in the fact that they were together. Now, as they ate, the rest of the world intruded and the spectre of their predicament loomed large. They fell to discussing the extraordinary events of the past few days and Larry listened incredulously to Bel's account of Walter's marriage to Vera.

To Larry, it was all very simple.

'I'll come back with you tomorrow,' he said. 'I'll tell Walter that I love you and we are going to be married. Then we'll leave and come back here and –' As Bel began to protest he said, 'What can he say? You are free to marry whoever and whenever you wish.'

'But I can't just leave him! You know I can't.'

'Why not? I don't want you anywhere near that Howard lunatic a moment longer. God knows what he might do.'

227

'But Larry, Walter's *ill*! I can't just abandon him. Mrs Banks won't stay unless I'm there – although what good she thinks I'll be in an emergency I don't quite know.'

'We'll hire a nurse then.'

'But if Howard –'

'Damn it, Bel!' He looked hurt. 'Anyone would think you *wanted* to stay with him.'

'Larry, I can't just walk out. If you could see him, you'd be shocked. You'd –'

'I'm already shocked! And not in the way you think. I'm shocked that he has made such a fool of you. Letting you live in sin all these years. I thought he had more integrity. Oh, yes, I *am* shocked!'

His face was flushed, his blue eyes dark. She had never seen him angry before. At least, not with *her*. 'Larry, darling, don't let's quarrel.'

'Well, don't be so unreasonable! I can't bear to think of you staying on in that place with him when you don't have to and when *I* love you and *I* want you here with me. I should have expected you to jump at the chance. Leave him, Bel.'

She looked at him sadly. 'He's ill and he's frightened. He –'

'Whose fault is all that? It's his own fault.'

'Larry! He's your brother! Oh, please don't be too hard on him. You've always said how much you owed him. You've always been close. And whatever would your father say? Larry, *please*! There's so much at stake here. I want somehow to sort it all out so that we do as little damage to other people as possible. We have to think it out very carefully. *Very* carefully. Don't let's go rushing in, making everything worse.'

'Can it get any worse?' he demanded.

'Of course it can. Walter could have a worse heart attack. Walter could *kill himself*! He looks quite desperate enough.'

Larry's expression changed. '*Kill himself*? Walter? Surely not.'

'Larry, you haven't seen him lately. He's in a very bad way, physically and emotionally. I didn't feel I should leave him, but I was so longing to see you again. It seemed so incredible that we had ever been happy, that afternoon at Hampton Court –'

He smiled suddenly. 'It was rather splendid, wasn't it? Everything. You in particular. I've decided to buy another motor so that we can nip off whenever we please. I might even buy a houseboat. On the "never-never", of course. Oh, Bel, my dearest girl. I do love you so much.' He leaned forward and kissed her. 'I'm sorry I was ratty. I'm so impatient. I could hardly believe your letter. Knowing that you and Walter were never married, thinking how much easier it makes it for us. I wanted to cheer and shout and sing. I shan't be prepared to wait long, you know. I love you.'

'I know. I'd marry you this very moment if it were possible, but I do want to get all this . . . this nastiness out of the way first. We do want to start off in the way we mean to go on, don't we? Decent and above-board.'

He grinned. 'All correct and shipshape! Aye, aye, sir!'

'Stop mocking me, you beast!'

'I'm sorry.' He tried to look penitent but his mouth twitched.

'I love you, Larry.'

'Ditto! Ditto! Etcetera! Et –'

She laughed. 'Stop it, Larry. I'm trying to be serious about – well, about everything.'

'It's called "Parva Sed Apta".'

'What is?'

'The houseboat that's for sale; the one I might buy.'

'Larry –'

'It means "Small But Enough!"'

She looked at him, catching a hint of amusement in his voice.

He said, 'Not a very suitable name!'

Light dawned. 'Larry! You – of all the conceited –' She began to laugh. 'That's a *very* cheeky thing to say. You have a really wicked mind! But I like the name. "Parva Sed Apta." Yes. It has class!'

He said, 'I like to see you smile and hear you laugh. When we're married I shall see to it that you are never unhappy again. Never sad, never bored, never worried.' He was not joking now. 'I promise you I shall do everything to make you happy. You will *never* regret marrying me, Bel.' He grinned. 'Let's go back to bed!'

'What? And let all this food go to waste?' She looked at the half-eaten meal.

'*You're* going to waste!' He stood up and held out his hands and gently pulled her to her feet. Then he lifted her into his arms.

'You're not protesting, then!' he said.

'I'm giving in gracefully,' she told him. 'It's what I do best!'

*

The Bell in Cotton End, known to the locals as 'Betsy's Bunker', was full to overflowing. The three barmaids in the snug were rushed off their feet, serving beers and whiskies for the men and rum and lemon for the women. The large room was crammed with customers, most of whom worked at the Royal Airship Works. Some men leaned on the bar, others stood, held upright by the crush. A lucky few, mostly women, sat at tables. The low ceiling was darkened by years of nicotine, but the walls were cheerful with photographs of the various airships that had made aviation history. Pinned up between them were several ancient pencil sketches of airmen which were now, years on, curling at the edges. In pride of place above the bar was a small replica of the pennant which graced the tail of the R100.

The date was the ninth of September and, although the talk wandered from subject to subject, it always came back to the forthcoming flight trials of the R101. Amid the haze of tobacco smoke, eager faces gleamed with excitement as the discussion revolved as always around the prospect of seeing their beloved airship taken out of the hangar at last and moored to its mast. Then, at the appointed time, she would rise like a bird into the sky, taking their hearts with her. A definite division had developed among the customers – there were those who had been chosen to fly on the airship and those who had not. Howard, standing beside Peggy, was unable to claim fellowship with the lucky few because no one must know that Alf Comber was going to cry off at the very last moment with a feigned illness and relinquish his place.

It was gone ten o'clock and nearly closing time, and most of the customers had reached that desired state in which, fleetingly, they could forget their troubles and believe themselves to be happy. A few, however, had taken on board one drink too many and were teetering on the edge of belligerence. Howard was one of these and he loomed over Peggy and her girl-friend, Brenda, wondering what the latter saw in her fiancé, John. In Howard's eyes, John was an overweight, ignorant loud-mouth. With a set scowl, Howard listened half-heartedly, understanding odd snippets of conversation but missing others.

'. . . so it'll be up to the Air Council. Listen, old son. They have to give the Permit to Fly . . .'

'. . . as long as the weather's decent, and September can be nasty . . .'

'. . . the faults they found at Hendon Air Pageant have been pretty well hushed up . . .'

Howard said suddenly, 'They'll be lucky to get that reversible airscrew before the end of the month!' He blinked, daring John to argue.

'They'll get it!' said John.

'Huh! You reckon, do you?' He stared grimly into John's face. 'Those engines will never be right.'

'Course they will!'

'They won't! They were designed for bloody trains, not a bloody airship!'

'So what? They've been adapted. You're talking through your hat!'

Howard's thoughts moved sluggishly, dulled by the alcohol. 'What faults?' he demanded, suddenly recalling an earlier comment. 'What faults at Hendon?'

Several faces turned towards them and John said, 'Didn't you hear?'

'How could I hear if they were hushed up?' His scowl deepened.

Peggy said, 'He wasn't up here then, John. Give the man a chance.'

'Oh, no. Sorry, old son. Well, the airship played them up merry hell, but luckily everyone on the ground was watching the fixed wing planes so they didn't notice. 101 dived a couple of times and they only just got her nose up again in time.'

'Crikey!' Howard shook his head.

'She did it again on the way home but it was never in the papers.'

Howard wanted an argument. 'But *someone* must have seen it. A ruddy great airship can't just dive without someone noticing!' He looked at John's small brown eyes with a growing feeling of dislike. The man was such a fool, he thought dourly. Got a big opinion of himself, but he knew next to nothing. Howard wanted to knock the stupid grin from his face.

'If anyone saw it, they might have thought it was meant to happen, like part of the trials. You know, *needing* to know what happens when she dives? How well does she respond to the elevator wheel? My uncle knows somebody who knows the girl who typed the report, and he says she says—'

Howard longed to tell them that his father was one of the consultant designers and knew more about the airship than all of them put together, but he had told Peggy his father was dead. Instead he mimicked, 'He says, she says!'

Peggy dug her elbow into him. 'Shut up, Howard. I want to hear it.'

He said, 'Shut up yourself!' Bossy little boot!

Brenda, annoyed for John, said, 'You just might learn something, Howard.'

'And I might not.' Howard tightened his mouth irritably. Women!

John went on regardless. 'He says she says that they were all a bit worried.'

'And that's it?' Howard demanded. He looked at Brenda. 'And I'm supposed to learn something from that *vital* piece of information?'

'Who cares what you learn!' Brenda tossed her head. 'Probably too thick to learn—'

Peggy said, 'Don't you call my chap thick!!'

Howard was losing track of the conversation, but he felt that things were going wrong. In an attempt to change the subject he dredged his mind for another snippet. 'Didn't someone say that Dowding was going on to the Air Control Board?' he asked.

'Air Vice Marshal to you!'

'He could shake 'em up a bit!'

There was a murmur of agreement.

'He was a bloody good pilot—'

'But does he know anything about *airships?*'

'Ah! Now you're asking!'

'It's a different beast!'

Howard puddled a finger in some spilt beer on the table and struggled to reclaim his earlier mood. He reminded himself how lucky he was. Here in the pub, among so

233

many like-minded people, he could relax and talk about airships to his heart's content. For a while, at least, he could forget about his father and *her*, and enjoy himself like any other young man of his age. With a few beers, he could obliterate the memories of the last few weeks and the business of the broken window. That had probably been a mistake, he saw that now, but at the time he had lost his temper and it had seemed a good idea. It had given his father something to think about and had shown them both that he, Howard, was someone to be reckoned with. At least they had not sent the police round after him, and that had been a relief. It would have been too awful to end up in jail just as he had made sure of his flight to India! He thought of his mother. Perhaps, after all, she would be pleased to see him settled here, accepted, among his friends. She had always worried about him being on his own so much. He hoped she was enjoying herself in France; he would write to her and tell her to look out for the airship, but he mustn't tell her until later that he was actually *aboard* it. That would give her such a thrill.

Smiling at the thought, he gave Peggy a half-hearted kiss and stared around. He was *one of them*, he had a girl-friend and he had finally handed over the ten pounds to Alf Comber. He was going to fly with the R101.

Just then the proprietor, resplendent in a red velvet waistcoat, appeared behind the bar, vigorously waving a handbell.

'Time, gents and ladies, please!' he called amid loud boos and a few catcalls. There was the usual rush for a last drink, but he shook his head amid groans of disbelief.

Peggy wriggled free and said, 'He gets earlier every night, he does!'

'He puts the clocks on!'

They all laughed at this unoriginal sally.

'Did he call last orders? I never heard him!'

To prolong the mood of cheerful bonhomie, Howard

raised his half-empty glass and said, 'Here's to the jolly old 101 and may God bless all who sail in her!'

Peggy laughed. 'It should be champagne,' she told him. 'It's champagne they smash over ships, isn't it?'

She leaned over and whispered something in Brenda's ear and they both screeched with laughter.

Howard looked at them suspiciously. What the hell were they laughing at? An unpleasant idea occurred to him. Had Peggy told her about the money? Because he'd sworn her to secrecy. If she had told that stupid girl-friend she'd be sorry! He said, 'What are you two whispering about? Out with it!'

John said, 'Tell Uncle Howard!'

The girls shook their heads and continued to giggle.

'*Tell* me, I said!' Howard wagged a finger in front of Peggy's nose, but this merely reduced them to hysterics and he eyed them blearily. 'Silly cows!'

Why did women have to be so bloody stupid, he wondered and a little of his joy faded. Peggy was supposed to be on *his* side, wasn't she? So why whisper secrets to that chinless friend of hers? He couldn't stand girls who giggled. He had a good mind to walk out on Brenda and John. Yes, that would wipe the smile off their faces.

He stubbed out his cigarette and said abruptly, 'We're off, then!'

No one else in the pub had made a move and they all stared at him in surprise.

Peggy said, 'Hang on, Howard! What's the hurry?'

'I'm going now, that's why!' He was beginning to feel a little queasy and suddenly a bit of fresh air seemed rather appealing. He breathed heavily. 'Come on, Peg. Get your skates on. We're off.'

She hesitated, dismayed by his rapid change of mood. 'Oh, Howard! Can't we wait for the others?'

Howard glared at her. So much for bloody loyalty, he reflected angrily. Just because he'd said he'd marry her she

235

thought she could answer back; thought she could throw her weight around.

'Please yourself,' he said and turned on his heel. As he pushed his way towards the door he heard her say, 'Howard!' and then her girlfriend said, 'Let him go, Peggy. He can't boss you about!'

Stupid, *stupid* cow, that Brenda! Outside in the damp street he waited, his collar turned up, his hands thrust into his pockets. The cool air made him feel worse than ever. He was sure she would come after him; she knew which side her bread was buttered. Long minutes passed while he muttered to himself and swore under his breath. Bloody, *bloody* women!

'Come *on!*' he told her, but she didn't come out. Well, that settled it. She would never see her ten quid again! He wouldn't throw her over just yet because in two days' time it would be Mrs C's whist night, and he was on to a good thing there, but she could say goodbye to her money and she would certainly never be Mrs Howard Roberts. He toyed with the idea of dragging her out of the pub bodily, but then all her friends would chime in and in his present state he decided he couldn't face it. She wasn't worth the effort.

Giving up, he started to walk down the middle of the road a little unsteadily, his mood darkening with every step. Vaguely he heard a car engine turn over, but as he stumbled along he was unaware that about fifty yards behind him the car followed. When at last he noticed the dawdling motor behind him he stepped on to the grass verge to let it pass. To his surprise it slowed to a stop as it drew level and the door swung open.

Someone said, 'Howard! Get in!'

'You *what?*' he said, startled. The voice was vaguely familiar, but in the darkness he could not recognise the car. He leaned down and peered in. '*Dad!*' he cried, taken completely by surprise.

'Get in, quickly. We have to talk.'

Howard backed away, recovering a little. 'I thought you were ill,' he told Walter accusingly. 'They said you were in bed!'

'I have been ill——'

'Good! I'm glad to hear it!'

'I've come out especially to find you.'

'So now you have.' He wanted to walk away, to frustrate his father, but his curiosity held him there a little longer. That and the chance to upset him. If only he didn't feel so ill. 'Talk about what?' he asked. If this was about the broken window, there was no way he was going to pay for it.

'About the money you need.'

Now Howard gave him his full attention. If his father didn't know that he had borrowed the money from Peggy, he might lend him another ten. But was it worth an earful? Did he want to listen to a telling-off' Not really.

'Why aren't you in bed then?' he demanded, playing for time, trying to decide what to do.

'The house is empty. I dressed and came out – against doctor's orders, but I wanted to see you. We must talk, Howard. For God's sake, *get in!*'

Sullenly Howard climbed in and sat down. Posh car, he thought resentfully. So this is how *they* drove around. For Howard it was a motorbike, and for his mother the buses. He was pleased to be reminded that he had a justifiable grudge.

'Thank you.'

The car glided forward and Howard asked, 'Where are we going?' because it would be just like his father to drive miles and then leave him to walk back to Shortstown. That's the sort of man he was.

'Not far. To somewhere quiet where we won't be disturbed.'

Howard sneaked a sideways look. Now that his eyes

were getting used to the gloom he was shocked to see how thin his father looked. His cheeks seemed to have sunk in and his eyes looked too big for the rest of his face.

He said, 'I saw the doctor's car outside your house. I watch your house sometimes.' Let him put *that* in his pipe and smoke it! 'I said I was a neighbour.'

Walter made no answer as they turned off the main road and drove along a lane. Then they turned off on to a track that ran into a wood.

'This will do.' He stopped the car and half turned in his seat. As he did so his knee touched Howard's leg. Was his father trembling? Fear or cold? He suddenly saw that beneath Walter's shirt he was still wearing pyjamas.

Howard said, 'You should be at home in bed,' and then wished the words unsaid. They were too caring. What did he care if his father caught a chill? He could catch pneumonia for all he cared.

'Listen, Howard.' Walter's eyes were bright in the darkness and his voice shook. 'I want to help you. I want you to believe that—'

'Help me? That's a laugh! All I needed was ten measly pounds and you wouldn't—'

'You didn't give me time to read the letter, Howard. I was in London when it arrived.'

'I bet!' Howard wondered if it could be true.

'I had just arrived home and was about to have my dinner when the rock—'

'All right! I know.'

'I would have given you the money. I've brought it with me – but first I want to know the truth, Howard, because I can't really help unless I do. Please tell me – is there a girl involved? Because if so, I will understand. These things happen . . .'

'Look who's talking!' cried Howard, suddenly incensed. 'If these things didn't happen *I* wouldn't be here now, would I? Of course they bloody happen!'

238

Walter wound his window down. What was the matter with him, Howard wondered uneasily. He couldn't be hot, surely, unless he was feverish. Unless perhaps he really was ill. Maybe he was going to *die*? The thought jolted Howard unpleasantly.

'Howard, I don't want to quarrel with you. You've been a fool and you've overstepped the mark, and I can't pretend I'm not angry and upset but you're still my son. I've been thinking a lot since I've been ill and more than anything . . .' His voice broke suddenly. 'More than anything I want us somehow to be – to be the friends we once were. All those years ago. It can't be—'

Howard fought against his momentary weakness. He *hated* this man, and with good reason. 'Friends? I don't remember being *friends*! Not with you.' He stabbed a finger in his father's direction. 'I remember being sick with worry when you came to visit in case you found fault with me or Mum. I remember dreading my school reports in case they weren't good enough for you. I remember—' His own voice had changed its pitch and he stopped and drew a deep breath. 'I remember you criticising me and Mum.'

'Criticise your mother? I most certainly never did!'

'You *did!*' Howard's eyes blazed. 'You came one day and Mum had spent ages making a special salad and . . .' His eyes blurred with tears.

'And what?'

'And you called it rabbits' food! And you *laughed!*' Howard could see it so clearly: his father's scornful face, and his mother trying to hide her disappointment. He could recall his own humiliation that they had somehow failed yet another test.

'But that – it must have been a joke, that's all. I didn't mean—'

'It wasn't funny!' Howard brushed away the tears.

'Howard, that was years ago. All that is in the past. I want a fresh start.'

239

'We were never friends.'

In a tired voice Walter said, 'I thought we were, once.'

'Well, you thought wrong,' Howard said bitterly. 'I remember dreading Prize Day because you wouldn't be there and all the kids would notice. I remember when I was nine you forgot my birthday, and Mum kept pretending that it had got lost in the post, but it never came. And when I asked Mum when her wedding anniversary was she trotted out this bit of paper all in French and pretended it was a wedding certificate!'

'Howard, it *was*!'

'Pull the other leg!'

There was a silence between them. Howard was furious. Did his father think he was a complete idiot? If he was married to his mother, then . . . 'So you're living in sin with *her*, are you? Oh, yes! I'm sure! She'd love that!'

After a hesitation his father said, 'Bel knows now and, naturally, it's upset her, but I'm not here to talk about Bel or your mother. Howard,—'

He stopped suddenly and put a hand to his chest and Howard looked at him anxiously. Was he *really* ill?

'I mean this, Howard, very sincerely. Things have gone very badly between us and I accept some – no, I accept *most* of the blame. I want you to know how sorry I am.'

'*I'd* feel sorry with a rock through my window!'

'Not because of that—'

Howard said roughly, 'Oh, cut it out, Dad! I don't want to hear all this stuff. I don't care any more. You don't matter to me the way you did. You said you wanted to help me so do it, give me the money and drive me home.'

'Not until we can talk sensibly about all this—'

'There's nothing to talk about. Give me the—'

'Howard! Please!' He began to cough, a thin, racking sound. 'I'm really not up to this – I'm really not well. I need to sort things out with you, and then get back to bed.

I can't bear the thought that we cannot salvage something from this terrible mess.'

He stopped again, and drew a deep breath. Howard wondered what he was ill *with*, but wouldn't ask. It might be catching.

'Howard, I told Bel about you. She knows that I care about you and she thought perhaps you and she and – it was her own idea – that you might meet—'

Howard laughed shortly. 'We've already met. Didn't she tell you? I walked into your garden, bold as brass, and—'

'I mean meet properly, under happier circumstances.'

Howard's mouth fell open. 'What? You thought *what*? Me and *her*? Do you know what that would do to Mum? Her only son fraternising with the enemy? I wouldn't do that to her. God, you're a bigger fool than I thought you were.'

When Walter relapsed once more into silence, Howard said, 'I've not told Mum yet about what I've found out. Because *I* don't want to hurt her. Not like you; I *care* about her.'

'Oh, Howard, do you think I don't care? I've written to your mother, to tell her everything.' The voice was very low now and rather hoarse. 'I want it all to be out in the open. A fresh start for all of us. Oh, God! This is harder than I thought. If only you would see—'

'Well, I don't see!'

Suddenly his father fumbled in the dash and took out a cigarette case. He offered Howard a cigarette.

'No, thanks!'

With trembling fingers Walter struck a match and in the small light Howard saw how haggard he was. So thin. He felt a moment's fear, which he quickly thrust from him, and said, 'I've had enough of this. Give me the money and I'll walk home.'

'Howard, tell me about the girl. You can confide—'

'The money, damn you!' He thrust out his hand, but his father shook his head.

'Then *bugger* you!' cried Howard. He fumbled with the car door and almost fell out. He put out a hand to steady himself but, feeling the wet undergrowth, withdrew it hastily. From the other side of the car his father appeared, saying, 'Wait, Howard. Please! Don't go!'

'You never meant to give me any money! You lying sod!' cried Howard, and he was shocked to feel sudden tears coursing down his face. He took a few steps towards his father, who looked incredibly small and frail. Around them the trees dripped moisture and twigs snapped underfoot. 'It was just a trick, wasn't it, to get me here! To give me one of your lousy lectures. Well, sod you! You know what you can do with your bloody money. Stuff it up your arse!' He gulped in lungfuls of air between his sobs. That would teach him. His father hated coarse language; his mother was always telling Howard that his father was a gentleman.

'Howard! Don't! It wasn't!' He fumbled in the pocket of his overcoat and drew out an envelope. 'Here's the money! Take it, please. There's fifty pounds!'

Beside himself now, Howard rushed forward, snatched the envelope from his father's hand and threw it on to the ground. 'I don't want it! I want nothing from you! Can't you understand. *I hate you!*' He stamped the envelope into the ground as his father watched helplessly.

'Please . . . No! Oh, don't, Howard, *Please!*'

Raging inwardly, Howard glanced up at him and was sickened. This was a man he could barely recognise, a father who had lost his authority. He wanted the man he had respected all those years. Furiously Howard grabbed him by the shoulders and shook him violently.

'You aren't my father!' he shouted. 'You aren't!'

'Howard! Don't – please.' The voice, so piteously thin, increased Howard's desperation. He lost control completely and slammed the frail figure against a tree. Then with his free hand he punched the haggard face again and again until his anger was suddenly spent. At last he released his victim and stepped back, trembling, appalled by his own violence.

'Howard . . .' The word was hardly audible as his father slid to the ground.

Howard breathed heavily, gasping for air as his rage ebbed away. He was shaking uncontrollably as he stared at the crumpled figure that was his father.

He said, 'Dad?' and his voice quivered with shock. 'Don't do this to me! Dad? *Dad*! Don't—' He was panting, sobbing, frightened But mostly he was frightened. He looked around fearfully. The wood and the darkness seemed to close in upon him. He dashed the tears from his face and took a few steps forward. All his anger had evaporated and Howard came to a momentous decision. When his father sat up he would tell him he was sorry. Yes, he would apologise. The thought made him feel a little better. He would agree to make a fresh start. His father loved him and would forgive him. He said, 'Dad? Please, Dad?'

He waited a long time and then forced himself to kneel beside the still figure.

'Dad?' His father was lying twisted with one leg under him and his face turned upwards to the dark sky. He didn't answer and he didn't move. Carefully Howard felt in Walter's pocket for the cigarette lighter. He knelt beside his father and examined him by the light of the small wavering flame. There was something dark trickling from Walter's mouth. Blood! Howard screamed. The sound seemed to echo through the dark wood and he looked round fearfully, but he was still alone. He touched his father's face, then lifted one of his hands. It was limp. Lifeless. *Lifeless? Not dead, surely*. He ran back to the car and climbed inside, shivering violently. It all seemed impossible. Incredible. Half an hour ago he had been sitting in the pub with his arm round Peggy and – and now *this*. He whispered, 'What shall I do, Dad?' If he called an ambulance and his father was dead, they would call him a murderer. If he didn't and his father was alive, he would tell the police and Howard would go to prison for grievous bodily harm or maybe attempted murder. Or he could run; he could hide. He could take the money and go abroad – but what about his flight on the airship? He would not let them cheat him out of that. He must go to India. But how?

They would be looking for him . . . or would they? How would they know it was him? His father could have been out in his car – he could have given someone a lift – a stranger. Or he could have crashed the car – Howard could make it look like an accident and then disappear. But he would need money . . .

'Oh, God!'

He scrambled out of the car and began a frantic search for the money. Fifty pounds! His father had been going to give him fifty pounds! So he *had* meant to help him. He stumbled to and fro across the damp ground until at last he found the sodden envelope. He stuffed it into his pocket and stood staring round him. He must keep a cool head.

'Think, Howard!' he told himself and swallowed hard, nodding his head in affirmation. If he kept cool and didn't panic, he would . . .

'Fifty pounds! Oh, *Dad!*'

His father had meant to help him, so surely he must have loved him – and now he was dead . . . But what to do? It seemed as though his mind moved in slow motion. If only he hadn't drunk so much.

'Think!' he urged himself. He must make it look like an accident. A car crash, not a murder. They must think that the car had run out of control and crashed, and his father had been thrown out. He put a shaking hand to his head. What must he do? He must drive the car into a nearby tree.

244

He had never driven a car, but he supposed it was not too difficult. Nervously, his heart thumping, Howard climbed out of the car and took hold of the starting handle. He gave it a couple of awkward turns and then it fired. The engine turned over and he almost wept with relief. Returning to the driver's side, he seated himself at the controls and put the car into reverse. It moved with a jump and then more slowly. After some difficulty Howard manoeuvred it into line with the tree next to his father, then closed his eyes. He muttered a brief prayer and put his foot down hard. The car hesitated, then shot forward and hit the tree. The windscreen shattered and Howard was thrown through it, ending up sprawled across the bonnet with a gash in his face.

'Oh, Lord!' He touched his face gingerly and discovered that he was bleeding. He sat there, dazed. There was a pain in his left shoulder too and he groaned, afraid even to move.

'You *fool!*' he told himself. 'Now you're hurt, too.' He hadn't intended that to happen; had anybody heard the crash, and if so would they venture out to investigate? With infinite care he slid from the bonnet of the wrecked car to the ground and took a few deep breaths.

'Not thinking straight!' he told himself.' Not thinking . . .'

After a moment he turned once more to his father and knelt down. Perhaps he was just unconscious? Fear sharpened his mind and he thought frantically. He would make it look like a robbery. He found a wallet and removed all the money, then felt in all the pockets and found his father's half-hunter watch. He had known it all his life, this watch; his father had taught him to tell the time on it. On the back it had his father's initials and the words 'From your loving father' — which was Howard's grandfather. The one he had never seen, and who had never even known he had a grandson. He slipped the watch into his own pocket.

'Dad? *Dad!* I'm going now,' he said. 'I'm sorry about everything.' He crossed himself in case his father really was dead, then wiped the blood from his face and said, 'Look at me, Dad! What a state I'm in!' He leaned down and brushed his lips against his father's hair in a clumsy farewell kiss.

Then, sobbing quietly, he made his way through the trees, away from the village, into the welcoming darkness.

*

Mrs Banks glanced sleepily at the clock beside her bed and sat bolt upright. She had overslept, something she never did. But last night Mr Roberts had told her to take an evening off, and she had gone to the cinema in Bedford to see Greta Garbo in her first ever 'talkie'. Her voice wasn't at all how Mrs Banks had imagined it, but once she got used to it she had enjoyed the story. She had cried buckets, and was looking forward to telling Mrs Roberts all about it when she came back from London. Then, being all alone in the house except for an invalid, she hadn't slept very well thinking of that dreadful Howard and wondering what *he* was up to. She'd spotted him a few days back, talking to the doctor, bold as brass. The *cheek* of the man! She rubbed the sleep from her eyes.

'Nearly seven!' she grumbled, annoyed with herself, as she threw back the bedclothes. A quick wash would have to do for today – what her mother had called an 'up-and-a-downer' – with one ear open for Mr Robert's bell. He sometimes woke early and needed something before she had had a chance to get the kitchen range going or prepare his breakfast tray.

'Porridge' she decided, 'and a bit of haddock.' Good thing he liked fish, because fish was light and on the doctor's list of approved foods. And she must tidy up his room before the doctor arrived. Not that she cared over-much for this new man – he *would* insist on fresh air, and opened the window without so much as a by-your-leave.

He might be a bit handsome, but he knew it and his eyes were all over the place, and she'd seen him eyeing Mrs Roberts. But a bit of Ronuk polish would make the bedroom smell nice, and he wouldn't be able to find fault with *her*.

She pulled on her clothes and hurried along the landing then put her ear to the main bedroom. Not a sound. Thank the Lord for that! She tiptoed past and went downstairs and was soon on her hands and knees in front of the grate, coaxing a few flames. Blowing on it until she felt faint, she finally thought it safe to leave it and turned her attention to the porridge and the haddock. While that was cooking, she buttered some brown bread cut very thin, keeping an eye on the clock. He would be awake by now, cleaning his teeth and having a splash with cold water. Funny how men liked the agony of cold water first thing in the morning. Presumably they considered it manly. She preferred a drop of hot with it herself. At ten the nurse would be along and she would give him a blanket-bath – which he hated. Poor Mr Roberts! She grinned. But the nurse had been a blessing, really, even though she was only part-time. 'The field marshal', the master called her! And she was a bit on the tough side, but then nurses couldn't afford to be too softhearted or they'd be crying their eyes out every time they lost a patient.

'Well, we're all set!' she told herself, admiring the tray with its clean lace cloth and a napkin folded like a fan. These little touches meant a lot to an invalid. She carried it upstairs, knocked on the door – and knocked again.

'Mr Roberts!' she called.

There was still no answer. Must be in the bathroom, she thought, and hesitated, waiting to hear the toilet flush. The master did hate to be seen wandering to and fro in his pyjamas. He was a very proud man. She would give him time to get back into bed and then pretend she had only just arrived.

Still no sound. Funny . . .

'Mr Roberts!' The porridge and the haddock were getting cold. '*Mr Roberts*!' she cried, raising her voice.

A horrible suspicion entered her mind. He had been taken ill in the night! She pushed open the door and saw the bed; it looked as though it had been slept in, but – the bathroom door was ajar and he wasn't in there. Her eyes strayed to the wardrobe and then she gave a gasp of dismay. The wardrobe door was open, so what was going on? Had he dressed and gone downstairs without her hearing him? Quickly, she set the tray down on the bedside table and examined the wardrobe. His overcoat was missing, and so were his brogues. A quick glance at the bed told her his pyjamas were missing. So had he put his clothes on over his pyjamas? It was so unlike him. And where *was* he? She rushed to the window. Surely he wasn't in the garden in this damp weather? He'd catch his death!

There was no sign of him and Mrs Banks sat down heavily on the edge of the bed.

'Lordy! What's he up to?' Had he had a brainstorm and gone wandering off? Her uncle's neighbour had done that – wandered out of the house and been run over by a tram. But he was senile, and Mr Roberts still had all his wits about him. But a brainstorm . . . With increasing agitation she searched the house and then returned to the kitchen.

She said breathlessly, 'Well, I don't know!' and waited for her heart to stop thumping. What to do? She could telephone Mrs Roberts, but there was no point in alarming her until she was sure. Ah! She smiled suddenly. His office! Maybe he had gone early to his office to collect something. She let out a relieved sigh. Now that made sense; that must be it. But why he had gone gallivanting off like that, she had no idea. The doctor would be furious; he had only been allowing him out of bed for half an hour at a time, and here was the master nipping off to the R.A.W. behind his back. And without telling her. It was so thoughtless.

'Tut!' She thought of the wasted breakfast and in a rush of pique decided to eat it herself. When he got back she would have to scramble him a couple of eggs. She went upstairs to collect the tray and sat beside the kitchen stove to eat the food. And no matter what he said, she would tell Mrs Roberts. It really wasn't good enough to frighten her like this. Her heart had gone all of a tiswas, banging away like anything. It was enough to give *her* a heart attack, let alone him.

'The car!' Of course, he must have taken the car. She abandoned the haddock and hurried out to the garage. So she was right! The car had gone. Now, suddenly, she knew what to do. She went back into the house and looked in the telephone book for the R.A.W. number. As she did so, she grumbled, for the telephone was newly installed and she hated using it. Answering it wasn't so bad, but making a call always flummoxed her. They never seemed to say the right thing at the other end.

She found the number and dialled the operator.

'Can I help you?'

The polite voice sounded so superior. Probably his secretary. Mrs Banks took a deep breath. 'Yes, please. It's Mr Roberts. I wondered if he's come into the—'

'What number do you want?'

Of course; she hadn't yet reached the office. 'Sorry. I forgot. I mean, I'm a bit worried about—'

'What number do you require, caller?'

'Oh, yes! Sorry. Cardington — oh dear! The page has turned itself over. It's the R.A.W. number. It's the—'

'R.A.W. I am trying to connect you.'

Mrs Banks scowled at the receiver. They didn't even let you finish a sentence. She heard a ringing sound and opened her mouth, but at once the operator said, 'Sorry. The line's engaged. Please call back later.'

'No, I can't. I think it's—' There was a click and the line went dead. 'I think it's an emergency,' Mrs Banks finished lamely. No manners, these telephone people. She had just replaced the receiver when the telephone rang and she jumped visibly. Maybe Mrs Roberts was ringing back to apologise.

'Hullo?' she said breathlessly. 'It's me.'

'Mrs Banks? It's Bel Roberts here. I just—'

'Oh, Mrs Roberts! Thank goodness. At least—' All her good intentions flew out of the window. There was no point in protecting her mistress; she might as well know now instead of later. 'It's Mr Roberts, ma'am. I was just trying to telephone to his office, but they're so rude, these girls. In such a hurry. Mr Roberts wasn't in his bed this morning and his—'

'What? Not in his bed? What are you talking about?'

Mrs Banks cursed her clumsiness. She should have led up to it gradually. 'He wasn't in bed when I went in with his tray this morning, and his clothes are gone. At least, some of them—'

'Gone? Gone where? What are you talking about?'

'That's just it, ma'am. I don't know. I thought he'd maybe gone to the office – and the car's not in the garage, so I think he's got himself dressed, and I was just trying to reach him at the R.A.W. so as not to worry you, but the line's engaged and you know how snooty these operators are.'

'*Wait!*' There was a pause. 'You say my husband's not in his bed but has dressed and gone out in the car? Are you sure?'

'Well, of course I'm sure,' Mrs Banks snorted indignantly. That is, he's not anywhere in the house. I could ring the office again – or you could?' She waited hopefully.

'I'll do that. And you wait there by the telephone, please. If he's not at the office . . . What on earth possessed him to get out of bed? It doesn't make any sense. But hang up, Mrs Banks, and let me ring his office.'

Mrs Banks relinquished responsibility with a sigh of relief. Now it was up to Mrs Roberts. She had done her best. While she waited for the telephone to ring again she began to wonder what they would do if Mister Roberts *had* gone funny in the head. That would be a disaster for everyone, but certainly for him because how could he go to India in that state? And *why* did all this have to happen when she was alone in the house with him? Not that anyone could blame *her*. The master had given her the night off and – she frowned suddenly. Now that was a bit of a coincidence, that was . . . R-r-ring. She grabbed the telephone, startled.

'Mrs Banks?'

'Yes? Is Mr Roberts at work?'

'No, he's not. They haven't seen him since he was taken ill originally, and they've no idea where he might be. We're coming down on the next train . . . What? Oh, yes!' She seemed to be talking to someone else. 'We might come by car. Anyway, we'll be with you as soon as possible, but you must stay put. Someone must be there in case he suddenly turns up. And you could ring the hospital in case there's been an accident—'

'Oh, no!' cried Mrs Banks, horrified by the idea that she should talk to the hospital. 'I mean, wouldn't it be better if you spoke to them? Being his wife, I mean. I really don't think—'

'Oh, very well. I'll do that now. But if he comes home, put him straight back to bed and call the doctor.'

Mrs Banks groaned inwardly. Telephone here, telephone there! Lordy! How she hated the thought of it. But she would have to persevere. Mr Roberts was always saying they must all move with the times . . .

'And give him something warm to drink, Mrs Banks. Or maybe a brandy. And something to eat. I can't imagine where he's gone. My head's just spinning! Oh, and when the nurse comes, tell her what's happened and keep her

251

there, even if my husband's still missing. We shall need her, so don't let her go again. And try not to worry.'

The line went dead and slowly Mrs Banks replaced the receiver on its rest and set the telephone back on the table.

Try not to worry! Fat chance! Undecided what to do next, she sat down beside the telephone table and stared at the hatstand. Why had Mr Roberts given her the evening off? Had he meant to get rid of her so that he could sneak off somewhere? Was he really *missing*? Was it what the papers called foul play? She felt her flesh creep at the idea that, while she slept, evil things had been happening in the house.

'Poor Mr Roberts!' she said. If only she had thought to look in at him when she came back from the pictures. But then he had told her not to bother, so was that part of a plot? He had said he was going to take a sleeping pill and shouldn't be disturbed. So while he was sleeping anybody could have bundled him away and taken the car to make it look normal . . . or nearly normal. That awful Howard might be to blame, might even be part of a gang. The idea sent shivers down her spine. She would have to remember all this when the mistress arrived.

Her eye caught his bowler hat, the one he wore when he had meetings in the city or with his bank manager. She took it from its hook and turned it slowly in her hands.

'Where's your master?' she asked. She pressed the smooth crown against her face and wondered if he would ever wear it again.

*

Half an hour later she had abandoned her post by the telephone, had ensconced herself on the sofa by the sitting-room window, and had poured herself a large brandy, for medicinal purposes. She certainly needed it, she thought, sipping it crossly. There had been no telephone call, and she was still alone in the house which was now beginning

252

to feel distinctly creepy. The thought of Howard haunted her, and she had not dared look in the cupboards or the attic in case he was the villain and was lurking somewhere, waiting his chance with her. She had tried to carry on with her work, but her mind was too distracted. She'd started to tidy the main bedroom, but had then dropped the sheets as though burned. Suppose the police had to be called in? The bed might be full of clues. She dare not sweep the carpets or plump up the cushions for the same reason. Her fingerprints would be over everything, but at least no one would accuse her of anything because she had an alibi. She had been in the cinema and had seen the postman and his wife there, and they had been on the last bus with her coming back to Cardington. Thank the Lord!

She had just started to toy with a new and rather startling idea that maybe the master had run off with another woman when she heard a car in the drive and, rushing to the window, saw that it was the mistress with Mr Roberts' brother. She threw the remains of the brandy on to the fern in the window and pushed the glass back in the cabinet; she would have to wash it later.

Rushing to the front door, she threw it open and called 'Any news, ma'am?'

Mrs Roberts came up the steps looking white and frightened and said, 'Not a thing, but they are looking for the car.'

Not a word about 'poor Mrs Banks'! Not a 'thank you' for all she had done. Mrs Banks sniffed her disapproval. The young Mr Roberts, however, gave her a smile and patted her arm. 'A nasty fright for you, Mrs Banks. And all alone.'

'I was a bit scared, sir, and I don't mind admitting it.' She loved his eyes, that deep, deep blue. If she'd been a younger woman, she could have set her cap at him.

'We won't leave you alone any more,' he assured her.

'I'll be staying until tomorrow, and Mrs Roberts will wait here at home until my brother turns up.'

'I do hope he's all right, sir. You hear such terrible things.'

Now that reinforcements had arrived Mrs Banks' courage faltered and she heard her voice quiver. Tears filled her eyes. The fact that they had rushed down from London made it all seem much worse somehow.

Mrs Roberts came back down the stairs and saw her being comforted.

'Poor Mrs Banks,' she said. 'I'm sorry you've had to bear all this alone. You've been absolutely splendid. Do you think you could make us a pot of tea? And a few biscuits? We haven't had time for breakfast.'

Glad of something to do, Mrs Banks wiped her eyes and was soon back in the kitchen, spooning tea into the teapot and feeling reassured by the familiar surroundings. She was just closing the tea-caddy when an astonishing thought struck her. It made her feel rather odd. On the telephone, Mrs Roberts had said, '*We'll* do this' and '*We'll* do that,' and she and the young Mr Roberts had come down together. And she had said, 'What? Oh, yes' to somebody . . .

The mistress and young Mr Roberts *had been together.*

Chapter Twelve

MARIE WENT INTO HER Father's room two days later with something akin to trepidation. She had been 'sent for' with a message from Emily, and she thought she knew the reason behind her father's uncharacteristic behaviour. Larry had telephoned her earlier and, with Bel's permission, had told her everything albeit briefly. He had given her strict instructions, however, that their father was to be told as little as possible until there was some positive news about Walter. Her brief was 'to use her common sense'. Assuming an air of innocent cheerfulness, she breezed into her father's room.

'Good morning, Father,' she began. 'I hear you want to talk to me . . .'

He said, 'Sit down, Marie.' His tone was grim and one glance at his expression prepared her for the worst. 'I want to know,' he said, slowly and deliberately,' what the hell is going on – and don't try to fob me off because I am not a fool. I know there's something wrong, and I strongly object to being "sheltered" from whatever it is.'

Marie hesitated, unnerved by the directness of his approach and the look in his eye. She had always found her father an imposing figure and now she felt like a child again, about to be interrogated for juvenile misdeeds. He had rarely needed to chastise her; a few well-chosen phrases and a certain cold look in his eyes had always been enough to quell any childish thoughts of rebellion. Today, even though he was bedridden, she was still aware of his power to intimidate her and this awareness irked her. What *exactly* was she to tell him, she wondered? Larry had been somewhat unspecific. All she could recall of their conversation on the telephone was that she was not to distress George unless it was really necessary. If Walter had not been found by the end of the day she was to break the news as gently as possible the following morning. She had not expected her father to get wind of the problem so quickly – unless he had somehow overheard her conversation with Larry . . .

'Marie!' He snapped impatient fingers in front of her face. 'I may be old but I've still got my wits about me and I demand to be told what's happening – and something *is*! I may be stuck in bed all day but I'm hardly senile. Larry's been avoiding me like the plague and Bel has—'

'I'm sorry, Father.' She floundered momentarily. What was he referring to? Had he discovered about Larry and Bel, or was he uneasy about Walter? Her own conscience was far from clear, and secretly she suspected that Walter had somehow found out about Larry and Bel and had decided to take his own life. If so, the responsibility for the tragedy rested with her and the thought terrified her. 'We just thought, Father, that until we knew more—'

'So there *is* something. I knew it!'

'We know nothing for certain yet, Father. We didn't want to upset you—'

'It's Larry and Bel, isn't it?'

The question startled her. 'I . . . no, it's—'

'Goddam it, girl, *tell* me!' he thundered. 'I've seen a change in her. No, don't pretend you haven't noticed. And at the mention of his name she lights up like a beacon.

They're in love and don't try to tell me otherwise. It's true, isn't it?'

She nodded.

'I knew it. Bel and Larry.' He sighed deeply. 'Poor Walter.'

Surprised by his perception, Marie wondered whether it was fair to keep the rest of the news from him. Perhaps he was right. He was as fit as any of them to receive bad news. He had certainly taken the confirmation of Bel's affair with no apparent harm – but then he had already suspected, so it was hardly a shock. The silence lengthened ominously.

'How long has it been going on? Did you know about it?'

'A matter of weeks, that's all, and yes, I knew.'

'Knowing you, you encouraged them!'

She swallowed hard, afraid of his wrath if he should ever learn that it was her interference that had initially sparked the affair. To delay any chance that her own behaviour would come to light, she said, 'It's Walter, Father.'

'Walter?' His eyes widened. 'You mean he's *worse*? Does he know about them? Oh, God!'

'No, no. At least we don't think so. He's—'

'Does he know or doesn't he? What's the matter with you, girl? You're nowhere near as bright as Larry, but you can surely answer a simple question?'

Marie flinched at this unexpected attack. *She* knew she was at fault, but *he* didn't so why was he punishing her by these cruel comments? 'We don't think Walter knows,' she said.

'Well, heaven be praised for small mercies.' He glared at her. 'Poor Walter. He's got so much on his mind at the moment with the airship. It will break his heart if he isn't well enough for that flight. He's lived with that dream for so long.'

Marie struggled with her hurt feelings. Why did they always kill the messenger, she thought bitterly. And whose fault was it if she were not as clever as Larry? All her life she had been made to feel that she was Larry's inferior. A duffer at sums, a rabbit at sports. Only she knew how hard she had tried to be his equal, and how bitter the realisation that she never would. Suddenly she wanted to strike back at her father. 'Father, you're missing the point because you won't let me tell you. We don't think Walter knows about them but . . . it's just that he, Walter, is missing.'

'Missing? Walter?'

Seeing the lack of comprehension on his face she rushed on. 'While Bel was in London on Tuesday he gave the housekeeper the evening off and dressed and . . . and went out—'

He was staring at her, his face suddenly twisted with anxiety. 'Walter went out? But he's ill; he's had a heart attack. What's got into him?' He narrowed his eyes, peering into Marie's face suspiciously. 'Oh, my God! He's not *dead*?' he whispered. All the colour drained from his face and she at once regretted her premature revelation. If anything happened to her father . . .

'Not dead, Marie? Tell me he's not dead!'

'No, no! Not dead. But he took the car and nobody knows where he went. They're trying to trace the car – the police, I mean.'

He stared at her and she watched a variety of expressions flit across his face as he considered her information. 'So you think he's left Bel. That he *did* know about her and Larry?' He shook his head wearily and Marie could see that it had struck him hard. He looked up. 'Is that it?'

Marie hesitated. It had never occurred to her that Walter might have left Bel, though now it seemed a possibility. But only one of many, and her father was ignorant of so much. She took a sudden decision. Larry was wrong about him; her father deserved nothing less than the truth.

'It's a little more complicated than that, Father,' she told him. 'It seems there was a son by an earlier marriage – at least, an earlier relationship.' Now he was looking thunderstruck. 'No, actually it *was* a marriage. I'm afraid, Father, that Bel and Walter were not legally married. It's all been a dreadful mess—'

'Bel had a son?' He was frowning, plucking unhappily at the bedclothes with his fingers. Marie could see that he had not quite grasped the extent of the problem.

'Not Bel, Father. Walter.'

There was another silence while he stared at her wide-eyed. He looked badly shaken . . . stricken. She was beginning to reproach herself; she had handled this very badly and Larry would be furious.

'Not married?' he said at last. 'Of course they were married. I won't believe otherwise.'

She shrugged. 'I'm only telling you what Larry told me.'

Larry had told her everything and Marie herself had had a hard time coming to terms with it all. 'I know,' she sympathised. 'It sounds incredible but—'

'It sounds bloody impossible!' he growled. 'Bel and Walter not married after all these years?'

She put a hand on his. 'Shall I get you a drink?'

'I don't need a drink, dammit! I need to know it all so I can think it out. There has to be something I can do – that we can do – to help. Poor Walter; he must have taken this very hard. Bel and Larry! I kept thinking it and then telling myself I was imagining it.'

'It's the boy, Father. His name's Howard and he's a bit unpredictable. The police think—'

'The *police*?' He stared at her, shocked. 'They've called in the police? God almighty!'

She ploughed resolutely on. 'The police think that Walter and the boy have gone somewhere together – maybe to thrash things out. Because the boy's missing, too; he didn't turn up for work, and his girl-friend hasn't seen him.'

259

'Ah, yes! The boy.' Her father seized the idea gratefully. 'That's probably what's happened. They're holed up in a hotel somewhere.' He frowned. 'How old is this boy?'

'About twenty.'

'Twenty, eh? Can you credit that?' He smiled suddenly and for a moment his eyes brightened. 'I've had a grandson for twenty years and never knew it. I expect Walter's worried about him. Mind you, Walter wasn't always an angel although he'd come to his senses by that age. But you should have seen him around fourteen or so. A bit cheeky, always answering back and thought he knew it all. He got in with a couple of brothers who were a very bad influence, and for a while we did worry about him. Luckily they moved house to another part of London, and Walter was his old self again. A drink, did you say? I think I could drink a cup of tea.'

She was beginning to feel the need for a drink herself. 'What about a cup of tea with a dash of whisky?'

He nodded distractedly and she rang for Emily and ordered some tea. For a while neither of them spoke. Marie had kept only one thing back, and this she had so far kept to herself. As soon as she had heard that Walter was missing, she had rushed off to visit Karma.

Hawk-eyed, her father said, 'What is it now? I can see it on your face. What else?'

'It's nothing.'

'You're a bad liar.' His voice was cold again.

Reluctantly she confessed. 'I went to see Karma.'

'That crazy woman? More fool you, then.' He held up a hand. 'And I don't want to hear any gibberish. If you can't see what quacks those people are, you've less brains than I thought. Karma! Even the name's phony.'

Marie sighed, saying nothing, relieved now that she had not allowed herself to talk about it. She had come away shaking, shattered by Karma's prediction. The clairvoyant had felt violence of some kind. She had also forecast an unexpected death in the family.

*

Wednesday the 17th dawned with a faint mist over the meadows and a sky that threatened rain at any moment. Prue Harris glanced at the clouds and decided to get her walk over before the heavens opened. She pulled on wellington boots and struggled into an ancient macintosh. Settling an old felt hat on her grey hair, she took up her stick and let herself out of the house. Always an early riser, she believed in fitness and, nearing seventy, took a morning constitutional whenever the weather was not too inclement. Sometimes she walked along the road and cut across Benton's fields; alternatively she walked through the wood, coming out beside the old quarry and back along the road. Either way gave her thirty minutes of healthy exercise before breakfast and set her up for the day.

As she set off she patted her pocket to see if the paper bag was still there. Mushrooms grew in the long grass around the quarry and she sometimes found three or four to put with her breakfast bacon. Striding in the direction of the wood she breathed deeply, filling her lungs with clean air and feeling it sharpen her mind. She was alone and liked it that way. Marriage had never interested her, and neither had she wanted to share her life with another woman. She was self-sufficient and happy to be so. She hummed to herself, something from 'Hymns of Praise', and swung her stick briskly to and fro. She did not lean upon it, but brought it with her to deter any dogs who ventured too close. Cats she could take to, but dogs bored her. She found them sycophantic and fussy, and gave short quarter to any that presumed to challenge her.

A few motors passed her, and a bicycle, but it was still too early for most folk to be about. Prue abided by the maxim, 'Early to bed, early to rise', and it was now just

261

after dawn. As she turned off the road she changed to another hymn.

'Soldiers of Christ arise
And put your armour on . . .'

She sang loudly and out of tune and thoroughly enjoyed herself. Later, if it did not rain, she would prune the yellow rose and maybe rake the lawn clear of leaves. If it did rain she would check the apples in the loft and make some lavender bags for the Christmas bazaar.

'The secret of the Lord is theirs,
Their soul is Christ's abode . . .'

It was wet underfoot and her wellington boots squelched through layers of dead leaves while large drops of moisture from the trees pattered on to her hat. She had gone about two hundred yards when she saw the car, and at first she regarded it with surprise and some dismay. Courting couples had been known to park along this stretch of track but not at this time in the morning. She moved a little closer and noticed that its bonnet was pressed into a tree – and that the windscreen was broken.

'Oh dear!' she muttered, and peered through the window to see if the unfortunate driver was still there. The car was empty. Presumably the driver had made his way to the nearest garage and they would send someone along to mend it – or tow it to the garage, or whatever they did to broken motor cars. Prue had never been inside a car and had no wish to do so, but she was curious. They were noisome things, motors, always tooting their horns and belching smoke and frightening the livestock, but this one did have a certain neatness of design which appealed to her. She liked the leather seats and the shiny chrome and the little driver's wheel. She made her way round the car to the other side and saw something lying beside the tree.

'Oh, no!' she exclaimed. This must be the driver, but if so he looked remarkably still. She leaned over and saw the swollen face, the bruises and the flies around the staring eyes.

262

'Now there's a thing!' she said, startled. She regarded the prone figure compassionately. Poor man. He looked so lonely lying there, so neglected. She leaned down to get a better look at his face and her hat fell on to him. She picked it up gingerly and continued to scrutinise his face for signs of life. He looked vaguely familiar but she could not put a name to him. She tapped his knee with her stick.

'Excuse me.' There was no reaction. Dead, she thought with a little sigh. How very sad. 'I'll tell someone,' she told him. She almost said, 'Stay there', but bit back the words just in time. It occurred to her that now her walk had been cut short she would have to forego the mushrooms. Straightening up she replaced her hat, frowning as she did so. She did so hate interruptions to her routine. This was an emergency, however, and she would have to report the accident to the police. No doubt they would ask her all sorts of questions, so she must be ready with the answers. She turned away, tutting quietly to herself . . . She would have to abandon her walk and go straight to the police station. The poor man could not be left there in that unhappy state a moment longer than was necessary.

On the way back she rehearsed what she would say. She had only been into the police station once before to report a lost umbrella – and on that occasion she had not been overly impressed. They had never found the umbrella. It began to rain and she quickened her pace, thinking of the poor, dead man who would be getting a soaking. At her age she had seen death at close quarters many times, but only in the respectability of a bed and surrounded by suitably grieving relatives.

'Poor man!' she said again.

In Prue's opinion, lying under a tree in the rain was not a fitting way to end one's days.

*

Later that same day in Cardington Bel was alone in Walter's

263

study, carefully going through his papers. Larry had only been able to stay for one night, and since his departure time had hung heavily. It was five days since Walter had disappeared and she was trying desperately to keep busy. Whenever her thoughts were not engaged, Karma's words returned to haunt her. 'The "W" and "H" entwines in everlasting peace . . .' Now she wondered if this could mean anything as sinister as a suicide pact. Walter had suffered emotionally and the boy was a little unstable, to put it kindly – and yet she was not convinced. Had only Walter been missing she might possibly have thought he had killed himself, although she had never thought of him as a coward. If suicide *was* the coward's way out . . . She doubted it. Surely it required great courage to end your own life? The police had told her that most suicides left a note by way of explanation, and they had found none. But since Howard was obviously involved it seemed too great a coincidence that they were both missing. The police had made enquiries outside their region and no hospital had admitted anyone answering to Walter or Howard's description. So an accident appeared unlikely. The number of the car had been circulated without eliciting any response. The police had suggested that they might have driven away together somewhere to thrash out their problems, and Bel clung to this small hope. George had suggested that Walter might be suffering from amnesia and would be found eventually, but if that were the case where was Howard? They seemed to have vanished from the face of the earth, and as time passed her hopes faded.

Today she had decided, albeit reluctantly, to take a closer look at Walter's affairs, since she now knew that they were far from normal. In a way, it seemed like a tacit admission that he was dead, but she had steeled herself to investigate in the hope that they might provide a clue which could solve the mystery. She had already discovered some letters from Vera, his wife, and a few, in a childish hand, from Howard; these had been tucked away in a locked drawer to which she had found the key. She had also found what she now knew to be her own spurious marriage licence, signed by A.F. Barrett, the ship's captain, and witnessed by two of the crew. She now knew too that Vera lived in Deal in Kent, and she was seriously considering travelling down to visit her. Vera should know that her husband was missing. But that would mean revealing her own existence as well as the vulnerability of her position, and if Walter were still alive he might resent her interference. Bel had no wish to make matters worse than they already were. And if she herself were going to leave Walter for Larry, which she intended to do, then Vera might be allowed to remain in blissful ignorance of her existence.

Bel was also wondering how much she should tell the police if Walter were not found. She had already omitted to inform them that she was not his legal wife, but at some stage concealing such evidence would look highly suspicious. If her relationship with Larry were to be revealed, that too might give the police cause for thought.

From the back of the bureau she withdrew a small, rolled bundle which turned out to be Howard's school reports, the pages browned with age, the spidery writing faded. Bel found her eyes filling with tears as she read them.

'Tries hard. A delightful boy . . .'

'Has made a tremendous effort with his arithmetic . . .'

'Howard wants to please. A very willing child . . .'

Oh, Howard! she thought, with a sigh. Where had all the sweetness gone? Was it possible that a delightful boy so eager to please could become vicious and unpredictable? If so, then how had the good in him been replaced by the evil? It was all so *sad*. She came across a school photograph and saw a small, round face with large blue eyes, the small mouth twisted into a hesitant smile. He was dwarfed by a very new-looking blazer, shirt and striped school tie. Had he been sent away to boarding-school, lonely and home-sick? Presumably Walter had wanted him to attend his old school. The boy looked so vulnerable. Perhaps they bullied him. Poor Vera! She must have been so proud of her son and so full of hope for his future. Walter, too, must have wished he could acknowledge the boy publicly.

A few more photographs fell from a slim folder and with a jolt she saw one of Howard with his mother, but the only likeness was in the small, timid mouth. The boy was so very much like Walter! The same eyes and nose, the same broad forehead; even the same way of holding his head. He was clutching a teddy bear and smiling shyly into the camera. His large eyes were fringed with long lashes and he looked about four years old; the mother was holding his shoulders and leaning over him a little, as though to protect him. Bel stared at the photograph, hypnotised. So that gentle-looking woman was Walter's wife? Well, if Walter were still alive the time would come when he might spend more time with her. If . . . if. . . .

Downstairs the bell rang and she waited, listening, for Mrs Banks to tell her who it was. Footsteps sounded on the stairs and Bel went out on to the landing to meet her.

'It's the police, ma'am. Sergeant Callohan and another one.'

Bel froze.

'Ma'am! They want to see you.'

'What about?' Her voice sounded strange.

'They didn't say.'

Slowly Bel went down the stairs. The thick-set man she recognised as Sergeant Callohan was waiting in the hall with a younger constable, and they had both removed their helmets. The younger man was introduced as Constable Wilmott; he looked very young, with fair hair and light blue eyes. Not trusting herself to speak, she led the way into the sitting room and, leaving the housekeeper outside, closed the door. If it was bad news she didn't want Mrs Banks having hysterics. She would break it to her gently when they had gone.

Sergeant Callohan said, 'Do please sit down, Mrs Roberts. We have some news of your husband.'

The constable was staring at her, fiddling with his helmet which he held in his hands.

Bel, swallowing hard, did not move. 'Bad news?' She watched the sergeant's face.

'I'm afraid so, Mrs Roberts.'

She sat down abruptly.

'We have found him not far from here, in woodland. I'm sorry to have to tell you that he's dead.'

For a moment the word rang in her brain, meaningless. Dead. The word she had been resisting for the past five days. Walter was *dead*.

The sergeant said, 'We're very sorry. Please accept our condolences.'

The constable said nothing, but he looked very pale.

'Dead,' said Bel quietly. 'Walter—' She felt terribly cold and glanced at the fire to see if it had gone out – but, of course, it was September and it had been unlit all through the summer. 'Walter is dead,' she repeated. If she heard it often enough she might believe it, she thought, beginning to shiver. Slowly she shifted her gaze back to the sergeant. 'But how did he . . .' She couldn't frame the word 'die'. 'How did it happen?'

The sergeant sat down opposite her, nodded to the constable to do the same and then took out a notebook. Avoiding her eyes he referred to it. 'He was found in a nearby wood, lying at the base of a tree . . . His car had apparently crashed into the tree, but that is not necessarily what happened. . . . He was found by a retired schoolmistress, one Prudence Harris, while she was walking alone in the woods. . . .'

She heard herself say 'Alone in the woods.' There was a

huge pounding within her head and her chest felt too small for the ache within it. Suddenly she could hardly breathe.

The sergeant's voice came as though from a great distance. 'Tell the housekeeper to bring some sal volatile.'

To Bel he repeated, 'We are so sorry, Mrs Roberts. It's a bad business.'

She looked at him. 'And the boy, Howard?'

'There was no sign of him.'

She took a deep breath. 'So was it an accident?' Not a suicide. Thank God!

'We – it's too early to be sure, but we don't think so.' Something in his voice made her glance at him sharply. 'The body was lying outside the car—'

The body. '*My husband*, you mean.' Was Walter already a non-person, she thought, shocked.

'Your husband, that is,' he corrected himself hurriedly. 'Both of the car doors were shut. It seems unlikely that the car crashing could have thrown the body through the window in that direction . . . Ah!' He turned gratefully towards the door. 'Here comes your housekeeper.'

Mrs Banks stood with the bottle of sal volatile clutched tightly in her hands and looked directly at Bel. 'Is it Mr Roberts, ma'am?'

'Yes, I'm afraid so,' said Bel. 'He's – he's been killed. It may have been an accident.'

Mrs Banks said, 'Oh, my Lord!' and swayed on her feet.

The sergeant said, 'Take her outside, constable, and keep an eye on her. It's been a nasty shock.'

Bel watched as the young policeman guided the housekeeper from the room. She took the sal volatile with her, but Bel was already feeling a little better.

She said, 'So if it wasn't an accident, could it be *murder*?' There was something obscene about the word, she thought dully.

'It's a possibility we cannot rule out. It may have been a robbery which went wrong. There was a wallet on the –

on him, but there was no money in it. Did he habitually carry anything else with him, Mrs Roberts?'

'He usually carried a watch, a gold half-hunter . . .' Was it remotely possible that the smiling boy in the photograph had killed his father? That the 'willing child', the 'delightful boy', had committed a murder? Oh, Walter! Poor, *dear* Walter! She closed her eyes as the first scalding tears rolled down her face. 'He was—' she began. 'We were . . .' She stopped, unsure exactly what she was trying to say.

'There was no watch on him. It's too early to say, Mrs Roberts, but we may have a murder made to look like a robbery. It's a very confusing scene, and I'm afraid that at some stage we shall need your co-operation.'

She nodded through her tears; she heard him but the words made very little sense. All she could think of was that Walter was dead. He would never speak to her again, nor could he listen to anything that she might want to say to him. And suddenly there were so many things she wanted to tell him. That what he had done was not so very terrible; that everyone made mistakes and no one was blameless; that somehow they could sort out the muddle and life could go on without all the guilt and remorse. But at least he hadn't known about her and Larry, and for that she felt immensely grateful. He had been spared that final blow.

The sergeant was looking at her expectantly, and Bel said, 'I'm sorry. What was that?'

'I said, "Did he leave a note anywhere?" They sometimes do if it's a suicide.'

The inquisition was beginning, thought Bel wearily, and the questions would come thick and fast. She had had no part in the crime, but there was so much to hide. She must think carefully about her answers, and yet she dare not withhold anything. The truth was bizarre enough and anything less than the truth might well appear suspicious. She would tell the whole truth and nothing but the truth, and try to hurt as few people as possible. She and Larry had been lovers, but in the unusual circumstances they had not actually broken any code, moral or criminal. With an effort she stopped crying, wiped her eyes, put away her handkerchief and looked at the sergeant, frowning. 'A suicide? You don't mean you think he drove *himself* into the tree?'

'It's not likely, I admit, but at this stage we mustn't rule out anything. My people will be examining the scene, but any ideas or theories you might have could prove invaluable. Naturally you might not feel up to talking just now, but the sooner the better. Time is crucial, you see. If we are looking for a murderer hours, minutes even, can make the difference between an arrest and an unsolved crime.'

'Yes, of course.' She gave him a direct look. 'Actually, sergeant, there is a great deal to tell you. I think we should start right away. No, I haven't found a note but there are some aspects of this that you should understand.' She thought his expression changed but that could have been her imagination. At all costs she must remain calm. 'I must begin at the beginning . . .'

Chapter Thirteen

MRS SIDNEY WAS STARTLED To see a policeman on her doorstep. Most policemen were bad news, but this one had nice grey eyes He also had a notebook in his hand, and for a nasty moment she thought he might have come about the 'second-hand' bike her youngest son had just acquired from a man in a pub. Well, if asked, she would know nothing about it. 'What do *you* want?' she asked sharply.

'We need to speak to your neighbour, Mrs Vera Roberts – or maybe her son, Howard Roberts. We've knocked but there's no reply. I thought perhaps you might know . . .' He left the sentence unfinished.

She hid her relief. 'Well *she's* gone away to her sister's in France and he's got himself a job somewhere. He's been gone a couple of weeks, although I did see him a few days ago. Popped back for something, I suppose. Like all lads his age, got a head like a sieve. Why are you lot after them, then? What have they been up to?'

'We don't think they've been up to anything, Mrs . . .'

'Sidney. I should hope not, but you never know these days. Saw it in the paper only yesterday, an old woman was done in by her own grandson for her savings. Dreadful! You should be out looking for people like him instead of—'

But the policeman was writing. He looked very young, with the beginnings of a moustache. She wondered for a moment what it was about the police force that attracted so many good-looking young men When his pencil was once more at rest he asked her exactly when she had last seen Howard Roberts.

'Oh, it must have been Tuesday morning – no, tell a lie, it was Wednesday. Middle of the morning. He looked terrible; got a bandage on his head. Been in a fight, he said. Some chaps at the pub calling his girl names, or something like that. Trust Howard. He always did have a quick temper, although it never lasted with him. Lovely little kid, he was. Used to play with my boys when she'd let him out. Kept to themselves, they did, mostly. She didn't hold with playing in the street. You sure he hasn't done anything?'

The policeman gave her a polite smile and said, 'We hope not,' in a voice that meant he wasn't saying any more.

'We'd like to speak to Vera Roberts when she returns,' he went on. 'I'll put a note through her letter-box. You've no idea when she'll be coming back?'

'A few weeks, maybe. The husband asked me the same question. All she said was "sometime", as much as to say, "You'll see me when you see me!" Know what I mean? Very vague really, but I'm looking after her cat; that's how I know.' She gave him a long look. He seemed rather interested in the fact that the husband had been down looking for them. Perhaps there *was* something funny going on after all.

'Well, thank you, Mrs Sidney. You've been very helpful.'

'Have I?' She rather wished she hadn't. They were all the same, the police. She wouldn't trust them further than she could throw them.

*

Peggy glared at the man on the doorstep. He didn't look like a policeman; he wasn't in uniform, but he did have a posh voice. '*You'd* like to talk to him, would you? Well, so would I. There's quite a lot I'd like to say to him.' She folded her arms belligerently. 'Because he's scarpered with my money, that's why. Ten quid I lent him because he said we were going to be married. And now he's gone and disappeared, and I'm left right in the cart. Cheating little baskit! I'd like to get my hands on him before you do and that's the truth.'

She paused to take another breath and the policeman asked her if she knew where Howard might have gone.

'No, I don't. If I did I'd be after him, and so would my Mum. She's hopping mad and if I'm – well, if he's got me in any trouble she'll *kill* him! If I don't get to him first.' Her lips quivered suddenly. 'He was so handsome and everything and he said he loved me. He was going to buy me a ring and everything and – and now he's buggered off with my savings.'

'So you haven't heard from him? No letter?'

'Nothing!'

'If you *do* hear from him, I'd like you to let me know. Ask for me at the police house. The moment he gets in touch – if he does.'

Her eyes widened. 'Why? I mean, he hasn't *done* anything, has he? I mean, nothing bad. I don't mean like me and him, but something really bad?'

'We hope not, miss. We're just making a few routine enquiries.'

She stared at him suspiciously. The phrase had an ominous ring to it. Routine enquiries usually meant that they weren't at all routine, that something dreadful had happened. And he wasn't an ordinary bobby so he must be a detective. Her mouth fell open suddenly.

'You don't mean — it's not about that old boy they found in the wood, is it? Not *Howard!*'

The policeman shook his head. 'At this stage we can't rule anything—'

He face fell. 'Gordon Bennet!' she whispered. 'Not *my* Howard—'

'Nothing's definite, miss. These are only—'

'I know. Routine enquiries.'

'It's just that they both disappeared on the same day and—'

'Disappeared?' She gave a little scream. 'You don't mean Howard might be dead too?' As the policeman hesitated she said, 'You *do* think that! You *do*! You think they've both been murdered!'

She began to cry and he looked uncomfortable and offered a clean handkerchief. She accepted it gratefully, and listened to the familiar phrases as he hurriedly closed his notebook. He promised to keep her 'informed of developments' and she watched him go with relief. After he'd gone she closed the front door and with her back against it, stared along the hall, white-faced. If Howard had got himself murdered and she was in the club, Mum would be really, really mad. She'd *kill* him! Except that she wouldn't be able to if he was already dead. 'Oh, Howard!' she moaned. 'Don't, please, *don't* do this to me!'

*

Alf Comber was talking to his fiancée about bridesmaids, without much enthusiasm, when the police called to ask him a few questions. Just 'routine enquiries', because Howard Roberts was missing and did Mr Comber have any idea when he was coming back or where he had gone? No, Mr Comber didn't. And wouldn't have said if he did know. Alf felt a bit guilty about swapping places with Howard on the India trip, because it was definitely out of order — strictly against company policy, but the policeman

274

didn't ask about that so he kept quiet. Say nothing about the ten pounds, either. Say as little as possible, that was his motto. He had never had a run-in with the police, so he had no reason to distrust them. On the other hand, he had no reason to trust them either.

'Was Howard Roberts a close friend of yours, Mr Comber?'

'No, not close.'

'Had he been working long for the R.A.W.?'

'No, not long.'

'Did he mention any friends he might be visiting?'

'No, he didn't.'

'You don't seem too helpful, Mr Comber.'

Alf shrugged.

'What sort of man was he? Peace-loving? Secretive? Violent?'

'Not really.'

'Thank you for your help, Mr Comber. Perhaps if you hear from him you would be kind enough to let us know? This is a *serious* case, and it is in your own interest to help the police with their enquiries.'

He nearly said, 'Is it?' but thought better of it.

When the policeman had gone Alf's fiancée, who had been listening, asked, 'What was all that about?'

'Don't you start!' said Alf.

'What do they want with him? What's he done?'

'How the hell do I know?'

'I was only asking.'

'Well, don't!'

'Alf!' She pouted.

He gave her bottom a pat to sweeten her up and said, 'D'you want to talk about this wedding or not?'

'Course I do, love.'

''Cause I'm up to here with it!' He put a flat hand up to his chin. He was sorry now that he'd gone along with the white wedding idea; should have said 'No' and meant it, but it was too late now. He'd given up the trip of a lifetime for her, so she'd have to make it up to him.

'*Alf!* Don't be like that.'

'Well, get on with it then.'

She opened her mouth to argue, but he gave her a look and she smiled instead. She had a lovely smile and he felt a flicker of hope.

'Well, it's almost all settled, Alf. I just need to decide on the head-dresses. Flowers look pretty but ribbons are cheaper, and Mum reckons if she ruched them up into bows and things and sort of twined them round . . .'

Alf nodded vaguely and tried unsuccessfully to forget Howard Roberts and concentrate his mind on the approaching wedding.

*

Mrs Croft was mortified to learn from the police sergeant that her lodger was being hunted in connection with a suspicious death. She felt it cast a slur on her personally as a landlady, but they assured her that she would soon find another lodger if young Mr Roberts was not coming back. She told them all she knew, and insisted that he had paid his rent on time and had enjoyed his food. She couldn't understand why he'd told her all those lies about his father being dead for years if the poor man was alive and well. Knocked off his motor-bike by a bus or some such – that's what he'd said. Still, that's the way some folk were. Tell you a lie as soon as look at you, but with him being good-looking you didn't expect it, somehow. . . . When had she last seen him? Well, he'd gone out to the pub one evening, that would have been the Tuesday, and never come back. She'd thought it a bit queer at the time. Oh, and she'd done a bit of washing for him and charged him ninepence, which he had said was fair, and the laundry would have charged half as much again. Just a few shirts and under-pants and vests. And socks, of course. He was quite a smart dresser. And *likeable*. Hard to believe . . . His habits? Once or twice he had come home late and a bit rowdy, but young men were like that. He had been courting her niece, too – Peggy, her name was. Peggy's mother was in a right state about it. Such a trusting girl, Peggy, and to think she'd been alone with him more than once and now he was a suspicious character. Mind you, she had wondered once or twice what they got up to when she was out of an evening playing whist, but she couldn't be watching them all the time. She wasn't his mother and she hadn't got eyes in the back of her head. She supposed they could search his room if they wanted to, but she had tidied it so her own fingerprints would be all over everything . . .

*

Mrs Banks sat in the kitchen reading the newspaper and was not reassured by what she read. The editor of the magazine *The Aeroplane* had written an article, strongly criticising the R101 and giving his opinion that she was not ready to fly to India and doubted whether she would get further than Ismailia.

'Dearie me!' she muttered. 'He doesn't mince his words. Let's hope he's wrong.' She wondered if the mistress had seen the article. Not that it mattered much now, because poor Mr Roberts was murdered and wouldn't be on the flight. But he had been so proud of the airship; she didn't want it to disgrace him after all the work he'd put in on it. She lowered the newspaper and thought about the disclosures of the past few days. It all seemed very dreadful and she was almost afraid to open the paper – there was so much about poor Mrs Roberts not being properly married, and Mr Roberts having another wife, and that young wretch Howard being his son. She had written to her sister about it – a really long letter – and sent her the cuttings from the local paper where they were making so much of it with great big headlines and photographs and everything.

Not that anyone could point a finger at *her*; she was just the housekeeper. And the reporter had got her name all wrong and called her Elise Banks instead of Elsie, not that she really minded – Elise sounded rather grand.

She supposed that Mrs Roberts and young Mr Roberts would be getting married. At first she'd been a bit taken aback and embarrassed by what had been going on, but since poor Mrs Roberts *wasn't* Mrs Roberts it was all right. And Mrs Roberts said they would still need her, so there was no question of her having to look for another position. She would feel a lot better when the funeral was over. Seeing someone lowered into the ground was so settling somehow. Definite. She'd felt that when her mother went. Once she'd been laid to rest it all seemed bearable. Perhaps it was the lovely flowers. She did hope that in spite of being murdered, Mr Roberts would have a lot of flowers. And Miss Roberts was coming, but not the father. He was bedridden, not to mention the shock to his system. Poor old soul; it was a dreadful way to lose your eldest son. She had told the police all she knew and they seemed very nice and efficient, but she did hope they would hurry up and catch that terrible Howard before he killed someone else – that is, if it *was* him, and all the papers thought it was and so did the police. They wanted him to 'help them with their enquiries' but everyone knew what they meant. And there were scientists in the hospital laboratories testing just about everything, and they'd practically taken poor Mr Roberts' car to pieces looking for evidence. Not that he would ever drive it again, poor man.

She sighed. He'd been a good man to work for, not like some, and she was sorry he'd gone. But he'd gone to a better place. That's what vicars always said at funerals and you must believe it. If you couldn't believe vicars and policemen, who *could* you believe?

*

When the pathologist's report was issued it confirmed that

death was due to multiple injuries to the head and face, one of which had fractured the back of the skull. Such injuries could not have been caused accidentally, nor could they have been self-inflicted. Immediately a full murder enquiry swung into action. The local police established a 'murder room' in the second bedroom of the local police house, and this was hastily furnished with the bare essentials. The church hall lent a couple of trestle tables and some folding chairs. A blackboard and easel were borrowed from the local school and various photographs of the victim and the victim's family were pinned to the board. A large map of the area was tacked to the wall and a smaller one showed the R.A.W. flying field in case that proved to be significant. A set of metal drawers contained the few files so far created and on one of the tables there was a typewriter and a pristine ream of foolscap paper. Tea would be brewed on a small primus stove and mugs stood nearby on a tray, alongside a tea-caddy, a tin of condensed milk and a single spoon.

The Cardington police were not particularly pleased that someone was being sent down from C.I.D. at Scotland Yard to mastermind the investigation. Detective Chief Inspector Carter, in his late thirties, was a well-set man with thinning ginger hair. His sergeant, a thin, taciturn man by the name of Paul, was also resented. They had no option, however, but to bow to the policies of their superiors, and secretly one or two were grateful for the expertise that the C.I.D. might be able to offer. The murder of one of their most illustrious residents could not go unsolved, and they were unhappily aware of the intense interest from both the national newspapers and the B.B.C. At a time when the world's press was focusing on the R101, a scandal on their doorstep was highly undesirable and an early arrest was vital.

The two men arrived in Cardington on Friday September 19th, and at once Detective Chief Inspector Carter shut himself away with all the files. On September 20th he called a conference of all the staff who were involved in the enquiry. Waiting for the last members to arrive, he surveyed his men with a jaundiced eye. He hated working with officers whose capabilities he could not yet know and this lot, he thought, looked no worse but no better than many other local teams he had worked with. Time would tell. The entire team consisted of only eight officers. Stingy bastards! He had hoped for at least a dozen. Still, he must make the best of a bad bargain. He nodded to his own sergeant, Derek Paul, hand-picked for the job because they had worked well together over a number of years. Paul closed one eye in an almost imperceptible wink. Carter then looked at the others with a critical eye. Local sergeants Callohan; Harris, a slow, heavy-looking man and Wills, wiry, in his early forties. In addition there were three constables – Pritty, Shadd and Wilmott. Carter looked them over and decided to give them the benefit of the doubt. He liked to think his reputation had gone before him, but if not they would soon find out that he was a hard man when crossed. The proverbial fools were not suffered gladly by him.

Once they were all present he gave them his usual pep talk, told someone to put the kettle on, then read them the coroner's report and asked for comments.

Sergeant Harris said thoughtfully, 'The bruising suggests a temper or a drunken frenzy – or the settling of an old score with his father.' Seeing that Carter had raised his eyebrows he added quickly, 'That's assuming the son did it. We think he did, don't we?'

Carter said, 'Rule number one – never take anything for granted. True, the son is number one suspect until we find him murdered; then we think again. At this stage we mustn't rule out the possibility of a coincidence here. A stranger could have killed the father, and the son might have taken off for any number of reasons. Could be coincidence but, like you, I doubt it.'

Eagerly Sergeant Wills said, 'We could put Constable Pritty on house-to-house enquiries for any stranger in the vicinity on or before the night of the murder.'

Pritty, his features at odds with his name, groaned loudly but was quickly silenced by a withering look from Carter. 'Yes, sir,' he said hastily.

'Probable time of the murder is——?' asked Wilmott.

Carter glared at him. 'You shouldn't need to bloody ask!' He extended his scowl to take in everyone. 'Let's get this straight. I mean to catch this bastard and nail him to the wall. And you're here to help me do it; I haven't got time to spoonfeed anyone. You do your homework; you keep yourselves up-to-date. You don't . . .' he turned back to Wilmott '. . . ask bloody silly questions. And I want all reports in on time. If you can't type, at least make it *legible*. You get back here and you write up your findings and you don't go home until it's done. This is a murder enquiry, not a picnic. Everyone got that?' There was a hurried murmur of agreement. 'OK. Now, to answer that question. It was most probably the ninth. Late at night on the ninth, or the early morning of the tenth. Christ, he's had a long time to get clear. We'll need a lot of luck on this one. You, Wilmott, can get over to the hospital first thing tomorrow and see what the lab boys have got for us, if anything. If there had been a struggle *something* ought to show up, but not all the results were in.' He rubbed his face tiredly and consulted his notes again. 'We've got a dark thread from the passenger seat but no doubt Roberts – or whoever' – he corrected himself quickly – 'will have destroyed his clothing. If he didn't panic, that is, which he might have done. And if he had enough money to buy replacements.'

Wills said, 'He'd been home remember, sir. Back to Deal. He could have picked up clean clothes there.'

'OK. Get down there and see if the mother's back. She'd know if his clothes were missing.'

'Right, sir. I'll do that.'

281

Carter frowned. Was he missing something here, he wondered suddenly. 'Bit of a coincidence, that,' he mused, thinking aloud for the benefit of his colleagues. 'Mother disappears, supposedly in France but no one has an address there. Then son murders father and also disappears. Could be a link.' He shrugged. 'A conspiracy to murder? I doubt it somehow.'

No one argued with him. He looked at Paul, who said, 'Not for my money.'

Carter returned to his checklist. 'Usual enquiries at ferry ports. See when the mother sailed for France – and if she came back. She may have disappeared into the woodwork. She has to be told her husband's dead.' He steepled his hands, frowning. 'Funny business, this bigamy. Unusual, that. I suppose they're not stringing us along. Someone check out the wedding on board the ship. It was years ago, but it needs doing.' He glanced round.

His own sergeant said, 'I'll do it.'

'Good. Try to find the captain. There's always the possibility that it's the wife and lover conspiring. Stranger things have happened.'

Callohan asked 'The real wife, d'you mean, or the non-wife?'

'Isobel Roberts, so-called.'

Constable Shadd raised a tentative hand. 'I know this is a long shot, sir, but it's a bit of a coincidence that the victim worked for the R.A.W. and the airship is due to fly to India at the end of this month.' There was a chorus of disbelief, but he ploughed doggedly on. 'I mean, sir, there might be someone wanting to discredit the whole opera-tion.' To a further chorus of doubt he insisted, 'It *could* be!'

Carter silenced them with a wave of his hand. 'It may be a long shot, but Shadd's quite right. *Anything* has to be considered.' He smiled at Shadd who, red-faced, brightened immediately. 'You get yourself over to the R.A.W. tomor-row and talk to the big cheese, whoever he is. Ask him about Roberts and his contribution, and sound him out on the remote possibility of someone trying to sabotage the project. If that was the motive I'd expect them to go for someone bigger, but that's just an opinion. And maybe they couldn't reach anyone bigger.' He glanced round him. 'Any other ideas? I want to hear *all* your thoughts on the matter. Not just those you think might be relevant, *all* your thoughts. This trail has probably gone cold and we'll need to *feel* our way into it. We'll have to follow up every single lead. My hunch is that it's the son, but we won't rule out anything else. Now, Wilmott—'

'Sir!'

'When you're done at forensics, double-check the hospitals admissions in the area. There was blood on the coat of the victim that wasn't his own, so maybe there was a struggle. We'll need to nail the murderer before we can match the samples. If it was a genuine crash, then the murderer might have been injured too and might have needed stitches.'

'Right, sir. But chances are he wouldn't have used his own name.'

'You might get a description though, if he had acted suspiciously and drawn attention to himself.' He pursed his lips, still thinking along the familiar lines. 'I'd like all roads covered between here and Deal since we know he went home. A notice asking for information and random checks too. Someone might have given a lift to a man with a facial injury or cut hands.' He glanced round hopelessly. 'There's a hell of a lot to cover with a team this small, but I'll keep pressing for some more men. We'll have to hope that the radio appeal for information will get results.' He consulted his notes again. 'Sergeant Callohan, I see you broke the news to the widow. Go back to her with a lot of questions – and the housekeeper, too. Separately, naturally—'

Callohan said stiffly, 'I do know the rudiments of police investigation, sir!'

Ignoring the comment, Carter finished his sentence '—
and we'll see if they tally with the earlier replies.'

Shadd, inspired by his earlier success, asked, 'What
about the lover? Laurence Roberts.'

'I was coming to him. I'll visit him tomorrow.' He
looked around. 'Is anyone watching the house, in case the
murderer returns to create further mayhem? No? Well, I'll
see if we can borrow someone from Bedford to keep an
eye on the place. Our resources are going to be stretched
to the limits.'

He drummed his fingers absentmindedly on the table-
top, awaiting inspiration. He'd been drafted to Cardington
within hours of finding the killer of a West End prostitute,
and that enquiry had kept him from his bed for the best
part of nine days. He was used to snatching the odd hour's
sleep where and when he could, but today he was feeling
particularly exhausted. He glanced at Wilmott. 'Make us all
a cuppa, would you? Mine's very sweet.' He didn't say
'please'. That would teach the young idiot to ask stupid
questions.

Wilmott, blushing, made himself busy while Carter re-
viewed the crime, scanning the coroner's report. 'Bruising
could have been done by a fist and most probably was. A
soft, blunt instrument is how the coroner describes it . . .
let's see . . . But the blows themselves would not have been
enough to cause death under normal circumstances. The
recent heart attack played a large part in weakening the
victim who may, or may not, have suffered a second attack
. . .' He glanced up. 'So that raises the point that it may not
have been intentional which would, if proved, reduce the
charge to manslaughter.'

Someone said 'He's still dead, though!' and there was
some ragged laughter.

Carter did not smile. 'Since the car belonged to the
victim it's likely that he gave a lift to the murderer. Unless
he got into the car and the murderer was already hidden in

the rear – possible, I suppose. Or they got out of the car together and the crash was arranged afterwards. Or the crash was genuine and the murderer hurt himself by going through the windscreen.' He stared at the papers in his hand, his eyes unfocused as he tried to imagine the scene. 'Infinite possibilities,' he muttered. 'I shall get over to the scene of the crime again this afternoon, but I shall have to wait for one of you to get back – which is a nuisance, but can't be helped since we seem to be doing this on a bloody shoestring. This room must be manned at all times. I shall talk to the press and ask the public for information, and we don't want people trying to ring or call in and finding it unmanned. Sergeant Paul, have I forgotten anything?'

'I doubt it, sir. Can't think of anything.'

'Sergeant Callohan? Any comments you'd like to make. Anything I've overlooked?'

Still smarting from his earlier rebuff, Callohan stared grimly ahead and said, 'Not a thing, sir.'

As Wilmott came round with the mugs of tea Carter took his gratefully and said, 'Right, then. Don't take all day drinking it; there's a lot to be done. I shall want to see most of you here first thing tomorrow. Eight o'clock sharp.' He pretended not to notice the dismayed looks. 'I'll try to ring' – he consulted the file – 'this Prudence Harris and ask her to call in.' He looked enquiringly at Sergeant Callohan, who said, 'Nice old girl. She taught my mother. Very proper. Observant. Keen on nature study and once wrote a book about funguses – or is it fungi? She's on the telephone, her number's on the pad there.'

'Thanks. Right.' He gave them a very brief smile and held his mug of tea aloft in a mock toast. 'Here's to an early arrest!'

*

Carter parked his car just off the road and walked along the track taken by the victim's vehicle on the night of the

285

murder, trying to visualise the sequence of events. Let's assume it was Roberts and his son in the car. Then had they previously arranged to meet somewhere? The suspect had been in the pub with friends that night and, according to several witnesses, he was still there when 'Time' was called. So did he go to the victim's house and persuade him to get out of his sick-bed? Most unlikely. The house-keeper said she was given the night off *unexpectedly*, so probably the victim decided to go and find – or meet – the suspect. Did he simply *guess* he might be in the pub and wait nearby?

He came in sight of the wrecked car and stopped to look at it. Had it been travelling fast enough to kill them both? It must have been travelling at a fair rate to do that much damage, so the speed must have been deliberate. Could the victim have planned to kill both of them? Possible – but where was the motive? Unlikely to be a double suicide. The young man would hardly agree to be driven into a tree! Unless he had no idea that that was in his father's mind. Or he was mentally unstable . . . but that could be ruled out. The foreman at R.A.W. had said he was bright enough and a good worker; 'keen' was the word he used. A young man *keen* on his job doesn't kill himself. But he might, and probably did, hold a grudge against his father, and this meeting was somehow connected to that relation-ship. Odd that his father had never acknowledged at work that the boy was his son. Unless he didn't *want* him to work there . . . or didn't *know* that he was working there. Then found out! He found out and met the boy – the son almost no one knew existed – to persuade him to push off and not embarrass him further. . . .

He passed the POLICE sign, said, 'Morning!' to the constable who was on duty and stepped under the rope that cordoned off the area of the crash.

'Morning, sir!'

'Not that it is.'

'No, sir, but at least it's not raining.'

'Was it raining on the night of the murder?'

'I'm afraid I don't remember, sir.'

'Hmm!'

The constable blew on his fingers to hide his nervousness.

Carter considered. The girl-friend said the suspect had had 'a fair bit' to drink, they had had 'a tiny tiff', and he had stalked out of the pub. So could he have contrived that tiff so that he could meet his father at a pre-arranged time? No, because she said he had wanted her to leave with him.

He said, 'I don't suppose there were any footprints in all this muck?' He kicked the decaying leaves irritably.

'I think not, sir but I don't know. I'm on loan from Bedford.'

'Ah! And you've been here all the time?'

'After the second day, sir.'

'And has anyone visited the scene who couldn't be accounted for? Anyone at all?'

'No, sir. Just us and the press boys. Cameras flashing everywhere!'

Carter nodded and cast a quick eye over the ground. 'No souvenir hunters?'

'No, sir.'

Carter smiled suddenly. 'No one to brighten your days, then? Must be a dreary job. Well, We're finished here. I'll get the car towed away this afternoon and then you can go back to Bedford.'

'Thank you, sir!' The constable brightened considerably.

'Did someone drop you off here?'

'Yes, sir.'

'I'll see that you get picked up. And take the rope and all the gubbins with you.'

Carter looked inside the car, then climbed in and sat in the driver's seat. What were they saying to each other?

What *happened* to spark the murder if it wasn't premeditated? Could they all be wrong? Suppose Roberts meant to silence the son and they fought and the son won? And then panicked, wondering who would believe him? That would be self-defence. A different kettle of fish altogether. The father had a lot to lose. His marriage – bearing in mind that Roberts didn't know about the lover – unless he'd guessed or someone was lying, and that was always a possibility. But if so, then who? Certainly the victim's reputation was at stake, not to mention the bad press for the R101.

He sounded the horn and the constable jumped.

'Sorry!' Carter smiled.

'That's OK, sir.'

He got out of the car and shut the door. Had the victim been killed here or had it happened elsewhere? Perhaps the vehicle was simply used to transport the body from A to B . . . He looked at the distance between the tree that had been hit by the car and the tree where they found the body, and thought that it could not have been thrown that far at that angle. It was no accident. There had been an assault outside the car. But who had assaulted who? Had a very sick man assaulted his very fit son? Unlikely. Had a son assaulted his very sick father? He turned to the constable and said, 'I'm off! I'll see to that tow and when the car's gone you can push off. I'll square it with your superior.'

He walked back to the car with the thanks of the constable ringing in his ears. As he switched on the ignition he thought about the first wife, the *real* wife . . . Had she found out and conspired with the son . . . and then done a rather neat disappearing trick? He closed his eyes despairingly, then opened them and reversed the car carefully. Why, just for once, couldn't he have a case that was cut and dried?

*

Once the coroner's report had given the police sufficient

288

grounds to call Walter's death murder, his body was released to his family. The funeral was arranged for 2 o'clock on the 24th September and Larry and Marie travelled to Cardington in Larry's motor. Bel was dreading it. The police had warned her that the press would be there plus a great many sightseers, as well as Walter's many colleagues from R.A.W. and his friends and acquaintances from both London and the village. His body lay in a mahogony coffin in the spare bedroom and, at Bel's request, the lid had been left open. After the violent manner of his death, both Marie and Larry had wanted to see their brother looking peaceful in the hope that they could remember him that way. The bruises had been well disguised and the funeral directors had managed to make him look almost normal. A swelling over his right eye had refused to subside but his colour was normal and, as Marie said wistfully, he might have been sleeping. Flowers had been arriving for the past twenty-four hours – blue irises from his father, white roses from Bel and red and white chrysanthemums from Marie and Larry. There were sprays of flowers, bouquets and baskets as well as a number of posies from local people, and from the Royal Airship Works there was a circular wreath in red, white and blue.

Mrs Banks, in between brief bouts of weeping, busied herself with a cold collation for forty-five people – close friends, family and a few colleagues – helped by Mrs Parks, who had begged to be allowed to come to Cardington to pay her last respects. It was almost 2 o'clock and Bel, Larry and Marie sat together in the sitting room waiting for the cars to arrive. Bel wore a black suit with a small hat and a half veil; Marie wore a black coat and hat. They talked sporadically, trying to keep each others' spirits up, aware that the worst was still to come, when Walter would be sealed into his coffin and laid to rest in the cold earth.

Marie said, 'Well, at least it isn't raining. That's always so frightfully depressing.'

Bel could only nod but Larry said,' I just wish he had been able to go on the flight. If this had to happen it could have been a few weeks from now and then he would have died happy.'

Marie asked 'Happy? How could he die happy? If your son kills you I don't see—'

'You know what I mean. He would have lived to see his dream come true and that would have been something. Poor Walter! Now even that has been snatched away from him.'

Marie said to Bel, 'Did you think what I thought when I saw all the flowers? Red, white and blue? Karma said she saw all the flowers and the music. Well, Walter has been sent all these flowers, and there'll be music in the church.'

Bel looked startled. 'You mean she foresaw this? The murder?'

'I don't know, but she did say she saw black and more black – and look at the three of us today!'

'And we thought by "all the flowers" she meant the reception in Karachi!' Bel frowned. 'But Walter didn't fall from a great height – at least not as far as we know.'

Marie was reluctant to relinquish her line of thought. 'Suppose he did somehow fall – or was pushed? And then dumped in the wood and—'

'Oh, Marie, *don't*!' cried Bel. 'Isn't it bad enough already without you making it worse?' Her voice trembled and Larry put his arm around her.

'Bear up, sweetheart,' he whispered. 'This has to be one of the worst days. Tomorrow it will all seem just a little better, a little more bearable.' He kissed her.

Marie said, 'I still can't get used to thinking of you as a couple. I can't get it into my head about Walter and Vera.'

Bel looked up, fighting back tears. 'I do wish the police could have found Vera. She should have been here. Walter was her husband and she has every right to be at his funeral. More right than I have, in fact. When the police suggested asking the solicitor, I did think we might be getting somewhere, but even he only had the Deal address.'

Surprised, Marie said 'But you wouldn't want her to be here, surely? You can't want to be *friends* with her!'

'Why not? She has done me no wrong and I haven't wronged her deliberately. We are both innocent in that way. I feel so desperately sorry for her.'

Larry shrugged. 'Maybe she's better off in ignorance until all the fuss dies down. I can hardly imagine her attending the funeral with all the press and the B.B.C. present. It would be a nightmare for her, knowing that the police are hunting for her son.'

Marie agreed. 'Especially as she would then find out about you and Walter. No, Larry's right. She's better off in France with her sister, oblivious of everything. She'll have to know some time, poor soul. As soon as she sets foot back in England, I daresay—'

'Or books her return ticket . . .'

Bel sighed deeply. 'The police are going to descend on her. Oh, God! I think it's going to hit her more than any of us; she'll lose both of them.' She glanced at her watch. 'It's five past two! Where are they?'

As if in answer to her question the first of the cars rolled to a halt outside the front door, pursued at a run by members of the press with their cameras at the ready. Bel thought of them as vultures, but she knew they were only doing their job. She appreciated, too, the fact that the publicity they gave to the murder might well prompt someone to come forward with a vital piece of evidence. Mrs Banks went hurrying to the front door and Bel made her excuses and ran up to the bedroom. She took a long, last look at the man she thought she had married.

'I loved you the only way I could,' she told him shakily She leaned forward and kissed his forehead and two tears fell on to his face. She brushed them away with trembling fingers.' 'Goodbye, my dear. God bless!' she whispered and then straightened up as the door opened and Mrs Banks ushered in the men from the undertaker's.

From the sitting-room window Bel, Larry and Marie watched the coffin loaded into the hearse, then went out together to climb into the second car. Immediately the reporters were all around them.

'How do you feel, Mrs Roberts?'

'A quick photograph, please, Mrs Roberts!'

'Is this a sad day for you?'

'How do you feel towards your husband's son?'

'Was it a shock? . . . Do you want to see him hang? . . . Do you feel betrayed? . . .'

She wanted to shout, 'Go away! Leave us in peace, for God's sake!' but how could any of the family be 'in peace' again? Circumstances had conspired against them to ensure that the past would always be with them; the memories of the last few weeks would haunt them. And there was probably worse to come; they would find Howard and he would stand trial and the suffering would continue.

The car followed the hearse and Bel, Larry and Marie sat together, their faces pale and set. At the entrance to the drive two policemen waited and one held a single flower.

Suddenly, seeing the flower, Bel had the strangest feeling. She said, 'My God!' and began to wind the window down, calling to the driver, 'Wait a minute! Stop the car!' She looked up at the policeman and said, 'That pink rose. Who sent it?'

He looked confused. 'Actually, we were told to remove it—'

'It's from him, isn't it. From Howard?'

Larry exclaimed 'What? He's had the gall . . .'

Bel opened the door of the car. 'I want to see the card,' she said, 'and I don't want an argument.'

Reluctantly he held it out to her. Written in a hurried scrawl she read the words: 'Forgive me. I love you.' There

292

was no name. Bel stared at the rose. Ophelia. In her mind's
eye she saw Howard standing in the garden at Cardington,
his hands in his pockets, the wind rustling his hair. What
she had seen in him then was the likeness to Walter. And
he knew Walter's favourite rose – and today Howard had
sent him one. Choked, she held out her hand. 'I'll take it,
thank you,' she said, keeping her voice steady with an
effort.

'But our orders are . . .'

The press were once more crowding round and Marie
was urging her to get back into the car. Larry got out and
stood beside her. The policeman was explaining that they
would need to find out where the flower came from. She
said sharply, 'The florist will have the details. You don't
need the rose. *Please*!'

While flash-bulbs popped and the questions from the
press were redoubled, Bel waited for the two policemen to
confer. Then one said quietly,' Do you think it wise, Mrs
Roberts?'

'I don't know,' she admitted, 'but I feel in my heart that,
in spite of everything, my hus— that Walter would want it
on his grave. Don't you?' She swallowed hard. 'For all the
happy times?'

He shrugged. 'If you say so.'

He placed the rose in her outstretched hand and as he
did so a single petal fell to the ground.

Chapter Fourteen

I N   T H E   N O.   1   S H E D   the following day, the work
on the R101 was nearing completion and those responsible for her turned their sights towards the all-important
test flight. Everything that could be done in the limited
time available had been done, and all that was needed was
a Permit to Fly. This meant only that certain prerequisites
had been met and the airship was considered airworthy;
permission was granted for her to become airborne in
order that her trials proper could begin. The airship with
her new bay had never been tested, and that would have to
be done before she could be allowed to set off for India.
The weather was now going to be a crucial factor in the
programme of tests set out for the R101, but before they
could begin she had to be 'walked out' of her shed, and
this was not as as easy as it sounded. It did, in fact, involve
enormous risks. The size of the vast shed meant that winds
gusted round it in an unpredictable manner, and a fierce
gust could swing the giant hull with terrific force against
the door or the side of the shed, with disastrous results. In
an attempt to avoid such a disaster a white line had been
painted down the middle of the floor so that the hundreds
of walkers could keep to a straight line while they tugged
the huge airship forward.

To the intense dismay of all concerned, the inclement

weather continued so that on the next day, September 26th, the R101 was still confined to her shed. They began the task of 'gassing her up' – hydrogen was pumped into her gas bags which were constantly monitored for signs of leaks. The gas valves were checked and rechecked and finally declared satisfactory. Various tests were undertaken for lift and trim, and the designers were much heartened by the results. By the end of the day they judged her ready to fly, but the weather did not improve and four crucial days passed while the designers and crew fretted helplessly and the airship remained in her shed. The decision was taken to use the interval for loading the provisions and stores, since there would now be no time for this *after* the trials.

The Permit to Fly was issued, but the time for the test flight was rapidly dwindling. What should have been a forty-eight-hour flight was reduced to only twenty-four-hour. Understandably neither Flight Lieutenant Irwin, the ship's captain, nor Lieutenant Commander Atherstone were happy about this reduction but, apart from delaying the scheduled flight to India, there was nothing they could do about it. Lord Dowding would travel on the ship on her final test and, if convinced by her performance, would issue the Certificate of Airworthiness. Ideally the ship should be tested at speed, in bad weather, in daylight and at night. This now seemed extremely unlikely.

But at last the wind died away and in the early hours of the 1st of October the moment they had all been waiting for arrived. Bus-loads of 'walkers' had arrived, many of them airmen from the R.A.F. station at Henlow, and had taken up their positions in the shed. Crowds watched eagerly from the airfield's perimeter as the silver nose of the airship appeared, like a shy animal peering from its burrow. A cheer went up, but it was much too early for congratulations. The R101 was seven hundred and seventy-seven feet long and had cost around a million pounds. The slightest error could damage her hull, and the walkers were well aware of the importance of their contribution. Inch by inch, foot by foot, yard by precious yard, the ship was eased out from the gloom of her shed into the daylight.

Amongst the crowd Peggy watched breathlessly, clinging to the arm of her aunt. Mrs Croft let out a sigh of real pleasure as the huge silver-grey shape was revealed in all her glory.

'Oh, Auntie!' cried Peggy. 'She's wonderful!'

'And about time too!' said Mrs Croft, but her own face shone with excitement as the huge craft hovered above the heads of the walkers, her silver skin reflecting the autumn sunlight. From the ranks of the waiting press hundreds of cameras flashed, recording the momentous occasion for the rest of the world. The R101 was larger in every respect than any ship that had preceded her, and those who had laboured over her for so long felt justifiably proud.

The giant airship now had to be raised to two hundred feet. She could then be edged forward so that her nose could lock into the top of the mooring mast. When this docking was completed, she would remain tethered until ready to fly.

'Look!' cried Peggy. 'Look at her nose!'

A hawser was being played out and this extended until it reached the ground.

Mrs Croft pointed to the top of the mooring mast from which a similar hawser was descending. Each hawser was quickly connected so that the airship was now loosely tethered to the mast.

'Now what on earth . . .' Mrs Croft muttered.

Two more cables were lowered from the airship's nose and these were grasped by two of the team on the ground.

'It's to hold her steady,' Peggy told her, 'while she goes up.'

The engines were started and slowly the airship was driven backwards while at the same time water ballast was released to allow her to gain height. More ropes were dropped from along her length.

'See the rollers on the ground?' Peggy pointed. 'They'll tie the ropes to those to stop her swinging around too much. They weigh two tons each, they do.'

'Two tons? Never!'

'They *do*! Howard told me.'

Mrs Croft said 'Howard!' She turned to frown at her niece. 'Don't talk to me about that young man, after what he's done.'

Peggy's mouth drooped. 'We don't know for sure,' she protested, but her aunt's face had assumed its familiar expression of disapproval and she decided not to pursue the subject.

The crowd watched breathlessly as the mechanism at the top of the mast slowly wound in the hawser until the airship was floating level with it. It was then a matter of closing the gap, but at last a roar of relief went up from the spectators as the airship swung at her mast.

'She's made it!' cried Peggy, and she and her aunt exchanged delighted smiles. Around them the crowd whooped and cheered, and there was a rush from the press enclosure as the reporters raced each other to the row of temporary telephones which had been installed for their use. Among the crowd, those thoughtful enough to have brought a picnic now tucked in; the others went hungry. No one would leave the flying ground until their marvellous creation had taken to the skies.

The next few hours passed with a series of minor delays requiring last minute adjustments, but the eagerly awaited moment finally arrived. At half-past four in the afternoon the R101 was detached from her mooring mast and, with a toss of her silver nose, was finally free of all constraints. Stunned with admiration, the ecstatic crowds stared upwards as the improved version of the R101 took to the sky for the first time.

*

From the window at Cardington Bel watched the airship with a heavy heart. If only Walter were still alive . . . If only he were aboard her . . . But instead he was dead and buried and would never share in the triumph to which he had devoted so much of his life.

Behind her Marie said, 'She looks like a giant fish – or a cigar.'

Bel shook her head. 'Too plump for a cigar,' she said. She wished Marie would go back to London, but knew that her sister-in-law felt she was needed here, to 'get Bel through the worst of it', as she had put it. The funeral had passed without incident, apart from the rose which Howard had sent. The police had traced that to a florist in Bedford, and Marie was convinced that he was still lurking in the area, preparing for further mischief.

Marie said, 'Your father would have liked to see that, too,' and Bel nodded without answering. What was it about airships, she wondered, that caught at men's hearts and held them in thrall? Ever since her father's death she had resisted them in her mind, trying only to see them as vast flying machines. Now, however, seeing the R101 sleek against the pale sky, she was forced to concede defeat. To put a machine that size into the air and steer it from A to B was the ultimate achievement against all the odds. It was the struggle against the elements. It was . . .

Marie slipped an arm round her waist. 'It was tough – the will,' she said. 'I didn't say anything at the time, but I was shocked.'

Bel shook her head. 'I was not his wife. Why should he leave everything to me?' She spoke as lightly as she could, grateful to Marie for raising the forbidden subject. Her own sense of shock and rejection at the will's contents was beginning to fade, and Bel knew that discussion of the subject could not be deferred indefinitely.

Walter had left Bel the house in Cardington and various investments. The London flat was to be sold and the proceeds shared between Vera and Howard. It had been a tremendous shock, but Bel was coming to terms with her new status as 'second wife' and was trying hard not to feel hurt. There were three letters, one each for Bel, Vera and Howard. Walter was nothing if not methodical, Bel now reflected ruefully. Hers had been written at a time when she was unaware of Vera's existence, and it explained the true state of affairs. This was followed by an abject apology and a heart-rending plea for forgiveness.

Marie sat on the arm of the settee and shook her head. 'I just feel that you came out of it a very poor second. It was too bad of him.'

With her eyes still on the airship Bel said, 'Vera didn't have a proper marriage either, remember. She must have been terribly lonely all these years. She must have felt neglected and unloved. Maybe that was his way of compensating her. Howard, too. I had Walter – or thought I did. I was never lonely or neglected.'

'You were! Walter was always at Cardington. You never saw him.'

'It's not the same and you know it.'

Bel put a hand to her head, which was beginning to ache. She was sleeping badly and her waking moments were filled with uncertainty about the future and a nagging anxiety about the whereabouts of Walter's killer. Journalists rang constantly wanting interviews or, failing that, answers to questions. Was she fearful for her own life? Did she think the police would catch the murderer? How had she felt when she first discovered that she was never married? At first she had tried to parry the questions, but now she hung up on them. The police called in daily with a progress report. Friends wrote letters. She felt that she would have crumpled beneath the weight of so much unwelcome attention if she had not been able to lean on Larry. He had been a constant support, a rock in a troubled sea. He telephoned every day and came up at weekends when Marie returned to London to be with their father.

As though reading her thoughts, Marie said, 'At least you've got Larry. You will marry him, won't you, Bel? I mean, you won't let any of this change your feelings towards him. He was totally blameless, although I admit he didn't know it.'

'You mean how guilty am I feeling?' Slowly Bel turned from the window. 'Well, since you ask, I don't feel too happy about what we did and I wish we could have waited a few months. Then we could have fallen in love without—'

'You *didn't* betray Walter. He wasn't your husband!'

'That ought to comfort me, but it doesn't. Not really. When I think about it I do feel rather cheap. And don't lecture me, Marie, because there's no way you can possibly understand.'

Marie's eyes darkened with the unspoken reproof. 'I know what you really mean,' she said. 'You blame me – for starting you and Larry—' She bit her lip.

Bel sighed. 'If I'm honest I suppose I do, *but* I do know how irrational that is so please don't take it to heart. Look, Marie, hindsight makes everything clearer and we can all look back and wish something undone or unsaid. But we can't undo anything, and that's life.'

Neither spoke for a while and then Marie said, 'I wondered if we could go to the flying field and watch her when she takes off for India. I think Walter would have liked us to see her. Can you face it? She's due to leave on Saturday, and Larry will be here. I could stay on a day or two. Father wouldn't mind. You could get passes for all of us; it would be something to tell our grandchildren—!'

'You mean *your* grandchildren.'

'I didn't mean – oh, Bel! You and Larry might have a child; you can't know for sure.'

'Can't I?' said Bel and then regretted the bitterness that she heard in her voice. But Marie had touched a raw nerve. Bel desperately wanted to give Larry a child, but knowing that Vera had borne Walter's son seemed to underline her own inability to conceive. 'I'm sorry. Let's not talk about it.' As Marie opened her mouth Bel added quickly, 'Yes, let's go and wave her off. It's the least we can do and anyway, it will be fun.'

Anything to take her mind off her many problems, she thought wearily, but almost immediately regretted agreeing. Now Marie would stay on, wanting to travel back in Larry's car, and Bel would not have Larry to herself at all. She cursed her own stupidity and then, in turn, cursed her selfishness. Of course it was right that Walter's close family should watch the beginning of the historic flight. Bel herself was not even a part of the family. Oh, God! She closed her eyes, defeated. Tired and confused and utterly wretched, she was wallowing in self-pity and she hated herself for it.

*

Vera walked back towards the farmhouse, trying not to mind that there was no letter from Howard. It was the 3rd of October and soon she would be going home. He probably thought it was not worth writing now in case the letter arrived after she'd left for Calais. She had walked to the farm gate every day to collect the post. It was funny, the way they did things in France: the postman left the letters in a little box on a pole outside the gate. She had teased Pierre about it, pretending that the French postmen were too lazy to walk to the front door. He was nice, Pierre – nicer than she'd expected – and Evie was happier than she'd expected, so that was all right. Although they

301

had had some sort of argument yesterday – not that she had been able to understand it, because they shut themselves away in the bedroom and gabbled away in French, but Evie had ended up in tears and they'd both done a bit of shouting. When it had gone quiet and she guessed it was all over, she had gone in with a cup of tea for them and they had both looked at her as though she was a man from Mars or something. Evie had been reading the newspaper and she suddenly screwed it up and pushed it into the fire. Odd, that. And Pierre had put both his hands over his face, almost as if he didn't want to see her. All a bit embarrassing, really, and it made her wonder whether or not she was outstaying her welcome. But then, afterwards, they were extra nice to her and they both said again that there was a home for her there, with them, if she ever felt the need. They'd gone on and on about it and that was a bit odd, too. They were very kind, but she was longing to get back home.

Vera was still glad she'd come, though. She felt a much stronger person – the sort of person who can travel and do things. Walter would be impressed when she showed him some of the picture postcards she had bought of Beauvais and Allonne. And Edouard was really sweet. A sweet, good man. They kept pretending he wanted to flirt with her, but she was not having any of that nonsense; she had told him about Walter, so he knew she was not free for anything like that. Still, she did like him and she wouldn't pretend she didn't. She was going to challenge Walter to a game of chess when he next came to visit; she was getting rather good at it; Edouard said she was a 'natural' at chess. But she did think Howard could have dropped her a line. Boys are so thoughtless; not like daughters. What did they say? 'A son is a son 'til he takes a wife; a daughter's a daughter for the rest of her life!' Not that she would swap Howard for a daughter, but she did wish he was a bit more loving. A letter from home would have been a big excitement. She had written to him once, but then she couldn't find his Shortstown address and had to write what she could from memory, and then just before she posted it she knew it wasn't right and had kept the letter back. She would post it as soon as she got home. It wouldn't matter, because he'd be busy and making new friends up there and he might even have met Walter. If so, she did hope they had been sensible about it all. They were both grown men. No doubt she would find a letter from Walter when she got back. She realised now that she *should* have told him where she was going because he might be cross, but at the time she had wanted to declare her independence. Now it seemed a bit silly, but it was done. Oh, well; no good crying over spilt milk. She ought to be worrying herself sick, but it all seemed so far away, as though England was another planet.

And she had told Evie and Pierre that they *must* come to England as soon as they could afford it. She would put them in her room in the double bed, and she would go in Howard's room, and she would make such a fuss of them. She sighed and, lifting the latch, let herself into the little kitchen. Picking up her knitting, she muttered, 'Oh, Howard! Is it really too much trouble to write your mother a letter?'

*

Evie and Pierre lay whispering together in bed that night. They spoke in French, although they both knew it was impossible for anyone outside the room to overhear the conversation. The previous day, they had learned from an English newspaper that Walter had been found dead in a wood, possibly murdered. They had also learned that the main suspect was Vera's son. The shock of this double tragedy had been tremendous, but, worse still was the problem of how to break the terrible news to Vera. They had delayed, arguing passionately about the best course of action. Evie wanted a few days to 'think things out', but Pierre wanted to face the problem head on.

'It will be kinder to her in the long run,' he argued yet again. 'It is terrible and sad, but some time she will have to know. If we tell her we can help her through the worst of it. We can—'

'But she'll want to go straight home! I know her, Pierre. She'll say she must be at home so that she can help Howard if he needs her—'

'Help him *how*? What can she do, Evie, to help him? The police will be watching the house; they will be opening her letters. She will be hounded by the newspaper men and interviewed by the police. For Vera it will be a nightmare.'

'So why send her back to all that? Why not let her stay here in blissful ignorance for just a few days longer?'

'Because she is due to go back soon anyway, and unless we tell her what is happening she will go home knowing nothing! What a shock *that* would be. Poor Vera!' He put his arms round his wife. 'I know it's hard for us to do what's right, but we need to be strong. For her sake, Evie.'

'Oh, God, Pierre! I don't think I can take much more – our own nephew a murderer!'

'Don't talk like that. We *have* to take what life sends our way. Somehow we have to live through it.'

'But she's always been so . . . so timid and nervous. I know her better than you, Pierre. I'm her sister and I know what this will do to her. If she goes back to England I ought to go with her. Or both of us.'

'Evie! We've been over this before. We don't have the money for even one fare, and how can we leave the farm?'

'We could borrow it. We could ask Edouard to feed the animals.'

'And how could we pay back the money?'

'I could go with her. That would be only one fare – but I wouldn't want to go without you. Oh, why did this have to happen? *Why*? Poor Vera! It will kill her! I know it will. And what if they catch Howard and – and . . .'

'And hang him? I don't know. If he killed Walter then he deserves to be punished.'

'But *did* he really?' She sat up suddenly. 'Oh, Pierre! Suppose he comes *here*! To us. To his mother. What would we do?' She gave a little cry of fear and began to tremble violently.

He said, 'But why should he? He won't come here.' But he, too, sounded alarmed at the idea.

'To be with his mother – to ask for help! He might be coming already! Would we hide him, Pierre? Would we have to lie to the police and – oh! That's an offence, isn't it? We would be in serious trouble then. Oh, God! I can't bear this.'

'Then let's tell her first thing in the morning. It will be best.'

He tried to pull her back beneath the warm bedclothes, but she resisted him.

'You see, Pierre, I keep telling myself that once she knows, the rest of her life will be poisoned. It will be the end of her happiness. No husband. No son. How could she bear it? She would not want to go on living. There would be no purpose to her life.'

'There is always a purpose to life, Evie. Always.'

'She might become religious. She might join something—'

'Be a nun, d'you mean?' Evie's voice rose in protest. 'Vera, a nun?'

'No, no! I meant a church group. Helping the needy. Someone must need help. There's the Salvation Army. She might join that. You could suggest it to her. She might fill her life that way.'

Evie was suddenly hopeful. 'Do you think she might?'

'I don't know, do I? I'm not clever.'

'Yes, you are!'

'Not in that way. But she could come here to us; we've told her that. You know she would be welcome.'

305

'You're so kind, Pierre. Such a dear man. I'm so lucky. I wish Vera had never met Walter, but I can't wish we'd never come on that trip or I'd never have met you.' She slid down into the bed again and pressed a kiss into his neck.

He said, 'If we tell her, we might persuade her never to go back. To write to the solicitor and say sell the house and send her the money. We could do up her bedroom here – a nice carpet, new curtains. I could put up a few bookshelves.'

Evie thought about it. At last she said slowly, 'One more day and *then* we'll tell her. I promise. She's so looking forward to watching the airship go over. Let her see that.'

'But Walter won't be on it.'

'Let her think he is. Let her be happy and excited, just for tomorrow.'

Pierre was doubtful about the wisdom of her idea, but it was awkward because they had already arranged a little celebration for the occasion; Edouard was coming round and they would cut into the new ham and open a bottle or two of the wine. Then they would watch the airship with Vera's husband on board go past on its way to India. The papers suggested that the airship should pass over Beauvais around midnight.

'Please, Pierre,' Evie begged. 'Then first thing the next morning we'll break it all to her.'

Reluctantly he nodded. They would have to keep up the pretence that all was well for another day. He shrugged mentally, said, 'First thing the next morning, then,' and it was agreed.

*

The 4th of October arrived with hardly any wind but overcast clouds. At the meteorological office at Cardington there were frequent meetings, and there was little comfort

306

to be found in the forecast. The weather could go either way, and all they could do was pray that it would not deteriorate further. It had finally been decided that the R101 would leave her mast some time that evening, probably around seven. There were still a few last-minute stores to be loaded – fresh produce for the galley and flowers for the passenger rooms – and these had to be hauled up in the lift which operated inside the mooring mast. Within the hull final checks were being made and riggers were everywhere; in the excitement nobody noticed that Alf Comber was not among them. Flowers were arranged on the tables in the dining room, beds were made up in the cabins and small toiletries were distributed to the bathrooms. Engines were given a last-minute inspection, especially the starboard forward engine which had performed badly during the test flight and was still giving some concern.

People had been converging on the area since first light. All the major roads into Bedfordshire were subjected to a continuous stream of traffic heading towards Cardington, and the police were on duty at every major junction. By mid-morning huge crowds fringed the airfield, kept in place by a contingent of police specially drafted in for the occasion. Journalists and reporters for the B.B.C. and other radio stations watched from a small but privileged enclosure. Marie, Larry and Bel, on police advice, watched from Larry's car which was one of the few allowed to park within the confines of the airfield.

Marie read aloud from the morning's newspaper. '. . . The passengers will arrive during the afternoon. These are few but impressive. Lord Thompson, Secretary of State for Air; Squadron Leader Palstra who represents the Australian Government—'

Larry said, 'I suppose that means she'll be off to Australia next!'

'. . . Squadron Leader O'Neill, representing the Indian Government; Sir Sefton Brancker O.B.E.—'

Bel said, 'He's the Director of Civil Aviation. Walter spoke often about him.'

'. . . And a Major Bishop, the Chief Inspector, Aircraft Industry Development.'

Larry said, 'You've forgotten Thompson's valet!'

'And the valet. Only six in all!' said Bel. 'A terribly select group.'

An urgent banging on the car window made them all look up. A photographer took a shot of their startled faces before a policeman grabbed his arm and hurried him away.

'Silly little man!' said Marie with a quick glance at Bel.

Bel said, 'I'm OK. Truly. I'm finding it very interesting.'

Leaving the car under the watchful eye of a policeman, they made their way through the crowds to the R.A.W. canteen where they had been invited to lunch. By the time they returned to the car it was mid-afternoon and they were dismayed to see that the weather was breaking up. Gusts of wind buffeted the airship so that she tugged at the mooring mast like an animal anxious to escape its tether. Bel eyed her anxiously as she loomed overhead in the fading light. There was something almost ominous about the giant presence, she thought, and was aware of a growing knot of apprehension within her.

Marie squeezed her arm. 'Cheer up, dear old thing!' she urged. 'It might never happen!'

'I'm all right!'

'You don't look it,' Marie told her. 'Remember this is a time of celebration, so no tears!'

Bel managed a smile and at that moment all the lights came on in the airship – white from the windows of the passenger deck, red and green from the navigation lights at either end of the hull. These, combined with the red light at the top of the mooring mast, gave her a more cheerful appearance. Lights also went on in the mast itself and several searchlights were suddenly trained on the airship. This gave the crowd a chance to applaud and Larry smiled.

'They're loving it,' he remarked. 'It's certainly a day to remember; something to tell the grandchildren.'

Bel nodded, trying to quell her uneasiness. There were still several hours to go before the flight was due to start, but the weather continued to worsen. The wind had strengthened noticeably and there were occasional flurries of rain. As the sky darkened the lights from the airship above glowed oddly on the upturned faces of the crowd below.

Larry caught sight of a group of policemen conferring and hurried across to find out if there was any news. He came back visibly relieved.

'They're not waiting for the official departure time. They're getting ready to go now.'

'Thank heavens for that!' said Bel.

A murmur of excitement ran through the crowd as the news spread and all eyes were strained as 'goodbyes' were said on the ground and those who were to fly were hurried up the mast in the elevator to make their way along the enclosed catwalk into the airship. At last it seemed that everyone was aboard and the moment had arrived. But the forward starboard engine was turned over again and again without starting. Larry wound down the windows so that they could hear as well as see.

Marie said, 'God! No! That would be too humiliating for words!'

Bells rang within the airship and they could imagine the frenzied activity. Suddenly there was a burst of noise and a shower of sparks and the reluctant engine began to throb. One by one the other engines started up until all were running satisfactorily. A roar of relief went up from the spectators and people could be seen hugging each other. Union Jacks were waved and triumphant fists were thrust upwards towards the R101.

Bel thought, 'I'm watching it for you, Walter,' and wondered if it were possible that somehow his spirit was watching too. Then the airship drifted slightly away from her mast and an 'Aah!' of delight rose from those on the ground. Suddenly her nose went down and for a long moment seemed unwilling to lift. The 'Aah!' turned to a groan.

Bel said, 'Oh, my God, Larry!' and he put an arm around her.

Marie whispered, 'If the wind blows her against the mast—'

'Don't say it!' cried Bel. With one hand to her throat she cried, 'Rise, damn you! Rise!'

Water ballast fell suddenly from below the bow, splashing down like a waterfall, and to the relief of all concerned the nose lifted abruptly. The airship shivered, turned safely away, and then the engine note changed and she was moving under full power.

Instinctively Larry, Bel and Marie scrambled out of the car and stood huddled together in the cold, damp air, watching her go. As she began to turn south a gust of wind hit her and she rolled. They could see the passengers silhouetted against the interior lights, waving their hands in farewell to family and friends they were leaving behind.

Marie said, 'It'll be champagne all the way!'

Bel nodded, choked with emotion, unable to speak. The airship turned still further and for a few seconds the searchlights found the pennant at the rear, a tiny splash of red, white and blue fluttering bravely in the cold, dark air. As the minutes ticked slowly by, the R101 drew steadily away from them until she was obscured by the lowering clouds. As she vanished from their sight the weary crowd fell silent, seemingly bereft.

'God speed!' whispered Bel and, as Larry hugged her, she was surprised to find her eyes full of the forbidden tears.

*

Howard, jammed between two of the R101's gas bags, grinned as they became airborne and gave the thumbs-up sign to no one in particular. He'd done it! He'd stowed away on his father's airship and was on his way to India. They would never find him there; he had beaten them. His grin broadened.

'That to the police!' he muttered, sticking up two fingers in a rude gesture of defiance. Not that it had been easy, because it hadn't, but he had gone about it in a sensible way, planning it well in advance. Planning! That was the all-important word. While the police were keeping a watch on the ferry ports and trains he had stayed low, moving from place to place along the East coast, never staying longer than a day anywhere. Never giving anyone a chance to become suspicious or ask awkward questions. He had grown a beard, which rather suited him although it had a gingery tone to it but maybe, generations ago, his ancestors had been Vikings. He had let his hair grow – had to, really, because he didn't want to hang about in any barber's shop in case they were on the lookout for him. The cut on his face was healing, although not very well. It should have been stitched, but he dared not approach a doctor or a hospital. So he would have a bad scar which might make him look a bit gangsterish, but he didn't mind that. He'd buy himself some decent togs when he reached India – if they sold good togs there. His knowledge of the Indian continent was confined to what he had been taught at school and somewhat sketchy but anyway, he'd buy the best he could find. He was travelling light, with nothing except what he stood up in. There was no way he could have smuggled a suitcase aboard!

The airship rolled suddenly and he held his breath. Gas could leak from the gas valves during a roll – he had heard them talking about it before . . . He swallowed. Before all that happened. He wondered if the police had traced his pink rose. Not that it would do any good because he'd moved on by then. He wondered if his mother knew yet that his father was dead. Quite likely she didn't. She'd be expecting to see his father fly over in the R101, and instead she would be seeing *him*! Not *seeing* him, of course, and not knowing, but later on he would write to her from India – no address, of course – and let her know that he was all right and that he had been on the airship. She might have to show it to the police, but even if she did they wouldn't know where to start looking. India was a very big place and he'd use another name. He'd been trying out a few new names while on the run and had finally settled on James Carlington! He grinned again. He'd just changed one letter, so nobody would make the connection with the R.A.W. But *he* knew. He would always know, and wherever he went in the world the name would always link him with home.

The airship pitched suddenly and Howard clung to the nearest girder to steady himself. It wouldn't do to be thrown through the roof of the dining room, slap into the middle of the VIPs! Below him he could hear footseps and voices as various members of the crew scurried to and fro on their different errands. No doubt Alf would be mad when he knew. That is, if he had still stayed away. Not that there was any need, because Alf must have thought that poor old Howard Roberts was going to miss his big chance. He was probably laughing to himself, for now he had the ten pounds *and* the trip to India. Lucky sod! Howard sighed. Somehow he would let the riggers know he was aboard; he wanted *somebody* to know how clever he had been. A stowaway on the R101! It would have made all the headlines if only he hadn't . . . if only his father hadn't died on him. For a moment the dreadful vision returned; he saw his father's eyes wide with horror, and heard his feeble voice. 'Howard! Don't – please!' He swallowed hard, closed his eyes and waited for the vision to fade. It was so unfair. He hadn't meant to do it. He began to count rapidly to concentrate his mind on something else . . .

'Twenty-one, twenty-two, twenty-three—' There! It had gone. He breathed a sigh of relief and tried to remember what he had been thinking about. Ah, yes! The riggers. If they knew he was on board, there was nothing much they could do. They could hardly toss him over the side! They could report him but they wouldn't; they would keep their mouths shut. They'd think it a bit of a giggle, and they might tell people when they got back to England, but it wouldn't matter then. Howard would have vanished. But the captain must never know . . . not during the outward journey anyway. If he knew he would have to arrest him – not for being a stowaway, but for being a suspected murderer. Howard shook his head vigorously. No, the captain must remain in blissful ignorance. That way Howard would make it to India.

He took a large slab of Nestlés chocolate from his back pocket and broke off a line of four. Nestlé's Superfine! He loved it. Not that this would last him for the whole trip, but he might get one of the crew to bring him some grub – he had enough money to bribe anyone. His father's wallet had contained seventy-three pounds, although most of that had gone on cheap lodgings in the seaside towns along the East coast. And a pound to that miserly old devil in the Austin who would only give him a lift if he gave something towards the petrol. Crook!

The airship rolled again and the thought of the gas was beginning to bother him; he began to wonder if hydrogen did anything to your lungs and, if so, was it doing anything to his. And what if it *was* leaking out? If she lost enough they would lose height. Already he imagined she was moving sluggishly, but that was probably because of the rain which was now lashing the airship with a loud drumming noise. If the rain wasn't so noisy he'd be able to hear the gramophone. It certainly was raining. The envelope would absorb a certain amount of water and some would run down to replenish the water ballast. The question was, how much water would the envelope take up? Water was very heavy stuff. Oh, well, that was their problem. He was just along for the ride! He chewed the chocolate and reflected that if only he hadn't been wanted by the police he might have been a hero, with his photograph in the paper like the chap on the R34. Ballantyne, his name was. Howard could just remember it. It was 1919, when the R34 flew to America. His father had been so proud – not that he'd been on it but he knew the ship's captain, Major Scott. Howard smiled at the memory. A man had delivered a bottle of champagne to their house so that he and his Mum could celebrate, and his mother hadn't known how to open it. She'd wasted half, getting the cork out, and then it had gushed out everywhere. That was in the days before mooring masts, when someone had had to parachute down to the landing ground from the airship to organise the ground crew. Nobody ever knew how to secure an airship in those days. His father had gone on and on about it. He frowned. Captain Pritchard, it was. No, *Major* Pritchard! The first man to actually land on American soil. No, the first man to land from the air . . . or to parachute down. Something like that.

He grabbed the girder as the ship bucked suddenly, then steadied herself.

'Christ Almighty!' he muttered. 'Like a ruddy horse!' Like a bucking bronco! He broke off another piece of chocolate and thought that maybe, after the stewards had all gone to bed, he might creep down and help himself to a bottle of beer.

*

The night of the 4th of October Evie, Vera, Edouard and

314

Pierre stayed up until midnight, peering from the downstairs window. At last it was agreed that maybe because of the bad weather she was crossing France by a different route. They knew she was on her way because they had heard it on the news, but if she had chosen another route at the last minute there was no point in sitting up any longer. They should go to bed, said Pierre. Evie agreed and Edouard shrugged. Only Vera wanted to stay up but at last she, too, was persuaded to abandon their vigil.

'You'll read all about it in the morning,' Edouard told her kindly as he set off towards his own house. 'Good night! Sleep well!'

Vera said her 'Good nights' also but, once in her bedroom, she made no effort to get undressed. She wrapped herself in a blanket from the bed and settled herself on a chair by the window. The others might give up if they wanted to, but she wanted to be able to tell Walter that she had seen the R101 fly over France. She took her little travelling clock and propped it against the windowsill; she would be able to tell him the exact time at which he had passed Beauvais, even though he was probably in bed by now. She could imagine him, curled up in the tiny bunk, full of good food and wine. And snoring! She smiled. She had teased him that one and only night they had slept together. 'What a noise!' she had protested, exaggerating wildly. 'Like a blessed saw!' Poor Walter, he had been so embarrassed. She wished afterwards that she hadn't said anything about it; it might have put him off sharing a bed.

She stared out into the cloudy night and wondered how well the ship was sailing in the storm. A bit of a bumpy ride, most probably. Like being on a ferry in a rough sea – only air instead of water. Her thoughts drifted to Evie, and she did hope they had made up their quarrel. They both seemed so edgy and weren't saying much although this evening had been a bit more cheerful. A glance at the clock told her that it was twenty-past one. Surely it couldn't take all this time to fly from Cardington and cross the Channel? Maybe Pierre was right and they had changed the route. Well, she would give it another hour or so and then give up. Mustn't doze off in case she missed it. . . .

Journey Log Book
. . . Time – 02.00 hours . . . Altitude – 1200 ft . . . True Air Speed – 53 knots . . . Weather – moderate rain . . . Position – Beauvais . . . Duration from start – 07 hr 24 m . . . Wind Force – 50 mph . . .

Officer of the Watch, Steff, finished entering up the figures in the airship's log book. He could have added 'turbulent conditions' but didn't. He could have said that the airship's progress was lamentably slow and that they were two and a half hours behind schedule. Still, it was just possible, *if* the weather improved, to make their scheduled arrival over Ismailia by early evening of the 6th.

The watch was changed, the passengers had gone to bed, the R101 was still airborne despite the pounding of wind and rain. True she was lurching along, making difficult headway with the fierce side wind, but she was coping with it. *Just.* In the control car there was a query about the accuracy of the altimeter. Were they actually as high as they thought? Meanwhile, the engineers Cook, Savory and Binks relieved their counterparts, Blake, Hastings and Bell. Leech, a senior engineer, had checked all the engines. He was off duty now and, in the empty stateroom, he poured himself a well-deserved drink. . . .

*

Vera ran screaming to bang on the door of her sister's bedroom. 'It's here! It's here!' she cried and then she rushed out into the garden to stare up at the airship which had suddenly loomed up so dramatically out of the darkness. She could see the row of lights from the passenger

316

deck and the control car. Clutching her coat around her with one hand, she waved frantically with the other. In a frenzy of excitement she yelled above the howling wind: 'Walter! It's me! Walter!' although she knew he would be asleep, and even if he wasn't he could not hear her. If truth were told she found the airship disappointing, but she would never, *never* tell him so. After all she was hardly seeing her at her best. The R101 was like a wild thing, a ghost, grey among the dark clouds, being blown almost sideways in the teeth of the gale, her engines grinding and roaring with the effort. And she was low. Surprisingly low. Vera thought that if it had been daylight she might have seen him at one of the windows.

'Walter! Oh, Walter!' She wished she could think of something more inspiring to shout at such a historic moment. Perhaps 'God Save the King' – but that would sound a bit melodramatic. She heard Evie and Pierre rush out of the farmhouse and the door swung to with a crash.

'Look at her!' she shouted, her words swept away by the wind.

Then, inexplicably, the airship dived towards the ground and they all screamed out in fright. When she straightened up Vera cried, 'Oh, Evie! For a minute I thought she was—'

Lashed by the rain, they stood together in the dark, windswept yard, staring up at the clumsy giant that floated above them.

Evie said, 'She's coming down so low!'

'Is she trying to land?' said Pierre.

And then, unbelievably, the R101 dived again. In a voice that was little more than a whisper Vera cried, 'Oh, Walter! *Darling!*'

Evie said, 'Please! No!' and Pierre muttered something in French that Vera could not understand. Then the R101 was so low there was no going back and she went out of sight behind some trees. There was a long, slithering sound and then the unmistakable crunch of collapsing metal.

'*Walter!*' Vera screamed.

Then there was a tremendous explosion, followed by two more.

Evie said, 'She's *crashed*!' in a tone of utter disbelief, and then the wrecked airship was suddenly a ball of fire lighting up the surrounding countryside with a fierce, white light.

Vera stammered, 'Oh, my love!'

As they watched, shocked and silent, red and orange flames leaped hundreds of feet into the air from a white-hot centre and were reflected by the low grey clouds. Smoke billowed, curling and swirling, swept into the surrounding darkness by the wind that still gusted erratically, fanning the intense blaze. They felt a huge draught around them as the hungry fire sucked in the surrounding air. Faintly they heard the crack of twisting metal and small fragments of burning debris fell like bright rain, hissing into the wet undergrowth. Vera dropped her coat and began to run towards the gate.

Evie found her voice. 'Don't, Vera. Come back! He's not on it! Vera! Walter's not on it!'

But Vera could make no sense of the words. She only knew that the man she loved was being burned alive in that terrible fire, and if there was the slightest chance she must be there to help him. She had reached the gate before Pierre caught up with her and then she fought him to be allowed to go on. She must be there, to be near Walter.

'Vera! Vera, Listen! He was not on the airship! Walter, your husband! He was not on it!'

Vera heard him but the words failed to register in her stricken mind. She pulled herself free from his restraining hands and stumbled on towards that fearful glow. They could hear the metal twisting, and the roar of the flames was something she would never forget. 'Walter!' she cried.

As she ran her foot caught in something and suddenly

she found herself sprawling in the wet grass. Sobbing, exhausted, she was struggling to her feet again when Pierre reached her and pulled her into his arms.

'He's not there!' Pierre insisted.

'Not there?' she sobbed. 'How can you be so sure? Oh, Walter! *Walter!*' But her strength seemed suddenly to desert her and she lay in his arms with her face against his chest.

'Come back to the house,' he said gently. 'We'll tell you everything then. A drop of brandy, and then I swear we will tell you everything.'

*

Vera sipped her brandy, her eyes dull with shock and pain. They had told her that Walter had been found dead in a car crash. Their faces were so sad that she knew it was the truth. Pierre had put another log on the fire and was busying himself with it, coaxing a bit of warmth from the dying embers. Evie watched her anxiously.

Vera said slowly, 'So he's dead anyway?'

'Yes.'

'Poor Walter.'

Evie swallowed. 'We put off telling you, Vera. It was my fault; it was all so dreadful.' Pierre said, 'Go on, Evie,' in a quiet sort of voice and Vera gave him a quick look.

'Go on what?'

Her sister said, 'One thing at a time.'

Pierre said, 'You're just prolonging the agony!'

Vera's heart lurched and she took another sip of brandy. Pierre reached out and refilled all three glasses.

'Look, Vera,' said Evie, and her voice was shaking. 'There's more bad news, I'm afraid. You'll have to be very brave.' She leaned forward and touched Vera's knee and Vera swung it away as though she had contaminated it in some way. 'Walter's death wasn't an accident. It was supposed to look like an accident but . . . but—'

She looked at her husband and Vera wanted to scream at

319

her, but she was too busy trying to understand what Evie was saying. 'He wouldn't,' she said. 'Not Walter. He would never, *never*—'

'Not that,' said Pierre. 'Not suicide, Vera. Walter was killed by someone. Someone murdered him.'

Evie turned on him. 'Oh, Pierre! You needn't have said it like that!' Her voice broke. 'Not right out like that!'

Vera blinked. She felt that this could not really be happening. 'All those people!' she whispered. 'All burning like that. That's horrible.'

Pierre had pulled the curtains so that the light from the flames was no longer visible. What a terrible death that must be . . . Now he said, 'It must have happened so quickly, I don't suppose they suffered long. It was probably over in a few seconds.'

'Do you think anyone escaped?' She looked at Evie who was sobbing now, tears trickling through the hands which covered her face.

There were so many things to think about, Vera thought, dazed. Pierre had been so sure that Walter was dead. *Already dead.* Not lost in the airship. She asked, 'Who'd want to kill Walter? What's he done?'

Evie gave a cry that was half a moan and half a sigh. 'I can't,' she whispered.

Pierre drew a deep breath. 'I'm sorry, Vera, but the police think it was Howard.'

'Oh, now, that's silly!' cried Vera, knowing that *couldn't* be right. 'Not Howard, Pierre. Not *my* Howard. Kill his own father? That's nonsense.'

Pierre looked years older, she thought suddenly; his face was grey and lined. Poor man.

He went on, 'The police think that Howard and Walter quarrelled about something, and that Howard lost his temper and they . . . they struggled.' He paused.

Vera did not help him. She hardened her heart. This was turning out to be a dreadful night, really dreadful. If Pierre had things he wanted to say, let him get on with it; she was past caring. Walter was dead and there was nothing left for her. It was all over.

Pierre went on, 'Walter had been ill with a slight heart attack—'

She sat up, startled. 'A heart attack! Oh, my God!'

Pierre and Vera exchanged a quick look. 'He – he was at his house in Cardington and they think that he dressed and went out to meet Howard, in the car. You see?'

Vera stared at him. No, she didn't see. She didn't see anything. She felt sick. If only she could cry, but the tears wouldn't come. Her mother used to say, 'That's right. You have a good cry!' As though that would make it all right! A good job her mother wasn't alive to know all these goings-on. Poor soul. Vera took a deep breath and then another, and thought how nice it would be if she could faint and not know any more. Or drop down dead. Why shouldn't *she* have a heart attack?

Evie said, 'That's enough, Pierre. Don't say any more. In the morning we'll get the doctor.'

'We could get him now,' said Pierre. 'I could fetch Monsier Albert. She needs something to make her sleep.'

'They'll all be at the crash.'

'The funeral!' cried Vera. 'Walter's funeral!' She put a hand over her mouth and thought that at least she had a decent black coat. She could take off the fur, which was getting raggy, and maybe sew on a new piece.

'We don't know,' said Vera. 'The coroner has to release the – his body. Probably by now . . .'

Evie's voice trailed into silence and Vera thought she had never known such a terrible evening. First the crash and then all these stories about . . . Her head was spinning. She swallowed the last of the brandy, and heard herself ask, 'Is there any more for me to know?' Even her voice sounded like someone else's.

Evie said, 'No!'

But Pierre answered, 'Yes, there is.' To his wife he said, 'Better get it all over with now.' To Vera he went on, 'You'll have to know some time. Walter was living with another woman, Vera – not married to him, but she thought she was. She didn't know about you. The police think Howard may have found out and tried to punish the woman. Maybe that made Walter angry. There, that's all of it. It's terrible.' His own voice cracked suddenly and he got up and stumbled out of the room.

The two women stared at each other, then at last Vera stammered, 'Another woman? *Walter?*'

Evie nodded.

Vera could hardly take it in. There were so many terrible things that she needed to grieve about, she hardly knew where to start. Walter and another woman! So he'd lied to her. She had asked him once who ironed his shirts. The laundry, he'd said, quick as a flash. 'Well,' she'd told him, 'you're paying them too much!' There were creases down the front. She had never let Howard wear a shirt like that. Another painful thought struck her. 'Did they have any children?'

'No.'

'Well, that's something.' The brandy was wonderfully warming and she could see now why some people took to drink. After a long silence she asked, 'How long have you known? Was it in that newspaper?'

Evie nodded. 'I couldn't bear for you to know. It was my fault.'

'Was there a photograph? Of her?'

'Yes.'

'Was she— What was she like? Pretty?'

'You know what newspaper photos are like. Sort of pretty. But she didn't know, Vera. You can't help feeling sorry for her. She didn't know about you and Howard, not for years and years. The paper said she was badly shocked. All those years and they weren't properly married! When she found out, at first she thought *you* were "the other woman". Then she discovered *she* was.'

'What's her name?'

'Isobel.'

Vera smiled tiredly. 'Is a bell necessary on a bicycle? That's what we used to say when we were kids. D'you remember, Evie? Is a bell . . .' Suddenly the thought of her childhood, in those far-off innocent days, brought home to her like a blow against her heart just how far her life had travelled away from her dreams. She was aware of a deep cry somewhere inside her, full of anguish and the misery of rejection. Suddenly tears seemed to rush upwards into her eyes and force themselves from beneath her eyelids. They came with such force that they spurted out, spattering her knees, and the ugly, keening sound that she heard was her own heartbreak. As she sobbed uncontrollably she was aware of Evie kneeling beside her and sobbing with her, cuddling her awkwardly.

'You can stay with us, Vera,' Evie told her. 'Don't go back. We want you to stay with us. One day we could all be happy again. Please don't go back.'

They cried for a long time. At some stage Pierre came back and stood beside them, his large hands resting on her shoulders. Then he went away again. After what seemed a lifetime, Vera found that she could stop crying and she blew her nose.

Evie said, 'Please stay with us, Vera.'

'I think—'

'Yes?'

Vera looked at her slowly. 'I think I'm going to be sick!'

She was, immediately, just like that, and afterwards she realised how much better she felt, as though she had got rid of all the evil in the whole world. And the rest of the night was a bit of a blur. Pierre slept in her little room, and she slept with Evie in their double bed in case she needed anything.

When she woke it was 3 oclock in the afternoon and, although her head ached and her eyelids were red and swollen, she could hear the birds singing. She pulled on her dressing gown and went down to the kitchen on wobbly legs, but there was no one about. She made her way outside and looked around, and to her astonishment the air seemed to be full of silver specks which glinted in the sunlight. There was something magical about it and, wonderingly, she held out her hand and one of the specks settled in her palm.

It was ash from the burning airship.

Chapter Fifteen

A FTER WATCHING the departure of the R101, Bel decided to travel back to London with Larry and Marie, having first obtained permission from Detective Chief Inspector Carter. He had questioned all three of them and had their statements, so there was no reason why they could not leave the area. Mrs Banks had been given two days off, so that she need not remain there alone.

On the morning of the 5th of October Bel awoke in the London flat to find Larry beside her, holding a cup of tea in his hand. They had spent the night together, and Bel was shocked to realise how late she had slept.

She struggled up on to one elbow and said, 'You're dressed!'

'Some of us have chambers to go to!' he smiled. As she took the tea he leaned over and kissed her. 'Last night was wonderful,' he told her. 'I'm glad they've never passed a law against it!'

Bel smiled at the memory. 'I'd break it!' she said, putting the cup on the bedside table. 'Oh, dear! Do you have to go in today? It's Sunday! A day of rest.'

He sat down on the edge of the bed and held her close. I should have worked on Saturday, but didn't. We've got cases coming up tomorrow and Meade won't be very happy if the spadework's not done.'

'The day will seem so long without you. There must be *some* way I can persuade you to stay!'

He sat back, grinning at her, and she thought how lucky she was to have this bright, wonderful person to love her. And to love. When all this misery was over they could be truly happy together. Now, when they made love, she felt that illogical twinge of conscience that they should dare to snatch a little happiness while others suffered.

He said, 'Don't tempt me, Bel. I'm very weak-willed where you're concerned.'

'I'm sorry, darling. I know you have to go.'

'And you'll go round and see Father, won't you? He'll be in desperate need of someone to talk to, and Marie will probably be off to Geraldine's again.'

'Of course I will. And I want to write a letter to Vera. She must come back to England some time and we need to make contact; she's going to need a lot of support. I just hope she'll accept it from me.'

'You're a sweetie! I love you!' he said, dropping a kiss on the top of her head. 'I must fly.'

When he had gone Bel sipped her tea and allowed herself the luxury of thinking about him. Remembering the way he made love to her, how he caressed her, the passionate things he whispered, the wild sweet promises he made to love her 'For ever and a day!' She smiled and thought with satisfaction of the pleasure she could give him, the love she could return now without guilt, and the plans they were making for the future. Probably they would never have a child, but they had talked about the problem and agreed not to let such a disappointment cloud their pleasure in each other. 'I have you', Larry had told her gently, 'I'm not greedy!' Hopefully Marie would marry eventually and produce a family. Being an aunt and uncle to her children would be fun.

'Oh, Larry, my dearest Larry! I'll love you "til the cows

come home"!' Bel whispered, smiling. Her father had said that to her so many times; that he would love his darling daughter 'til the cows come home!' That had been his promise, their private joke, until death took him from her.

Bel bathed and dressed, eager to see the morning's paper for the first news of the airship's progress. She had made up her mind that despite the manner of Walter's death, he should not become someone to be whispered about, a sad skeleton in the family cupboard. All she could do for him now was to keep his memory alive. She intended to make a start today by beginning a scrapbook about the flight, so that one day Marie's children could learn about their uncle's involvement with the R101. She was also on the lookout for a souvenir to mark the event – possibly a special issue mug or plate. She imagined Larry seated on the floor with his arms around a small boy and girl, telling them about the R101 and showing them the pictures. The airships would be history by the time the children were old enough to understand, which was a sad thought. But Larry would make a wonderful uncle, she thought, determined to be cheerful. She went downstairs to find Mrs Parks standing in the middle of the hallway with the day's newspaper in her hand. On hearing Bel come down the stairs she looked up slowly, her face rigid with shock.

'Ma'am! Oh, *ma'am!*'

Bel's stomach lurched. 'What is it now?' she asked, her tone sharp with irritation.

'Oh! Mrs Roberts, ma'am!' Her voice shook. 'It's the airship. It's crashed!'

Bel frowned, finding the prospect quite unacceptable. '*Our* airship? Surely not!' Yet even as she denied it something within her grew cold with apprehension. They stared at one another and then the housekeeper handed Bel the newspaper. 'It's crashed!' she repeated. 'Read the STOP PRESS bit. Lordy! Whatever next?'

Still unable to believe it, Bel read the brief report with horror.

'. . . R101 crashes near Beauvais, France. Sunday 2.09 a.m. Fireball. Few survivors expected.'

'Oh, my God!' It was true. The R101 — *crashed*? It was almost unbelievable. *Few survivors expected*? She said, 'Walter would have been killed!' but as soon as she uttered the words she realised how meaningless they were. Walter was dead already; he had merely exchanged one terrible end for another.

'Oh, ma'am! Isn't it dreadful! There just aren't any words — it's just terrible. A fireball! That lovely airship and all those poor people burned to death!'

Bel nodded, still unwilling to accept that the giant airship had indeed gone; that the result of years of work and hope had been so quickly obliterated. The pride of Britain's aviation industry, with the eyes of the world upon it, had lasted less than a day and Bel knew, more than most, just what the disaster would mean. Walter had spelled it out to her time and again. There would now be no more money made available to the industry. The R100 had shown the way, but the R101 could not follow. The disaster signalled the certain end of the airship industry; the end of an era.

Mrs Parks said, 'Good thing Mr Roberts *isn't* alive. He'd have been so upset.'

Bel nodded again, still unable to express her feelings in words. Yes, Walter would have been 'upset', she thought. That was the understatement of the year. He would have been devastated. As the silence lengthened, the telephone rang and they both jumped.

Bel said, 'I'll answer it. You get some breakfast, Mrs Parks, for both of us. Some scrambled eggs will do.'

She picked up the telephone and put the receiver to her ear. 'Bel Roberts.'

It was Detective Chief Inspector Carter. 'I thought you'd like to know of several developments, Mrs Roberts,' he told her briskly. 'I expect by now you have heard about the R101.'

'I've just seen a newspaper. I can't believe it.'

'I'm flying out there. They seem to think they have one body unaccounted for. They believe it could be Howard Roberts. The bodies are, of course, badly charred—'

Bel winced but said nothing.

'They are having to make identifications by any object found on the bodies that have survived the fire. One of them had a gold half-hunter watch. It was distorted by the heat, but there were some words engraved on the back. Your husband's name and something indecipherable that—'

She interrupted him. 'Walter did have a half-hunter, given to him by his father.'

'Howard could have taken it from your husband on the night of the murder. Or it might have been given to him before things turned nasty.'

Bel tried to focus her thoughts. 'That's possible, but how on earth could Howard get on to the airship? I don't understand that at all.'

'It seems he has been working at the R.A.W., but only for a week or so. I have been asking a few questions and apparently it happened once before. A young rigger named Ballantyne stowed away on the R34. It made the headlines, of course. In spite of all the security, Howard may have decided to try the same thing.'

'And succeeded!'

'So it would seem. Somehow he slipped through security. God knows how, because we we had alerted the R.A.W. that we were looking for him. Though I must admit it seemed a long shot at the time. Most people in Howard's shoes would want to put as large a distance as possible between themselves and the scene of the crime. He was cleverer than we thought; presumably he meant to skip ship at some stage and disappear. Ironic, when you think of it.'

'Isn't it?' Recovering slowly from the second shock of the morning, Bel's thoughts moved quickly now. 'But his poor mother! Oh, God! Hasn't that poor woman had enough?'

'That's the way of it, I'm afraid.' His voice was flat and unemotional. 'Anyway, the other piece of news is that the ferry have traced a booking for Vera Roberts for tomorrow. Now we'll be at Dover to meet her. She'll have heard about the crash presumably, and may suppose that her husband was involved. It depends where she has been in France and how much English news she knows. We'll keep you informed.'

'She may be all alone. She'll need someone to help her through the worst of it.' Bel thought of Vera's double loss and her heart ached for the woman she had never met. 'I'd like to think I could help her, but I'm probably the very last person she would want to see!'

'I'm afraid so. But don't worry. We'll look after her.'

'Thank you. So we can assume that if it *is* Howard, then he is no longer in this vicinity. I mean, he is no longer a threat.' She felt reassured and then immediately guilty.

'You can assume that the unfortunate lad is no longer anything,' Carter told her, 'except charred remains. But in a way it might have been a merciful release. All the passengers and many of the crew were asleep in their beds, and hydrogen burns with such a tremendous heat. They reckon that before anyone was able to wake up and register what was happening they were most likely . . . consumed. Almost instantaneous, which would have been a reasonably merciful way to go. If we had caught up with Howard, he'd have had to stand trial and possibly hang. He was spared all that, and so was his mother. Look on the bright side, Mrs Roberts.' He hung up and Bel replaced the receiver on its rest.

'The "*bright* side"?' she muttered. 'Is there a bright side?' And 'charred remains'; she was deeply shocked. Once again Howard's image appeared uninvited, hands in his pockets, strolling across the grass. She remembered how afterwards she had recognised the likeness to Walter. Howard had been Walter's and Vera's son, and now he was nothing. Charred remains! She thought the dreadful phrase would haunt her. But perhaps the policeman was right in one respect. A long trial would have been agony for his mother, and Bel was glad Walter was no longer alive to see what had happened to his son. How strange if fate had arranged things differently and both father and son had perished in that terrible fire.

'Karma!' she muttered. No doubt Marie would claim that the strange little woman had foreseen all this – and who was she, Bel, to deny it? The 'W' and 'H' were undoubtedly entwined now in everlasting peace. And the airship had fallen from a great height. She shivered. If Karma had seen all these things, then Bel pitied her. For who would choose to foresee all the tragedies of the world? She was glad that she did not have the gift of prophecy.

*

The scene at Allonne where the R101 had crashed was one that shocked even Carter, who had seen so many awful sights. He stood alone, horribly moved by the twisted skeleton of the world's largest airship. The rear half, with the framework of the tail fin virtually intact, lay across a ploughed field, but the bow was buried in a low, wooded slope. With narrowed eyes, he tried to reconstruct in his mind the airship's last moments. It looked as thought it might have slid along before the bow reached the fairly insignificant rise in the ground. Then, presumably, the

331

bow was compressed into the present tangle of metal. At that point numerous girders would have snapped, gas bags would have been ruptured and a spark could have ignited the escaping hydrogen. The pungent smell of burning still filled the air – a mixture of hot metal, burnt vegetation, burning fuel and something too awful even to contemplate. Cremation on a scale hitherto unimagined, Carter thought bitterly and, as the scale of the disaster finally impressed itself on his mind, he fought with an instinctive urge to run from the scene He stared slowly around him. The trees that had survived the inferno remained as blackened trunks and all the leaves had gone. Small groups of people huddled together. The collars of their coats were upturned against the weather; their heads, in a variety of caps and trilbys, were bent in earnest conversation. Some had turned their backs on the devastation, others averted their eyes. Two kneeling figures in white coats were examining something on the ground. Here and there a solitary person, like himself, wandered amongst the debris or wrote furiously in a notebook. A film crew hovered unhappily on the fringes of the roped-off area, watching three men in blue overalls as they attempted to approach the wreckage from which wisps of smoke still wavered skywards. The camera whirred as they were beaten back by the residual heat and retreated reluctantly across the parched ground.

Carter noted that a small contingent of the French police were there, as were the representatives of the R.A.W. and members of the investigative teams from both sides of the Channel. A lone ambulance stood by, although all hope of finding more than the six survivors had long since gone; its bright red cross provided the only splash of colour in an otherwise grim landscape. All plant life for yards in all directions had been burnt or singed to a dull brown or black, and the smell of smoke hung in the air, stinging Carter's throat and nose. There was, he thought, an awesome silence about the place. It was so much worse than he had expected, and it moved him.

A reporter came up to him and took his photograph. Carter scowled. 'Must you?' he said.

'*Daily Express*,' said the man, undeterred. He shook his head as he looked around. 'What a bloody mess! Never seen anything like it. And yet, take a look at the tail. Still intact, and yesterday there was the pennant still flying, hardly touched by the flames. That was some photograph!' He shook his head. 'Of course, they're blaming the weather.'

'Well, it was a foul night.'

'Amazing that *anyone* got out of that little lot alive, but six of them did. Mind you, two poor beggars are in hospital and might not make it.'

'Where are the bodies that they got out yesterday?'

'They're in the Town Hall in Beauvais. What the Frogs call the "Mairie". Mairie equals Mayor. See? But they're moving them by train tomorrow to Boulogne. It's been declared a national day of mourning.' He looked at Carter through narrowed eyes. 'You police?'

Carter nodded.

'I can always tell.' He tapped the side of his nose. 'If you want to see them, you'd best get over there at the double. They're under a military guard – Red Cross, soldiers and gendarmes. Forty-seven dead and one of the riggers not expected to survive the night. Poor bloody devils, all of them!' He shook his head in despair. 'It's wicked. *Wicked*! How could such a thing happen. What went wrong? Someone's to blame. And yet look at it!' He waved a hand towards the wrecked airship. 'The frame didn't break up. It's still whole. Twisted but not in pieces, if you take my meaning. So if it didn't break up in the air, was it struck by lightning? Did it spring a leak and then – boom? Crash?' He moved his hand in a dramatic downward curve. 'You tell me!'

Carter tore his gaze away and shook himself mentally as though to dispel the uncomfortable image. 'I must get over to the Town Hall.'

'Just ask for the Mairie.'

'Thanks.'

Carter strode away across the field and pushed his way through the crowds who were being held back by French police. He struggled back along the road which was jammed with cars and asked directions He hoped for Howard's sake that his end had been as quick as possible. Difficult to wish a death like that on even the worst villain.

*

Vera arrived back in England on Wednesday the 8th of October. To her surprise, she was met by a police sergeant who took her by car to the police station, where Detective Chief Inspector Carter broke the news of Howard's death as gently as he could. She didn't cry; she was past tears. Inside she was still numb with shock and she guessed that some time it would all hurt her more than it did now. For the present, she was thankful to feel nothing, grateful for the pause between hurt and pain. The policeman gave her the watch which had once been Walter's, and for the first time for nearly a week she smiled. Holding it in her hands she thought that this sad little watch had been near to her son, tucked in a pocket close to him. Walter's watch had been with him at the end so he had not been quite alone. She stared at the watch, which was now mis-shapen and lacking glass.

'The hands are still there,' she said wonderingly.

Carter said, 'Hard to believe, after all it's been through, but they still turn.' He demonstrated the small miracle and she gave a shaky little laugh.

'A bit like me,' she said. 'After all I've heard in the last week – but bits of me still work!'

She wasn't sure about her heart. She knew *that* was

broken beyond repair. But she thanked Mr Carter for the watch and he sent her home in a police car. She told the sergeant she had no relatives and didn't much care for her neighbours, but there were some letters on the mat inside the front door and she gathered them up dutifully and put them on the hall stand. As soon as they went into the kitchen the cat jumped up on the sill outside, mewing a welcome, and she opened the window and let him in.

She smiled again. 'I'll be all right now, sergeant. I'll make myself a pot of tea.'

He looked at her doubtfully. 'I shall ask if one of the local men can look in on you each day – just in case you need any help.'

'You're very kind,' she told him.

He stayed for a cup of tea and a few very stale biscuits, and he did his best to make her feel better. He had wanted her to see a doctor, suggesting that she might need something to help her to sleep, but she had said, 'No, thank you' very firmly and finally he had gone away.

It was wonderful to be home. Everything looked so normal, as though nothing had changed. In fact her whole life had changed but here, in her little kitchen, she was soothed by its ordinariness. One of the letters was from somebody called Isobel Hammond. It began, 'My dear Vera, You will not be expecting a letter from me . . .'

Vera exclaimed, 'Isobel *Hammond*?' She read on:

> . . . but I feel I must write to you. This has been such a terrible time for both of us and we have both lost a man we loved . . .

'It's *her*!' said Vera. 'Calling herself Hammond.'

> . . . a man I thought I had married. A man you *had* married. I believe that he loved us both. Poor Walter.

It was all such a muddle that I can find it in my heart to forgive him. I expect you will too . . .

'Yes, I will. I do' said Vera impulsively. The cat jumped into her lap and she scratched the furry head distractedly.

I know that you will be worried about your son and I hope that somehow things can work out better than we might expect . . .

Vera looked at the date on the letter. It had been written before the crash, before they knew. She swallowed hard and read on:

I envy you your boy. We had no children, and I now know that Walter was very fond of Howard. This is such a difficult letter to write, but you will see that I no longer call myself Roberts. Hammond is my maiden name. If, as I hope, you bear me no ill-will, perhaps we could meet and be friends. Oddly, in the circumstances, we have a lot in common.

You probably don't know yet about the will, although there should be a solicitor's letter waiting for you when you get home. If you need help of any kind, please telephone. Or come to Cardington and stay for a few days. I'm sure you will want to see Walter's grave . . .

Vera raised her eyebrows. Yes, she *did* want to see Walter's grave. She would want to put some flowers on it. Isobel Hammond. What a strange woman. She would write and tell Evie all about her. And what an amazing letter. Did she, Vera, want to be friends with Walter's . . . what was she exactly? A bit of fluff? No, no. That was not a very nice way of putting it. Lady friend, perhaps?

336

'Well!' she said to the cat. 'I shall think about it. Who knows?'

She was surprised about the will because she hadn't given that a thought. Perhaps Walter had left her something. And the bit about the grave had come as a shock. Still, it was her own fault for rushing off to France like that, all hoity-toity and not telling anyone. Now they had buried him in Cardington instead of Deal. She would have to think about that, too. At least Isobel wasn't still pretending to be Mrs Roberts, so she couldn't be all bad. She took a deep breath and read to the end of the letter:

Do please get in touch.

Yours with respect, Bel Hammond.

'With respect?' Vera shrugged. Difficult to know what else she could have said. She put the letter back in the envelope and decided to save the rest until later. She was desperately tired and she could not face any more unpleasant surprises. As she poured herself another cup of tea there was a knock at the door and she was surprised to see the policeman back again.

He said 'I forgot to tell you, Mrs Roberts, that there will be a funeral for the victims of the crash on Saturday up at Cardington. If you feel up to it and *want* to attend, we can take you there.'

'Saturday, you say?' Vera hesitated. She had been longing for the peace and quiet of her own home, but maybe Walter would have wanted her to attend. She wondered if she could bear it.

She asked, 'Will *she* be there? The Hammond woman?' Evie had said she was 'sort of pretty' and Vera was curious.

'I don't know. It's certainly possible because, as you know, Walter Roberts was so closely involved with the airship and as his—' He caught himself just in time. 'That

337

is, Mrs – I mean *Miss* Hammond, would have known a lot about the airship.'

'I might want to meet her. She wrote to me. A nice sort of letter. I might go.'

He tried to hide his surprise and Vera suddenly realised that if her name was known there would be fingers pointed in her direction and whispers behind hands. 'That's Vera Roberts, the mother of Howard. The wife of Walter . . .' Could she cope with that sort of thing? For a moment she almost answered, 'No', but then she lifted her head defiantly. She was not ashamed of either of them; she *loved* them both, no matter what they had done, and she would always love them – and she would tell the whole world if it wanted to know!

'A meeting would be possible, I'm sure,' he said. He smiled. 'Sleep on it,' he advised. 'I'll call round in the morning and see if you've decided.'

When he had gone she made herself a very large bowl of porridge, because she had promised Evie and Pierre that if they allowed her to come home on her own she would look after herself and not get run down. The porridge went down a treat and it made her sleepy. First thing in the morning she would go round to Mrs Sidney and thank her for looking after the cat. And she would buy her a box of Black Magic chocolates.

Tomorrow was another day, she told herself gently. She had survived this far. She could survive anything. Although it was only half-past eight she filled a hot water bottle, wrapped it in its knitted cover and carried it up to bed.

*

Bel had just finished lunch on the following Friday when Mrs Banks rushed into the dining room looking very flustered.

'Ma,am! There's a lady to see you. She says her name's Mrs Roberts and that you said she could come!'

338

Bel stared at her. 'Mrs *Roberts*?'

'Yes, ma'am.' Mrs Banks was flushed with excitement. 'I think it's *her*!'

Very slowly Bel stood up. '*Vera* Roberts?'

'She just said *Mrs* Roberts. She looks a funny little—'

'Please! That's enough.' Bel held up a hand to stop further confidences. Whatever her own feelings, Bel knew she could not allow her housekeeper to comment adversely upon Walter's wife.

Mrs Banks registered the rebuff but made no further comment. She asked, 'Should I show her in?'

Bel hesitated, although there was no way she could now refuse to see Vera, and she could not deny that she was curious. 'Yes. That is ... *No!* Let me think.' Bel was overcome by a sense of confusion and something akin to panic. To gain time she whispered 'Mrs Vera Roberts' and wondered what on earth they could say to one another without increasing the hurt that each had suffered. Walter's wife was *here*. Of course, she *had* said Vera could come and visit. It had seemed a good idea at the time, but she had not really expected her to avail herself of the invitation; had certainly not expected her to react so quickly. It had seemed most unlikely that Vera would *want* to visit.

Mrs Banks said again, 'Shall I show her in?'

Bel tidied her hair self-consciously, not meeting the other woman's eyes. 'I'll let her in myself.' Ignoring her housekeeper's disappointment, Bel glanced at the table and the remains of the lunch. 'Mrs Roberts may not have eaten. If necessary, can you find something for her?'

'Yes, ma'am, but is she ... you know—' She looked appealingly at Bel.

'Yes, she's Walter's legal wife,' Bel told her. 'She's Howard's mother.' And without giving the housekeeper a chance to respond she hurried past to the front door to greet her unexpected visitor.

She saw a small, tidy woman whose mousy hair was

tucked under a neat felt hat. Her face was pale and drawn, and her soft brown eyes showed signs of recent tears. She had once been pretty, Bel decided, with a good complexion, but she could see no likeness to Howard who had obviously inherited only his father's looks. Vera's black coat with the fur trim at the collar was hardly fashionable, and her well-polished shoes could at best be described as 'sensible'. Bel was immediately aware of her own fashionably styled hair, her expensive black dress and suede shoes. Illogically, the difference in their ages made her feel ashamed. This woman had borne Walter his only child and had struggled alone to rear the boy. Vera Roberts was *entitled* to look a little frayed and worn. Bel knew that she was staring, but could not tear her gaze away. It was hard to imagine Walter married to this woman, but then she could not imagine him married to any woman other than herself.

Vera returned her stare for a moment. 'Geoffrey's daughter!' she said. 'You are so like him.'

Bel nodded wordlessly.

'You of all people!' said Vera. 'You've got his eyes.' She shook her head and repeated, 'Geoffrey's girl. After all these years—' She swallowed nervously. 'You said I could come. I hope you meant it. There's something we have to talk about.' Her voice was quiet but determined.

Bel found herself wondering how anyone so unworldly had coped with the terrible pressures of the past week, and was conscious of unwilling admiration. A 'funny little thing' perhaps, but there was more to her than was at first obvious. Bel opened the door wider and Walter's wife stepped into the house. Her eyes went at once, with obvious surprise, to the parquet floor, the highly polished furniture and the two good pictures that hung on the wall.

Bel wondered uneasily about the little house at Deal. 'I'm very glad you came.'

'The police brought me by car. They've been so kind.'

'It's very brave of you. I – I'd like you to know how

340

sorry I am – for all your troubles.' The words came out in a clumsy rush and sounded trite and insincere.

'Thank you.'

Mrs Banks, hovering nearby, now rushed forward to help Vera off with her coat, trying hard not to stare at the visitor.

'It's a nice house,' said Vera, 'but it must take a lot of heating.'

'I suppose it does.' Bel had never thought about it.

'Walter always did have good taste – in houses and things, I mean.'

Vera's tone had sharpened and Bel wondered how to take the remark. Did Vera mean that she could only approve his taste in furniture but not his taste in women? Was she preparing to be difficult? And what was this 'something' they had to talk about? Just how aggressive was Walter's 'funny little' wife, she wondered unhappily. Perhaps her invitation to Vera had been a mistake. If so, it was too late now for regrets and she asked, 'Have you had any lunch? I'm afraid I've just finished, but Mrs Banks says she can manage something for you. It would be no trouble.'

'I had a snack in the station tea-room. A rather dry sandwich, but food doesn't taste like food at the moment, no matter how good it is. It's funny, that.'

In her black tweed skirt and hand-knitted cardigan Vera looked positively frail, and Bel found herself praying that somehow they could be friends and not enemies. She led her into the sitting room and asked Mrs Banks to bring a tray of tea and some cake. She and Vera sat in the armchairs on either side of the fire.

Vera held out her hands and Bel, with an unexpected tug at her heart, found herself examining the thin gold band on her left hand. Vera's wedding ring was thinner than her own wide band, and there was no engagement ring. On her right hand, however, she wore a dress ring of

341

small pearls set in gold. Bel found herself concealing her own expensively adorned hands in her lap.

Vera forced a smile. 'I do like a bit of fire,' she said with unconscious irony. 'It's always so comforting. I never could bear to stint the coal like some folk do. Walter used to say—' She stopped abruptly and pressed her lips together. 'I'm sorry. I . . . This is a very nice room.'

'Thank you.'

There was a long, uncomfortable silence. Bel felt that she should take the initiative, but this fragile little woman had somehow stolen it from her. She was the wife, that was it. No matter how grand Bel's house was, nor how beautiful her jewellery, Vera was the legal wife. It might almost be argued that Bel's presence in this house had come about by false pretences.

Vera said, 'It was kind of you to write to me. I felt so sorry when I knew – for you, I mean. Not being married. It must have been a shock.'

'Yes, it was. But by that time—' She stopped abruptly, appalled. She had been on the verge of discussing Larry.

Vera waited.

'I'm sorry. It was nothing.'

Vera's face expressed disbelief, but she merely gave a little shrug.

Bel said, 'I was hoping no one need know, but of course the papers have got hold of the facts. I should have realised. In the circumstances, once the police knew, it was inevitable.' She fell silent, annoyed with herself; she must not let this woman see how vulnerable she felt.

'We've given them a nice little story.' Vera's mouth tightened.

'I'm afraid so. Something to talk about over their tea and cakes!' Bel took a deep breath. 'Howard was so like his father.'

'Yes. It used to annoy him – Howard, I mean. Because he wanted nothing to do with him towards the end.' She glanced up from the fire. 'They can break your heart. Children. And yet you wouldn't be without them. If I could go back . . .' She drew a deep breath and looked at Bel defiantly. 'I'd do it all over again. That's how foolish I am.' She clasped her hands around her knees as she leaned forward a little. 'You could say Walter made fools of us both, but I don't ever want to think like that. I want to think—' Her voice broke suddenly and she swallowed. 'I want to believe that he did it all for the best. You put it nicely in your letter, that he loved us both but got himself into a muddle. I think we should cling on to that, don't you?'

Saddened by the woman's obvious distress, Bel could only nod.

Vera went on, 'I've come about the graves. I don't think you should have buried Walter without my permission, especially not here in Cardington. I feel he should be nearer to me so that I can put flowers on his grave whenever I feel like it.' As Bel hesitated, Vera continued, 'I also want Howard to be buried in the same grave. They were father and son and I think it best. I've told the police he is not to go in that mass grave with the other victims.' She gave Bel a long, straight look. 'I don't care what you or anybody else thinks about Howard, he was my son and I loved him and I'll go on loving his memory. If he killed Walter it must have been an accident. It *must* have been!'

'I'm sure it was, Mrs – may I call you Vera?'

'Yes.'

'I don't think Howard could have known how ill Walter was. Walter had no business to be out of bed, out in the car, that cold night. He must have wanted very desperately to talk to Howard because he loved him. He told me that, that he wanted them to be friends again. He thought the world of him, you know.'

'I always knew that.'

343

'But children growing up get funny ideas.'

'Oh, they do! They do!' Vera sat back, rubbing her eyes tiredly. 'And what can you do? You can't give them a good smacking at that age even if you want to. Howard was so difficult. He needed his father; a stern hand. Some boys are like that. They just go off the rails and, given time, you can get them back on line again. Poor Howard just ran out of time.'

Mrs Banks appeared with the tray, and a few minutes later Vera had drunk her first cup of tea and Bel was pleased to see her eating a large slice of coffee cake with some signs of enjoyment.

Vera said, 'I sometimes wished he'd been a girl, but then he wouldn't have been Howard and he was such a dear little boy. You'd have loved him – oh! No, you couldn't have. Sorry!'

'In the circumstances it's a good thing that we didn't have any children,' said Bel.

Vera considered this, then she said, 'I feel a bit greedy, eating alone. Why don't you have some cake? It's very good.'

To please her, Bel did so and for a while they ate in companionable silence. Then Bel asked, 'Do you want to know how Walter and I became involved? He didn't mean it to happen; he only meant to have you and Howard in his life.' Without waiting for an answer, she explained briefly about her father's death and the way it had brought her and Walter together.

Vera listened without interrupting, then said, 'So that was it. You were Geoffrey's daughter. Walter thought the world of Geoffrey, you know. They made a pact when they were boys, never to marry.' She laughed. 'And then Geoffrey let the side down. I suppose he thought Walter would have forgotten the pact. Then, as though marrying wasn't enough, Geoffrey produced a child!'

'Me.'

344

'You. Little did anyone know how it would end. Fate can play nasty tricks.'

After another long silence Bel said, 'Of course I must bow to your wishes about Walter's grave. I have no right to decide. But I thought he would want to be near his beloved Cardington, near the R.A.W. and the flying field. It meant so much to him. But it's quite possible to have his coffin taken down to Kent for re-interment, if that's what you wish. It might be expensive but there's plenty of money – that is, Walter left you very well provided for in his will. You need never worry again about money.'

'I've got a little job, two mornings a week in a grocer's shop. I didn't tell Walter because he was so set against the idea of his wife having to work. You needn't worry on my account. I shan't starve.'

'But you will be comfortably off. You could give up the job if you wished; you could move.'

'Move? Where to?' She looked surprised, wiping cake crumbs from her mouth with the napkin.

Bel shrugged. 'I don't know. I thought that if you wanted a fresh start, perhaps?'

Vera said, 'Howard was crazy about that place, too – the R.A.W., I mean. It was all they talked about in the early years. Airships and more airships. Then, of course, Howard wanted to work there and that would have been a bit awkward for Walter. But I see what you mean about the grave. Maybe I'll leave well alone and Howard can go in with his father.'

'They should be together.'

'*I'll* decide that,' Vera said sharply.

'I'm sorry.'

'No, *I'm* sorry. There was no need to snap your head off.' Vera shook her head. 'Oh, dear! If Walter could see us now! Whatever would he say?' She allowed herself the ghost of a smile. 'Would he be pleased, d'you think?'

'I don't see why not.'

345

'I suppose not.'

Bel steeled herself. 'There's something else I want to tell you ... because you'll find out anyway. I'm going to marry Walter's half-brother, Laurence.'

'His half-brother? You mean you—' For a moment Vera looked affronted. 'You and Laurence were ... well!' She subjected Bel to a long, hard stare which made her feel most uncomfortable, but then suddenly she shrugged. 'Why shouldn't you? You're a *single* woman.' She straightened her back. 'Even I have an admirer,' she told Bel 'His name's Edouard. He's French but he's a good man.'

Bel said, 'Then one day – who knows, Vera? Walter wouldn't want you to be lonely.'

'I've always been lonely!' The sharpness was there again.

'I meant that Walter surely wouldn't begrudge you a little companionship, as you get older. He might even feel that you deserve it and be glad for you. He always had your welfare at heart.'

'How would you know?'

'I know *now* because Walter made it quite plain. When he told me, he told everything.'

'He was like that. No half-measures.'

They were silent for a while, busy with their own thoughts.

Vera said, 'I could never live in France. England's my home. It may not be perfect, but I belong here.' She stood up suddenly. 'I have to go round to Mrs Croft, to collect Howard's things. If I could spent tonight and tomorrow night with you – then I could attend the funeral.'

'Of course you can. And I could take you to the solicitor this afternoon. You must receive your copy of the will.'

Vera busied herself, brushing imaginary crumbs from her skirt. 'I'm glad we've met. At least you're a nice, *reasonable* sort of person – not at all how I imagined.'

346

Bel took her hands and held them. 'Walter was very lucky with his women!' she said.

The words hung in the air for a long moment and then they both managed a shaky laugh.

Chapter Sixteen

MRS CROFT OPENED the door and stared at the woman on the doorstep. 'What?' she demanded irritably. She was feeling hot and bothered with that silly little girl, and her heart was banging like a drum. The last thing she needed was some stranger turning up out of the blue, as if she didn't have enough to worry about.

'I'm Mrs Roberts, Howard's mother. I believe he used to lodge with you?'

'What? *Howard's* mother?' She peered at her suspiciously. 'The Howard that was my lodger. That got himself—' She stopped herself just in time.

'He spoke very highly of your cooking,' the woman said with a faint smile.

Howard's *mother*! Mrs Croft snorted. Well, she looked a poor little thing, but then she'd had a bad time of it lately. 'It's a bit inconvenient right now,' she began. One thing at a time, she told herself crossly. She would have to come back later. Framing these words in her mind, she became aware of footsteps behind her, and then Peggy was poking her nose in.

Peggy said, '*My* Howard's mother?'

'You get back in the kitchen, Peggy,' said Mrs Croft. 'I haven't finished with you yet!' The woman on the doorstep turned to Peggy 'What d'you mean – *your* Howard?'

Peggy pushed herself forward. 'We were engaged, Howard and me. Well, sort of engaged. He said he was going to marry me and so I—'

Mrs Croft said, 'Hush, you silly girl! No one's talking to you.'

'I won't hush! It's the truth and you know it. I *told* you at the time and you said, "Lovely" and I said—'

'I said "Lovely"? I never did! And I never thought you'd be so daft as to—'

Mrs Roberts said, 'I really came for his things. His clothes and whatever else he had.'

Mrs Croft glanced from her to Peggy and suddenly made up her mind. 'Perhaps you'd better come in,' she said. 'There's something you ought to hear.'

They sat down in the kitchen with Howard's mother still in her black coat. Her eyes and nose were red, but she sat very straight. Peggy sat white-faced at the table, twisting a damp handkerchief between nervous fingers, while Mrs Croft remained standing with her hands on her hips. Awkwardly, they stared at their visitor.

'What is it I ought to hear?' she asked to break the silence.

Mrs Croft stabbed a finger in Peggy's direction. 'This is my niece. She's just been telling me – well, *you* tell her, Peg. It's your problem, not mine, thank goodness, though what your ma will say when she hears I don't know! And take that look off your face! Tears won't help you. Just get on with it.'

'It was me and Howard,' said Peggy, looking earnestly at Vera. 'We were in love and—'

Mrs Croft snorted. 'In love! Listen to the girl!'

Peggy persevered. 'We loved each other and Howard wanted to buy me a ring and do everything properly—'

The woman was visibly shocked. 'My son wanted to marry you?' she protested. 'He never said anything to me.'

349

'They'd only known each other five minutes!' put in Mrs Croft.

Peggy said 'It was longer than that! You know it was. Anyway,' she turned back to Vera, 'he asked me to marry him, sort of, and I said I would. I mean he was going to do it properly when he'd bought the ring, because he said he wanted it all to be romantic and I believed him. Why shouldn't I? And I lent him some money – most of my savings—'

The woman stiffened. 'How much money? I'll pay you back. Nobody's going to say that my son ran up debts.'

Mrs Croft hastily revised her opinion of Howard's mother. Offering to pay it back before she even knew how much!

'Ten pounds,' explained Peggy. 'I can prove it. You can look at my savings book!'

'I have to see the solicitor this afternoon, but I will pay you back in a day or two. I'm sorry if you've been worried. Ten pounds is a lot of money. And I'm sure Howard was fond of you if he said he was but, as your aunt says, you hadn't known each other long. I'm sure you'll meet someone else.'

Mrs Croft said, 'Hang on a minute. She hasn't got to the important bit.'

Peggy flushed. 'We – well, because I knew we were going to be married I – he wanted to . . . you know . . . and in the end I let him. Because he *was* going to marry me,' she ended lamely.

Now Mrs Roberts was staring at her. 'You and my Howard?' she whispered.

Mrs Croft sank on to the nearest chair. 'You tell me!' she said. 'Young people these days have no sense of sin. They wasn't brought up like us with the fear of God in them. Not that my sister hasn't done her best, 'cos she has, but if I'd as much as *looked* at a man that way my pa would have walloped me. Young people today—'

Peggy protested, 'It wasn't like that! It wasn't like a sin.'

350

Howard's mother had put a hand to her mouth. 'So are you saying that you might be – be having my son's child? Is that it?' Her expression was incredulous, her eyes wide with shock.

Peggy scowled. 'I don't *know*! All I said to Auntie was, what would I do if I *was*? She just went off the deep end!'

Mrs Croft wagged a furious finger. 'I should think I would go off the deep end, with Howard not here to marry you and your dad likely to chuck you out!'

Peggy's eyes filled with tears and she dabbed at them ineffectually with the damp handkerchief.

Mrs Croft looked her visitor straight in the eye. 'And she's *not* coming to live with me. That's what she's after. Oh, I know you, Peggy, so don't look at me like that as though you don't know what I'm on about. I can't do with a baby around the place; I've got lodgings to run, and only one spare bedroom as well you know. If you've been that daft – well! You make your bed and you get to lie on it!'

Peggy said, 'But it might not be a . . . a baby after all.'

'Well, it won't be an elephant, will it? Don't talk so daft, girl.'

Peggy flushed. 'It's not *funny*!' she protested hotly. 'I meant it might not be *anything*. I meant—'

Mrs Roberts asked, 'When will you know? When were you due?'

'Two days ago,' Peggy confessed, shamefaced.

Mrs Croft glared at her, open-mouthed. 'Why you little cheapskate! You told me you wasn't sure. Now you say two days ago!'

'I meant it should have come, but it didn't, so it might be a day or two late though it usually isn't late and I wasn't sure . . .' She began to cry.

Mrs Croft wanted to shake the silly girl. Daft as a brush and always had been. Not that her mother was any great shakes, but they'd spoiled the girl rotten when she was a baby and now look at her.

351

Howard's mother said briskly, 'Well, you'll have to take her to a doctor in a month or two, but just let's suppose the worst has happened. Or the best!'

'The best?' Mrs Croft glanced at Peggy, whose tears flowed faster.

Mrs Roberts took an envelope from her handbag and wrote carefully on it. Peggy, noticing, looked at her in alarm.

'If that's one of them doctors, I'm not going! I *want* the baby! I just don't know what to do about – about anything!'

Mrs Croft said, 'No girl in her right mind wants a baby without a husband, and *they* don't grow on trees.'

'This is my address in Deal.' She handed the paper to Peggy. 'If you're having my boy's child I shall want to know about it. You understand? And I'll want you to have it. You can come and live with me for a while and if, later on, you meet someone else, another man, and he doesn't want the child – I'll have it. I'll adopt it.'

Mrs Croft said, 'Adopt Peg's kid? Well, now, I don't know what to say.'

Peggy, startled by the speed of events, stopped crying. 'But – but I . . .'

Howard's mother said, 'No buts, Peggy. My husband has left me comfortably off, so I'm told, so we'll manage pretty well. If Howard loved you, then so shall I.' She stood up. 'Nobody will ever say that Howard's child was a burden. *Never.* So don't cry any more. It'll be all right, I tell you. Come here, Peggy.' She held out her arms and, after a moment's uncertainty, Peggy stood up and was duly hugged. 'Howard's baby! Who'd have thought it! Howard, a father!' Smiling suddenly, she held Peggy at arm's length. 'Now you *will* tell me. You promise?'

Mrs Croft said, 'If she doesn't, *I* will. There'll be hell to pay when my brother-in-law finds out, so she'll be well out of it at your place.' Her heart had stopped thumping and she was beginning to feel a little better as she smiled and breathed a deep sigh of relief. Howard's mother! Of all the people to turn up, today of all days. Fate played some odd tricks, but this one looked as though it would work out for the best after all. Life was funny that way. She looked at Peggy and the girl was grinning like a Cheshire cat! And well she might!

'Stop grinning, Peg,' she told her niece, 'and say "Thank you" to Mrs Roberts. It looks like it's your lucky day.'

*

The forty-seven coffins containing the survivors of the crash were brought back to England in the destroyer H.M.S. *Tempest*. They travelled through the darkness to arrive in Dover in the early hours of Wednesday the 8th of October. From there they went to the Westminster mortuary, where they were later joined by the coffin containing the body of Rigger Church, who had died from his wounds in the hospital at Beauvais.

The whole country was plunged into mourning and on Friday, when the coffins were laid in state in Westminster Hall, thousands of people thronged London to pay their last respects to the dead. The queue extended for more than a mile as people waited silently to file through the Hall in a final tribute. The pennant of the R101, most of which had miraculously escaped the flames, was exhibited on the altar of St Paul's Cathedral. After the memorial service at Westminster Abbey and a similar service at Westminster Cathedral for the victims who were Roman Catholics, the forty-eight coffins were carried slowly through the streets of London to Euston Station. It was an impressive but moving procession, and it was watched by half a million people.

Later that same day, Bel waited outside St Mary's Church in Cardington with Marie on her right and Vera on her left; Larry was on Vera's left. All the employees of the

353

R.A.W. were there, and the townspeople of Cardington swelled the crowd as they waited to offer prayers for the dead. Soon they would see for themselves the sad proof, if any were needed, of the end to all their hopes for the R101. Suddenly, at exactly 2 o'clock, a flight of aircraft and then a second flight split the sky above them, timed to appear as the first coffin was taken from the train at Bedford Station. As they roared overhead, they signalled to the waiting thousands who lined the route from Bedford to Cardington that the final journey of those intrepid airmen had begun. The funeral procession was led by a small contingent of police and a detachment of the Royal Air Force bearing reversed arms. Behind them came the convoy of grey lorries, each carrying two coffins; these were covered with Union Jacks but the flags were almost invisible beneath the hundreds of wreaths sent from virtually every corner of the world. For the final half-hour of the journey the church bell tolled mournfully, but just before 4 o'clock the procession arrived at the little church.

Standing within sight of the large communal grave, Bel was aware that Walter's own grave was only a short distance away. She took hold of Vera's hand and squeezed it gently. Vera was holding up remarkably well, she thought with a flicker of admiration. She caught Larry's eye and smiled. How strange, she thought, that Walter was not one of these tragic victims. Yet, if he had died in the crash, that might have been stranger still, for then he would have died in the same way as Geoffrey – killed by one of the elegant monsters they had worked so hard to create. She caught Marie's eye.

'Karma!' whispered Marie, with a nod towards the banks of bronze and white chrysanthemums which lined the grave. With a tilt of the head she indicated the first of the coffins, draped in red, white and blue, now being carried to its final resting place.

Bel sighed and the band began to play 'Abide With Me'.

354

Somehow Vera remained dry-eyed, but then the vicar of Cardington began the burial service. In his clear voice the well-known words rang out in the twilight.

'I am the Resurrection and the Life . . . The Lord giveth and the Lord taketh away . . .'

A huge, gulping sob was suddenly torn from Vera but before Bel could react, Larry's arms had gone round Walter's widow, and it was Larry who whispered the much needed words of comfort.

*

In Cardington, almost a year to the day from the funeral, Bel walked down Church Lane towards the two small boys who were trying to bring down conkers from the large horse-chestnut which flanked the church gate. With Larry beside her, she turned left into the churchyard and walked along the path towards St Mary's. The afternoon sun warmed the stonework of the walls and picked out the stone tracery which spanned the doorway. The lawn between the low gravestones had recently been cut, and the smell of fresh grass scented the air. Bel and Larry had been married for six months and now lived in a flat in London, near to Larry's chambers. Inevitably, Bel's thoughts were drawn back to the events of the previous twelve months which had seen so many changes in all their lives. The house in Cardington had been sold, as had the London flat. With the sale of these two homes it seemed to Bel that most of her past life had been snatched away – lost in the flurry of estate agents, potential buyers and the inevitable drawing-together of Walter's personal estate.

Larry touched her arm. 'Don't look so sad!' he whispered.

'Just memories,' she told him. 'Ghosts from the past.' She shook herself mentally. Larry was right. The past could never be undone, nor could it be forgotten, but life was full of promise and their love for each other burned as brightly as ever.

Ahead of them Vera walked next to Peggy, who carried Howard's three-month-old daughter, Jessica. It was the child's christening which had united them all on this occasion. If Walter and Bel had been married, this would be her grandchild, Bel thought wistfully. But no; there would have been no children and no grandchildren. It was Vera who had ensured the continuation of the Roberts family line; Vera who claimed the title of 'grandmother' and who richly deserved the joys with which the little girl had already enriched her stricken life. For it was Vera who had given Peggy a home when her furious parents turned her out; Vera who had encouraged and cared for her through a pregnancy fraught with difficulties, and who had assisted the midwife when the baby finally arrived. The three generations now lived in Vera's attractive cottage on the Bedford road. Bel could never begrudge Vera her happiness.

Behind Larry and Bel, Detective Chief Inspector Carter walked hand in hand with Marie. Theirs had been an unlikely, somewhat tempestuous relationship, Bel reflected, but one which had somehow survived. It now appeared destined to last longer than anyone could have expected. George, amused, had termed it 'a nine-day wonder', but after nearly a year had professed himself pleasantly surprised at the policeman's 'staying power'. Now Bel turned towards them and said, 'A perfect day. Someone up there is smiling on us at last.'

Marie nodded. 'I hope Walter's ghost is watching.'

Bel laughed. 'No doubt Karma can tell you that!'

John Carter joined in the laughter. 'Don't encourage her,' he begged. 'I'm trying to convince her that it's so much hocus-pocus.'

Marie pouted, turning towards Bel. 'But it's *not*, dear old thing!' she insisted. 'Last week—' She broke off suddenly, staring at two people who rounded the corner of the church and walked hesitantly towards them. 'Good Lord! Isn't that . . .?'

Everyone turned. The man and woman who approached were Peggy's father and mother, chivvied along by a determined Mrs Croft. Bel felt a rush of apprehension. Vera had insisted that Peggy's parents should be invited to the christening despite their earlier, unhelpful behaviour. Peggy had been unwilling to include them, convinced that there would be a family row which would mar the occasion. She had finally given in to please Vera and now, judging by the shamefaced expressions on their faces, it seemed that a reconciliation was the more likely outcome. Vera had been right, thought Bel, and was again surprised by her perspicacity.

'It's amazing what a child can achieve!' she whispered to Larry, who slid his arm around her waist by way of reply.

Peggy had gone very red but at that moment, as if on cue, the vicar appeared from within the church and began to shake hands with everyone.

Peggy's mother sidled closer to her daughter and Bel caught her whispered words: 'Your father's that sorry, love. He wants to be friends, but you know the way he is.'

Peggy said, 'I know.' Her mouth was set in a tight, unforgiving line.

'We made a mistake, Peggy love.'

'Yes, you did.'

'But Mrs Roberts said you were willing to let bygones be bygones?'

'She said it, not me.' Peggy was clutching the baby to her, preventing her mother from seeing it. With a flash of understanding, Bel realised that Peggy was enjoying her moment of triumph.

Her father spoke gruffly: 'Well, if we're not wanted—'

Peggy hesitated, and Bel smiled. The young mother was

obviously longing to show off the baby and earn her parents' approval.

She said, 'Well, if Vera invited you—'

'She did, love,' her mother insisted. 'That's why we're here. We never would have come otherwise. Well, I mean, we couldn't, could we?'

Before Peggy could prolong the agony, Vera intervened and shook hands with Peggy's mother and then her father. 'Of course you must be here,' she told them firmly. 'I've told Peggy. Children get lonely. They need their family around them, and one grandmother is not enough. The more love they get the better, I say.'

Peggy's father looked at her soberly. 'I daresay I was a bit hasty . . .' He blurted out the words as though they had weighed heavily upon him for a long time.

'*A bit!*' cried Peggy. 'You were more than a *bit* hasty. You were blooming awful. You were—'

His wife said, 'Peggy, love, we do know we should have been a bit more . . . well, *thoughtful*, but your father was that upset.'

'Upset?' Her words tumbled out. 'What about me? Wasn't I upset? How d'you think I felt, with a baby on the way—'

The baby whimpered suddenly and Vera promptly took her from Peggy's unresisting arms. 'Hush now, Peg. You've frightened the poor little love.' To the baby she said, 'Are they quarrelling on your special day, then. What a shame!' She rocked the baby, crooning softly, and at once they were all contrite.

Bel watched with a feeling of envy as the past was set aside with hugs and a few tears, and the grandparents took their first ecstatic look at Jessica.

A few minutes later, at the vicar's bidding, the little party – restored to good humour – moved obediently into the church. Bel glanced round the familiar interior, struck by its timeless, unchanging peace. She took a few steps forward and gazed down the aisle towards the altar. In the comparative gloom, the slim columns soared to the wooden ceiling, the neat rows of oak pews exactly as she remembered them. She and Walter had worshipped here on many occasions; she could see the pew where they had so often stood together, hymn books in hand. Walter had had a good voice and he sang well. Walter Roberts and his *wife*. A highly respected couple . . . She was aware of a tightening in her throat as the memories crowded back, unchecked. But then Walter had fallen from grace, and his carefully preserved world had collapsed around him . . . Her gaze moved upwards to the wall where, framed and glazed, the pennant of the R101 was displayed. The Union Jack and the roundel of the Royal Air Force stood out boldly from the pale blue ground. All that remained of a once proud craft. Walter's dream. She thought of the monument that now marked the grave of the victims, and of the grave where father and son shared eternity . . .

'Bel!'

She turned at Larry's voice and saw that the rest of the group were assembled around the hexagonal font. As the vicar mounted the two steps, she hurried to join them. Bel, as godmother, was at once entrusted with the baby who mercifully appeared quite unfazed by the event. As the child was thrust into her arms she felt her pulse quicken. Walter's grand-daughter was beautiful, she thought, and the knowledge that he would never see her brought a lump to her throat. Dark blue eyes stared up at the light which filtered through one of the stained-glass windows of the baptistry. The service began, but Bel heard nothing. She had eyes only for the child, who felt incredibly small and helpless in her arms. For an agonised moment her own childlessness mocked her as she stared down at the tiny, puckered face with its halo of fine blond hair. At the sight of the small clenched fists her throat tightened. She would never have a child of her own but this little girl, born out of so much grief and anger, was her niece. Or *half*-niece! At least she was *kin*. And she was her god-daughter. Jessica would come to visit, George would love her, and she and Larry could take her to the zoo and the pantomime.

The solemn words reverberated round the church and the family answered, the soothing ritual of the familiar service binding them together. Peggy's mother was crying softly, and even the irrepressible Marie appeared moved by the occasion. The vicar took the baby from Bel's arms and gently trailed water over her forehead.

'I name this child Jessica Vera . . .'

The baby smiled and beneath the long christening robe the small legs kicked excitedly. As Larry reached discreetly for Bel's hand, she felt a surge of hope. Returning the pressure of his fingers, she looked down at the baby and smiled. Jessica Vera, she thought, with a surge of hope. The new life signalled a fresh beginning for all of them.